Shameless Duke

League of Dukes Book Four

BY
SCARLETT SCOTT

Shameless Duke
League of Dukes Book Four

ISBN: 978-1-689135-52-8

Edited by Grace Bradley
Proofread by CM Wright
Cover Design by Wicked Smart Designs

For more information, contact author Scarlett Scott.
www.scarslettscottauthor.com

Lucien, Duke of Arden, is on the brink of disaster, about to lose everything he worked so hard to attain as the leader of the Special League. When Home Office obliges him to join forces with a Pinkerton agent to keep his position, he is determined to send the fellow back to American shores faster than he can say "Yankee Doodle." There's just one small problem with his flawless plan to undermine the unwanted agent...

Hazel Montgomery has spent the last ten years as a Pinkerton detective, fighting to be treated as an equal to her male counterparts, and the list of her successful cases is as long as the Mississippi River. She is not about to allow a supercilious duke to condescend to her. If Arden does not want her assistance, he can take his arrogance and go back to his fancy drawing room where he belongs.

Their clash is as instant as it is inevitable. When a fresh wave of bombings hits London, and the danger intensifies, Lucien and Hazel must work together to bring a new ring of Fenians to justice. The more time they spend in each other's company, the more the underlying attraction between them sizzles, until it bursts into uncontrollable flames.

Haunted by past tragedy, Lucien vowed long ago never to fall in love. Hazel's sole rule in life is to trust no one. But soon, the cold duke and the bold American find themselves locked in a battle for the greatest prize of all—each other's hearts.

Dedication

To all the Hazels and women who dare.

What do they mean, these marks,
if not how to calibrate ourselves in the
endless dark of night's sky,
to find out where we've been,
where we're going?
~ "Astrolabe" by Scarlett Scott

Chapter One

1882

$\mathcal{A}$ S FAR AS Lucien was concerned, Mr. H.E. Montgomery could go to the devil.

Not only was the American interloper unwanted, but he was also late. Lucien despised tardiness. It was enough of an indignity the Home Office had foisted the Pinkerton agent upon him as a proposed—he shuddered—*partner*. But now, the fellow could not even be bothered to appear at the appointed time for their first meeting.

Lucien removed his pocket watch from his waistcoat and glared at the ticking hands, which revealed Mr. H.E. Montgomery, celebrated Pinkerton and new fellow leader of the Special League, was precisely forty-seven seconds tardy.

"Unacceptable," he muttered to himself, his irritation mounting with each passing second.

Lucien attempted to distract himself by once more turning his attention back to the compendium of Montgomery's cases as a Pinkerton, a career which appeared to extend at least a decade into the past. The fellow had successfully routed murderers and thieves, and in recent years, had infiltrated a cutthroat band of New York City Fenians known as the Emerald Club.

All well and good. All perfectly fine. He had no doubt Mr. Montgomery was more than capable of performing his job in America. But England was a great deal different, and this was Lucien's bloody territory. He had been leading investigations into the dangerous network of Fenians threatening England, at home and abroad, on his own for months now. He had done a damned good job of seeing a number of Fenians arrested, the threat they posed to the public effectively extinguished by his hand. Indeed, if it were not for The Incident, Home Office would never have made such a humiliating demand.

Being forced to accept this Yankee agent was an anathema to him.

Particularly since the man was now—Lucien checked his watch—one minute and seventeen seconds late.

A knock sounded on his study door at last, and the portal opened to reveal the expressionless countenance of his butler, Reynolds.

"Has Montgomery arrived?" he asked, his irritation mounting.

"You do have a visitor, Your Grace," said Reynolds with a furrowing of his brow. "However, I am afraid it is not a Mr. Montgomery at all, but rather—"

"*Miss* Montgomery," drawled a distinctly feminine voice.

An equally feminine figure, clad in a smart navy gown and a jaunty hat atop her head, rudely brushed past Reynolds and sailed into Lucien's study. The creature who sauntered across the chamber and approached his desk was decidedly not who Lucien had been expecting.

"Forgive me, Your Grace," Reynolds said in a strangled tone. "I am afraid Miss Montgomery refused to wait until I ascertained if you were receiving callers."

"You need not speak of me as if I am absent from the room," the woman admonished his butler, fixing the unfortunate domestic with a look designed to convey her supreme irritation. "I am standing right here, and I do assure you both my ears and my wits are in perfect working order."

She turned back to Lucien, standing over his desk in a startlingly authoritative fashion. Though she was slim, she was tall, and she possessed a commanding air at odds with what one expected of a genteel lady.

"Does everyone in England have a guard dog posted at the door?" she demanded of Lucien, without preamble.

Then again, it was becoming increasingly apparent the woman before him, despite being fashionably garbed, was no genteel lady.

Lucien spared a glance for poor Reynolds, who hovered at the threshold, for once appearing uncertain of the protocol. To the domestic's credit, it was not a daily occurrence for the butler to be routed, then thoroughly browbeaten, by a brash American female.

"That will be all, Reynolds." Lucien waited for his butler to make his discreet exit before turning back to his unexpected visitor. "Please do—" She settled herself into one of the chairs opposite his desk without a hint of grace. "Sit."

"Thank you." She thrust her gloved hand forward. "It is a pleasure to make your acquaintance at last, sir. I have heard a great deal about your work."

He frowned, staring at her hand. He supposed she meant for him to shake it, so he did, against his better judgment. "Indeed, Miss Montgomery. It is a pleasure to make your acquaintance as well, though I must admit your appearance here is unexpected. I presume you are Mr. Montgomery's sister?"

She frowned back at him. "Who the hell is Mr. Montgomery?"

She was still holding his hand, shaking it with a grip which was strong and altogether unladylike. He did not wear gloves, and though she did, the warmth of her skin burned into his. It seemed somehow intimate. Too intimate. He extricated himself from her grasp, tamping down the unwanted reaction.

What manner of female was this, dressed as a lady, yet unpardonably rude? Shockingly pretty, in spite of her abrasive personality? And why had she asked him who Mr. Montgomery was? Or, to be precise, *who the hell* Mr. Montgomery was?

He cleared his throat, feeling rather disconcerted, which was unlike himself, but this astonishing creature had him at sixes and sevens. "Forgive me, Miss Montgomery, but I presumed, since I was to meet with Mr. Montgomery, and you share the fellow's surname, surely the two of you must be familiars, if not relations."

Icy blue eyes, studded with long dark lashes, met his unflinchingly. "There is no Mr. Montgomery, Mr. Arden."

Mr. Arden?

He was so flummoxed by the sheer effrontery of the woman, it took him an extra second to realize everything she had just said. "Of course there is a Mr. Montgomery," he snapped. "Madam, I do not know what game you are playing at, but I am not amused. I suggest you take your leave at once. I have neither the time nor the inclination to engage in riddles. Furthermore, I am the Duke of Arden, *not* Mr. Arden. My correct form of address is *Your Grace*."

She pursed her lips, and he noted—quite involuntarily—how full they were, how sensual. "I am aware of the proper form of address for a duke, Your Grace. I was merely making a point."

What the devil? A disconcerting sense of unease slid down his spine.

"A point," he repeated. "Would you care to elaborate, madam?"

She sighed. "I am beginning to discover your need for my aid, Your Grace. Very well, if I must explain, I chose the wrong form of address for you, just as you have done for me. As you can plainly see, I am *Miss* Montgomery, decidedly *not* a mister."

"*You* are H.E. Montgomery," he said, the unease blossoming, radiating throughout his entire body.

She smiled, and damnation if that smile did not hit him, first in the gut, then somewhere distinctively lower. "Miss Hazel Elizabeth Montgomery, Pinkerton agent, at your service."

"But you are a woman," he said stupidly.

An evident observation, but he could not keep it from bursting forth from him. In all his correspondence with the Home Office, in every debriefing he had suffered in the wake of The Incident, he had been told to expect the famed H.E. Montgomery, arriving to act as his partner in the Special League, being diverted from assignment in New York City.

He had never once been told to expect a female.

Miss Montgomery made a great show of glancing down at her person, feigning surprise as she did so. "Why, I am a woman. How shocking, Your Grace! You *do* have women in England, I presume?"

A maddening, ill-mannered woman, he added silently. He noted again the drawl giving her words their foreign lilt and wondered what part of her country she hailed from. And then he reminded himself it did not matter, for there was no way he was going to accept this creature as his partner in the League, and after today, he would likely never set eyes upon her again.

"Yes, Miss Montgomery," he replied, careful to keep his tone as frigid as possible. "We *do* have women in England, and they are all far more refined than you."

A mocking smile curved her mouth, drawing his attention to the fullness of her lower lip, the perfectly defined Cupid's bow of the upper. *Damnation*, this would not do. He could not continue to notice the woman's mouth. It was an aberration, surely, for a creature this bold, vexing, and masculine in conduct to possess lips so supple and pink. Likely, it was the only softness she possessed.

But then his gaze dipped to her bosom—also involuntarily—and he had to admit Miss Montgomery owned other distinctly soft areas beyond her mouth. And his trousers seemed suddenly tight.

A burst of self-loathing struck him square in the chest.

The mocking smile blossomed, growing wider. "I cannot argue the point with you, Mr. Arden, as I am woefully lacking in knowledge concerning refined English women. Undoubtedly, it would not be considered refined of me to acknowledge I noticed your gaze dropping to my bosom."

He almost swallowed his tongue. His spine stiffened, and he pinned his most ducal, frigid stare upon her. "I do beg your pardon, Miss Montgomery."

"Beg my pardon all you like, Mr. Arden." She waved a hand in the air as if she were swatting a fly. Truly, the woman owned *not a modicum* of grace. "You are staring at me in a manner I find insulting. More insulting than the thinly veiled slurs you have already delivered verbally, in fact. I will thank you to look upon me in the same fashion as you would any man."

Mr. Arden.

He did not even know where to begin. Surely the woman before him was a poor jest on the part of the Home Office. Perhaps an attempt to test his mettle.

"You may address me as *Your Grace*," he informed her coldly. "If I am to treat you with respect, I expect it to be reciprocated."

"I will reciprocate when you begin," she said with false sweetness.

Her voice, deceptively pleasing and mellifluous, the unhurried drawl of her words, all settled over him in a way he could not like. The woman was irritating. Unnerving. Maddening.

"Mr. Arden," she added.

Damn it all to hell.

"Madam, you are one more *Mr. Arden* away from being tossed out of my home."

She raised a brow. "Tossed? Truly? Who will do the tossing, Mr. Arden? Your guard dog? I cannot think him the sort to toss about ladies, despite the low regard his employer holds them in. Surely not you?"

Irritation lanced him. "It is an *expression*, Miss Montgomery. Surely you have those in America?"

She continued studying him in that bold, assessing manner of hers, and the strange urge to sit straighter in his chair struck him. He could not shake the feeling this woman was taking his measure.

And finding him lacking.

"Of course we do." She began plucking off her gloves then, one finger at a time, and he watched, mesmerized and horrified. "See here, sir. We have wasted enough precious time on circling each other with our daggers drawn. There is far more important work to be done, so let us be candid. If we are to be partners, you cannot think of me as a female."

Partners. He swallowed a bitter lump of resentment. "Madam, we will never be partners."

"We are already partners, sir." Her tone was cool. Stubborn.

No, they damn well were not. Nor would they ever be, if

he had any say in the matter. And he certainly intended to have one. A very long, very precise, very vehement say.

"Prospective partners," he said. "The Home Office will need to issue final approval, as will I."

The last was not true, for The Incident had significantly reduced his authority, but this creature need not know that. Inexplicably, his gaze settled upon her hands. They were small, the nails neat. She wore a gold ring, studded with a small pearl, upon her left hand, but no other adornment. Her fingers were fine-boned, almost delicate, in stark contrast to her brash personality. He had not previously found this part of a woman's body intriguing before, but he could not deny the subtle rush of warmth the sight of them provoked within him.

"Have you found fault with my hands, Mr. Arden?" she asked in her airy drawl.

Confound it.

"Your Grace," he corrected. "You have removed your gloves."

"I cannot turn pages whilst I am wearing gloves." She bent down to retrieve something from the floor, then re-emerged with a satchel he had somehow failed to notice upon her earlier entrance. "Perhaps it is because I am not *refined*."

The woman had a true gift for nettling him. He had never in his life met a female more irksome than this one. Lucien watched as she produced a thin gold chain, hidden at her neck by the high décolletage of her gown, by plucking it free from her bodice. A key hung from the end of it, which she thrust into a lock on her satchel.

Astounding. The woman had secreted a key in her bloody bosom. What was next? A pistol beneath her hat? A dagger from her shoe? And why did the sight of that key, which he knew instinctively would be warm from the heat of her flesh, taunt him? Why did his own fingers itch to touch it?

"Precisely what is it you are doing, madam?" he asked, forcing an edge of steel into his tone.

She rummaged about in the satchel, before extracting a leather-bound journal. She placed it atop his desk, then slid it toward him. "Producing some case notes I have prepared for you. While I do not officially begin in my capacity as your partner until tomorrow, you will have had ample time to review the results of my recent work in New York City. I have made some interesting discoveries concerning future plots here in London."

Her response, and the journal itself, took him by surprise. Despite her brazen nature, she appeared to take her work seriously. And if the notes he had read regarding her past cases were any indication, she was an excellent agent.

He flipped the journal open to a random page. Her penmanship was tidy and concise, bereft of ornamentation. He snapped it closed. "While I appreciate the offer, Miss Montgomery, I am afraid I do not believe our...*partnership* will be necessary."

The mere word "partnership" felt bitter and distasteful upon his tongue, far more because it was being used in conjunction with this conundrum of a female. She locked her satchel and dropped her key back into its hiding place—snug in her ample breasts—once more as he looked on in horrified silence. Slowly, methodically, she pulled her gloves back on.

"Madam?" he prodded into the silence, pushing the journal back across his desk. "I believe you will want to take this with you on your return journey to America."

"You will wish to read it," she said. "Do not be pigheaded, Mr. Arden. It ill becomes you."

She had just delivered two more insults to him without batting her long dark lashes. He ground his teeth. What in the hell had the Home Office been thinking, saddling him with this…*this*…

Damnation! He could not even think of a word in the English language fitting enough to be used to describe her.

"I very much doubt you could have uncovered any evidence I have not already received from my own men in New York City." He gave her a tight smile, refusing to descend to her level this time.

It was true, after all. He possessed a vast network of agents scattered across America, Ireland, and England. He knew the Fenians were plotting once more. Thus far, most of their bombing campaigns—efforts to strong-arm England into giving Ireland Home Rule—had either failed abysmally in their ability to inflict damage, or had been stopped by Special League investigations.

There was nothing, he was certain, this vulgar American Pinkerton agent could tell him which he did not already know.

"Of course, Mr. Arden." Her expression became pinched. "Your *men*."

He did not like the implication in her tone. It was true he had been shocked to discover H.E. Montgomery was in fact *Miss Hazel Elizabeth* Montgomery, rather than the man he had supposed her to be. But he did not entirely object to her being female, though admittedly, he had been taken aback to discover H.E. Montgomery was a woman. Rather, he objected to the notion of being forced to share his power with anyone, let alone her.

Plainly put, he did not like her. He had not liked her when he had supposed her to be Mr. Montgomery, and neither did he like her as Miss Montgomery. The Special League was his now, and given enough time to make reparations for The Incident, Lucien was certain the Home Office's faith in him as a leader would be restored. The

Incident aside, his record was impeccable. He had imprisoned dozens of Fenians since taking on his position, ensuring the safety of the queen's men, women, and children to the best of his ability.

"I mean you no insult, madam," he said, making his best effort at kindness, though Lord knew the creature before him deserved none. If she called him *Mr. Arden* one more time, he would gather her over his shoulder and personally haul her from his home. "What I meant to say, is that I fear the Home Office made the wrong decision in bringing an American agent to London to aid our cause. You are best served in your homeland. Our concerns here are better answered by myself and the agents beneath me. I will be speaking to the Home Office later today, and I am confident they will agree with my concerns in the matter."

"The Home Office was very clear on the matter when I spoke with them prior to my arrival here," she said, flashing him a smug smile. "I enjoyed a lovely discussion with the Duke of Winchelsea, Mr. Arden. It is the reason for my tardiness."

Her revelation sank in his gut like a leaden weight.

"Once again, I would remind you I am the Duke of Arden," he gritted. "You may refer to me as Duke or Arden or Your Grace, Miss Montgomery."

She stood abruptly, smile still in place, clutching her satchel as if it were a weapon. "As I said, I will address you with respect when you treat me with the same. Now, if you will excuse me, I find I am plum tired from all my travels. I will leave my journal with you. If you would be so kind as to point me in the direction of my lodging?"

Plum tired.

The woman was a menace. But at least she was leaving at last. The weight in his gut lightened incrementally.

He stood. "I am afraid I do not know your hotel, madam. You may inquire with my butler, Reynolds. He ought to be able to assist you."

"Oh, I am not staying in a hotel," she informed him brightly. "I am staying here. With you."

The hell she was. "That is out of the question, madam."

"There was a recent spate of thefts at the hotel where I was meant to stay." She tilted her head, considering him as if she found him pitiful. "The Home Office has deemed it best I stay here, as your guest, until further notice. We cannot afford for my documents to be stolen and find their way into the wrong hands, you understand, Mr. Arden. Now then, will you be showing me to my room, or would you prefer me to inquire with the guard dog?"

He clenched his jaw so hard, it ached.

Abomination, he decided grimly. *That* was the perfect word to describe Miss Hazel Montgomery.

Chapter Two

*H*AZEL FROWNED DOWN at the words she had written in her journal beneath the heading *Lucien West, Duke of Arden.*

> *Arrogant.*
> *Condescending.*
> *Devilishly handsome.*

The last two words did not belong in her catalog, and the sight of them, penned in her own hand, aggrieved her mightily.

Why, it was as if her mind betrayed her.

Whenever she began a new case, it was her habit—a tactic established years ago, at the beginning of her career as a Pinkerton agent, but one which had stood the test of time—to make copious notes on all involved in the case. Suspects, friends, family members, fellow detectives, the law… Hazel recorded everyone, categorized them, studied them. Her mind functioned at its greatest potential when she was organized.

Lists. Her mind wanted *lists.*

Her fellow agents found her an oddity, she knew. Not just because she was a female, but a *peculiar* female at that, the sort who had no desire to become some man's blushing bride. The sort who chose to find her own fortune, her own destiny. The sort who relied upon herself, upon her cunning, wit, daring, and determination. The sort who earned her own money and paid for the bread on her table and the roof over her head.

But strange or not, she had established a history. Not a failed case in a decade, with the exception of one. And she believed, quite firmly, her success was due to the familiarity she had with herself. It was the sort of familiarity which only could be had by years of living on her own, years of depending upon herself. She had learned a long time ago to trust no one else, to be her own best ally at all times.

Hazel had been depending upon herself from the time she was old enough to walk. Had learned to listen to the needs of her convoluted, confusing, complex mind. If her mind required lists, she gave it lists, by God.

One thing she did *not* do, was allow herself to feel any emotions toward her fellow agents or the suspects she investigated. She had allowed it to happen once, in the early stages of her career, and she would never forget the painful lesson she had learned. There was no place for subjectivity as a Pinkerton agent. Each moment was one of life or death, decision versus indecision, truth warring with deceit, right over wrong.

Proverbs said *pride goeth before destruction, and an haughty spirit before a fall*, but Hazel believed firmly it was not pride, but rather an inability to see past one's nose, which caused destruction. She chose objectivity over subjectivity, without fail.

Which was why she put the metal tip of her pen to paper now and struck through the unwanted third item on the list. Heaving a sigh, she dipped her pen back into ink and continued her list.

Devilishly handsome.

Icy.

Forbidding.

Suffering from an abundance of self-confidence.

Yes, there was that. The Duke of Arden thought himself invincible. She had spotted it from the moment she had first set eyes upon him when she had entered his study.

She frowned down at the sudden ink blot, which fell from her nib and marred the page.

"Oh, hell," she muttered.

Now she would have to tear out the sheet and begin again. The ink stain ruined it all. Hazel tore the bound page in one hasty rip, then crumpled it and set it aside.

She began again.

Lucien West, Duke of Arden.

Arrogant.

Forbidding.

Suffering from an abundance of self-confidence.

Strongly objects to being referred to as "Mr. Arden."

She could not repress her smile as she wrote the last. Her intentional needling of him had proven fruitful indeed. Not only had it revealed a great deal to her about him, but it had also been vastly entertaining to watch the flush of anger steal over his sharp cheekbones. To witness him shifting in his seat, to note the ferocious slant of his brows, the pursing of his lips, the grinding of his teeth, and the tensing of his jaw.

Yet another necessity Hazel had learned during the course of her years as a Pinkerton agent: always study your fellow agents and detectives. It was the key, not only to working well with others, but to understanding their weaknesses and being able to fill the holes they inevitably left in an investigation accordingly, before it was too late.

And the Duke of Arden possessed a waterfall of weaknesses.

A gushing geyser of them after she'd had enough time to study him and anticipate his reactions. He was surprisingly easy to manipulate. Though, to herself alone, she would admit some of her manipulations had been for her own pleasure, and had nothing whatsoever to do with her role as his partner.

A role he resented her for obtaining.

He had not been expecting a woman, and he had made no effort to hide that fact. Nor had he expected her to be a guest of his. Her smile deepened at the thought of her most successful manipulation of the duke. The Home Office did not give a damn where she laid her head at night, and she knew it. Nor had there been any thefts in the hotel at which she had been scheduled to stay. But she had been struck as she sat there in Arden's study, the subject of his unnerving perusal, by the notion she should see how far she could push him.

Staying as a guest in his home seemed an excellent choice.

He had been too polite to deny her. Not an hour earlier, Arden's butler, a man who seemed to view smiling as a sin, had escorted her to the chamber in which she now found herself. Naturally, though she had extended the offer to him, the duke would never deign to stoop so low as to show her to a room, as if he were no better than a servant himself. His sense of self-importance, likely ingrained in him since birth, would not allow it.

Easily manipulated, she added to her list. No surprise on that account; most men were, especially by fluttering lashes and feminine praise.

Pompous.

Strong.

Damn it all, where had the last item on her list emerged from?

She once more crossed out and continued on.

Strong.

Dark hair.

Emerald eyes.

Possessed of an authoritative manner.

No, this simply would not do. It made the Duke of Arden sound like a marital prospect, and Hazel had decidedly not suffered sailing over an ocean, then riding a train across England, merely so she could find herself a husband. Not only did she not want to marry, but she also had a purpose.

The information she had gleaned when she had posed as Mrs. Eliza Jane Mulligan in New York City would prove crucial to her work here in London. Of that, she was certain. If only her partner was as sure. She thought once more of the manner in which he had carelessly paged through her journal before dismissing it earlier, and returned to her list with a new resolve.

Emerald eyes.

Possessed of an authoritative manner.

Exceedingly rude.

Yes, no question about it, the man was insufferably dis-courteous. She ought to enjoy outsmarting him as she had, making an utter fool of him. For today, her story would hold true. Likely, by tomorrow, the truth of it would reign free, and she would then find herself landing on her rump after all, just as he had promised.

Had she already written arrogant? A cursory perusal of her list suggested she had. But if there was anyone she had ever crossed paths with who deserved a double listing of the word arrogant more, she could not think of one.

Arrogant, she added for the second time.

A quick, unexpected rap sounded at her door before she could proceed any further.

Some foolishness inside her convinced Hazel it was the Duke of Arden, coming to apologize for his earlier treatment of her. A second knock sounded, and she gave up the effort, simply snapping the journal shut. With a sigh, she stuffed her pen back into the inkwell before rising.

Hazel made her way to the door and opened it, startled to find yet another servant hovering in the hallway before her, this time, a female, who appeared similar in age to Hazel. A ready, if sheepish, smile was pinned to her lips.

"Miss Montgomery," the servant greeted. "My name is Bunton. I am here to help you in dressing for dinner this evening. May I take the liberty of unpacking your trunks while you are otherwise engaged as well?"

Unpacking her trunks? Either the Duke of Arden believed her flummery, or this was his way of testing her. She decided the answer did not signify, for she traveled lightly—one trunk only—and no one had ever helped her to dress herself since she had been a babe in swaddling. What a lark! But then, this place *was* called Lark House, was it not? Fitting.

She did not hesitate with her answer. "I do thank you, Bunton, but no. Please advise the Duke of Arden that I will not require his peculiar sense of hospitality. I will do for myself, just as I always have."

Bunton blinked, seeming uncertain of how to proceed.

She lingered on the threshold, speechless. Hazel supposed most guests of the Duke of Arden would be elegant societal lords and ladies, who expected servants, such as the woman before her, to aid them in their unpacking and dressing. What a fantastical notion.

"I am afraid I cannot relay such a message to His Grace on your behalf, Miss Montgomery," the domestic replied at last, her tone stiff.

"Thank you then," she tried again, smiling, though she was weary, and she wanted nothing more than to return to her work. "You may go. I am otherwise occupied."

Hazel had never particularly enjoyed the company of others. Not since Adam, that was. But she would not think of him now, for fear she would spend the rest of the evening wallowing in melancholy, rather than formulating her battle plan.

And a battle plan was precisely what her latest assignment would entail, there was no question of that.

But Bunton was still lingering, her expression fraught with concern. "I was told to assist you, Miss Montgomery, and directly by His Grace." She looked as if she had been about to say more, but paused, attempting to compose herself.

Hazel's eyes narrowed upon the poor woman, who clearly lived in fear of her employer. It would seem she had another trait to add to her notes concerning Arden: *Tyrant.*

"No need to overset yourself, my dear," she said soothingly. Over the years, her work as an agent had enabled her to hone her skill of reading others, and the woman before her was clearly distraught. "Come along inside then, won't you? I have already unpacked my trunk, but there is no reason why you cannot have a seat and keep me company."

Indeed, now that she thought upon it, suffering more social interaction this day would prove most worthwhile, if it garnered her additional understanding of the Duke of Arden. He had made his distaste for her—a *female*—as his partner apparent. She would need to fight him at every turn to prove her worth, and the more ammunition she had in her reserves, the better it would suit her.

Bunton entered the chamber, closing the door softly at her back. "Thank you, Miss Montgomery. I am new to my position, but I would not like to displease His Grace. The duke has never spoken to me directly before today, and I do wish to keep this post."

Hazel knew the necessity of earning her bread and board more than anyone. "I understand, Bunton. Forgive me for being churlish. You see, I am not a cheerful traveler. Ships make me ill, and I fear railways are little better. I have landed in an unfamiliar country, and I am tired and disagreeable and decidedly in need of sustenance. I am famished."

"Dinner is to be served in an hour, madam, but I can fetch you something from the kitchens now if you wish," Bunton said then, ripping Hazel from the murky distractions of her past. "Regardless of what you decide, we should have ample time to prepare you for dinner, Miss Montgomery."

Hazel glanced down at her navy gown, one of the finest dresses she owned. She had donned it early that morning, but it was holding up rather well, she thought. Few wrinkles to show for all the carriages and chairs she had inhabited. And it had cost a handsome penny too, as it was made by a fine dress maker back in New York. Handsome gowns were one of Hazel's few indulgences. Gowns and sweets. And baths. Hot, delightful baths, such a rarity and a delight...

"What preparing have we need for, Bunton?" she asked. "I am already dressed for dinner."

Bunton appeared crestfallen. "Madam, forgive me. Is this not a day gown?"

Hazel sighed. Her hands itched to return to her journal, to take up pen once more and set the nib to paper. Her work loomed before her like a gaping, voracious maw. There was no more disconcerting time than the beginning of a new assignment, when she needed to lay the foundation, organize her existing knowledge so she could build upon it with her inquiries and investigations, brick by brick. Always daunting, yet forever thrilling.

She had no wish to be tormented over a matter as trivial as the gown she wore. "It is indeed a day gown, but a very fine one, Bunton. It will do."

Bunton's expression tightened with disappointment. "Very well, Miss Montgomery. Perhaps I may see to getting you a light repast while you wait, if you do not wish my aid in your toilette?"

Guilt skewered Hazel. "I do have one gown, Bunton, which may be a more suitable choice for dinner."

It was her finest gown, the gown she knew showed off her figure to perfection, cut and draped with skillful precision. Fashioned in rich cream silk moiré, accented with cornflower-blue, and trimmed with antique lace, it had been sent to New York all the way from Paris. The dress had cost so much of her wages, she had eschewed dinner for two months just to pay for the frivolous confection.

Only to never wear it. It had accompanied her on her journey because of its value. She hated to leave the thing behind.

She ought not wear the dress now either. Not for the first time, and certainly not for the Duke of Arden. And yet, something within her longed to feel the luxurious silk against her skin. To don the extravagance she had not dared dream she would ever own as if it were her armor...

"Perhaps you could show it to me, Miss Montgomery?

And then, I can see to your hair."

Hazel frowned. "What is wrong with my hair, Bunton?"

Bunton blinked again. "Nothing at all, Miss Montgomery. It is perfectly lovely as it is."

She quirked a brow. "But?"

A flush tinged Bunton's pale cheeks. "But perhaps I could dress it for you. His Grace requested me to aid you, Miss Montgomery. I mean to uphold my duty."

Hazel's frown deepened. She was beginning to think she ought to have closed the door neatly in the domestic's face when the woman had first appeared. If she had, Hazel could have continued on with her solitude and her research. But now, Bunton stood before her with expectations.

Damn it all to hell.

She sighed. "Very well, Bunton. Do what you must."

LUCIEN WONDERED IF he should have armed himself prior to joining Miss Montgomery for dinner. He watched her attacking the food upon her plate with a vigor he had never before witnessed. His curious house guest and unwanted partner-of-the-moment was overdressed in a silk evening gown, her hair worn in a more becoming style, which was captured at her nape. The lush femininity of her form and the extravagant gown were at odds with the voracious manner in which she consumed her dinner.

Right now, he very much pitied the *haricot verts.*

Her gaze met his, delivering a shock he felt to his core. She raised a brow, as if in challenge. "Is something amiss?"

Yes, something was amiss. He had an American interloper seated across from him at his dinner table. A strange, rude woman, who had either never been taught not to spear her vegetables as if she were harpooning a whale upon her fine porcelain plate, or just did not give a damn. She was yet another punishment he had suffered in the wake of The Incident, along with the surrendering of his pride and self-respect. He could not look upon her without being reminded of his own faults.

But he, too, had been rude, he realized belatedly, for he had been staring at her in horrified fascination. He cleared his throat. "Forgive me, Miss Montgomery, but I could not help but to note the intensity with which you consume your repast. Are you angry with this course in particular, or is it all the courses in general?"

More rudeness from him, but he could not help it. Miss Montgomery irked him. Her presence at his dinner table, within his very home, nettled him. He resented her. In truth, he resented himself.

Her cheeks flushed, an embarrassed tinge of red stealing over the creamy skin. She stared at him for an indeterminate span of time, long enough he had to tamp down the urge to squirm in his seat, much like a lad whose nursemaid had caught him sneaking his dinner to the family pet.

"Hungry, Mr. Arden, not angry. I am merely hungry," she said at last.

And he felt, instantly, a sharp, stinging sensation he recognized at once: Shame. He wanted to say something remorseful. To fill the silence with an apology. But his lips refused to form it.

"This is the first meal I have had the occasion to partake in today," she added, flummoxing him even more. "Between my arrival, my time at the Home Office, and my visit to you, I have been kept quite busy. I had not realized how famished I had become until I sat down. I do realize I am more…vigorous than most females. But my constitution has always stood me in excellent stead, so I'll not apologize for it now."

She was vexed with him. Lucien saw it in the way her mouth tightened and her eyes darkened. Rightfully so. For the first time since her unexpected arrival in his study—Miss Montgomery, that was, rather than the gentleman he had prepared himself to meet—it occurred to him she was not to blame for her interference in his life. After all, the Home Office had offered her the position aiding him in leading the League. The Home Office had courted her, had brought her over the sea, had landed her in his midst like a bloody pestilence.

He clenched his jaw, stemming the disastrous tide of his thoughts. Lucien could not bring himself to apologize, but he knew he must swallow his bitterness and offer something.

"Do not let me stand in the way of your vigor, Miss Montgomery," he said, his tone stilted. He noted her plate was empty, and he turned to a footman, who presided over the entire odd affair. "The next course, if you please."

When the servant had taken his leave, Miss Montgomery took a healthy gulp of her wine at last. Lucien had noted she had yet to touch it during the course of their meal, though she had shown great enthusiasm for every morsel of food. When she was finished, her tongue flicked slowly over her upper lip.

Once drawn there, his attention remained riveted upon the perfect bow of her pink pout. The sight of her tongue should not have affected him, and yet, his cock twitched. He swallowed, reaching for his own wine, then poured a healthy portion down his throat.

"How can there be yet another course?" Miss Montgomery asked, providing him a source of distraction he appreciated.

"That was but the *relevé*," he told her. "The *entremêts* are next. Shall I call them off? If you are famished, however, surely you would wish to partake?"

She smiled at him, and that rare transformative curve of her lips hit him squarely in the chest. "Of course I wish to partake, Arden. My mind works best when my stomach is happy."

He blinked, taken aback by her artless honesty. "Very well then."

"Have you perused my notes?" she asked, assessing him in that frank manner she had. Utterly guileless.

Maddening, really.

The woman before him was no lady. If Great Aunt Hortense had not been dining that evening with the ladies of her beloved hospital charity, she would have been properly horrified by Miss Montgomery's manners. Of course, she would also be horrified to know he was dining alone with an unwed female. But he would deal with his aunt's indignation later, when the time came. Procrastination was his favorite form of art when it came to the beloved dragon.

For now, back to Miss Montgomery's notes.

"I have read a portion of them," he told her, having no intention of discussing the matter over the next remove while a servant hovered. "They are...copious."

In truth, he had not perused them beyond the initial glance he had cast over them earlier during their awkward interview. And he had no intention of reading them either, for he was not about to share his duties with Miss Montgomery. Indeed, the mere notion of seeing the frothy tiers of her silken skirts as she entered a carriage on her way back to America filled him with a searing sense of satisfaction.

"Copious," she repeated now, disrupting his fantasy of her exodus.

"Would you prefer voluminous?" he asked, as the next

dishes were laid before them.

The urge to discomfit her, to ruffle her feathers, could not be dismissed. Even if he had no intention of working alongside her, he could not deny a part of him found her an oddity. Intriguing, even.

"They are detailed and rife with important information," she informed him coolly, before turning her attention to the dish before her and attacking it just as surely as she had her *haricot verts*.

The remainder of the dinner continued in polite silence. When the dessert course had been whisked away, Lucien dismissed the footman, leaving himself and Miss Montgomery alone in the drawing room. It was deuced odd, sharing the table with a female other than his aunt and his sister, Violet. But Violet was now the Duchess of Strathmore and damned unlikely to be sharing his table any time soon, thanks to The Incident. He sipped his port, drowning the disagreeable thought with spirits, an ineffective panacea though it was.

Miss Montgomery had accepted port and had remained at the table along with him, as if she too were a gentleman. She watched him now, that icy gaze of hers assessing. "You did not read my journal, did you?"

The warmth which had begun to unfurl within him from the port died. Blast the woman. He took another sip, returning her regard frankly.

"No."

Her lips compressed. "Nor do you have any intention of reading it."

The last was a statement rather than a question. She seemed an intelligent woman. Indeed, if the list of successful cases she had completed was an indication, she was quite smart. Therefore, he would not prevaricate.

"No." He savored another sip port.

Her spine stiffened, her eyes blazing with irritation. "Do you doubt my abilities because I am a woman, Mr. Arden?"

Again with the bloody *mister* nonsense.

He sighed. "You may call me Arden, madam."

"I do believe I already informed you the circumstances required for me to refer to you by your silly title."

He placed his glass on the table with more force than necessary, the sound echoing through the chamber. "Need I remind you that you are a guest in my home, madam?"

"What has that got to do with me calling you Mr. Arden?" she returned.

He ground his molars. The woman certainly knew how to goad him. "If I did not respect you, I would not be seated here at the table with you now. I would not have seen you comfortably settled in a guest chamber for the evening nor provided you with an attendant. I would not have listened to you natter through the soup course."

"I did not speak a word during the soup course."

Perhaps she had not. His mind was heavy with troubles, and the vexing female before him was the last complication he needed to add to his burdens. All he knew was, at some point, she had returned to the topic of her damnable journal once more, and they had not left it ever since.

He frowned. "You may as well have. Your eyes speak for you."

That much was true. Her unusual light-blue gaze was everywhere, always observing, and seeing far too much, he had no doubt.

"What a strange man you are, Mr. Arden," she said, her tone contemplative.

He bristled. "You will call me Arden, madam, or I shall throw you over my shoulder and cart you to the carriage myself."

"Let us strike a bargain," she suggested, seemingly unaffected by his threat.

Perhaps she did not think he would manhandle her. Certainly, the gentleman within him would not dare to commit such a sin. But as he watched her now, pique swelling within him, he could not help but to believe himself capable of it.

And worse, that he would savor the moment.

For a beat, he imagined himself rising from his chair, then closing the distance between them, hauling her from her seat, and sending her over his shoulder. His hands would settle upon her rump, and he would stride to the door while she protested. Perhaps she would squirm, attempting to escape him as she continued to refer to him as Mr. Arden, and he would be forced to deliver a swat to her bottom to make her still…

Damnation. He drained the remnants of his port. She was speaking, he realized, whilst he had been fantasizing about her removal from his home. And how his fantasy had become so suddenly sensual in nature, he did not wish to know.

"What do you say, sir?" she asked, watching him expectantly.

Her bloody bargain. He had drowned out the sound of her proposal with his own disgraceful thoughts.

Lucien cleared his throat, as irritated with himself as he was with Miss Montgomery. "Repeat the bargain, if you would, madam."

"Of course." Her smile widened knowingly. "I promise to call you 'Arden,' and in return, you promise to read my journal."

Oh, she thought she was clever, his determined American thorn-in-the-side. But he was far craftier than she supposed. Far more skilled in the art of dismantling his opponents, tearing them apart, piece by piece. And there was no mistake here; this woman, lush and feminine and unassuming though she appeared, was very much not just his opponent, but perhaps even his rival. It had occurred to him the Home Office, whilst in the midst of making the Special League an official branch of Scotland Yard, may be looking for a replacement.

That perhaps H.E. Montgomery would usurp him, unthinkable though it was.

For he had only just begun.

"Let us drink to the bargain," he said, smiling into her eyes as he refilled his glass, before raising it aloft.

For if he had to guess, he would wager Miss Hazel Elizabeth Montgomery did not imbibe often. Everything about her neat precise scrawl and rigid attention to detail, suggested a woman who very much needed to be in control of herself and others at all times. And she had failed to touch her port thus far.

But she lifted her glass now, because her pride would not allow otherwise, just as he had suspected.

"I will indeed drink to that, Arden."

And then she did, swallowing nearly half the contents of her glass in one go, before suppressing her shudder, though her effort was obvious to him. He grinned at her. At long last, he had found the solution to his problem. He was going to make certain Miss Hazel Elizabeth Montgomery was thoroughly in her cups before the night was over.

Preferably, so soused she could not bear to rouse herself from bed—and for their all-important meeting with the Home Office—the next morning. No more abomination, no more bloody journal.

He raised his glass to his lips, taking a small measured sip, and damn it if his port didn't taste just a bit like victory.

Chapter Three

*H*AZEL GROANED, OPENING her eyes slowly, before blinking the room around her into distinct objects rather than hazy blurs. Her mouth was dry and bitter. Her stomach heaved. Her head pounded. In all, she felt as if her body had been relentlessly trampled by an invading army. She felt...*miserable*. That was the word.

What had happened? Where was she? When would the world cease swaying as if she were on a ship?

Lord God, was she still aboard that infernal ship? Was not nine days at sea, handsome cabin on a White Star Line steamer aside, enough?

No. Remembrance descended upon her mind with the torpidity of a lame mare. She was in an elegant chamber at the Duke of Arden's townhome, Lark House. Not to be confused with his many vast country holdings, of which there were no doubt legion. Because he was a duke, and he was icy and arrogant, and of course he owned more than one home— stately and extravagant though this one was.

She, meanwhile, had never called any place home since she'd been a girl. In truth, she had never possessed a home at all. Sometimes, not even a roof over her head or a dry place to sleep.

Her stomach rolled once more, much as it had when she'd been aboard the ship. Perhaps this was a lingering effect of her sea voyage, which had been merciless and punishing. She had cast up her accounts so many times during the arduous trip over stormy waters, she could still taste her own bile on her tongue even now.

Or was that her own bile she was tasting at this very moment? Had she vomited recently? The disgusting taste in her mouth certainly suggested she had. To corroborate, along came a murky reminiscence of the Duke of Arden procuring a chamber pot for her. Of his worried, yet still unbearably handsome, countenance, and of her clutching him before she lost her balance...

She had not vomited upon him, had she?

She searched her mind for the memory, for the answer, as she cringed and her stomach clenched yet again. Her mind was blank. What was this malady she suffered? Belated or prolonged seasickness? Perhaps the combination of her travel and her interactions with the condescending Duke of Arden had simply worn her out. There had been the seemingly endless sea voyage, followed by a seven-hour train ride from Liverpool to London; all more than enough to drive anyone to the edge of madness.

Surely those were the sole explanations for her failure to rise at dawn as was her customary habit. Those were the only reasons why she instead had awakened—*good sweet God*—with the sun bright and high on the other side of the window dressings.

What time was it? She had a meeting with Arden and the Duke of Winchelsea from the Home Office this morning, the first in her official capacity as Arden's partner. She could not afford to be late. And if there was one thing Hazel loathed more than deceptions, it was tardiness.

Her head thumped with increased vigor, her wretchedness mounting. How much wine had she consumed with dinner and its endless courses? And afterward, following the Duke of Arden's lead, not just sampling his port, but attempting to keep paces with him? Had he not asked her to toast to their bargain? And what else had he asked of her?

A surge of new memories returned to her then, hazy and indistinct. What a cake she had made of herself. Shame and regret stung her as if she had twin live coals in her belly.

She recalled laughing uncontrollably. Hiccupping into her hand. She remembered leaning upon Arden for support, the seemingly infinite journey up a set of stairs and down a never ending hall to her chamber. The smell of him, she recalled that as well, citrus and musk, with a hint of soap. Delightful, really. Not at all like hair grease and unwashed armpits like most of the men she had been in proximity with over the years.

The reminder of those disagreeable scents made her stomach lurch painfully now, as if she were smelling them in truth. Clutching her abdomen, she rolled over with another groan. *Dear Lord*, she needed a chamber pot. *Had* Arden given her one, offering it to her much like an olive branch the night before? Or was that memory born in her fanciful imagination, a product of her dreams?

Hazel swallowed against the sickness threatening to unburden itself from her throat. There was no mistaking her reaction, she feared. Her physical ailments, coupled with the fragments of lucid memory she possessed from the night before, all pointed to one inevitable truth.

The night before, she had been drunker than the husband of a temperance woman who had just been laid into the ground. *Yes*, she had. The time for denying her egregious lack of control and gross misconduct was at an end. She must face the truth of what she had done.

And what she had done was drink herself silly. She had

been unprofessional, even if goaded into it by Arden. Which she had, undeniably. She had allowed him to provoke her, and she saw it so plainly by the ugly morning light: her weakness, him taking advantage of the vulnerability in her defenses, as any opponent worth his salt would. As she would have done in his stead, had their situations been reversed. But that was rather a moot point.

Because the damage had already been done, the battle lines distinctly drawn. Hazel rolled from the bed, falling clumsily to the floor, and landed upon her hands and knees. The Axminster was thick, although not plush enough to blunt the sting of pain. But there was no time for pain. A more fervent need rolled up from her gut, demanding an answer.

She required the chamber pot her faded recollections had Arden proffering to her the evening before. *How humiliating.* He had been in this very room with her, the room where she would sleep, the room containing a bed.

Her hands seized the pot not a moment too soon, her mind grimly taking note after she had finished retching, that even the Duke of Arden's chamber pot was fancy.

"WHERE IS MISS Montgomery?"

Lucien knew a momentary spear of guilt, sharp and stinging, in his chest before he squelched it. He had no cause to feel guilt, he reminded himself, when the infernal woman had deceived him and cozened her way into staying at his home.

Careful to keep his face an expressionless mask of impassivity, he met the gaze of the Duke of Winchelsea, his primary contact at the Home Office, and the man responsible for saddling Lucien with The Abomination, which was how he vowed to think of her from this moment forward. It was far safer to think of her in those terms, after all, than to think of her as Miss Montgomery.

If he called her The Abomination, he would not be forced to recall the way her silk gown had clung lovingly to her generous bosom and sweetly curved waist. Nor would he recall her warmth, that suppressed feminine flesh heating his hand through her bodice, when he had escorted her to her chamber last night. She had not been wearing a corset, and he could not fathom how a dress could hug her body so well, without the boning and lacing which seemed to be the standard armament of all females.

Damn it, there he went again, thinking about The Abomination's lush form.

"Arden?" Winchelsea repeated, his irritated tone cutting through Lucien's tortured musings. "Have you received word from her this morning? When last we spoke, she assured me she would be here this morning at ten o'clock."

Though Winchelsea was a diplomat, his demeanor was often haughty and detached. Lucien resented the extension of the Home Office's power into the Special League under the aegis of the duke, and he suspected Winchelsea resented him in equal measure.

He extracted his pocket watch and glanced at the time. "I am afraid I have not, and it would appear she is one quarter hour late."

Because he had gotten her thoroughly soused the night before, refilling her port glass until she had no longer resembled the determined detective who had appeared in his study. Until she had been glassy-eyed, giggling, and hiccupping. Until she had required an escort to her chamber, and he had given her one, and she had clung to him like a lover, her breasts crushing into his arm.

Her nipples had been hard. He wished he had never

discovered the revelation. He also wished he was not thinking of those tempting peaks now, as he was seated across from the Duke of Winchelsea.

"This is most distressing," Winchelsea offered, his tone grim.

Lucien silently agreed. Thinking of The Abomination's breasts was not just distressing, it was the height of lunacy. But he and the duke were ruminating upon different matters entirely.

The door opened before he could gather his wits enough for a response, revealing none other than The Abomination herself, dressed in a somber gray gown, which failed to perform the same feats as her dress the previous evening at dinner had. Thank Christ for that. She wore the same jaunty hat upon her head she had worn for his first meeting with her, and she strode into the room with the same sense of purpose.

But there was no mistaking her pallor. Guilt attempted to break free inside him once more as he recalled helping her find the chamber pot the night before. A servant could have done just as well, but The Abomination had been clinging to him with the persistence of an ivy vine, and he *had* been responsible for her sorry state. He wondered now if she had spent the morning casting up her accounts.

And then he brutally reminded himself of the discovery he had inadvertently made during innocent conversation with the Duke of Winchelsea. The Abomination had been assigned a room at a hotel. She had not been ordered to stay at Lark House, which meant her story about thefts at the hotel had been pure fabrication. Which also meant she had deceived him with malicious intent. If anything, she deserved the punishment she had received this morning. After all, he had not poured the bloody port down her gullet.

Belatedly, Lucien stood in deference, along with Winchelsea, as she sailed across the office. Just as she had the day before, she marched forward, hand outstretched. The duke accepted her handshake with nary a hint of hesitation.

"Forgive me for my lack of punctuality this morning, Your Graces," she said. "I fear I did not allow sufficient time to arrange for my transportation. With no omnibus nearby, I had to hire a Hansom cab instead."

Had the woman truly imagined she would find an omnibus outside his door? And was it Lucien's imagination, or was her honeyed drawl dipped in an extra coating of sugar for the Duke of Winchelsea's benefit? And why had she yet to glance in his direction? Her bright gaze was settled upon Winchelsea with the fervent dedication of a lover.

That thought gave him pause. Frowning, he cast a glance over Winchelsea. He was a man in his early thirties with a reputation for being rigid, harsh, and unforgiving, one wife in the grave, and if Lucien recalled correctly, a daughter. The man was unyielding and cold. Hardly the sort a woman who bore the personality of a gale of wind would be drawn to. *Surely* she was not interested in the duke?

"Perhaps you ought to have risen earlier," Lucien suggested to her, his tone cool, for he could not suppress his irritation.

Her presence was an anchor in the room, and Lucien had done his damnedest to make certain she would fail to appear. But appear she had, and even in her shapeless dress and ashen complexion, Winchelsea was looking upon her with undisguised appreciation. Indeed, it was the warmest regard Lucien had ever seen the devil cast upon anyone. Worse, she continued to invade his own thoughts, and his arm would not forget the graze of her nipples. Nor would his mind stop wondering if she wore a corset today.

Blast. She had, it would seem, thwarted him once more.

Perhaps *abomination* was not a strong enough descriptor.

The woman was a plague.

A pestilence.

An interference he neither wanted nor needed.

Her gaze flicked to his at last, and the anger he saw sparkling in their depths was unmistakable. He had prodded her with his words. Goaded her even, and had issued a challenge. Surely she would pick up his tossed gauntlet in acceptance and announce to the Duke of Winchelsea what Lucien had done to her the previous evening. For, thorn in his lion's paw or not, Miss Montgomery was a smart woman. By now, she would have realized what he had been about. She would have known his machinations had led to the sickness roiling in her gut.

"I fear I was more exhausted from my travels than I had realized, Your Grace," she told him sweetly. "Sea voyages require a fortuitous constitution. Next time, I shall be armed with the weapon of experience, however. I shall not fall prey to such naïveté."

He understood the double meaning in her words and the challenge in her frank stare. She was not going to tell Winchelsea Lucien had foisted so much port upon her the night before, she'd spent the morning undoubtedly on her knees before the chamber pot.

Part of him rather wished she had, for then they could dismantle this farce, and he could convince Winchelsea and the rest of the Home Office he had no need for a partner. Specifically, that he had no need for The Abomination, a woman who had allowed her pride to lead her foolishly into his trap on the very night of her arrival in London.

"I have no doubt your voyage was arduous, Miss Montgomery," Winchelsea said, the picture of a beau flattering the lady he had asked to dance at a ball. "Fortunately, you are here in London for the foreseeable future, and I am sure time and some proper rest shall aid you."

Good God, was Winchelsea *courting* The Abomination? Had he chosen her for the position based upon having seen her photograph? Had the Duke of Winchelsea met her during his trip to New York City in the wake of The Incident? Perhaps *that* was the reason Arden had been given such a bloody curse.

Lucien must have made a noise of disgust, for The Abomination and Winchelsea both looked at him askance. Though the urge was a childish one, he was struck by the sudden desire to point a finger at the bane of his existence and announce she had been late on her first day due to over-imbibing his port. Clearly, the woman brought out the very worst in him.

He swallowed, and when he finally forced himself to speak, he was unable to entirely expunge the bitterness from his tone. "Let us have a seat and carry on with the meeting, shall we? I have urgent matters requiring my attention today."

"As do we all, Arden," Winchelsea reminded him coolly, an edge of chastisement to his tone.

Lucien bristled, but he said nothing, for the man was his superior, and whilst Lucien had once believed the duke possessed relatively little authority over the League, he had discovered quite differently not so long ago. Of course, Lucien had never almost managed to get one of his own men killed before, never mind the man was a peer of the realm, the Duke of Strathmore. And Lucien's brother-in-law.

Lucien sat, as did The Abomination, with her standard lack of grace. He'd had occasion to watch her seat herself thrice now, and each time was just as sudden and artless as the last. She sat as she did everything, as if she were waging war.

An odd female, to be sure. Why he chose that moment to once more recall the curve of her waist in his palm and the silk-covered abrasion of her nipples against his upper arm, he could not say. His reaction to her was baffling.

"Now then, Miss Montgomery," Winchelsea began with an overly familiar smile—a bloody *smile*—aimed in The Abomination's direction. "Your reputation precedes you as an incredibly successful Pinkerton agent, and the history of your cases is impeccable, as is your work with the Emerald Club."

"Thank you, Winchelsea," she said, a becoming flush finally giving her pale cheeks some color.

Lucien gritted his teeth, tamping down a caustic reply. Was The Abomination batting her eyelashes at Winchelsea? *Lord God*, if this entire forced partnership was founded solely upon the Duke of Winchelsea's desire to get beneath Miss Montgomery's cursed skirts...

"Have you finished familiarizing yourself with Miss Montgomery's work with the Emerald Club, Arden?" Winchelsea asked then.

Damnation. Of course he had not, because at the time he had received them, along with the devastating information he would be forced to accept a partner in running the Special League, he had been certain he would not need to bother acquainting himself with the background of someone he would see dismissed posthaste.

And nothing had changed, other than the unexpected realization that H.E. Montgomery was a woman.

A woman with responsive nipples and beautiful eyes.

Decidedly unwanted thought, that.

Lucien forced himself to answer Winchelsea. "I have worked my way through most of it, yes."

"And?" Winchelsea prodded.

"I have only just provided him with my notes," The Abomination chimed in. "They are far more detailed in their reporting than the summaries the agency provided to you previously. I expect the duke will require some time to pore over my copious scribblings."

Lucien's gaze swiveled to her. She tilted her head, regarding him with such intensity, the need to look away gripped him. Once more, she was smoothing things over. Making no effort to blacken his eye before the Duke of Winchelsea. This too was unexpected.

He did not like being taken aback, and it seemed for the past few months, his life had been rocked by one surprise after the next. First, his incorrect belief the Duke of Strathmore was a double agent, when in truth, the man he had taken under his wing was the true traitor. Then, his sister Violet, not just taking up the cudgels for Strathmore, but running away with him and marrying him.

The discovery, too late, that his own trusted man, Swift, had betrayed him. The inevitable reaction of the Home Office to his failure. Learning he would share his duties with a partner. Discovering the partner in question was a female. It never seemed to end.

But now, Miss Montgomery—correction, *The Abomination*—was surprising him as well. He especially did not like being surprised by his enemies. And he had no doubt the woman staring at him now was his foe. He recognized the hunger burning inside her. If he let her, she would not just share the reins with him, she would steal them from his hands and drive the carriage herself.

Straight into the ditch.

"I am certain Arden will devote himself to the task of reading your notes, Miss Montgomery," Winchelsea said pointedly, casting a sharp glance toward Lucien. "We are fortunate indeed to avail ourselves of the incredible mind and investigative abilities of Miss Montgomery. I trust the knowledge she brings us will enable us to make further arrests and secure the safety of not just London, but all England as well."

Winchelsea wished to *avail* himself of far more than The Abomination's mind and skill as an investigator. That much was apparent to Lucien. The ordinarily unflappable, relatively quiet, always serious duke had transformed into a smiling, blistering-eyed Lothario, who could not seem to wrest his gaze from Miss Montgomery for any length of time. His admiration was clear.

For a brief, sickening moment, Lucien wondered if perhaps The Abomination had ever sought purchase against the Duke of Winchelsea's wiry frame when she was not wearing a corset. If Winchelsea too knew the sensation of her generous breasts and her tight nipples grazing his arm. Had the duke kissed her? Had he already been beneath her skirts?

Because he could ill afford to exercise his anger, Lucien forced the unwanted thoughts from his mind. He could not worry nor wonder. And even if Winchelsea had already found his way beneath Miss Montgomery's skirts, what effect did it have upon Lucien? He was still just as determined as ever to rid himself of her.

"I trust your judgment," he said to his superior.

That, too, was a prevarication. But a necessary one. Lucien possessed enough experience with Winchelsea to know the man expected resolute loyalty.

"I am deeply honored by the faith you both place in my abilities," The Abomination said then, drawing Lucien's attention once more.

She was still pale, but also beautiful. Her neck was a smooth, elegant column. Her creamy skin called for a mouth. Her dark hair was swept into a haphazard chignon beneath her hat, but the rushed style did not detract in any manner from her allure. Even in her loose-fitting, unattractive gown, her inherent loveliness shone through. He could not seem to cease staring at her throat now that he had begun. Could not stop imagining pressing his lips there, his tongue flicking over her skin to learn the taste of her, the fragile beat of her heart beneath his mouth.

He did not want to be having these thoughts, did not wish for one moment to feel his cock stir as he sat before his immediate superior on an uncomfortable chair in Winchelsea's office. And yet, The Abomination met his gaze without hesitation, the blue of her eyes sinking into him like a blade.

"I have nothing but faith in your abilities, Miss Montgomery," he offered smoothly.

"In that, we are in complete agreement, Arden," Winchelsea said, sounding pleased.

Lucien noted the man's eyes had never once strayed from Miss Montgomery. And why should they? She was an entrancing woman. There was something about her which was quite unlike any lady Lucien had ever encountered: an assuredness, a confidence. She did not make any apologies for herself and who she was. Had she not been chosen as his unwanted partner, perhaps he would have been capable of appreciating her more. As it was, he dared not allow himself to feel even the base rush of lust which coursed through him whenever he was in her presence.

He told himself his reaction to her was foolish. After all, he had proven to himself this woman was not untouchable. She was susceptible to pride, to suggestion, to manipulation. Not the picture of womanly perfection Winchelsea would paint her. Not the solution to the dire straits in which they now found themselves, as the Fenians and their push for Irish Home Rule, by any means, grew more vociferous by the day.

"I am humbled by your faith in me," The Abomination said then, and while there was a distinct note of humility in her tone, he could not help but doubt her. "I hope I can prove myself to the both of you."

"I have no doubt you will," said Winchelsea with confidence, his statesman's smile and his gaze both fixated upon Miss Montgomery.

Everything Lucien longed to say roared through his mind, demanding to be said, and yet he subdued it all. Banished it. Forced himself to be polite.

"I second that sentiment," he told Winchelsea, as they all three got down to the business at hand.

But like his superior, Lucien's eyes were firmly upon Miss Montgomery when he spoke the words.

Chapter Four

$\mathcal{B}$ECAUSE HER HEAD was still aching as much as her pride, Hazel decided the best course of action was to ignore Arden. Following her meeting with the duke and Winchelsea, she slipped away and left the building, intent upon hiring another Hansom cab to take her back to Lark House, so she could pack her belongings and make her way to the hotel. Arden had proven himself a worthier opponent than she had initially supposed, and she did not like it.

He had made a fool of her, in fact.

And Hazel did not like that either.

"Miss Montgomery," his familiar baritone called out from behind her.

She spun about, somehow unprepared for the imposing sight of him, although she had just spent the better part of two hours in his presence. Even on the busy London street, he stood apart. He stared at her in that rude fashion of his, his gaze impervious, looking at her as if she were beneath his notice. An irritant. A pebble which had worked its way into his shoe.

"Mr. Arden." This time, she did not force a smile as she acknowledged him.

Nor did she bother to hide her displeasure. This man was her enemy. He had made that more than apparent when he had plied her with port the previous evening. His clear intention had been getting her so thoroughly drunk, she would be incapable of attending their meeting this morning.

But she had thwarted his labors. It had required a Herculean effort on her part, but realization had settled in after her stomach had stopped heaving. She'd splashed cold water on her face and dressed in haste, vowing to never again drink another drop of port so long as she lived.

Also, to never trust the Duke of Arden.

"My carriage is this way, Miss Montgomery," he announced in his crisp accent.

As fancy as his house, his china, his many-coursed dinners, and his chamber pot.

"Then you had best be finding it, Mr. Arden." She raised a brow, still feeling as if she had drunk poison the night before, but doing her damnedest not to allow it to show. "If you will excuse me, I am attempting to hire transportation of my own."

"That is unnecessary." His expression was grim, almost as if he found what he was about to say distasteful. "As we are both going to the same location, and as your safety is now a part of my duties, you will ride with me. One never knows what manner of cab driver one will find."

She was certain this was yet another ruse. Likely, he would lure her into his carriage, then attempt to throw her from it whilst it was in motion. "Was my safety your concern yesterday evening as well? Or this morning, for that matter?"

He stepped nearer to her, and though the jangling of tack and the busy sounds of the city surrounded them, she felt strangely as if they were alone. Arden absorbed all of her attention with his undeniable magnetism.

"I did warn you to pace yourself, did I not?" he asked, offering her his arm.

She ignored it. "My recollections suggest otherwise."

"Your recollections are faulty, in that case."

His gaze continued to burn into her, making her uncomfortable. She longed to squirm. Admittedly, her remembrance of the evening before was murky at best. She did not recall, for instance, how she had managed to undress herself, or even find her way to the bed. Fortunately, Bunton had dispelled her inner horror when she had reassured Hazel earlier *she* had been the one to aid her.

If the Duke of Arden had undressed her, Hazel would never had been able to look him in the eyes again.

But that was neither here nor there, for she was still standing opposite him, in the midst of a teeming city street, at a stalemate.

"Did you, or did you not, encourage me to drink enough port to drown a sailor?" she demanded.

"As I have never attempted to drown a sailor, I cannot help but think myself unqualified to answer that question." He smirked.

And Lord help her, but if a frowning Duke of Arden was handsome, a smirking Arden was somehow even more beautiful. Of course, she knew she was not meant to notice he was a man. It had been her policy ever since working amongst them for the last decade. Romance did not mingle well with detective work, and she had learned that bitter lesson long ago in the most brutal manner.

Still, she could not seem to ignore Arden's undeniable good looks, despite her determination to think of him in the same fashion she had all the other detectives she had worked with over the years. Despite his arrogance and his condescension. Despite his attempt to undermine her by filling her glass with port.

All of which just served to heighten her irritation with him.

"You knew I was going to be ill this morning," she countered.

The smirk deepened. "You *were* looking rather green by the time I escorted you to your chamber. But you seemed perfectly hale and hearty in the dining room. How was I to know you were an unseasoned novice when it comes to port consumption?"

Her eyes narrowed. The scoundrel was enjoying this, taking pleasure in her discomfort. "You knew."

"I suspected." He lowered his head toward her, getting closer still. "Just as I suspected you were lying about the Home Office wishing for you to stay at my home."

She truly had underestimated Arden, even more so than she had initially supposed. "I am leaving for my hotel upon my return. You have no need to worry I will impose upon your hospitality a moment longer."

"No, you will not," he said simply, as though his pronouncement was a predetermined conclusion. "You will be staying at Lark House for your tenure here, however long it lasts."

However long it lasts.

Ah, so that was Arden's game. He intended to chase her off, to send her running scared back to New York City. She had faced murderers and never once turned tail. But he would discover her mettle soon enough.

"I will not be staying at Lark House, Mr. Arden," she informed him coolly. After all, she need not give him further opportunities to do damage to her. "Now, if you will excuse me, I truly must get about the business of procuring my ride back to Lark House."

"You misunderstand me, Miss Montgomery," he said, still offering his arm as if he were a suitor. "After I relayed my concern for the criminal activities at your hotel to Winchelsea, he agreed with me that it is best if you stay at my home. He is concerned that your anonymity be preserved. Remaining at Lark House suits that purpose nicely."

It also suited Arden's purposes, she was sure. For the proof was there, in every word he had just uttered. Arden had routed her once more, using her prevarication about the hotel against her, appealing to Winchelsea after she had fled the office and making certain she would be required to remain beneath the same roof as him.

So he could attempt further sabotage. That much was without question.

"I will speak to Winchelsea myself," she said. "I will reassure him staying at my hotel is the only reasonable option."

"By admitting your little falsehoods to him?" Arden's tone was knowing. "Somehow, I cannot help but suspect doing so would prove a hindrance to your attempts to instill confidence in your abilities, but do go ahead, Miss Montgomery. I shall wait if you wish it. Or, we can cease conducting an argument on the side of the street like a pair of rival costermongers, and you can accompany me to my carriage."

He was right, damn him, and he knew it. His conceit was in full force. He waited, looking well-pleased with himself, and she supposed he ought to be. He had manipulated her into drinking too much port, made her late for her meeting, and had seen straight through her deceptions, using them against her.

Heaving a sigh of great displeasure, she glared at him, still refusing to accept his arm. She did not need to be squired about as if she were incapable of walking without a gentleman's escort. "Lead the way, Mr. Arden."

His sensual lips quirked into a victorious smile. "I am certain a woman with your extensive list of successful cases is not accustomed to being bested."

"I am a detective," she told him. "Not a woman."

The distinction was an important one. She could not allow it to be overlooked, regardless of the womanly way in which her body reacted to the duke's handsomeness. It was a natural physical reaction, she was sure, and something all women likely experienced whenever they looked upon him.

Until he opened his mouth.

"Detective," he said, his smile undiminished. "Forgive me, Miss Montgomery. I meant no insult."

And she was sure he had. "Well then, to the carriage if we must. As you said, it won't do to stand about all day when we have important work that must be done."

He caught her hand in his and placed it in the crook of his elbow. When she would have withdrawn it, he held tight. And then he began walking, without saying another word.

His strides were long, for he was taller than she. But she was taller than most women, and she had no trouble keeping up with him, in spite of the continued thumping in her head. Her mouth was dry, and she would give her left shoe for a cold lemonade at that particular moment.

He handed her up into the carriage first, in gentlemanly fashion, and she allowed it, though she ordinarily chose to buck convention. She wanted to be treated as a man's equal, not as a delicate burden. Self-reliance, and being the best detective she could possibly be, were her only goals in life. The aftereffects of her unfortunate run-in with port the evening before had left her weakened however.

She'd not had time to break her fast, and the omission was haunting her now. She flopped onto the leather bench, taking note of the detailed elegance inside the carriage. Polished leather squabs, well-padded and comfortable, an elegant interior, and a plush rug on the floor. Had she doubted, even for a moment, that the Duke of Arden's conveyance would be any less fancy than any other portion of his life she had glimpsed thus far?

He seated himself opposite her, and as he did so, his scent wafted over her, citrus and musk, mingled with leather. She breathed through her mouth instead of her nose, determined not to inhale him. *To hell with the man.* He was making everything about this assignment far more difficult than it needed to be.

Though the interior of the carriage was spacious, his legs were so long, his knees nearly brushed against the simple skirt of her gown. She stared at the encroaching appendages, oddly struck by the urge to lay her hand there, her palm flat. His thighs were muscular beneath his dark trousers. She swallowed as she imagined gliding her hand higher, absorbing the heat and strength of him. Higher still, all the way to his male length, which was clearly delineated and—

He cleared his throat pointedly, shifting on the carriage bench as he did so, as if he were suddenly uncomfortable. "Miss Montgomery."

The tightness in his voice, along with a husky edge of an emotion she could not define, forced her gaze upward to meet his. Her ears burned, and she was sure her face was red as a boiled beet. He had caught her staring at his legs, at his thighs, at his...

How shameful. She needed to recall her rules. She had not suffered such an egregious lapse in all the years since Adam. But she had been young then, so much younger, so ignorant of the ugliness the world held and how easily a heart could be broken, how easily a life could end.

"Forgive me," she said, finding her voice. "I was admiring the interior of your carriage. It is very fine."

She was not being completely dishonest, she reasoned, for she had been admiring something inside the carriage, against her better judgment, and his horseman's thighs *were* rather fine. Even though they were attached to the rest of him.

He shifted again, his gaze becoming more intense. "You were *admiring*, Miss Montgomery?"

She swallowed. That had been a poor choice of word. Obviously. "It is a handsome carriage," she said instead, glaring at him.

But that, too, was all wrong, and she knew it the moment the words emerged. *Damn it*, she had all but admitted she had been admiring Arden's thighs and found him handsome. Which she *had* been and she *did*, but she had not had a crumb of sustenance all day, and she was likely growing delusional.

Her stomach chose that moment to issue a demanding growl, so loudly, it could be heard distinctly, even above the din of the street and the sounds of their carriage rocking into motion. She pressed her hand over it, as if that would stave off future rumbles.

"You are looking wan," he observed unkindly. "Have you eaten anything today?"

How disagreeable of him to notice, then comment upon it as well. "My stomach was in no condition to partake in anything other than retching into a chamber pot, thanks to your generous hospitality yesterday."

"You do have a charming hiccup," he dared to say. "I would happily pour as much port for you as you would like following dinner this evening, just so I may have the opportunity to hear it again."

"Go to the devil," she growled. Her head was pounding, and it felt odd, almost as if it were too light for her neck. She wondered if she would need to retch again upon her return to Lark House.

As the carriage rocked, her stomach lurched, as if in warning. She bit her lip, thinking it would serve him right if she cast up her accounts all over the long legs and strong thighs she had been ogling. Lord knew no man's arrogance could withstand vomit.

"You are vexed because I outsmarted you." He raised a dark brow.

"Vexed does not begin to accurately describe my feelings for you at the moment, Mr. Arden." And yes, she took great joy in watching his nostrils flare once more, and his full lips turn down with displeasure, upon her deliberate confusion of his title. "But rest assured, try though you may, you will never be capable of outsmarting me. Not even the wiliest criminals have been able to escape me."

"I accept your challenge, Miss Montgomery."

"It was not a challenge, Mr. Arden," she grumbled, as pearls of sweat broke out on her brow, "but a promise."

"Sure of yourself, are you not?" His tone was amused.

Hazel saw nothing humorous in their current circumstances. She needed food, and she needed a chamber pot, and with each moment that dragged by, she was more and more uncertain which of those things she required first.

"I am secure in my abilities," she told him anyway.

She could not bear to allow him to think her weak. Or to imagine he had broken her. He had not. He *would* not. She was H.E. Montgomery, and she had faced murderers, without a hint of fear. She had infiltrated the Emerald Club. She had traveled an ocean to take on her biggest case yet. No duke too arrogant to accept a partner was going to scare her away.

"It is good you are, my dear Miss Montgomery," he told her smoothly, smiling his wolf's smile again. "For you will need to be."

BY THE TIME they returned to Lark House, Miss Montgomery's pallor had returned.

By the time he accompanied her into the entry hall, she began to crumple. There was no other word for it. One moment, she was striding boldly at his side, as if she were a general marching into battle, and the next, she was falling like a felled tree in the woods.

He reacted instinctively, catching her, before she toppled to the marble floor and struck her head. His aghast butler looked on as Lucien stood there, Miss Montgomery's drab skirts pooling around him, her unconscious form in his arms. She was heavier than she looked.

"Shall I fetch your physician, Your Grace?" Reynolds asked.

"Not yet," he said grimly. "I'm taking her to the salon. Have someone bring me a tray of food and some water. With haste, if you please."

He had a feeling he knew what had caused Miss Montgomery to suddenly swoon. It was nearly one o'clock in the afternoon, and she had yet to eat a thing after having spent the morning emptying her stomach into the chamber pot.

Because of *him*.

Guilt crashed over Lucien, and this time, he made no effort to dispel it. Even if she *had* deceived him, he had no cause to do her injury. Forcing her to grow so weak she fainted had decidedly not been his intent. Moreover, he had already gotten even with her for her deceptions by pressing Winchelsea to agree to the notion of Miss Montgomery staying at Lark House for her own safety. In truth, it was so Lucien could more easily continue in the task of ridding himself of the unwanted burden of her as his partner.

A burden he felt physically now, as he strode to the salon, carrying her. With ginger care, he laid her upon a divan. She had begun stirring already, and he had a feeling she was too stubborn to remain unconscious overly long. He removed her hat, then arranged her skirts so they draped over her legs, showing nary a hint of ankle.

Tending to her felt odd, and it occurred to him he had never before performed such personal tasks upon a female. Not even his sister Lettie, for Great Aunt Hortense had been an ever-present boon to aid him with raising his sister after the deaths of both of their parents. He briefly thought about fetching Aunt Hortense now and begging her assistance, but something overcame him: shame at his culpability in laying Miss Montgomery low, along with something else…

Some unfamiliar need to tend to Miss Montgomery himself. Some foreign sense of tenderness, the likes of which he had never felt for anyone other than Lettie. A tendril of dark hair had escaped Miss Montgomery's messy chignon, and he brushed it away from her forehead, before he could rethink the gesture.

She groaned, her dark lashes fluttering against her silken skin, as wakefulness returned to her. He noticed, quite against his will, that Miss Montgomery had a small trail of freckles over the bridge of her nose. And then his gaze dipped inevitably to her lips. They were the lips of a courtesan, lush and full and inviting. They reminded him of the manner in which she had been staring at him earlier in the carriage. At his cock.

At first, he had been convinced he was mistaken. But as he had observed her, watched her eyes widen, her pupils dilate, he had known he was not. Prim Miss Montgomery— the feisty enigma, who had just yesterday warned him *you cannot think of me as a female*—had been ogling his erection. An erection which had initially been caused by a disturbing combination of their discourse on the street and his proximity to her in the carriage.

But beneath her stare, he had swelled even more, until he had been forced to attempt to readjust himself and hope like hell she had not noticed. Or, if she had, since she was a Miss Montgomery rather than a Mrs., she would have no notion of what she had seen.

Her eyes opened at last, some of the color already having returned to her ashen cheeks. She looked adorably befuddled for a moment as her gaze traveled wildly about the chamber. A strange burst of warmth unfurled within him. Not longing or desire, but something else. Something more profound.

"Did you push me from the carriage while it was moving?" she asked groggily.

The warmth fled instantly. Was her opinion of him truly that low? "You think me capable of throwing you from a moving carriage, Miss Montgomery?"

She eyed him mulishly.

"You swooned," he snapped, irritated with himself as much as with her. "In the entry hall. I brought you here, to the salon."

She frowned at him, returning to her usual, troublesome self. "I do not swoon, Mr. Arden."

"Yes," he corrected her firmly, "you do. And furthermore, we had a bargain, if you will recall. Each time you refer to me as *Mr. Arden*, you are breaking it."

"You broke it when you attempted to poison me with port," she accused, as if she could not possibly wait to flee.

"I made no such attempt." True, he had known she would be ill this morning. And it had been his intention. But *poison* was rather a strong word. "You were in full possession of your faculties, madam. I held not one glass to your lips."

He should not have uttered the word *lips*. Because now, he could not resist looking at hers once more, and this time,

God save him, he wondered how they would feel beneath his.

He banished the unworthy thought immediately. There were scores of women in London, and kissing any one of them would be an infinitely better choice than kissing the frowning creature before him. Why then, was he still thinking about it, curse him?

"You may not have held the glass directly to my lips, but you knew what you were about, filling my glass whenever it was nearly empty. I do hope you are ashamed of yourself, though thus far, you have only seemed pleased." She finished delivering her impassioned chastisement as she worked her way into a sitting position.

Although the color had returned to her cheeks in full— owed to her dudgeon, unless he missed his guess—she was still weak. And she was not going anywhere until she bloody well broke her fast and drank some water.

He placed his hands upon her shoulders, staying her. "You will remain where you are. I have sent for a tray, which should be here shortly."

"I do not require a tray to be brought to me as if I am an invalid," she protested, but her voice was weak and tired.

Her mind was at war with her body. He had no qualms deciding the victor on her behalf. It would be her body, and she would eat the damned food he had procured for her.

"Whether or not you require such a thing, you are a guest in my home, and I cannot, in good conscience, allow you to go traipsing about in your weakened state." He kept his palms where they were, firmly pressed against her clavicles.

Such a position ought not seem intimate or incite any untoward sensations within him, and yet it did. She was warm and supple beneath his touch, and for a brief, maddening beat, he longed to run his hands over her without the barrier of her dress and undergarments between them.

"I do not traipse," she informed him with a raised brow, because she was the argumentative sort, this strange American conundrum.

"Very well, Miss Montgomery," he allowed, bending down even farther and lowering his head so they were eye to eye. Also a mistake, he realized at once. But it was too late to turn back now, for the damage had been done. "You do not swoon, and you do not traipse, but what you *will* do is listen to me. You require sustenance and rest, and you will have both."

She said nothing, her eyes going wide.

His grip on her shoulders tightened. "Do you understand me, Miss Montgomery? I have kept my silence, but I will do everything I have threatened you with, if you do not keep your arse planted upon that seat and eat the food that is brought to you. I will inform Winchelsea that the famed H.E. Montgomery is naught but a drunkard, who tippled so much port, she could not reach our meeting in time because she had spent the morning vomiting into my chamber pot. After she lied to me about her hotel being unsafe, and the Home Office demanding she stay as my guest here at Lark House."

"Mr. Arden, I am—"

"You are remaining precisely where you are," he inter- rupted in the voice he had often used with his headstrong sister, Violet.

Ah, Lettie. He hoped he could one day restore his relation- ship with her. That it was capable of being restored, after the damage he had inflicted upon it with The Incident. At least he knew she was happy now, and Strathmore, to his credit, seemed a doting and loving husband. Then again, he was required to be, else Lucien would feed him his own ballocks.

"How dare you presume to order me about?" Miss Mont- gomery demanded, pique making her cheeks flush even further.

Damn it if she wasn't lovely in her fit of irritation.

"I dare everything, madam," he informed her.

She was beneath his roof after all, and it was his rule here. Not hers. She struck him as a woman who was well-accustomed to not just being on her own, but to commanding all others in her presence. Perhaps that had worked well enough for her in America as a Pinkerton, but it would not work here at Lark House. These walls were his territory; this country was his to protect.

A knock at the door heralded the arrival of the tray he had requested at last, along with a reprieve for him from his ruinous, foolish path of thoughts. He accepted the tray from the servant and dismissed her, turning back to Miss Montgomery, who was already standing.

Until her face went ashen once more, and she flopped upon the divan in typical, graceless Miss Montgomery fashion. Somehow, she had ceased to be The Abomination, and this realization disturbed him. She had slipped past his defenses. He would rebuild his turrets, and build them higher.

He stalked toward her with grim intent, the tray outstretched, as if it were a weapon. When he reached the divan, he seated himself alongside her, resting the tray upon her lap.

"Your repast, Miss Montgomery," he announced.

She stared at him for longer than necessary, her gaze unfathomable. He wondered what her agile mind was thinking. What attempts to overpower and disarm him she was already formulating. Regardless of what they were, no matter how clever, she would never beat him. He would always win.

He was the Duke of Arden.

And the Duke of Arden did not lose.

Mistakes? He made them. Far too many to count. But

defeat was not and had never been an option. Defeat by Miss Hazel Elizabeth Montgomery? *Never.*

"I am not hungry," she announced, stoic.

"You do not think you are," he corrected her, for he had given the bottle a black eye many a time in his younger days. He was more than familiar with the aftereffects of overindulgence the day after making merry. And he knew the best cure for what ailed her was food. Food, water, and rest. Also, bed sport. But that was not going to happen.

No bloody chance.

Unless the Duke of Winchelsea clambered into her bedchamber window later on. Which was unlikely indeed, for many reasons. First, Winchelsea was too dignified for clambering. Second, the likelihood of the duke surviving such a clamber was poor, since Miss Montgomery was staying on the second floor, and Lark House did not possess any architectural marvels which would facilitate such an endeavor. Lucien knew, because his younger sister was beautiful, and he had been acting as her father for many years. A man who had been wild himself in his younger years knew what to look for when protecting his women.

And third, if Winchelsea attempted to bed Miss Montgomery beneath Lucien's own roof, Lucien would take great joy in beating the man to a pulp, regardless of whether or not he was Lucien's senior in the Home Office. He had little left to lose.

"I *know* I am not hungry," Miss Montgomery interrupted his tumultuous thoughts then. "I thank you for this tray, truly I do, but I cannot force myself to eat a bite."

Disturbed by the vein of his thoughts and the protective urge he inexplicably felt for the maddening woman at his side, Lucien clenched his jaw. Counted to fifteen. Inhaled, then exhaled.

Felt not at all like himself. But that was rather too bad. He was beginning to realize everything about Miss H.E. Montgomery left him bewildered, frustrated, and filled with...yearning.

No. Good God, no. Irritation. Yes, that was more apt. *Far* more apt. She filled him with irritation.

But he still wanted her to eat. She *had* to eat.

He picked up a cherry tartlet, then raised it to her lips. "A bite, Miss Montgomery."

"My fingers are in functioning order, Mr. Arden." She frowned at him.

Unmoved, he pressed the tartlet to her mouth. "Open."

To his amazement, she did, revealing a neat line of even, white teeth. And she took a bite. Her surrender should not have an effect upon him. But there had been something unbearably erotic in the way she had opened her mouth at his directive, accepting the tartlet. The manner in which she obeyed him. This somehow felt like more of a victory than tricking her into drinking too much port had.

He watched her chew the confection slowly, then swallow. "Better?" he asked.

Her lips pursed. "Do not pretend as if you care."

Her sharp retort almost made him smile. "I do care. I have no desire to be covered in your vomitus."

Desire. There was another word he should never utter in Miss Montgomery's presence. For even though it shared a sentence with *vomitus*, a splinter of warmth pierced him anyway.

"No one would deserve it more," she said sweetly, before reaching for the tray and seizing the glass of water.

She gulped down the contents with a gusto that did not surprise him. More tendrils of hair had escaped her chignon, framing her face in wild little curls. The sight of them entranced him. For some reason, he had supposed her hair to be straight. But now he wondered how the glossy mahogany strands would appear, unbound down her back. A riot of rebellious curls? Soft waves?

And then he reminded himself he must cease all such unwanted mental inquiries into Miss Montgomery as a woman. He was aiming to rid himself of her, not to seduce her, for God's sake.

She settled her water back upon the tray with a lusty sigh. "Not lemonade, but far preferable to port."

Lemonade. Of course she would prefer a drink which was tart. He ought to have guessed.

He held up the tartlet. "More?"

She eyed him warily. "I think I like you far better when you speak in one-word sentences, Mr. Arden."

"And I like you better when your mouth is otherwise occupied," he returned, only realizing the double entendre too late.

Devil take it, what was the matter with him? And why was he suddenly plagued by the notion of her mouth occupied by his? Or, even more wicked, by another part of his anatomy entirely?

She did not appear to take note of the secondary meaning however, simply giving him an admonishing look, before reaching for another tartlet and plucking it from the tray. Raising her brows, she took a bite.

He still held the half-eaten pastry he had fed her in his hand. It was apparent she had no intention of consuming the rest, or allowing him to feed it to her. He had to admit doing so had been a grave lapse in judgment. Because performing any task which required him to not just look at Miss Montgomery's mouth, but to get near enough to touch it was a horrible, disastrous idea.

Still watching her, he popped it into his own mouth. Her eyes dipped to his lips. A flush stole over her high cheekbones. He felt that gaze as if it were a touch. The steady thrum of longing, which had first struck him in the carriage on their return to Lark House, returned. Only this time, it was stronger. More insistent.

He swallowed. Miss Montgomery reached for her water. An uneasy silence settled between them which was far too intimate for his liking. What in the hell was he doing, sitting here mooning over the partner he did not want?

Turrets, he reminded himself. He needed to rebuild his. At once. He could not allow this maddening woman to storm his battlements and overtake the castle. He had worked far too hard, for far too long, to gain his position as the leader of the Special League. Commanding the agents charged with keeping England safe was everything he wanted. All he needed.

Lucien cleared his throat and stood. "I will leave you to finish your repast in peace, Miss Montgomery."

He offered her a bow, then began stalking from the room.

"Arden?"

Her drawl halted him. He turned back, taking in the sight of her, all disheveled and adorably rumpled, a tray laden with tartlets at her side. She had not called him Mr. Arden, and he rather wished she had. When she nettled him, it was much easier to recall his dislike for her.

"Yes, Miss Montgomery?" he demanded, when she said nothing more.

She smiled, and that simple curvature of her lips was a revelation. When she smiled at him in such a fashion, he found it difficult to not only think, but to breathe. Even in her horrid dress, with all her odd mannerisms and strange brash ways, she was bloody gorgeous.

"Thank you," she said.

Turrets.

He nodded. "You are welcome, Miss Montgomery."

Then he did the only thing he could do. He gave her his back and strode from the chamber, before he did something exceedingly foolish, such as sinking back into the divan and hauling her to him for a kiss. Licking the sweet taste of cherries from her lips and mouth. Discovering for certain whether or not she wore a corset today.

This would not do. Not at all. He increased his pace, fleeing as if an invading army followed in his wake. And in a manner, it did.

Turrets, he reminded himself grimly. *Turrets.*

Chapter Five

*T*HE DUKE OF Arden confounded her.

And Hazel did not like being confounded. She liked answers. Knowledge. She liked plans and lists, and people who acted exactly as she expected them to at all times. People who did not act out of character. People who did not surprise her with sudden kindness.

She did not like men who were supercilious and patronizing one moment, then tender and considerate the next. She did not like men who had tricked her into drinking so much port, she'd spent the next morning feeling as if she'd been run over by a railcar, then fed her cherry tartlets and stared at her lips.

She examined her reflection in the looking glass, nodding at herself. The ragged-looking waif of the day before was no longer in evidence. She had refreshed herself with a bath and had scraped her wayward hair into a neat braid pinned at her nape. Bunton had offered assistance once more, but Hazel had declined. She was self-sufficient, and she needed to remember that. It would not do for her to grow weak and complacent, accustomed to having someone wait upon her, as if she were a lady to the manor born.

Hazel Montgomery was not a lady to the manor born.

She was an orphan, who had been raised in squalor with other orphan children whose parents had either died, did not want them, or could not afford to feed them. Her childhood had unfolded beneath the dark cloud of civil war being fought all around her. She was a woman who had taught herself everything she knew, from reading and writing to shooting a pistol. And she could damn well dress herself.

This morning, she was dressed for battle, wearing the divided skirt she'd had made for herself in New York, and a fitted bodice covered by a jaunty jacket. It would not do for the Duke of Arden to think of her as a female, and neither would it do for her to think of him as a male. These garments were her armor. She had donned them often when working in partnership with her male colleagues, and while the trousers inevitably shocked, they also served their purpose, reminding her fellow agents she was an experienced detective worth her salt.

And she would remind the Duke of Arden of that too as they began their work together today. More importantly, she would eradicate from her mind the memory of the way he had looked at her mouth the day before. She would forget she had imagined, for one wild and foolish moment, what his lips would feel like moving over hers.

She would banish all such wayward thoughts and impulses, for they were beneath her. Her post was important, after all, in myriad ways. For Hazel, it was a much-needed increase in pay as much as it was an affirmation. Her case history spoke for itself, and though she had worked herself to the bone on those cases, she was proud of her work. She knew she was a damned good detective. But the Home Office had requested her specifically, and she considered that proof to all the men she had worked alongside who doubted her abilities.

Not only was she earning a greater salary, but she was also the agent who had been chosen from all the rank and file to represent the agency abroad. Although Pinkertons were regularly consulted by the English Home Office and their Special League devoted to Fenian containment, no Pinkerton before her had ever been asked to partner in leading the League itself. Had others before her been asked to provide consultation? *Yes.* To provide intelligence? *Also, yes.*

Lead the ranks of their London agents?

Impossible.

But *she* had. Hazel Elizabeth Montgomery, who had been fighting and clawing her way through life from the moment the mother she could not remember had abandoned her on an Atlanta street, had been asked—a woman, and one of few lady Pinkertons—to aid the League. Her reaction to the Duke of Arden was an aberration.

She was here not just to provide the intelligence she had sourced in New York, but to help guide the League's investigations in England accordingly. She would not allow herself to become distracted from that all-important duty. Because if there was one thing she wanted in her life upon the Lord's great earth, it was to prove to everyone that a woman could perform a job just as well as any man could.

Hazel had been doing so for ten years, and she intended to continue doing so for the next fifty, God willing.

She consulted the pocket watch she carried with her. Five minutes until her first true meeting with Arden. This time, she would be early. And this time, she would be well-armed, prepared for whatever nonsense and trickery he had in mind. She had kept her distance yesterday following her ignominious collapse, regrouping herself.

Briefly, she wondered whether his concern for her the day before had been feigned. Then, her overactive mind—restored, now that she'd had a restful night's sleep—began churning. And she wondered just how devious he was, how malicious his intent. Had his masculine interest in her been contrived? She had dealt with overtures often enough over the years to know when a man was attracted to her, and judging from his gaze, his intensity, and his mannerisms, Arden was very drawn to her.

Unless his interest had been merely a further attempt at her manipulation on his part? She wondered, not for the first time, how she had wound up on the divan. One moment, she had been walking at his side in the marbled mausoleum that served as an entry hall to Lark House, and the next, she had awakened laid out on a piece of furniture, a distraught-looking Arden hovering over her.

The notion of him carrying her in his arms made her uncomfortably aware, all over again, that she was a female and he was decidedly a male. It made her stomach tighten and tingle, made an insistent ache pulse between her thighs. But that sensation would have to go, because she could not abide being late, and she was scheduled to meet with Arden in his study in their first official capacity as partners in precisely— she checked her pocket watch again—two minutes.

"Damn it," she muttered.

Had she truly ruminated over the Duke of Arden for a full three minutes? Her vulnerability for the man—produced, no doubt, by a natural reaction to his handsome face and nothing more—had to be mown down like a field overrun by weeds. Mow it down, she would.

Beginning now.

With a final nod at her reflection in the glass and a straightening of her jacket, she set off in the direction of Arden's study.

SWEET GOD.

Lucien could do nothing but stare, transfixed, at Miss Montgomery as she strode across the expanse of his study wearing the most bewildering—and mouthwatering— costume he had ever seen upon a woman.

Her legs were encased in billowing trousers rather than skirts, coupled with a fitted bodice that, had he been viewing it alone, would have looked indistinguishable from the upper portion of any gown. It was fashioned of blue silk, with lace at the top that almost resembled a cravat in its frothy waterfall over her décolletage. Atop the bodice, she wore a cutaway jacket, which flapped in the breeze as she approached his desk with her unique sense of determination.

He stood, belatedly, offering her a formal bow. His tongue felt as if it were stuck to the roof of his mouth. Any hope he possessed that a subsequent look at her outlandish attire would render him horrified died a quick, merciless death when he straightened to his full height and settled his gaze upon her once more.

She was astounding.

Mesmerizing.

Damnation, her hips. Full and round, just as he had imagined they would be. Her legs, so long. Legs a man could well imagine wrapped around his waist. He wondered if her bodice was attached to her trousers. The whole effort appeared seamless, but surely it could not be so. And that thought inevitably led to him disrobing her in his mind. Surely she wore no corset beneath that bodice. He wondered if her nipples were hard once more, hiding beneath the safety of her jacket.

Christ, this was going to be torture. The Home Office had not just foisted a partner upon him. No, indeed. They had forced him to accept a determined, intelligent, fiercely independent, rebellious, beautiful female, whose body was a courtesan's dream, as his partner. And an American one, at that.

She bowed right back at him, startling him from his unacceptable ruminations concerning a woman he could not afford to want. Hers was not a full gentleman's bow, but rather a cursory, abbreviated thing. Halfway between a curtsy and a bow. Odd, to be sure. He hoped to God she never made such an awkward gesture should she find herself at a social gathering during her short stay in London.

Her incredibly short stay, he reminded himself bitterly. The woman before him—eccentric, endearing, and enticing though she may be—was his nemesis. He could not forget that bitter truth.

"Good morning, Arden," she said.

Ah, an overture on her part. She had not referred to him as *Mr.* Arden. He would have smiled had not the situation been so dire. It would seem all that was required to pierce Miss Montgomery's armor was cherry tartlets and a good night's sleep. He could manage that. Far less guilt-inducing than drowning her in port, after all.

"Good morning, Miss Montgomery," he returned, forcing himself to keep all hints of emotion and all traces of his reaction to her from his voice.

Doing so required every last speck of his self-restraint. Because those bloody trousers. And her legs. Lord in heaven, the woman's legs. He had known she was taller than most ladies, but the way those trousers clung to her curves and emphasized how *long* her legs were...

His cock was hard.

He had to sit.

Almost in unison, he and Miss Montgomery sank loudly and gracelessly into their respective seats. He stifled a groan. It was as if the dratted female had him so bollixed up, he had somehow begun taking on her alarming lack of polish and grace. What more havoc could the woman wreak upon him? What was next? Would he too be attacking his dinner as if it were about to flee his plate?

She stared at him, her back straight as a ramrod, unblinking. "Have you had the opportunity to review my notes?"

Bloody hell. Again with the journal. He had skimmed it once more following his hasty retreat from the salon the day before, but in truth, his blood had been pulsing in his veins, and desire had simmered through him with such insistence, he had been forced to take matters into his own hands in his chamber.

Shameful. Disgraceful even, but true. He had gripped his own cock to the thought of Miss Montgomery taking him into her mouth. He was not proud of himself. Not at all. What was wrong with him?

He forced the unwanted thoughts away, where they belonged. "I have perused them, yes."

She quirked a brow, looking distinctly unimpressed. "And what do you make of the threats against the railway system?"

Her question stole his breath, but this time, it had nothing to do with him mooning over her beauty, and everything to do with what she had just asked.

"Against the railway?"

Her brow hiked an inch upward. "Yes, precisely as I said, Arden."

Still not a mister. Simply Arden. And damned if he didn't enjoy the sound of his name in her sweet, syrupy drawl. Apparently, he had earned himself enough redemption to carry him over for now.

"I failed to read that portion," he told her honestly.

"Perhaps we ought to begin at the beginning." Her tone was steeped in disapproval.

Was she already attempting to wrest the reins from his more-than-capable hands? Surely not. He would remind her which of them was the leader of the League, and which of them was the new partner dredged up from the bowels of New York.

Lucien pinned her with a glare. "Perhaps you ought to allow me to decide where and how we begin, Miss Montgomery."

"This is not a matter of which of us possesses more power than the other, Arden," she said coolly. "This is a matter of your country's safety. You do realize that, do you not?"

He bristled at her implication he did not take this assignment seriously. The safety of England's men, women, and children had been his sole concern for years. Plucking the evil roots of the Fenian desire for destruction was his daily goal.

"Of course I realize how grave the danger is," he snapped. "Already, there have been innocent lives lost, among them a child and a leading political figure. I am doing my damnedest to make certain not one more drop of blood is shed, that there is not one more death."

"If you were doing your damnedest, then you would have read my notes," she returned, with equal vigor.

So much for the bloody cherry tartlets. Their sweetness had not lasted long.

"When was I to have possessed the time to read your voluminous scribble, Miss Montgomery?" he demanded, not caring if his voice dripped with acid. "I only received word I was being suddenly forced to accept a partner in leading the League a few days prior to your arrival."

She frowned at that. "Do you mean to suggest you did not know about my arrival until recently?"

He inclined his head, a rush of outrage bubbling to the surface with him at the reminder. "Yes."

"I see." She paused, seeming to contemplate his revelation, as if it had somehow given her a setback. "How much notice did you have when you received your previous partner, Arden?"

Here, too, was another source of indignation. "I had no partner."

Her full lips parted in surprise. "I am the first?"

"The first," he confirmed bitterly. *But rest assured, you will not last long, if I have anything to say about it.*

"Is that why your dislike for me is so strong?" she asked. "You resent me for the Home Office's decision to make you share your power with me?"

"I do not dislike you, and nor do I resent you." That was a half-truth. Part of him disliked and resented her very much. The other part of him wanted to peel her out of those indecent trousers, settle her before him on the desk, and feast upon her.

But most importantly, he would *never* share his power with her. Not ever.

"You do not fool me, Arden." She gave him a look laden with meaning. "Not when there is no port about for you to drown me in, anyway. You have a way of looking at me as if I am a fly you've found in your soup."

He almost laughed at her unexpected analogy. *Almost.* By God, the woman was strange. "You are a great deal larger than a fly, Miss Montgomery, and I should never wish to find you in my soup."

Her lips pursed in displeasure, her eyes narrowing upon him. "You misunderstand me deliberately, but I will not be swayed from my course. I want answers from you, Arden, and I want them now. If this partnership is to be successful, and I do not see any reason why it cannot—aside from your arrogant, condescending, obdurate nature—we must be honest with each other."

There was honesty. Ugly and altogether unwanted. Drat the female.

"You think me arrogant, condescending and obdurate, madam?" he asked tightly, offended in spite of himself.

"I *know* you are," she countered. "Fear not. I have worked with a great deal of men such as yourself over the course of my career as a Pinkerton. I am entirely prepared to deal with you."

"To deal with me," he repeated, thinking surely, *surely*, he could not have heard the woman before him correctly.

"You are having difficulty accepting the fact that you are being forced to accept a partner," she added. "To make matters worse, I am a woman. An American woman, at that. You consider me an interloper, and you think me intellectually and physically incapable of performing the same tasks as you, a man."

She spoke with such certainty, as if she already knew every word she spoke was irrefutable fact. But to his utter shame, he realized she was not entirely wrong. She had read him as if he were a book laid open before her.

"I am not pleased about being forced to accept a partner," he allowed, "as it casts a shadow over my abilities. Furthermore, forgive me, but I cannot help but to feel, down to my marrow, that a native Englishman will have a much better understanding of the current wave of Fenianism than an American."

If possible, she sat even straighter, and as well as she could read him, he could read her. She was infuriated. Arguing with her had not been his intention for this meeting, but it would seem they found themselves in dubious footing upon a slippery slope.

"Most of the men who have already been arrested, or who

are actively plotting now, are Americans with roots in Ireland," she countered, her voice firm.

He admired her tenacity. Her ability to find success in a predominantly male profession did not surprise him in the least, now he'd seen it in action. And he had to admit, she was correct about her assertion concerning the American ties to many of the Fenians who had been caught thus far. However, he still disagreed with part of her argument. Quite vehemently, in fact.

"That is an incontrovertible fact. However, running covert operations in a city you are familiar with is decidedly different from running them here in London." He tapped his fingers against the surface of his desk to drum away some of his vexation. "Surely you must admit the difference, Miss Montgomery."

"You fancy me from New York?" She laughed then, and the sound was rich and true and sultry.

Damn him if her laughter did not send a trill straight down his spine.

"Is that not where you hail from, Miss Montgomery?" he asked coldly, nettled by his reaction to her—all over again—and her amusement. No one laughed at him. He was the Duke of Arden, by God. Leader of the Special League.

"No," she said, the remnants of her luscious laugh lingering in an equally tempting smile. "I am originally from Atlanta, Georgia. Or, at least, that is where my recollections begin. I am an orphan, you see, no memories of my mother or father, and I am sure that is just as well. Atlanta is where I remained until the city was burned in the war. After that, I moved whenever and wherever I had to, a child of misfortune, as it were. I have found my home in a dozen states. I am not bound by geographical location, Mr. Arden."

He had returned to mister status once more. Somehow,

that concerned him far less than the notion of a young Miss Montgomery, in an orphanage within a burning city, in the midst of the chaos of war. Something inside him shifted.

Softened.

"How old were you?" he asked.

"When?" she asked, seemingly unaffected by the harrowing childhood she had just described.

"When your city burned," he clarified.

He knew he should not care. That he ought not waste his precious time on inquiring after personal details about her, which would never matter when she had been dismissed from her position and sailed back to America. And yet, unable to help himself all the same. He wanted to know more about this irksome, intriguing woman.

"Nine years old, or thereabouts," she said. "No one can be certain, since I was abandoned as a small child. No birth date on record for me, I am afraid."

"A girl," he concluded, thinking of how Miss Montgomery may have looked, bright-eyed, with a halo of dark ringlets around her heart-shaped face.

And despite his every instinct to the contrary, he allowed himself to entertain, just for a moment, a sense of kinship with her. Hidden deep within him was an orphan as well. His mother had died in his youth by her own hand, drowning herself in the North Sea. His father had died not many years later, leaving Lucien and Violet with no one in the world but each other.

And Aunt Hortense, of course, who was not to be forgotten.

But he related to Miss Montgomery, for he too knew what it was like to be motherless and fatherless. To be adrift in the world, without the guidance of those who should have loved him best.

"I was old enough to find my way when the time came," she said then, her gentle drawl dispersing his heavy thoughts. "I tell you this, not so you pity me, but so you see I have never called any place home. I find my home wherever I am, and I am not daunted by the prospect of conducting an investigation in a country I have only just recently arrived in. If anything, I am eager."

He believed her when she said those words. He did not discredit the vehemence in her voice, or the strength of her convictions. "My mother drowned herself in the sea when I was a lad," he found himself revealing to her.

Why, he had no idea. Merely that she was there, and for this brief moment, the connection between them seemed a bridge, and he was blindly crossing it. Reaching out, not an olive branch, but a hand, from one orphan to another.

But she did not wilt as most ladies would. Her eyes filled, not with sympathy, but with something far more valuable: understanding. "Perhaps you have more in common with this American interloper than you initially suspected, Arden."

He swallowed against the rush of bile which inevitably rose in his throat whenever he thought of his mother. How beautiful and pale she had been in death, how unlike herself. She had finally been at peace, but she had left him behind in torment.

"Perhaps," he allowed at last, gaining control over his emotions.

"Read my notes," she said. "Begin on page twenty-three. There is a man here in London going by the name of The Nightingale, who has been accepting funds and shipments of Atlas powder from the Emerald Club. The club is organizing an attempt to cause destruction on your railways using bombs hidden inside portmanteaus. I do not have more than that, other than the knowledge The Nightingale is not alone. My investigations suggest there are others, working in concert, all with strong connections to the Emerald Club."

Her words sent a different trill altogether down his spine. He recognized the icy claws of dread all too well. Either the woman before him was a fraudster, flush with false information, which would prove unreliable, or…

Or she was exactly who she seemed to be: an intelligent, resourceful creature, who had somehow infiltrated the ranks of one of the most secretive and dangerous Fenian organizations in America *and* mined crucial information, which could be used against the Fenians before it was too late.

He extracted her journal from where he had stored it, locked in one of his desk drawers. "I will read the bloody notes."

"Page twenty-three," she prodded.

"Page twenty-three," he agreed. Of course the woman knew by memory what information was contained on which page. He should not be surprised, and yet he was. Somehow, Miss H.E. Montgomery continually surprised, impressed, vexed, and confounded him.

"Excellent." She flashed him a beaming smile and stood, thrusting her hand out over his desk.

He was forced to stand as well, and to accept her handshake, even if it felt deuced odd, which it did. Her hand was bare in his, and he could not deny the spark which shot past his wrist and up his arm. Or the heat settling somewhere in the vicinity of his trousers.

"This is not a surrender, Miss Montgomery," he warned her, lest she think he was falling into her battle formation.

"I would never dream of such a hasty capitulation, Mr. Arden," she assured him, grinning as she pumped his hand with more vigor than a lady ought to possess, before releasing him. "I will leave you to your reading. I have some inquiries to make about town."

Jesus, the thought of her gadding about in those trousers... *No.*

"I shall accompany you," he decided grimly. "I will read the notes upon our return."

Her smile deepened. "I do not require your assistance, sir. I assure you."

Oh yes, yes she did. He'd be damned before he allowed her to go traipsing about London, alone, wearing those misbegotten trousers.

"Nevertheless," he said, trying to keep his voice even and smooth, "I am your partner, Miss Montgomery. My place is at your side."

She frowned at him, looking distinctly unimpressed. "Very well. If you must."

He placed her journal back within its locked drawer for safekeeping. "I must."

It was either that, or spend the rest of the afternoon pacing his study, worrying about what would become of her in those blasted trousers. He had no choice really. Not any more of a choice than he had in accepting her as his partner.

For now, he reminded himself. *For now.*

Chapter Six

THE DUKE OF Arden's mother had drowned herself in the sea.

This lone, awful thought would not leave Hazel's mind. Disliking him was difficult indeed, if not impossible, after his revelation. Even more so with him sitting across from her in his carriage once more, their knees nearly brushing with each sway of the conveyance. She ought to have worn one of her simpler shapeless day gowns, instead of her trousers, she thought grimly. Her skirts would have provided a sufficient barrier to ensure Arden's trousers could not accidentally glance over hers.

Damn it, she was staring at his knees once more, she realized, and from there, it would not be long before she was ogling his thighs. Her face heated. And not just his thighs. She forced her gaze to the window instead. Far more interesting sights and sounds awaited her in the bustling streets of London. Moreover, she had a job to perform, an investigation to conduct, and Arden was her partner.

She must stop mooning over his fine form and face. His masculine appeal had no bearing upon the tasks looming ahead of her. Firmly, she forced her mind to facts. Reaching into the interior pocket sewn into her coat, she extracted a list.

"A love letter?" Arden guessed into the silence which had settled between them.

She flicked an irritated glance in his direction. His lips were quirked, and in spite of her every intention to remain impervious to him, she could not deny the Duke of Arden was a handsome devil. Nor could she deny he had the ability to make her pulse quicken and send heat rolling through her.

"Do I seem like the sort of woman who would secret letters from a lovesick swain about her person?" she asked.

He quirked a brow. "You seem like the sort of woman who is as unpredictable as dynamite."

"Dynamite is predictable," she quarreled. "It explodes."

"Not when the mechanisms surrounding it fail to perform their functions," he pointed out. "For every explosion we have suffered at the hands of the Fenians, there have been at least half a dozen others, either foiled or faulty."

"I will concede the point," she allowed, holding her paper aloft. "But this is a list, and most decidedly not a love letter. During my investigation of the Emerald Club, I discovered there were locations repeatedly mentioned by the members, both in conversations I overheard, and in documents I was able to view, and I would like to visit each of them for myself."

He studied her with that piercing gaze of his. "The information I was given by the Home Office did not describe how you managed to find yourself within the Emerald Club."

"It was not me who infiltrated the club. It was Mrs. Eliza Jane Mulligan," she told him.

He blinked. "Who is Mrs. Mulligan?"

"You are looking at her." She grinned. "Or rather, another version of her. Mrs. Mulligan was a ruse, the sort I have used often. She was illiterate, and unfortunately, dull-witted. But her mother hailed from County Cork, and she excelled at hovering at the elbows of senior members, whisking away dinner plates and refilling glasses of wine."

Her assignments often required ruses, but pretending to be Mrs. Mulligan had been the most dangerous of all her cases yet. The Emerald Club was, to the impartial observer, a gentleman's social club like so many others. But behind its walls, a dangerous new faction of Fenians plotted destruction as amiably as they inquired after each other's womenfolk.

"How is your Ma, O'Bannon?"

"How many crackers can accompany next month's boat to Liverpool, Rourke?"

They had never imagined simple Mrs. Mulligan would know *crackers* was a euphemism for shipments of lignin dynamite. Oh, they had never spoken words such as *dynamite* or *bombs* directly. But there was great power in hiding in plain sight. When the men she served had gazed upon her, they had seen precisely what she wished them to see: a bespectacled woman with a cap upon her head, eyes always cast downward, a mother of five struggling to earn coin to fill her children's hungry bellies.

Arden's voice interrupted. "You disguised yourself and went amongst them?"

He sounded almost impressed. She dared not fool herself that he was.

"I played a role," she conceded. "Men such as these speak freely behind closed doors, and in the presence of each other, particularly when there is food and spirits involved. None of the other agents could hide themselves as well as I could. You see? We female detectives are every bit as capable of performing our jobs as our male counterparts."

His lips compressed. "I never suggested you were not, Miss Montgomery."

"Mmm." She hummed and glanced back down at her list. "There were implications."

"*Imagined* implications?" he persisted.

"Undeniable ones." Her gaze returned to him. "Your displeasure with me, for instance."

"My displeasure at having a partner," he corrected, "when I have been managing quite well without one."

"Obviously you were not managing *quite well*, else Winchelsea and the Home Office would not have chosen to give you me as your aid," she argued calmly, for it was the truth.

He tensed across the carriage, and it was so subtle, she sensed it more than she saw it. One slight tic of the muscle in his jaw, fleeting and then gone, betrayed him.

"My work has been impeccable and diligent, Miss Montgomery." His tone had grown markedly cold. "With the exception of The Incident."

For a moment, she forgot about her list. They were *en route* to Praed Street Station, one of the targets which had been bandied about quite readily by Emerald Club members. But Arden held all her attention. She had assumed the Special League had always been led by partners. But Arden's earlier words returned to her now, fueling her curiosity.

"Which incident?"

His countenance was grim. "I do not speak of it."

Naturally, that just made her want to speak of it more. She leaned forward. The action, coupled with an unexpected bump in the road, sent her to the edge of the bench. Her knees were suddenly entangled with his long legs, and the warmth he radiated seared her.

Hastily, she slid her bottom back to the proper position. Her cheeks went hot, but she did her best to pretend she was unaffected. "As your partner, I believe I ought to know, Arden."

His stare had fallen to her legs, and it did strange things to her equilibrium. A throbbing sense of urgency came to life within her. Her lungs felt as if they were too constricted, and her belly tightened. For one brief, dizzying moment, she imagined his hands on her thighs.

At last, his green eyes flicked to hers, impenetrable as ever. "As I said, I do not speak of it."

Was it her imagination, or did the carriage seem smaller? He dominated it with his body, his presence. Her discomfit was a source of great irritation for Hazel. She tolerated neither weakness nor distraction in herself, and she was currently allowing both to overtake her.

She forced her mind to the matter at hand, Arden's evasion. "If you do not tell me, I will ask Winchelsea."

His nostrils flared. "Is that a threat, Miss Montgomery?"

"I would never be foolish enough to threaten you, Arden." But she did have a well-known, unchecked habit of poking rattlers, and the Duke of Arden was certainly a rattler, amongst other things. Hazel offered him an encouraging smile. "Rather, it is a chance for you to unburden yourself on your own."

"The Duke of Winchelsea may be charmed when you flutter your lashes at him, but I am impervious to your wiles, madam," he said in his clipped aristocratic accent.

He thought she had wiles? Hazel nearly laughed aloud. She boasted a great many talents, but seducing gentlemen had never been one of them. Indeed, she had not even been interested in a man since Adam. Her reaction to Arden was an anomaly. Likely because the man himself was an anomaly. She had no doubt it would dispel soon enough.

"I am not attempting to lure you behind the barn for a kiss, Arden," she retorted. "I am asking for an explanation. If you have weaknesses, I need to know what they are, for your safety, as much as for my own."

"You are an odd woman, do you know that, Miss Montgomery?"

He was frowning at her, and she could not be certain if he called her "odd" as a compliment, or an insult. She frowned right back at him.

"And you are a stubborn man, Mr. Arden," she challenged, once more reverting to the manner in which she could nettle him best.

There was something about getting beneath the Duke of Arden's thick skin which appealed to her. She could not deny it.

The carriage came to an ill-timed stop.

"We have arrived at Praed Street Station," Arden announced.

And damn her hide, but Hazel was just as tempted to remain in the carriage, as she was to leave it and investigate the location. All the more reason to flee this enclosed space and create some much-needed breathing room between herself and Arden.

With great haste.

"Then let us not waste a moment more." She tucked her list back into her coat pocket. "We have much work ahead of us, and if my research is any indication, little time in which to accomplish it, if we wish to stop further attacks before they happen."

"THIS IS HIGHLY irregular," Aunt Hortense announced staunchly that evening following dinner. "I must insist that Miss Montgomery and I withdraw. It simply is not done for a lady to remain in the dining room for port and cigars."

Lucien frowned. Aunt Hortense's previous introduction to Miss Montgomery had been awkward. The notion of an unwed female as their guest had been blaspheme to her. And now, he had politely suggested to his aunt she retire to the drawing room alone, so he could confer with Miss Montgomery. His poor aunt had nearly swallowed her tongue.

"Dear Aunt, you know this pertains to Special League matters," he reminded her gently. "There is nothing about Miss Montgomery's presence here that is regular."

"I dare say not," replied his great aunt, the frigid chill of deepest, darkest winter in her voice.

She disapproved. He could not blame her. He disapproved as well.

But Miss Montgomery had been foisted upon him by the Home Office, and he had a duty to perform. Part of that duty was working alongside the lady in question. Without the hindrance of his lady aunt, who was as trapped in the decades of a bygone era as her attire. She still proudly wore her widow's weeds in the fashion of her halcyon days.

"There will be no cigars," he offered. "You know I cannot abide by the things."

"The lack of cigars is not at issue here, Arden," she argued shrewdly.

Perhaps she imagined Miss Montgomery a grasping American, who would attempt to trap him into marriage at the first opportunity. If Miss Montgomery had been a finely bred English lady, the sort of delicate flower who blossomed in drawing rooms and curtseyed before the queen, he would have agreed with Aunt Hortense. But there was something about Miss Montgomery—perhaps her mannerisms, perhaps her extensive history of experience working alongside other men before him—that put him at ease. He had no fear she would attempt to dupe him into unwanted nuptials. She hardly seemed the sort who would wish to wed, and he had vowed to never find himself trapped in the constraints of such an untenable institution.

"Lady Beaufort," Miss Montgomery interjected, before he could steer the conversation into safer waters, "you must forgive me for disrupting your household. Your hospitality has been most excellent, and I am ever so thankful to you for your kindness in humoring my presence here. Naturally, I do not wish to upset you. Perhaps I shall withdraw with you, then later, meet with Arden in his study. Would you be more amenable to such an arrangement?"

The woman's drawl was in full effect now, dripping in honey. She did have a certain, unusual charm about her. Even Aunt Hortense, who was ordinarily as indefatigable in her defense of propriety as a battleship, appeared to wilt just a bit beneath the force of so much charisma.

"Miss Montgomery, you are an unmarried female, and it simply is not done for you to be alone in the duke's presence," Aunt Hortense said at last, but her tone had lost some of its ice.

"I do realize you are unaccustomed to such an arrange-ment," Miss Montgomery continued gently, "but it is my occupation. I have been a detective for over a decade, my lady. I have worked in the company of gentlemen all this time. My honor remains intact."

"It is not your honor which concerns me, but that of my nephew's," Aunt Hortense snapped. "I have never in all my life seen a female who so dares to defy civility, as to garb herself as a gentleman. I can only imagine what you are capable of."

Bloody hell. Perhaps he ought to have sent her to live with Lettie and Strathmore. Her widow's portion was small, she had been living at Lark House for years, and Lucien loved her as he had once loved his mother. But this interference was not what he needed. Perhaps if he spoke to her alone, in private, later...

"My lady, your tongue is unbecoming," he chastised his aunt. "I must insist you apologize to Miss Montgomery."

"It is quite alright, Arden," Miss Montgomery reassured him, sending a smile in Aunt Hortense's direction. "I understand your concern, my lady. Even at home in America, I am not like most women. I can only imagine how strange I must seem here. But despite my lack of sophistication, I can assure you, the work I must attend to with Arden is of the utmost importance. Far more important than breaking a rule by remaining at the dining table for a glass of port."

"I do wish I could be so dismissive of rules, Miss Montgomery," his aunt said.

"Have you ever wondered if some rules were not meant to be broken, Lady Beaufort?" Miss Montgomery asked then.

"No," answered Aunt Hortense resolutely. "They exist for good reason. My poor sister, Felicity, learned that lesson in a most difficult fashion."

Oh, Christ. Not the tale of Great Aunt Felicity again. It was one of Aunt Hortense's most beloved sermons.

Lucien cleared his throat. "Forgive me, Aunt, but I must insist. Miss Montgomery and I have some matters requiring our attention. The Duke of Winchelsea is depending upon us."

"Winchelsea?" Aunt Hortense's brows rose.

For some godforsaken reason, his aunt was in awe of the duke. On the sole occasion upon which Lucien had entertained him at Lark House, Aunt Hortense had mooned over him like a young girl eyeing her first suitor. Her admiration for Winchelsea had irked him at the time, but he was not above using it in his favor now.

"Yes," he said smoothly. "Winchelsea himself decreed Miss Montgomery stay here at Lark House, and he has nothing but complete admiration for Miss Montgomery, as have I."

Perhaps the last bit was a lie. His feelings for his unwanted partner were confusing and jumbled at best. But Aunt Hortense need not know that.

"Well." Aunt Hortense rose from her seat with a dignified air. "I suppose I cannot help but to defer to Winchelsea. He is one of the finest statesmen of our age, after all."

"Thank you, Aunt. I bid you good evening."

Lucien wondered, not without a hint of bitterness, what Aunt Hortense considered *him* to be. But he stood all the same with a feeling of relief, and Miss Montgomery did as well. As his aunt took her reluctant leave, Lucien arranged for coffee and port to be brought round for them. Coffee for Miss Montgomery, port for himself. He would not get her soused this evening. Nor would she fall for his ruse a second time. She was far too intelligent for that.

When the servants had been dismissed, and the two of them were alone at last, Lucien sipped his port and stared at the vivacious conundrum that was H.E. Montgomery.

"That was a falsehood," she told him.

He quirked a brow. "Pardon?"

Her lips twitched, and he noted, not for the first time, how finely formed they were. How pink. How soft-looking.

"You told your poor aunt you admire me," she elaborated, an edge of admonishment in her voice.

"I do admire you," he countered, even though he had just entertained a similar thought himself. But as he said the words aloud, he realized they did indeed possess some truth. "I cannot think of another woman who would have convinced the Home Office to bestow upon her the depth of trust and respect that has been shown to you."

Her eyes searched his, her countenance unsmiling. "Your

aunt believes I am attempting to entrap you in marriage."

"My aunt lives and dies by the winds of propriety," he said. "She forgets I have no desire to play a role in polite society; not now, not ever. Scandal does not concern me. Rooting out those who would terrorize innocents, however, does."

She took a sip of her coffee, and he noted she had added neither sugar nor cream to it, instead, leaving it unadulterated.

"You have every right to be concerned," she said. "The information I obtained in New York City suggests a new wave of attacks is being planned. They are eager to rally in the wake of the capture and death of some of the key figures of the Fenian movement."

He nodded, turning his mind easily to the task at hand. They needed to unravel the plans of these would-be marauders before they could even begin. He thought of what she had revealed to him in their investigations.

"You are certain Praed Street and Charing Cross were referenced as potential targets for an explosive device to be planted?" he asked.

"I am utterly certain, Arden," she reassured him.

The information she had brought to him may indeed be true. Could possibly even be vital to the investigations the Special League would pursue moving forward. However, the Special League had recently arrested an entire ring of Fenians who had been plotting to lay bombs on the railways. He had to be certain her information was not old, and that the suspects in question had not already been removed from the streets before they could inflict damage. Lucien was not in the business of tilting at windmills.

"Who did you hear reference the locations, and when did you overhear it?" he asked next.

She took another delicate sip of her coffee before answering him, and his eyes tracked the movement of her creamy throat as she swallowed. "The Emerald Club is run by a man named Drummond McKenna. He has a handful of trusted associates he often confers with, and I overheard them speaking about Praed Street and Charing Cross in the week before I left my post and boarded the steamer for England. There was great displeasure among the ranks, following arrests made here in the last few months. I understand several of the suspects have turned Queen's evidence."

Blast. That was decidedly not what Lucien wished to hear, for it meant another round of plotting was likely underway. "Some of them have," he confirmed, "which in turn led to more arrests."

"McKenna was relieved he had never connected himself to the conspirators in a documented fashion," Miss Montgomery offered. "I was able to surreptitiously read some of his correspondence. He feels confident his name is unknown to police here in England."

McKenna was correct about that, for although Lucien was familiar with the Emerald Club's existence from his League connections in America, this was the first time he had ever heard of the man himself.

He frowned. There remained something deeply disturbing to him about the notion of Miss Montgomery infiltrating the ranks of such brutal men without any protection. "Did you conduct your investigation of the Emerald Club alone, or were there others?"

"Alone," she said simply, her stare turning challenging. "Although a fellow agent posed as my husband, it was deemed best by all that I infiltrate the Emerald Club alone. I have a flair for covert operations."

He would not argue the point, for there was no need. Miss Hazel Montgomery was clearly much more than he had initially supposed. He had to inwardly admit to a grudging respect for her, though he could not say for certain his pride would allow for a vocal affirmation. After all, he was still quite perturbed at having been forced to share his duties and authority with her.

Not, as she had suggested earlier, because she was female. But because he did not wish to be forced to adhere to the wishes of another, particularly when his greatest fear remained that those wishes could well be horribly wrong. However, he was quickly coming to a great many realizations where Miss Montgomery was concerned, and whilst he did not necessarily enjoy those realizations, he recognized their necessity.

As an agent himself, he no longer harbored any doubt that her reputation was as pristine as Winchelsea, and the documents he had been provided, suggested. Likely even more so. Scratch that. *Definitely* more so.

Her mind was formidable. Her determination was voracious. And when the woman wanted to find the answer to a question, she was relentless. Ruthless.

Breathtaking.

He struck the last thought from his mind, for it was unworthy, and the last thing he ought to be doing in this moment was waxing poetic over the partner he had never wanted. The partner he did not require. Indeed, the partner who had been unceremoniously forced upon him by a Home Office regime, which had lost its confidence in his abilities far too quickly. He could not forget that, nor could he allow himself to forget who she was.

"Your flair for the covert is not in question by me, Miss Montgomery," he told her.

"But my capability as your partner is?" she queried, sharp as a blade.

He hesitated. The answer was complicated. "Not your

capability, so much as my necessity for a partner."

Particularly one who made his cock stiff simply by sitting at his dinner table and calmly sipping coffee. His reaction to her was not just unwanted. It was wrong. Miss Montgomery may have a lovely face, a sharp complex mind, dark hair he wished to bury his face in, a lush bosom, and long legs he yearned to feel wrapped around him, but she was his *partner*.

The partner he had never, ever wanted.

The partner he now, *somehow*, desired. Merely not in the way he should. But lust had no place in his life. Reason, ration, fact—these mattered. Emotion, desire, vulnerability— these, he abhorred. These, he plucked from his life with attentive precision, never allowing one to remain long enough to bloom and produce fruit.

For the fruit would be rotten. Lucien's blood was tainted, and he knew it.

She took a sip of her coffee again now, and he could not help but note the manner in which she pursed her lips, then flicked her tongue over them to remove any traces of her drink.

Would she taste of coffee, bitter and dark? Would she taste of the raspberry fool they had consumed for dessert, sweet and light, slightly tart?

"There is a reason for my presence here," she reminded him, effectively piercing the fog of lust which had begun clouding his brain. "One you have alluded to, but have yet to share with me. After such a productive day, I cannot help but to hope you have changed your mind."

He took a fortifying sip of his port, hesitating with his response. "One productive day does not entitle you to my confidences, Miss Montgomery."

"I expect not." She watched him with a frank regard. "But I would rather hear it from your lips, than borrowed from the

Duke of Winchelsea's."

The notion of Miss Montgomery having anything at all to do with Winchelsea's lips was irksome. Belatedly, he realized his hands had clenched upon the table. He forced them to relax, then indulged in another drink of port.

"We were not finished discussing the railway targets," he reminded her.

The woman was vicious when she set her mind upon something. That much, he could discern already. She circled back to the source in relentless pursuit.

But somehow, his prompt had the desired effect. Miss Montgomery's mind returned to another favorite topic of hers, detective work. He could almost see the wheels of her mind begin to churn. Her eyes widened, an expression he was coming to realize indicated she had stumbled upon an idea.

"Have you any maps showing the railways, Arden?" she asked, her drawl cascading over his senses. "Being new to this city, I cannot help but to feel rather discombobulated after having been squired about in your carriage all day."

"I do," he confirmed, before he could think better of it.

The hour was growing later, after all, and closeting himself in his study, without the barrier of a dinner table and the possible disruption of servants dancing attendance upon them, seemed the very worst sort of idea.

"Excellent." She stood, beaming a smile at him that also brought with it a host of other worst sorts of ideas. "I find I have had more than enough coffee. Lead the way, if you please."

Turrets, he reminded himself with grim intent.

Chapter Seven

EITHER HAZEL WAS delirious in the wake of her world travels, coupled with a full day of investigative work, or the Duke of Arden was staring at her mouth. Her lips parted, a slow breath escaping her as her heart pounded.

The hour was late.

She and Arden had been alone in his study for an indeterminate span of time. The servants had all retired for the evening, leaving the house in a hushed state, which was interrupted by nothing save the ticking of a mantel clock and the occasional din of the street.

A frisson of awareness slid through her. A desperate, mad yearning pulsed from deep within. It was the sort of longing she had not experienced in years. The sort she never, as a rule, allowed herself to even contemplate. And for a wild moment, she imagined leaning toward Arden, brushing her lips over his.

Then she recalled why such fancies were not just wrong, but impossible. She cleared her throat and returned her gaze to the map laid out upon the surface of his massive desk. The London streets blurred, bisected by railways which formed the arteries of the city.

"Are the bulk of the railways underground, then?" she asked, even though she already knew the answer for herself, having pored over half a dozen London travel guides prior to her arrival.

"Most of them, yes," he answered, his voice sounding strained. "They run through a network of tunnels built beneath the city streets."

His finger, which had been still upon the map, traced over the railways, stopping just short of grazing hers where it lay over Leadenhall and Fenchurch Streets. She bit her lip, staring at his hand, so large and so near to hers. Another disastrous urge swept through her, strong and sudden. The impulse to slide her hand atop his, to touch his heat and strength, to feel a man's fingers laced through hers after so long... It was as overwhelming as it was ruinous.

"The Inner Circle," she forced herself to elaborate, irritated by the breathless state of her voice, clearly discernible to her own ears.

"So named, because they run in a circular pattern over most of the city's interior," he agreed. "From Aldgate here," he paused as his finger slid along the map, trailing over the stations as he named them, "to Bishopsgate, all the way to King's Cross, then onward to Baker Street...Praed Street Station..." He continued, until his finger reached Mansion House. This time, when he returned to Aldgate, his finger did graze hers, and there it lingered. "And back to Aldgate once more."

One small touch, his forefinger against hers, and she felt as if she had been set aflame. Her awareness of every sense was heightened to an almost painful level. The divine scent of citrus-laden musk struck her. Her heart beat faster. Heat pooled in her belly, and lower still, between her thighs. Her nipples went hard. She could hear the hitch in her own breathing, just above the ticking mantel clock and the frantic thud of her heart.

She ought to move her finger away, to sever the connection and effectively reverse whatever spell he had seemingly cast upon her. Yet, some wickedness within her considered moving away a retreat. A failure. And she could not bear to be bested by Arden. Could not possibly allow him to see how very much he affected her.

Hazel forced herself to remain still. To focus upon the case and the very real possibility the Emerald Club was about to send a group of men to London to wreak havoc upon the underground railway as she had been led to believe by her investigations.

"The trains run all day in steady intervals, correct?" she asked.

"Correct," he confirmed, his voice a deep rumble near her ear. "They begin at six o'clock in the morning and end close to midnight, with the fastest time in between trains running from eight o'clock in the morning through eight in the evening."

She swallowed, her gaze fixed upon the map, but in truth, also his finger, still touching hers. Why had he yet to move it? More importantly, why did she not simply remove hers?

"That is an incredibly high volume of daily travelers and stops," she observed.

"A staggering amount," he agreed, his baritone sending a shiver straight through her.

His voice seemed even nearer now. So too, the heat from his tall, masculine form. Inexplicably, the memory of his well-defined thighs, long legs, and broad shoulders hit her. *Pure, sensual torture.* Why did she torment herself? Even if she was attracted to the Duke of Arden, she could never act upon her wayward impulses.

Never, she told herself sternly. *Only think of what happened with Adam.*

Attempting to keep the tremor from her voice, she mustered up yet another query. Another means of distraction.

"How many, do you suppose, Arden?"

"I cannot begin to guess, Miss Montgomery. Something such as one hundred thousand passengers a day, I would venture to say."

"One hundred thousand in a day," she repeated, a swift rush of futility assailing her. "With so many people traveling about the city, and so many stops, it will be impossible to keep a bombing from occurring. Surveillance on such a grand scheme is difficult and costly, which is precisely what McKenna is counting upon."

Silence descended upon them once more. But still, neither of them moved. His presence burned into her back in the same way the fleshy pad of his lone finger seared hers.

"Unless we have names or aliases to trace, the best we can do is prepare ourselves for the inevitable." His tone was bleak. "And from what you have said, you have only one here in London."

The Nightingale, yes, and unfortunately, the trail leading to him was sparse at best. Though Arden's words were a reflection of the awful realization dawning in her own mind, she did not want to hear them. Before she had found herself in the vast, thriving metropolis of London, she had been hopeful her information could thwart the attacks almost certainly being plotted by McKenna. But what she had witnessed today, coupled with the map before her, and the knowledge she had gleaned from her guide book and Arden himself, suggested the impracticality of doing so.

"I do not know the identity of The Nightingale," she said, wishing she had more information to rely upon. But given the secrecy of the Emerald Club, it was a miracle she had managed to obtain what she had. "I overheard a discussion concerning a trip to London for two. This was in conjunction with discussion of Praed Street and other stations. McKenna's closest and most trusted friend is a man named William Flanagan, and though I do not have conclusive evidence of it, I suspect he is the man who is tasked with choosing members for various missions."

Deciding she had played the coward for too long, she lifted her finger from the map, then turned to face Arden. To her shock, he had drifted even closer than she had supposed, rendering them uncomfortably near. Uncomfortable in the most delicious way possible.

Her breath caught. His expression and gaze were both inscrutable, as if he were utterly unaffected. As if he did not feel the spark that had ignited deep inside her, burning into a roaring flame.

And perhaps he didn't.

But then she recalled the manner in which his gaze had feasted upon her lips, and she was certain he did. She had not consumed a drop of spirits this evening. She could not even blame the attraction she felt for Arden upon port consumption. And neither could she excuse it as a weakness somehow developed by her voyage across sea and land, respectively.

No, this was a weakness—an infirmity, as it were—of her own constitution. She alone was at fault. Well, she and the handsome, arrogant duke standing so near to her, his scent once more invading her senses. He was coming straight for her, and she was not certain she had the willpower, nor the desire, to stop him.

"Tomorrow is a new day, Miss Montgomery," Arden was saying in his pristine aristocrat's accent. Perfectly clipped, his baritone so lovely and deep, a tingle trilled through her. "Together, we will formulate a plan to anticipate the attacks you speak of. While we likely cannot stop these villains, we can make their evil tasks more difficult to carry out, if we put our minds to work upon it."

If there was one word in the English lexicon that rendered the Duke of Arden more handsome and irresistible than he already was, she had just discovered it: *together*. And another, equally lovely word: *we*.

Those two words combined seemed to suggest Arden was on his way to accepting her as his partner. Those words also made her want to kiss him. In truth, it wasn't just the words. It was also the way he was looking at her, respect gleaming in his eyes.

As a female Pinkerton agent, Hazel could count on one hand the number of times she had ever been considered an equal by the men she worked alongside. Even when she brought murderers and thieves to justice. Even when she disguised herself and conducted the sorts of complicated investigative missions her fellow male counterparts could never hope to even *imagine* on their own. She was forever being judged and found lacking by her fellow male agents who expected higher pay and fancied themselves far more effective detectives solely because they were men.

"Miss Montgomery?" His head dipped lower. His hands had found her waist.

Wrong, she reminded herself. *This is wrong. And foolish. And ruinous.* Romantic complications of any sort did not blend well with working as a detective, and no one knew that better than Hazel. Still, she could not stifle her desire.

She met his gaze. "Arden?"

She wanted to kiss him. For the first time in years, a man had somehow slipped past her defenses. It had been so long, in fact, since she had last felt such a foolish weakness, that she had believed herself incapable of it.

"The hour grows late," he said, offering up the voice of reason.

"Yes," she agreed, "it does."

She ought to excuse herself. Seek out her chamber. Get some much-needed rest. But instead, she remained where she was, temptation within reach. The longing inside her would not be satisfied. She was possessed by the fleeting suspicion that if she did not act now, she would forever regret not seizing the chance. There was no choice, not really.

Hazel closed the distance between them. She slammed her eyes shut and moved on instinct. One step, rising on her toes, the tilt of her head, her hands fluttering to his shoulders, was all it required. Simple gestures, taken separately.

But when her lips touched his, nothing was simple. Everything was alive and complex, sparking like electricity. His mouth was warm and supple, and her upper lip fit between his as if it had found its home. He groaned loud and low, the sound seemingly wrung from him against his will.

And then, his mouth moved. He did not just kiss her back; he consumed her. His lips took over, aggressive and bold, ravenous and insistent. He kissed her as she had never before been kissed, his mouth working hers open, his tongue slipping inside. Arden's kiss was carnal and dominating, and nothing like the teasing, languorous meeting of mouths she had once known, seemingly a lifetime ago.

This kiss promised pleasure. It promised hands skimming beneath her skirts. It promised forbidden touches in forbidden places, places that had not been brought to life in years.

She gave in to the urge to run her tongue along his. He tasted sweet, like raspberry fool and port. A sound she barely recognized as her own emerged from her throat. Breathy and needy. Her fingers dug into his shoulders. He had long since shucked his jacket, and he wore only shirtsleeves and a waistcoat. Beneath her bare hands, he was warm and vital and so very strong.

Hazel forgot all the reasons why she should never have

kissed the Duke of Arden. He deepened the kiss, his hands on her waist tightening as he stepped into her, bringing her body flush against his. She too had removed her jacket in the course of their work, and without the barrier of a corset beneath her bodice, her breasts crushed into his chest. Because she wore trousers, their limbs tangled.

She kissed him back with all the fervent need roaring to life within her. Urges that had lain dormant for far too long revived. An aching pulse between her thighs had her arching toward him, seeking contact, needing relief. But instead of relief, she only discovered more torture. He knew what she wanted, and he gave it to her, sliding his well-muscled thigh between hers.

The delicious friction made her remember how good it felt to be touched. How wondrous her body could feel. She thrust against him, wanting more. Wanting release. Her fingers had somehow found their way into his hair. Wavy and lustrous, it was softer than she had imagined. She held him to her, kissed him back with all the urgency swelling to a crescendo inside her.

One of his hands slid from her waist, cupping her breast, then kneading it. He found her nipple and rolled it between his thumb and forefinger, tugging it through the stiff silk of her bodice. His touch was gentle yet commanding, and while their kisses became more frenzied, he caressed her slowly, taking his time and prolonging her torment.

They wrestled for control. Hazel wanted more, faster, harder. She felt as if she were starving and he was the feast laid before her. She wanted to gorge herself on him, because the rational part of her mind recognized this madness between them could not be indulged in ever again. It was once and done. Later, she could blame the lateness of the hour, the many years since she had been touched by a man, the dizziness of her mind after nine days at sea. She could blame Arden's handsome face, and his expert kisses and knowing hands.

But Arden had his own pace. He nipped her lower lip, then licked away the sting, before fusing their mouths for a slower, deeper kiss. She sucked on his tongue, shamelessly rocking over his thigh as the pressure within her built. She was dimly aware of the buttons running down the front of her bodice coming undone.

She ought to stop him, but everything felt too good. Her eyes fluttered open at last, to find his startling green gaze burning into hers. She felt the shock and the connection of it deep inside. But still, she did nothing to stay his progress. She kissed him back, staring at him, her body moving rhythmically against his as, one by one, buttons slid from their moorings.

She kept kissing him as he opened her bodice completely. Kissed him as he peeled the sleeves down her arms, his hot hands gliding over her bare skin. Kissed him right back while he pulled her bodice from the waistband of her custom trousers and let it fall to the floor.

He tore his mouth from hers, his breathing harsh and ragged, his gaze never wavering, as he gripped her waist and lifted her, settling her bottom upon his desk. The crinkle of the map as she sat upon it reached her, and it ought to have been a reminder of what they were meant to be doing and why she was in his study alone with him.

But the Duke of Arden's mouth was ripe and dark from kissing her, and his eyes were eating her up as he nudged her knees apart, settling himself firmly between her legs. And then the ridge of his manhood pressed against her core.

She gasped. He was large, even through the layers separating them. She knew what it meant now, as she had in the carriage. He wanted her. And she knew too what the pulsing, aching hunger inside her meant. She wanted him too.

He cupped her cheek in a touch that was surprisingly gentle. Without speaking a word, he lowered his lips back down to hers. Her mouth clung to his. This time, she kept her eyes open. He rolled his hips, sending his length over her. She scooted nearer, thrusting against him without thought.

Later, she could writhe in agony when she thought of how she had behaved. Later, she could worry about the effect their actions would have upon their fledgling partnership. It had been years since a man had kissed her, years since she had been caressed, since she had been wanted.

And she did not want to stop.

His mouth left hers to trail kisses down her throat. He dragged her chemise down her shoulders, baring her breasts. Kissing behind her ear, he filled his hands with her, and she allowed it. Longed for it. She looked down at the erotic sight of his large hands upon her and watched as he kissed his way down the curve of one of her breasts. When his mouth closed over her nipple, she cried out.

He sucked, then flicked his tongue over the tight bud, sending a flood of sensation to her center. And still, she did not stop him. Instead, she sank her fingers into his hair, holding him there as he laved and suckled, torturing her flesh.

He angled his rigid manhood against her, pumping into her aching center, then sucked her other nipple into his mouth. It was too much. Years spent tamping down and ruthlessly ignoring her body's needs rendered her helpless beneath Arden's sensual onslaught.

She rocked against him, the friction making her lose control. She shattered as an intense burst of pleasure roared through her. Her inner muscles clenched and convulsed, and she spent, then and there, seated on Arden's study desk, grinding her body into his like an alley cat longing for her mate.

He made a low sound of need, his tongue flicking over her nipple, and still she felt no shame. Only a boneless, liquid sense of gratification. Until he released the turgid peak and straightened.

And she began to fall from her cloud. Ramifications returned like the ground rising up to meet her. What had she done? Not only had she trespassed over an all-important boundary between herself and her new partner, she had also allowed another man to touch her for the first time since Adam. Worse, she had enjoyed it. She had writhed against Arden without regard for what would happen afterward.

Her hands went to his chest, pushing him from her. She grasped her chemise and hauled it upward, covering herself. Hazel hopped down from his desk, searching blindly for her discarded bodice, for she could not walk the halls of Lark House in her underclothes. Any domestic who passed her would have no doubt as to what had just occurred.

The need to escape was every bit as strong and sudden as the fires of desire he had lit within her. She required as much distance as possible between herself and Arden. Not to mention those hands and the tempting protrusion of his manhood.

Her cheeks burned as she thought about how he had felt against her and how she had wanted more. About how desperately she had longed for what she had never even experienced with Adam. And how close she had come to almost allowing a man who she had only known for a short time make love to her. She found her bodice crumpled beneath his desk and sank to her knees, snatching it up.

"Miss Montgomery," Arden rasped, an undeniable note of apology edging his voice. "Hazel, I... Forgive me. I overstepped my bounds. I should never have touched you."

Somehow, the sound of her name in his clipped accent

seemed just as intimate as the torrid embrace they had just shared. She needed to go. To run. Flee. Gather up the tattered remnants of her pride and leave him to his crumpled map, cavernous study, and intricately carved desk. There was precious little solace in the belated realization that, like every other one of his possessions, the Duke of Arden's desk was also intolerably fancy.

She stood and thrust her arms into the sleeves. "I must beg your forgiveness as well. I do not know what came over me." Her hands shook as she attempted to fasten the buttons running down the front of her bodice.

"Allow me," he said, moving forward.

"No," she denied, still unable to look at him as she took a quick step in retreat.

Unfortunately for her, Arden's desk proved as unforgiving as it was immobile, and her rump slammed right into one of its sharp corners. Pain tore through her, but she bit her lip, refusing to allow herself to make a sound. Her pride was forcing her to smile and bear it. Her mind was counting down the seconds until she was alone.

"That seemed as if it would smart," he observed.

She scowled down at her bodice as she settled the last button into place only to realize she still had one more buttonhole to fill. Her entire bodice was off by one button, but she refused to unbutton herself all over again to repair it. Her ignominy was complete enough.

"I am perfectly well, Arden," she lied, hating the sound of her voice, breathless and husky. "If you will excuse me, I must retire."

Offering him something between a curtsy and a bow, she still avoided meeting his gaze. Swallowing down a great lump of shame, she turned on her heel and fled, ignoring the sound of his voice calling after her.

Chapter Eight

*C*HREE DAYS AFTER The Second Incident, Lucien arrived at the Duke of Winchelsea's residence for dinner, just as he preferred to be, punctual and alone. But when Winchelsea's butler announced him, and Lucien crossed the threshold of his superior's study, he discovered there was another guest who would be joining them for dinner.

A pair of wide blue eyes watched his entrance. To be precise, it was the same wide blue eyes to which he had been in close enough proximity to note the striations of deeper colors hidden within their depths: gray, violet, and cerulean. To be even more precise, it was the same pair of eyes he had stared into whilst she had rubbed her cunny all over his thigh until she spent.

Christ.

He had not expected her here, and his cock twitched at the sight of her, a testament to just how wrong he had been in telling himself what had happened three days ago in the late hours of the evening had been an aberration. That it had been nothing more than a rare lapse in judgment produced by the unfortunate combination of her nearness and the sight of her long legs in those infernal trousers.

He had spent the days since his folly avoiding Miss Montgomery. She was a creature of habit, which rendered the task easy. He rose before dawn and breakfasted before her. On the first day of his self-imposed isolation, he had spent hours in his study, poring over her notes. He began on page one, rather than on page twenty-three as she had previously advised, and what he learned as he worked his way through them, was the woman was even more intelligent than he had supposed, and impossibly brave as well. His admiration had grown.

So too his attraction.

Which meant maintaining his distance from her was all-important. Because, even though he was gradually beginning to see having Miss Montgomery's New York-gleaned information and enterprising mind aboard the Special League could be an asset, rather than a hindrance, he also knew his shockingly lewd behavior must never again be repeated.

Regardless of how desperately he wanted to haul her into his arms and kiss her breathless, before carrying her to the nearest bedchamber, where he could bed her to his heart's content.

"Arden." Winchelsea's voice pierced the thoughts weighing down upon him then.

Precisely the reminder he required. He could not stand here like a dolt, mooning over Miss Montgomery, while Winchelsea looked on. Nor could he continue making love to her with his eyes. This was precisely why he had been evading her for the last three days. Well, this and his own inherent weakness. He was drawn to Miss Montgomery, and there was no denying the all-consuming spark of attraction he felt whenever he looked upon her.

Or thought about her, for that matter. But that too, was neither here nor there. Lucien could control himself. He simply had to exercise his restraint. And perhaps find an accommodating bed partner to distract him from his recklessness.

What was she doing here, for Christ's sake? He had not been warned an invitation had been issued to her as well. By God, had she hired a hack? The thought vexed him immensely, but he battled his indignation and irritation, for neither was wanted, or needed, at the moment.

"Winchelsea," he greeted, inclining his head and performing an abbreviated bow in the direction of the blue-eyed curse, who haunted his every errant thought. "Miss Montgomery. I did not expect you."

She had risen from her seat at his entrance, but she did not offer him a curtsy in return. Instead, she executed her strange half-bow. "Your Grace. Nor was I expecting you."

He supposed they were even on that score. But quite lopsided on another. This was one of a few times she had paid his title deference, and it was not lost upon him. Odd though it was, he had to admit he rather missed her ordinary daring.

Was it his fanciful imagination, or had she grown more beautiful since that night in his study? Her cheeks were stained a pretty rose pink, her dark hair caught in a becoming Grecian braid, with wisps of curls framing her heart-shaped face. How had he failed to notice how delicately her brows were arched?

Her tongue wetted her lower lip.

And he knew she was not as calm and serene on the inside as her placid expression would suggest.

When he was seated in the chair at her side, facing Winchelsea, he could not help but note the manner in which his superior's gaze lingered upon Miss Montgomery. He thought of her responsiveness to him when they had been alone. Thought about the ardent manner in which she had kissed him, the way her hands had clawed at his shoulders first, and then his hair. The way she had opened her legs and wrapped them around his hips, meeting him thrust for thrust, while he sucked her nipples.

And he wondered. He wondered how long she and the duke had been alone before his arrival. He wondered if she had taken note of how prodigiously tall Winchelsea was, even taller than Lucien himself. The man was more beast than man, truly. He wondered why Winchelsea had issued a separate invitation to her. He wondered if Winchelsea had cornered her against his desk, taken her mouth as his own...

Christ! The mere notion made him ill.

And bloody furious.

He clenched his jaw tight. Beyond Winchelsea's sumptuously appointed study, it began to rain. A thorough, soaking rain, pelting the street outside, rattling against the windows. Lucien flicked a glance over the expensive carpets and all the dark leather and gilt. This was his first time at Winchelsea's residence, and he could not help but question the timing. Would he have been invited at all, if not for Miss Montgomery? More to the point, precisely *what* had Miss Montgomery been up to for the last few days while he had been isolating himself?

He had imagined she was keeping to herself, studying her maps and making her lists. But it occurred to him now he had never inquired after her whereabouts. He had not concerned himself with what she was doing, or with whom she was doing it. He had simply taken for granted she would remain within Lark House.

He was a fool. Doubly, it would seem.

"The Nightingale," Winchelsea said, bringing Lucien's attention back to where it belonged.

The Nightingale was the name of the contact the Emerald Club kept within England. Lucien had read the entirety of Miss Montgomery's notes. Twice.

He raised a brow. "What of him?"

"We need to discover his identity," Winchelsea elaborated. "Miss Montgomery feels the unearthing of this villain will prove essential to our ability to stave off attacks on our London railways."

Lucien turned toward Miss Montgomery. Their gazes clashed, and he saw everything reflected within hers for a brief, shattering moment, until she seemed to gather herself with a deep breath. Her lashes lowered, and when she tipped up her chin and met his gaze once more, he saw nary a hint of the vulnerability she had shown him merely seconds before.

He remembered every touch. The way she tasted. The sounds she made. The way her body had come to life against his. For as long as he lived, even if he never touched her again, he would never forget.

And he would be lying if he said he did not feel a stab of jealousy at the realization she had been sitting alone with the Duke of Winchelsea, formulating a plan without him. It hurt more than his pride.

"Is that so, Miss Montgomery?" he asked her directly, refusing to allow her to look away. "What else have you been telling Winchelsea in my absence?"

Inferring he was going to divulge the boundaries they had crossed together to Winchelsea was wrong, and he knew it well. But he would also be a liar if he claimed he did not enjoy the subtle lifting of her brows, the widening of her eyes, and the parting of her lips. Her spine stiffened. Her shoulders straightened.

Her full, lush mouth tightened then. "I related to Winchelsea the affable manner in which we have been able to coexist as partners of the Special League," she said formally, her tone bright. "I also told him how very grateful I am for the manner in which you have welcomed me, Your Grace. You have been so *warm*, so caring and solicitous. Indeed, without the guidance of your dexterous hands, I would never have been able to find my footing here so well."

Her words were laden with double entendres, the minx. He had riled her enough she had almost spilled their secrets then and there before Winchelsea.

Almost, but not quite.

He flashed her a smile he did not feel. "I am happy to know my dexterous hands have enabled you to find your...*footing*, my dear Miss Montgomery."

She pinned him with a glare. "I could not ask for a better partner," she seethed through gritted teeth.

"Nor could I," he growled right back at her.

"Shall we attend dinner?" Winchelsea asked hopefully, aiming his smile exclusively in the direction of Miss Montgomery. "I confess I am quite heartened that the two of you have settled into a working partnership with such ease."

Oh, they had settled into a partnership, Lucien thought grimly. But perhaps not in the manner Winchelsea would prefer.

"One can never be certain," his superior added, "given the disparity of station and nationality, to say nothing of the undeniable fact that Miss Montgomery is female. Though her record is flawless, and she is unparalleled in her successful cases."

"Men do not accept women as their equals," Miss Montgomery said, her gaze raking over Lucien. "There is no need to dance around the subject with me, Winchelsea, for I have been fighting against the current for the whole of my life. Resistance does not daunt me. Rather, it heightens my persistence. Whenever I am doubted, my determination to prove the naysayer wrong prevails."

Her words were meant as a reprimand toward him, and Lucien knew it. But she could not know he did not doubt her.

Nor could she know his respect for her capabilities was unparalleled. The woman before him was so much more than a lovely face and an amalgamation of luscious feminine curves. She was more than her kiss, more than the surrender she had given him. Far more than the way she made him feel. She was more than lust. She was also intelligent, brave, and a damned fine agent. Her sex did not matter one whit. She was incomparable.

How could she not see it? How had he not seen it before?

So many words crowded on his tongue, but he could not seem to formulate a proper response. And the Duke of Winchelsea was ever at the ready. He rose, circled his desk, and offered Miss Montgomery his arm. Lucien rose as well.

"Allow me to escort you to dinner, Miss Montgomery?" he asked with the air of a swain.

Devil take it. Lucien found himself scowling as he watched her settle a bright smile upon Winchelsea and take his proffered arm. And then he continued to scowl as Miss Montgomery and Winchelsea presented him their backs. She leaned her head toward the duke's and laughed.

The sound was beautiful. Melodious. It trilled down his spine. Had she ever laughed like that in his presence? And had she ever smiled at him thus? The bile rose in his throat, along with a vicious, rampaging surge of jealousy.

Three nights ago, he had held this vibrant, beautiful creature in his arms. He had kissed her, stripped her, suckled her nipples. He had brought her to a crashing, body-ravaging spend. And now, he was staring at her elegant back, forced to acknowledge her gown this evening was not at all shapeless, but rather well-fitted and crafted of fine silk, with the spare trim of ribbons and the occasional fringe.

Which was just as well, for this magnificent woman did not require adornments.

His gaze flitted to her waist. She was not wearing a corset this evening either. He could tell. And damn him if his cock didn't ache and throb at the realization.

"Arden?" she called to him in her honeyed drawl.

He realized, quite belatedly, that Winchelsea and Miss Montgomery had almost reached the door to the study, while he had remained rooted to the spot, misery overtaking him as he watched them go. This, surely, was his punishment for nearly losing his control in her presence. Perhaps she and Winchelsea would marry, and she would bear him a dozen dark-haired babes, who would grow to be seven feet tall and lumber about in an ungainly fashion.

Bloody fucking hell.

He brushed an imaginary speck of lint from his coat sleeve. "Lead the way."

Dinner proceeded in an unhurried fashion. The courses were uninspired and bland, but even had they been lovingly crafted by the finest French chef, Lucien would not have tasted them. Winchelsea hung upon every word Miss Montgomery spoke. Miss Montgomery avoided Lucien's gaze and consumed her dinner with considerably less gusto than she had evinced on previous occasions.

She laughed at Winchelsea's tepid attempts at making sallies.

She spoke fondly of New York City in her melodious drawl.

Lucien could not help but to think about how her sweet pink nipples matched the color of her lips.

"And that is when I fell from the tree," Miss Montgomery told Winchelsea with a laugh, currently in the midst of regaling him with tales of her girlhood.

She had been an orphan, he reminded himself, thinking once more of a young Miss Montgomery. Had she always been as determined as she was now, with more backbone than most gentlemen he knew? Against his will, he envisioned her as a girl, climbing a tree, intent upon her quarry. And he was charmed, in spite of himself.

The Duke of Winchelsea was smitten too, his glowing admiration for her evident upon his face. "Were you injured, Miss Montgomery?"

"Fortunately, the branch was low, and I landed on my feet," she concluded, smiling. "But I certainly learned my lesson. From that day on, I have never climbed a tree to pick an apple while wearing skirts."

Lucien would be willing to wager Lark House, and all his funds, she wore trousers instead. And that the damned woman *always* landed on her feet.

"An excellent lesson. We may consider ourselves fortunate you survived your apple-picking adventure unscathed and are here with us to tell the tale," Winchelsea said warmly, chuckling.

Far too warmly. Lucien cut his roast beef with more force than necessary. The sound of his cutlery on the china resonated through the room, sending two pairs of eyes in his direction. At last, that light-blue gaze was upon him.

He forced a smile to his lips, even as a memory of how responsive her mouth was beneath his struck him. He banished it and forced his attention back to their host. "We are very fortunate indeed, Winchelsea."

Just as fortunate there was a large expanse of dinner table between himself and Miss Montgomery. Else he could not be trusted to avoid hauling her to him for another kiss. His need for her had not abated in the days of distance he had enforced. To his utter horror, he found it had only grown. He had been given a small drop, and he wanted the entire bloody ocean.

Before further conversation could occur, the butler reappeared, bearing a missive for Winchelsea. "Forgive the interruption, sir, but I was informed by the courier that it was urgent."

"Thank you, Havilock. That will be all for now." Winchelsea accepted the note and read hastily, his face turning ashen.

The domestic bowed and beat a hasty retreat, gesturing for the footmen presiding over the dinner to accompany him. The door had scarcely closed upon them when Winchelsea looked up from the missive. His countenance was one Lucien recognized well. It was the same expression he had seen on the faces of men witnessing death for the first time; that odd, yet distinct blend of shock, numbness, and fear.

Something terrible had occurred. There was no question of it. Every muscle in Lucien's body tensed. Out of the periphery of his gaze, he noticed Miss Montgomery's back stiffen, her shoulders squaring, as if she were preparing herself for a blow. It would seem she was no stranger to such grim scenes as this.

"There have been two explosions this evening," Winchelsea announced. "They occurred just minutes apart."

"Where?" Miss Montgomery demanded, rising from her chair, as if she intended to storm to the location and find answers that very instant.

"Praed Street and Charing Cross stations," he elaborated grimly. "Dozens are feared injured, if not hundreds."

Shock washed over Lucien, followed closely by rage. Innocent men, women, and children going about their daily lives and performing a task as commonplace as sitting upon a train. And they had been wounded. *Damn it.*

"It was the Fenians," he said with certainty, swallowing down the bile rising in his throat. Would their bloodlust know no end? How could these few, dangerous zealots possibly believe they could win Irish Home Rule by the attempted slaughter of men and women going about the business of earning their daily bread?

"There can be no doubt," Miss Montgomery added.

Winchelsea interrupted. "Speculation is abounding, of course. We cannot be certain as to the cause, until a full investigation occurs. We must take care and maintain objectivity, so that we are certain the conclusion we reach cannot be questioned. The explosions may have been caused by gas."

"Were it but the one, I would concur," Lucien said. "Two explosions in one evening, at two different stations, separated by such distance, cannot be the work of an accident."

Miss Montgomery had been right. Her concerns and observations had been precise.

"It is just as I feared." Miss Montgomery's tone was resolute. "McKenna and the Emerald Club are responsible for this. I am certain. McKenna strikes like a snake, fast and deadly. I have witnessed him do it with business associates and club members who did not prove their loyalty sufficiently enough to appease him."

The man sounded like a viper himself.

"I fear we must put an end to our dinner," Winchelsea said, stating the obvious. "I need to meet the Scotland Yard director at the Praed Street station. As I understand it, there is much chaos and confusion."

"Of course." Lucien bowed. None of them had an appetite for food any longer, not after learning explosions had torn apart railway cars and injured innocent people. "Miss Montgomery and I will take our leave."

"I arrived by hired hack," she informed him coolly.

"But now, as my partner, and in this time of great tumult, you shall accompany me. Your safety requires it, would you not say so, Winchelsea?"

"Oh yes," the duke acquiesced, sounding partly distracted, partly in shock. "Allow Arden to escort you this evening, madam, if you please. It shall do my heart good to know you are safe."

Miss Montgomery's expression turned obstinate, and he sensed an argument. He knew her well enough by now to know she did not believe she required a man's protection. And he also knew she would not wish to be doing anything this evening other than investigating.

They were well-matched in that regard, for he too had every intention of digging for answers. The criminals responsible for these atrocities could still be within their reach, but time was essential.

"Of course she will allow me to escort her," he answered on her behalf, quirking a brow at her and daring her to challenge him. "Will you not, Miss Montgomery?"

She stared at him, searching his gaze, her pause far longer than necessary. "Of course," she relented at last, before turning her attention back to Winchelsea. "I would not dream of worrying you, Your Grace."

The smile she had given Winchelsea made Lucien grit his teeth. But he circled the dinner table and offered her his arm just the same. And then he swallowed his damnable pride, met her gaze, and asked the one question he would have sworn he would never put to his unwanted American partner. "What do you propose we do next?"

ONCE MORE, HAZEL found herself sitting opposite the Duke of Arden in the confines of his handsome carriage. And once more, his long legs nearly brushed against her skirts. Once more, the carriage smelled of leather and *him*. The stakes were different, far higher than ever, but her reaction to him was alarmingly the same.

She tried not to stare at the man, truly she did. In the softness of the lamps lighting his carriage, he was an alluring, shadowed mystery her eyes could not help but seek. At the Duke of Winchelsea's dinner table earlier, he had been cold and aloof, his jaw rigid. And he was no less tense now, given the grim circumstances in which they found themselves.

Her mind swarmed with facts, questions, and plans. She ought to have been sufficiently distracted by the seemingly Herculean task looming ahead of them. But looking anywhere other than upon Arden seemed an impossible feat when she had just suffered three whole days of being deprived of his presence.

He had been evading her.

Yes, she had taken note. On the first day, she had been relieved she would not be forced to look him in the eye following her shameless display in his study. She had devoted herself to combing through her notes and extracting key names, places, and anything else she could. She drafted a dozen assorted lists. She ate each meal in the still-disapproving company of Lady Beaufort, until dinner, when she had a tray delivered to her room, and fell asleep atop the covers long past midnight, only to wake up in the darkness with her face buried in a map of London.

By the second day, she had convinced herself she would apologize for her rash behavior, and promise him it would never be repeated, while urging him to do the same. She spent breakfast stabbing her eggs and sausage and glaring into her coffee. In between exchanging mindless pleasantries with his aunt, she wondered if he would join them, until the butler announced *His Grace* had already taken his meal an hour earlier. She decided to investigate the railways further on her own, and took great pleasure in wearing the divided skirts which made Lady Beaufort shudder, and hiring hacks all over town.

When the third day had arrived, her inner shame had swelled like a river after a torrent of rain. Arden was not merely too preoccupied with his duties concerning the League to speak with her, and it was blatantly apparent he regretted what had passed between them. So too did she, and though she had spent every lucid hour since her lapse of judgment and reason sternly admonishing herself against it ever happening again, the knowledge he could not bear to face her was nonetheless humiliating.

Her dinner invitation this evening from the Duke of Winchelsea had been a welcome distraction from her isolation. But she would never have accepted had she known Arden would also be in attendance.

"Tell me." Arden's deep, decadent baritone severed the silence and her musings both.

She jolted, grinding her molars to keep her cheeks from flushing as she realized she had been staring fixedly at him for Lord knew how long. "I beg your pardon?"

"Your thoughts," he elaborated. "Tell me what you are thinking. I can see the wheels of your mind working."

He supposed she was thinking of the bombings and their next step, which she was. But beyond the instinctive decision to visit all hotels surrounding the railway stations where the bombings had occurred, she knew not what step they should take next. And she had just spent the last few minutes ruminating upon *him*.

This would not do. She forced her thoughts to return to her duty, where they belonged.

"If the perpetrators responsible for the explosions are

indeed sent from the Emerald Club, as I suspect they are, then they are Americans," she said. "They will be staying at hotels under aliases. They will have arrived a few days prior to the day of the attacks. Common ruses in such circumstances is the pretense that one is a traveler, perhaps with family in the area, or a businessman. They will be traveling lightly, but not light enough to cause suspicion."

"And you believe them to be staying in hotels near where they laid their bombs?" he queried, his expression impenetrable, his tone harsh. "Why would they be so foolish? Surely they would predict the first places to be searched will be those nearest the crimes?"

"Not necessarily," she countered, grateful her mind could once more be turned toward a more worthy task. This, she reminded herself sternly—detective work—was what she was meant to do. "The hotels nearest to the railway stations will be most convenient. If one is carrying a portmanteau containing explosive powder, and an accompanying device which will explode it, one will not wish to travel far."

He inclined his head. "That is a fair point. However, would not the fear of discovery trump the fear of a premature explosion, or other such incident?"

"Valid question, Arden," she acknowledged. "But I have had ample time to acquaint myself with the way McKenna's mind works. If he is indeed the man behind this latest atrocity, I am convinced he will have sent a select handful of men, all of whom he trusts implicitly. Their primary goal is bomb detonation. A man carrying a bomb will be nervous; it is only natural. The shorter the distance he must travel to plant his bomb and relieve himself of his burden, the better. Therefore, McKenna's men will have lodged in the hotels nearest to the stations that were targets. If we are fortunate enough, they could even still be in residence."

Arden nodded. "If they carried out their plan as you suspect, they likely traveled on the railway themselves. The two explosions occurred just minutes apart, but the stations are too far in distance for the bombing to have been carried out by the same man. Having two suspects heightens our chances of at least apprehending one, and if we can get one, we can be certain the others too shall fall. Imprisoned men facing the threat of the gallows have a way of singing like canaries."

"Precisely." When he was not being an arrogant oaf, or kissing her senseless upon his desk, she appreciated Arden's quick wit. "All we need is to capture one of them, and he will lead us to the others, either with his confession to gain better favor for himself, or through the clues on his person and in his lodgings."

She and Arden could work well as partners, she knew, as long as she could keep her distance and stop thinking about his lips. Those were the forbidden sorts of thoughts she could not afford to entertain for a fellow agent. Most especially not for the Duke of Arden. And most especially not in this moment. She struck them from her mind, forbidding them to return.

The carriage slowed then, and Arden peered out the window. "We are almost to the Great Western Hotel by Praed Street Station," he observed with a grim air. "But there is rather a great deal of pandemonium in the streets from the look of it. We may be better served to disembark here and travel the remainder of the distance on foot, since time is of the essence."

"Then let us do that," she said, her decision instant. "Every minute which passes us by is one more minute in which the villains responsible for these dastardly acts can escape."

Arden rapped upon the carriage, bringing them to a halt,

and hastily relayed his orders to the driver. In no time, he was springing from the carriage and offering her a hand down as well. Into the sea of chaos they went, her hand firmly in the crook of his arm.

"Stay with me, and follow my lead," he told her tersely, his jaw tight, as they waded through the stricken men and women who had either been rescued from the afflicted railway or were searching for loved ones who had.

His hand covered hers, holding her tightly to him, and she tried to ignore the spark his touch produced. This was neither the time nor the place for her to indulge in unwanted longing. Through the crowd they went, snippets of conversation reaching her as they made their way.

"Please, sir, have you seen my daughter Miss Jenny Throckmorton? Blonde hair, brown eyes…"

"He was to have been making his way home from his shift, but he never arrived."

"The name is Tommy Weston. He was to be at the Edgware Road Station, but he never showed."

"Gas explosion is what they're saying."

"Fenians, more like."

The desperation and fear in those voices as they trickled to her were a lance to her heart. She could not shake the heavy weight of responsibility upon her shoulders as she and Arden made their path to the hotel. She ought to have done something more to prevent this day from happening. But she had not possessed any concrete knowledge of dates and times. Not enough.

And she could not help but wonder if the information and experience she had to offer the Special League would ever be enough. They were fighting a shadowy hydra. One which may well prove impossible to defeat.

At last, they slipped inside the hotel, an impressive edifice from both the outside and in, where the atmosphere was considerably less chaotic than the streets, and yet, still tense. A handful of gentlemen milled about in the lobby, some of them engaged in deep, distressed conversation.

A clerk at the front desk greeted them, appearing nervous to Hazel's well-trained eye. The young gentleman's eyes were darting about. She could not be certain just yet whether his reaction was caused by the fear of the unrest surrounding his general vicinity, or if it was because he had something to hide.

"Good evening, sir," Arden greeted him coolly. "We are here on behalf of—"

She squeezed his arm in warning and spoke over his voice, her instincts warning her with an edge too strong to ignore. "We are here to inquire as to whether or not you have an open room we are free to view. My husband acquired lodging for us at a different hotel, and I am afraid it did not meet my exacting standards. Some hotels in this city are not as concerned about keeping a tidy and clean space, I have discovered."

She took care to emphasize her drawl, so her words emerged slow as molasses and sweet as sugar. And when the young clerk's eyes settled upon her, she gave him a bold smile. It was a technique she had used often. Say far too much, make it apparent she was an outsider, lower the other person's guard, and smile at him as if he were a tall glass of lemonade she could not wait to devour.

Arden made a sound of protestation, likely displeased by the manner in which she had ignored his earlier edict to follow his lead. She remained unaffected. After all, had he truly expected her to obey him?

She patted Arden's hand and turned her false smile in his direction, telling herself she must look upon him as if he were a man she loved. When their gazes connected, something hot and unwanted flared to life, and she had to work to muster her thoughts. "Is that not right, my darling?"

He cleared his throat, then turned a ferocious frown upon the clerk, who was still staring at Hazel with wide-eyed confusion. "My wife wishes to see a room. You can accommodate her request, can you not?"

"Th-there was an explosion on th-the railway this evening, s-sir," the unfortunate clerk stuttered. "I-I do not know if we are allowing additional—"

"Have you rooms?" Arden snapped, clearly losing his patience.

And she did not blame him, for they were wasting precious time. But she had a plan she intended to see to fruition. Her instincts had never before led her astray.

"More importantly," she added, giving the clerk another slow and steady smile, "have you many American travelers who frequent your establishment, sir? Call me silly, if you wish, but I cannot help but think it wise to find lodging in a hotel where my fellow countrymen have also stayed."

"We…er, yes." The poor young man blinked, then shifted his gaze to the left once more. "Recently, we have had several Americans."

The young man's reaction to her query, coupled with his nervousness, told her everything she needed to know. There were Americans in residence, and it was quite likely some of them were responsible for the bombings today. And further, they had offered him money in exchange for some favors, which explained his awkward mannerisms and general anxiety.

"Excellent." She smiled so hard, her cheeks ached with the effort. "If you will but direct us to an open room, sir, I will have a look, then we will return directly."

"Er, room seven is not currently occupied," he said. "You may have a look there. The door is unlocked. It is to be found down the hall, just over there, on the left."

"Oh, but the Americans," she drawled. "I would very much like to know where they are staying, so that I may view a room comparable to theirs, as our expectations are likely to be similar. Tell me, if you please, where those who have most recently arrived are residing."

"Twelve and fourteen, but I do not believe there are any available apartments near those at the moment, madam." The clerk paused. "I do apologize."

Arden's hand tightened over hers, as if in warning.

But she preceded with her plans. "Thank you, sir. We shall have a look at room seven, as you say, then return forthwith."

Arden inclined his head toward the clerk, his only response, then led her away. When they were beyond earshot of the clerk, he made his irritation known.

"What the devil happened to you following my lead?" he growled softly.

"I never agreed to such a thing," she returned through her teeth.

"You were smiling at him as if he alone is responsible for hanging the sun in the sky each morning," he gritted.

Was the Duke of Arden *jealous*? She would be lying if she claimed the thought did not give her a trill down her spine. Even in the midst of their investigations, he was a potent force at her side. And she could not deny her reaction to him, any more than she could deny the longing he triggered within her. The man was a weakness she did not dare indulge in, but one that dogged her every step nonetheless.

"I was smiling at him as if he was a guilty-looking clerk, who was attempting to hide information at the behest of the Americans who paid handsomely for his silence," she countered. "He had information I wanted, but announcing we are here on behalf of the Home Office or the Special League was not going to accomplish our gaining that information. He would have put up a wall and refused to allow us to climb it. But this way, we not only have access to the hotel, but knowledge of where the current American guests are residing."

"I concede the merit of your approach, but that does not mean I like it." His tone was dark and low.

"You do not have to like it, Arden," she pointed out to him. It was true, after all. She was not his paramour, not his wife, and not a lady he was courting. What had transpired between them the other night in his study had decidedly muddied the waters, but nothing had changed, aside from the unwanted provocation of lust he stirred deep within her.

"You are correct," he clipped, his tone cold. "I do not have to like it, and neither do I have to respect it. Forgive me for suggesting otherwise. It is merely that, if you wish to use your wiles upon every male you encounter in the course of an investigation, I shall have to prepare myself."

They reached the apartments bearing the placard *Number 7* and paused. She cast a glance over her shoulder in the direction of the clerk and the main desk. They were decidedly out of sight.

"I have no intention of using my wiles, if indeed I possess any," she countered wryly.

"You possess them." His response was quick. "You most certainly possess them, Miss Montgomery."

Before she could respond, or even mull over Arden's assertion, a gentleman bearing a valise bustled around the corner and straight into their path. It happened so swiftly, none of them had the opportunity to stop before a collision ensued.

The man's valise fell to the ground with a loud, unnatural thump. It landed with such force, it split open, and the contents of the case spilled out, all over the polished hall.

"I beg your pardon," the man said, as he stooped to hastily stuff the contents of his valise back inside it. "I ought not to have been traveling without paying attention."

His accent gave him away. He was American. Of that, she had no doubt. And although he was on the wrong floor, that meant nothing. He had seemingly been in the act of moving to another destination with haste.

"Nonsense," Arden said easily, his tone congenial. "The fault is mine. I was determined that my wife ought to examine the apartments available here, for she found the last establishment sorely lacking."

"Indeed." The American was hunkered down, frantically stuffing the contents of his valise within it once more.

Hazel studied the papers and attempted to read every word she saw printed upon the pages. She spied a map of London. Innocuous enough in the possession of any traveler, but on an American, who seemed eager to escape after Fenian bombs had just exploded on the railways, it was damning indeed.

"Nonsense, sir." Arden bent down as well, snagging some of the papers. "Allow me to help you."

"No thank you!" the man protested, his tone vehement. *Too vehement.*

Before Hazel could even formulate another thought, the American stuffed a handful of his spilled belongings in his valise and abruptly broke into a run, sprinting for the lobby. Arden growled a curse.

"Wait here for me," he bit out, then ran after the man.

Chapter Nine

*I*F ARDEN THOUGHT Hazel was going to remain where she was and simply await his return, he was mistaken. One suspicious American, hell-bent upon leaving the hotel in a hurry, meant there could be more. She wasted no time in finding the staircase leading to the second floor and took the steps as quickly as she could. When she reached the top, a quick scan of the placards led her to her quarry.

Room twelve.

She offered a quick knock on the door, and when there was no answer forthcoming, she tried the latch. It was unlocked. Casting a glance either way down the empty hall, she hesitated not a moment, before slipping inside.

The room was bathed in shadows and lit by a lone gas lamp. She made her way about the chamber, looking for any shred of evidence—newspapers, correspondence, books, maps—but the room was spartanly kept, and indeed, looked as if it had never even been inhabited.

Swiftly, she left the chamber, intent upon investigating number fourteen as well. But when she reached the hall, she discovered a man leaving that particular room, a hat worn low over his brow, and a portmanteau in hand.

"Sir," she called out, belatedly recalling she had neglected to tuck her small pistol into her reticule before leaving for Winchelsea's townhome.

The man's head jerked up, and the luminaries in the hall cast light over his countenance. She barely suppressed her gasp of shock, for she knew the man staring back at her. She had served him at the Emerald Club in New York, when she had been disguised as Mrs. Mulligan.

Sean Flannery.

Although she had suspected the bombings this evening had been the products of the Emerald Club, seeing a member she knew so well, still rocked her.

"Have we met before, madam?" he asked, his eyes narrowing.

"I do not recall ever having met you before, sir," she lied, careful to mimic an English accent, clipped and precise. "Forgive my interruption. You seem to be going somewhere in haste. I was merely looking for an acquaintance of mine."

"You were in my room," said a deep voice behind her. "Why?"

The hackles on her neck rose as she slowly turned to face the man who had approached her from behind so soundlessly. Recognition hit her, along with a burst of dread. Thomas Mulroney, one of McKenna's most trusted men.

And she saw recognition flare in his eyes as well, along with a dawning comprehension. *Damnation*, she had no means of defending herself, and she was in the untenable position of facing two men who had potentially just caused dozens of people to be injured, or worse.

"What are you doing here, *Mrs. Mulligan?*" Mulroney asked, steel in his voice.

In the next moment, something blunt and sharp connected with the back of her skull. The force was sudden, unexpected, and painful. Her vision clouded, darkening at the edges, as she struggled to maintain consciousness. But a second forceful blow hit her just then. Her vision went black, stars burst before her eyes, and she felt her body go limp, just before the darkness claimed her.

LUCIEN WAS NOT one bit surprised when he returned to the place where he had left Miss Montgomery and found her gone. The bastard he had followed into the crowded street had managed to disappear with ease in the throng. One moment, Lucien had been gaining on him, and the next, he had vanished. Though he had done his damnedest to fight his way through the street and apprehend the fleeing American, Lucien had been forced to acknowledge he was losing valuable time.

He had retraced his steps, ignoring the sputtering questions and demands of the desk clerk as he strode down the hall in search of his "wife." Unfortunately, she was missing. Fortunately, he had a good idea of where he might find her, and unless he missed his guess, it would be somewhere in the vicinity of rooms twelve and fourteen.

He climbed the staircase two steps at a time, worry churning in his gut. If there were more Americans, and if they were indeed guilty of setting the bombs which had exploded on the railway that evening, Miss Montgomery approaching them alone would be not just foolhardy, but dangerous.

His fears were confirmed when he reached the second floor and discovered a prone female form. He recognized those skirts, damn it. Had she been shot? *Good, sweet God.* A sickening wave of dread hit him as he raced to her side. She was unmoving, lying facedown on the carpet. Lucien sank to his knees, fear knifing through him.

She was not dead. She could not be dead. He refused to believe it. She was too vibrant, too fearless. The thought of her lifeless stole all the saliva from his mouth. Made his gut cramp and terror roil through him.

No, no, no, no. It could not be.

"Hazel," he panted, forcing himself to remain calm only through the exertion of great control.

This was not the first time he had come upon one of his fellow agents incapacitated. He told himself there was no difference between Miss Montgomery and the rest of the men he had worked alongside over the years. Then he noticed the blood in her hair, and he told himself he was wrong. She *was* different, and not just because she was a woman, but because he *cared* about her.

He did not know when or how it had happened, but at some point between the moment she had first sauntered into his office and offered him her hand to shake, and now, she had managed to storm his battlements. Hands trembling, he rolled her onto her back with as much tender care as he could. She was unconscious, but her chest was rising and falling. *Thank Christ.*

"Hazel," he repeated, but she did not stir.

He was acutely aware of the tenuousness of their situation, and he knew he could not afford to remain in the hotel. They were on their own, she had been attacked, and the stakes were far too high. He had no way of knowing what had happened to her, or how badly she had been injured. All he did know was, whoever had done this to her could return.

Hunting down her assailant and the bastard who had bombed the railway—likely one and the same—would have to wait for another day. Hazel's welfare was his primary focus. Abruptly, he was reminded of another day, long ago, when he had held his mother's lifeless and waterlogged body in his arms.

She had walked into the North Sea, and though he had

done everything to find her and save her, his efforts had been too little, too late. She had drowned, just as she had wanted, though somehow, the ocean had mercifully washed her back ashore, so he could find her and bring her home one last time.

He had failed his mother, but he would not fail Hazel Montgomery.

"Hazel," he said again, gently patting her cheek. "Wake up for me, sweetheart. Come back to me."

She emitted a low moan of misery, her eyelids fluttering, as she struggled to come to. All signs indicated she had received a blow to the head, rather than having been shot. The foolish, brave woman. If she had remained where he had told her to, she would not have been attacked.

"There you are," he said, as a profound sense of relief hit him in the gut. "Open your eyes for me."

"Arden?" she croaked, her eyes opening at last, bright and blue, reflecting her confusion. She shuddered, her hand lifting to the back of her head. "What…happened?"

"You were attacked." He gathered her in his arms and stood. "But I have you now. All will be well."

It was a promise he would do his utmost to keep. As he carried her to the first floor of the hotel, he also vowed he would bring the bastards responsible for her pain, and the suffering of countless others, to justice. Even if it was the last thing he did upon this earth.

HAZEL'S HEAD FELT as if someone had taken a hammer to it. She clutched at Arden's shoulders, confused and disoriented, as he carried her down a set of steps as if she weighed no more than a babe in his arms. Awareness and lucidity returned to her slowly, in time with the pounding misery throbbing through her skull.

She was in the Great Western Hotel, she recalled, and she had run across Emerald Club members she recognized. But, most importantly, they had recognized her. Even without her disguise. Her voice was likely at fault, for she had interacted with Mulroney quite extensively in her capacity as Mrs. Mulligan. Someone had walloped her over the head, and she would be willing to wager her last nickel it had been Sean Flannery.

Hazel could not be certain which shocked her more: the recognition she had seen in Mulroney's gaze, the sudden knock to her head, or the realization she was being carried by the Duke of Arden. She blinked up at his rigid jawline and his harsh countenance.

What had become of Mulroney and Flannery? Had they been able to disappear, thanks to her misstep in turning her back upon Flannery? She could only hope not. But in truth, she feared she knew the answer. Arden seemed grim indeed.

"Arden," she managed to say, again vaguely aware of a commotion surrounding them in the lobby of the hotel.

A flurry of unfamiliar voices assailed her, much as it had earlier in the street.

"Excuse me, sir, you cannot simply…

"Good heavens! What has happened to her?"

"Is the lady unwell?"

"Touch her at your peril," Arden snarled at someone.

And then, they were once more in the chaos of the street. The glow of street lamps, and the sound of horses and jangling tack, mingled with dozens of voices and orders being issued by policemen.

"Arden, put me down," she tried again.

"Not now," he said, urgently, his expression taut. "We need to get you home."

She had no home. She wanted to tell him so, but all she could muster was a yawn. Her body felt weak, her mind was confused, and she could not deny how good and reassuring being held by Arden felt.

He was warm and strong and steady.

She snuggled against his chest, inhaling deeply of his divine scent. Later, if he questioned her, she could blame her indecent reaction upon her confusion. She had suffered at least two blows to the head, after all. Perhaps she could even convince herself the blows she had suffered were the reason for the warmth settling over her, and the undeniable feeling of *comfort* being in his arms gave her.

Even when her stomach was as tender as if it had been run over by the wheels of a carriage. What in the hell had they done after bludgeoning her? Even breathing hurt. A booted kick would have produced such an effect, she was sure. Her head ached, the throb of her heartbeat pulsing in her temples. The blows she had received had been substantial enough to make her lose consciousness. She blinked up at Arden's beautiful jawline, dizziness suddenly assailing her.

For the second time in her acquaintance with Arden, Hazel feared she would cast up her accounts all over him. The first time, it would have served him right. This time, however, she would feel guilty. After all, here he was, playing the role of knight, whisking her away to safety in his powerful arms.

She swallowed hard, forcing the lump of bile down her throat. She would not be ill. One slow inhale through her nostrils, one exhale. Her head ached more, but the wave of nausea subsided.

"What happened?" she forced herself to ask. "How did you find me?"

"There will be ample time for explanations later," Arden clipped as he continued striding to his destination. "Are you in a great deal of pain?"

He sounded slightly winded, and she had no doubt it was the effect of carting her about the streets taking its toll upon him. She was tall for a woman, and she knew it well. Her height had both haunted and aided her for all her life. She was certain she weighed more than enough to wind even the strongest and most able-bodied of men.

"It hurts to breathe," she admitted, though the confession pained her as much as her injuries did. "But I have survived worse scrapes."

"Falling from a tree, for instance."

Something about his quip touched her. His attempt at lightness, in such a time of darkness, warmed her insides. And, well, here was proof he had been listening to her silly stories earlier at dinner with Winchelsea. That warmed her too.

"That was nothing," she told him, her tongue and mind still feeling sluggish. "I landed—"

"On your feet," he finished for her. "Nary a broken bone for your troubles. I would suspect that is always the way of it for you, Hazel."

Hazel.

Arden had called her *Hazel* for the first time since the wickedness in his study. And something inside her was melting. It was a name she had never liked, merely the one she had been given by the mother who had not wanted her. But on the Duke of Arden's lips, Hazel sounded different. When he spoke her name, she wanted to be Hazel, rather than Miss Montgomery, or H.E., as all the other agents she had worked with called her.

But this reaction, this strange affinity for her name, this sudden thrill…? Whatever her unseen assailant had cudgeled her with, it must have addled her wits. For there was no other reason why Arden's use of her given name—spoken in his precise accent—should wrangle a sigh from her lips. But it did. She sighed and snuggled closer to him. Her head still ached, and breathing still hurt, but his scent of musky citrus had replaced the odors of the city, and his muscular, protective heat had replaced the lingering shock dogging her.

"I do not always land on my feet," she said at last before continuing, compelled to protest once more. "But you must put me down, Arden. I am capable of walking."

"No."

"Arden." Her protest was by rote. In truth, she did feel weak and dizzied, and the pain in her head was growing to a crescendo by the moment. She did not want to reach the safe haven of his carriage by her own locomotion. But for the sake of her pride, *by God*, she would.

"We are almost at my carriage now, Hazel. I would carry you back to New York myself if I had to, after seeing you lying on the floor in a crumpled, bleeding heap."

His vehemence took her by surprise. Another wave of nausea crashed over her, but she fought it back with as much determination as she had the first time. Unless she was mistaken, there was a protective note in his voice. Precisely what had Flannery and Mulroney done to her? A chill went down her spine, making her tremble.

"The last thing I remember, is something cracking against my skull, twice," she said. "Whatever happened afterward, I have no recollection. Do not concern yourself on my account."

His jaw clenched. "Hold tight to me now. We have reached the carriage."

He issued orders to the driver, then climbed into the conveyance, still carrying her as if she were helpless, until he deposited her gently upon the bench. Dizzied anew, she planted her palms against the leather, holding herself still, lest she collapse in a puddle upon the floor.

He settled at her side, rather than opposite her, then stared down at her, his countenance strained, pulled tight with lines of concern. "Miss Montgomery," was all he said.

She mourned the loss of her given name in much the same way she mourned the loss of his touch. "Arden," she returned, struggling against her aching head, her increasingly painful ribs, and the dizziness, which would not seem to leave her, now it had settled in like an unwanted guest. "You need not sit at my side as if I am an invalid. I have received injuries before, on many cases. This is not the first, nor will it be the last time, I expect. Attend to your duties."

"*You* are my duty," he gritted, his jaw clenching once more. "And I have already failed you once this evening. I will not do so again. I never should have left you there on your own. I chased the bloody miscreant into the street and promptly lost him in the crowds."

"Arden," she said again, reaching for his hand.

Neither of them wore gloves, for they had fled Winchelsea's townhome without bothering to attend to social niceties. Her gloves—and *Lord*, how she hated wearing gloves anyway—were likely discarded somewhere upon the Duke of Winchelsea's handsome carpet. They had been in her lap, but when she had sprung to her feet, they had been unceremoniously flung who knew where.

"Do not protest." His hand cupped her head, and she winced as his fingers gently probed her scalp. "You are bleeding. I need to get you home so a physician can tend to your wounds."

"I am fine," she assured him, even though her head felt as if it were a melon which had been busted open after being dropped from the roof of a tall building, and her ribs hurt as if the devil himself had danced a jig upon them.

"You are certainly *not* fine, Hazel." He cupped her face in his big hands, staring into her eyes with an intensity that cut straight through all her aches and pains to the heart of her. "And I alone take responsibility for what happened to you. I ought to have been there to protect you."

Her sense of independence—running through her like a river for all her life—objected. "I do not need anyone to protect me. I protect myself just as I always have, and if I fail in that, *I* am to blame. *I* alone have made an error in judgment. Do not feel responsible for my injuries, Arden. I am perfectly well. Do not accompany me because you feel beholden. Capturing the men responsible for the bombings is of far greater importance, and I fear I already bungled that."

"*I* bungled it," he growled.

His fingers probed a particularly sensitive area, and the moment he touched her there, she knew her scalp had been split open. Warm wetness trickled down her skin. *Blood.* She hissed a painful breath, then grimaced as her ribs reminded her they too had suffered a trauma. She suspected Flannery and Mulroney had acquainted her ribs and stomach with their boots.

Several times. How gracious of them.

But Arden was not responsible for her hasty decision to venture to the second floor of the hotel on her own, and she would not allow him to mistakenly imagine he was.

"I followed on my own though I was unarmed, and past experience strongly cautioned me against doing so," she argued. "You are not to blame for my knock over the head."

"This is more than a knock over the head," he argued, his voice cold, yet radiating with barely suppressed fury. "By the time I reached you, you were lying prone upon the ground, and I thought…"

He shuddered, not finishing his sentence.

A shocking realization occurred to her then: Arden had been concerned for her. What had happened had left him shaken. That was the reason for the grimness in his expression and the tenseness in his jaw. Could it be possible the Duke of Arden cared for her?

Her fingers tightened over his, the connection between them seeming, somehow, vital. "You reached me, and you carried me all the way to your carriage. You did everything in your power, and now I am safe. I have once more landed upon my feet."

He shook his head, and despite her attempt at levity, his sensual lips did not turn upward into a smile. "I reached you too late. It was my responsibility to remain at your side. Being beaten is not landing upon your feet, Hazel. When I find the man responsible for this, I will tear him limb from limb."

Her blood chilled at his menace-laden words. "There were two of them."

His stare never wavered from hers. "You saw them?"

She tried to nod, but her head hurt too much for the movement. Her eyes slid closed against the blinding flash of pain. "I know them."

"Christ, Hazel. Who are they?"

"Their names are Sean Flannery and Thomas Mulroney," she said faintly, as another burst of pain hit her when the carriage rattled over a bump in the road, jarring her. "Though I have no doubt they were traveling using aliases. You must tell Winchelsea. We need to find the list of guests at the hotel. It may not be too late to discover their travel plans. They will be leaving London soon, I would imagine, and they will have booked passage back to New York."

"You will be doing nothing, aside from being attended to by a doctor," he said sternly. "I will pass the information on to Winchelsea and put some of our men on their trail."

"We should find Winchelsea immediately," she protested, guilt skewering her at the delay she had already caused in not imparting the vital information to Arden as soon as she had regained consciousness. "I can describe them. Perhaps a sketch could be created."

"You will do nothing of the sort," he said, his tone firm. He slid an arm gently about her shoulders and settled her against him. "You will rest."

"I do not rest," she countered, though her eyes were still closed, and she was suddenly feeling incredibly weary.

"You do now," he insisted, and she felt the unmistakable, though swift, caress of his fingers upon her cheek. "How is your head, sweetheart?"

Had he just called her "*sweetheart*," or was that her confused and scattered wits betraying her? Playing tricks upon her?

She opened her eyes again, attempting to gather herself, but when she did, she was every bit as lost within the emerald depths of Arden's eyes as she had been before. She stared at him, taking in his handsome face, his regal bearing, his soldier's air.

Had any man ever been more potent in his allure? Not even Adam had drawn her to him with such intense magnetism. It was the sort of reaction which could drown a woman alive.

"My head aches," she told him honestly. "And my ribs are painful. But I am grateful to you, Arden, for charging after me and finding me. I would not be sitting here, if it were not for you."

"You are sitting here bleeding and wounded *because* of me," he argued stubbornly once more, his voice rife with disgust. "But I will make amends, to you, Hazel. This, I swear."

Chapter Ten

*J*UST AS HE should not have been surprised Hazel had refused to do as he had bid her that night in the hotel, he also knew he should not be surprised to find her stowing away in his carriage. But when he climbed inside the vehicle and saw her sitting there upon the leather bench, dressed in her outlandish trousers, of all things, he knew a brief moment of astonishment.

It was replaced quickly by outrage.

"Out," he ordered her.

Her supple lips fell open, no doubt in shock at his brusqueness. But she found her voice in no time. "No."

"Yes." He folded his arms over his chest. "Madam, Dr. Kelly was strict in his orders. You are to rest. You suffered a concussion. Moreover, there is a pair of vicious criminals on the loose in London, who know you are not what you claimed to be. You need to remain where you are safe and incapable of injuring yourself further."

She crossed her arms and glared at him. Due to the injuries she had sustained, she wore no hat today, and though her hair was dressed simply to also accommodate for her wounds, she had never looked lovelier.

"I told you I do not rest, Arden," she informed him. "If you are going to examine the scene today with the Scotland Yard investigators, I wish to accompany you."

"It is no place for a lady," he said, regretting the words the instant they emerged.

Her shoulders straightened. "Fortunately, I am not a lady."

"I meant to say it is no place for a woman who has so recently suffered such grievous injuries and is attempting to gad about the city, against the doctor's orders," he corrected. "Now out with you."

"No."

Devil take the woman. Did her stubborn foolishness know no bounds? "This is my carriage, Miss Montgomery, and you are trespassing."

"Very well." She rose from her seat. "I will hire a hack as before."

Damn it.

"You will do no such thing," he gritted.

She met his gaze, unflinching. "Either I will travel to the Praed Street station in your carriage, or I will hire a hack, Arden. Which would you prefer?"

"Clearly, I would prefer for you to do neither." He clenched his jaw. "You suffered terrible injuries yesterday. I have no wish for you to injure yourself further."

"I will not injure myself if I have you as my escort," she countered. "But if you want me to hire a hack, that can be accomplished as well."

It occurred to him she was more stubborn than a goat. He could either stand here, arguing with the infernal woman, or he could allow her to win and do his damnedest to keep her from landing herself in further scrapes.

"Sit down," he ordered her.

She beamed and settled herself back down with her signature lack of grace. Despite her complete disregard for the uniquely feminine art of gracefulness, she was the most mesmerizing, infuriating, *delicious* creature he had ever laid eyes upon. What he wouldn't give to have her in his bed. To watch her find her pleasure once more, but this time, to be inside her when she spent.

Bloody hell, this would not do. He had obligations, duties. *Honor*, he reminded himself. He had that as well. Or at least, he *had* possessed it, until a certain vexing American Pinkerton agent had forced her way into his life.

On a sigh at his own lack of control, Lucien entered the carriage and sat opposite her, knowing seating himself at her side, as he had done the day prior, was a danger he could not entertain. Her scent in the carriage—crisp clean soap, with just a hint of lavender, nothing so effusive as orris root or rose—was enough to affect him. She was too tempting, with her long legs on display and her hair uncovered. And so stubborn, he wanted to kiss her into submission, which he had also vowed he would never do again.

Desiring Hazel Montgomery was a very bad idea indeed.

One he could not afford to entertain.

"Thank you for the lemonade," she told him in her mellifluous drawl, as the carriage lurched forward and they set upon the same course they had taken the evening before.

He had inquired after her welfare with his domestics more times than he cared to admit, beginning the evening before, after she had been attended by Dr. Kelly, and through this morning. He had seen to it lemonade was sent on the tray delivered to her chamber, both for breakfast and for luncheon.

He rather regretted having allowed himself to indulge in the weakness he harbored for her, now that he was faced with it. But seeing her lying motionless on the floor of the Great Western Hotel yesterday had done something to him. It had not just taken him to the same vulnerable place he had dwelled within, all those years ago, when his mother had waded into the North Sea and left her children behind. It had proven to him that, regardless of how intently he tried to refrain from caring for anyone aside from his sister Violet and Great Aunt Hortense, he was not, in fact, a fortress.

It was the same lesson he should have learned already in the wake of The Incident. But it would seem he had not, and it had taken the American firebrand across from him being attacked to force him to realize his own faults.

He was more than aware of his faults now, all of them glaring, and he could not bear to accept her gratitude for a gesture he had made to slake his own rising guilt.

He did not meet her gaze, fiddling instead with his signet ring. "I am afraid I do not know what you refer to, Miss Montgomery."

"Come now, Arden," she chastised lowly, her honeyed drawl making his cock twitch to life. "You are the only one I mentioned my love of lemonade to."

Still, he had no wish to make an admission. "Perhaps you told the domestic who has been assisting you, and you merely do not recall."

"Bunton," she said.

He lifted his gaze to her at last, hating the way the mere sight of her sent a frisson of something decidedly unwanted straight through him. "I beg your pardon, madam?"

"The domestic assisting me," she elaborated, "is named Bunton. You seemed uncertain of the name of your own staff member. I aided you in the recollection."

"Bunton," he repeated, vaguely remembering his house-keeper recommending one of the more experienced maids for the task of assisting Miss Montgomery.

"Yes." She gave him a small smile. It was slow and secretive, beautiful and thrilling. He wanted to kiss it from her lips.

He refrained, settling for clenching his hands instead.

"Well," he said. "Surely it was Bunton who was responsible for the tea."

"Lemonade," she corrected him, with a knowing look.

"Lemonade then," he said dismissively, as if he could not be bothered to even recall the proper name of the beverage in question. In truth, he hoped the lemonade had buoyed her spirits and brought a touch of happiness back to her after all she had endured.

He glanced away from her, diverting his attention to the cityscape beyond the carriage window. London by the light of day seemed decidedly less menacing. So too the men responsible for the atrocities carried out on the railway the day before. They were mere men, all of them, and he would hunt them down and make them pay for what they had done.

"Why?" she asked.

Once more, she commanded his attention. He devoured her with his gaze. Her full, pink lips, her dark hair, those shockingly blue eyes. Those goddamn legs.

He jerked his gaze back to her lovely face. "What are you asking me, Miss Montgomery?"

"The lemonade was sent by you," she charged, without heat. "Why pretend otherwise?"

Because he could not bear to face what the longing for her, deep inside him, meant. He did not believe in love. He did not want a wife, had vowed to never take one. His blood was tainted. Tender affections toward any female on his part were dangerous indeed. They were not to be entertained. And if he needed a lover, one could be obtained, with far fewer complications than bedding Miss Montgomery would create.

"If you wish to believe I sent the lemonade, I shall not stop you," he said coolly, even as he wondered if she had found it to her liking. He had not a clue how a trousers-wearing Pinkerton agent, originally from Georgia, preferred her lemonade.

"It was delicious," she said, as if reading his thoughts.

He frowned at her.

"Thank you," she repeated, smiling at him once more, that coquette's smile he could not seem to gird himself against.

Bloody hell. Would her stubbornness know no end? And would his susceptibility to her prove a bottomless well? It would certainly seem so, on both counts.

Perhaps a change of subject was in order.

"I read your notes," he told her.

"All of them?"

"Yes."

Her brows rose, then she winced, as if in pain. "When?"

"Is your head paining you?" he asked. *Damn it,* she ought to have listened to him. She should have remained at Lark House, lying abed and plied with lemonade. She had worked hard enough, and suffered enough, for her dedication to her cause. The woman deserved a respite.

"My head is fine." She frowned at him. "When?"

"A few days ago," he admitted. "The day after…"

And then he realized what he had been about to say, so foolishly, and promptly stopped.

But Miss Montgomery pressed the matter. "The day after?"

"My study," he bit out, hating to even acknowledge what had occurred between them, because the mere thought of their heated session upon his desk was enough to make him as hard as coal. He had thought about it in all the intervening moments since. Especially when he was alone. In bed. Naked.

Fuck.

"You finally read my notes the day after what happened in your study," she repeated, her voice thick, her eyes dipping to

146

his mouth, before jerking back up to meet his gaze. "Was it because you felt guilty, Arden?"

"Guilty over what transpired between us?" He paused, considering his response, weighing his words. "Yes. I felt immeasurably guilty. I took advantage of you, and I dishonored you, without a thought for the consequences. You are my partner and worthy of my respect. A respect which I did not give you."

He meant what he said. As much as he had initially resented both her and the mere notion he was to be saddled with a partner, he could not help but to see she was an asset. She was intelligent and driven, compassionate and brave, loyal and fierce. The information she had gleaned in New York was valuable, and though they had not been able to stave off yesterday's bombings, he had no doubt she had provided them with information that would prove vital moving forward.

"You did not take advantage of me," she said then, interrupting his whirling thoughts and sending him reeling once again.

"Miss Montgomery," he protested, for he was still mired in confusion over what had happened between them.

Of course he had taken advantage of the situation. He had wanted to kiss her, and she was beautiful, and he had pressed his suit, without thought for the repercussions which would inevitably follow. He knew better than to dally with an unmarried female. His honor was important to him, and he deeply regretted allowing his lust to overrule his mind. And yet, there was also another part of him that knew, if given the opportunity, he would kiss her senseless all over again.

"You did not," she repeated, her voice low. Rife with an emotion he could not define. Husky, almost. Alluring, to be sure.

He had to resist his base impulses. "Regardless," he forced

himself to say, "my actions that day were inexcusable."

"I wanted you to kiss me," she blurted. "You cannot take advantage of someone who is willing. And not just willing, but *longing*. That is how I would describe the way you make me feel, Arden, in spite of myself, and in spite of all the rules I have created over my years working as a Pinkerton agent. I would forget my rules for you."

Her words resonated, sinking deep inside him, the blossom of something which felt a whole bloody lot like joy unfurling. Or perhaps it was lust. Or blind, sheer stupidity. He knew not, nor did he care to examine it. Hazel's words had settled within him, and the sudden urge to possess her seized him anew.

I would forget my rules for you.

God, yes.

He moved, shifting himself to her end of the carriage. He settled upon the bench at her side, cupping her face in his hands and looking into her eyes. What he saw glistening within those endless depths shook him.

Terrified him.

There was only one way to answer the fear and the need both.

He lowered his lips to hers and claimed hers in a kiss. She was soft, so soft; her cheeks in his palms, her lips beneath his. He forced himself to go slowly, to savor her. Just yesterday, she had been savaged, and he wanted to banish the memory of her lying helpless and lifeless on the floor with his mouth.

She did not hesitate, kissing him back, opening to him on a sigh. Her tongue played against his, and she tasted of sweetness and citrus and nothing had ever been more delicious. A fierce pulse of desire tightened his ballocks, testament to how badly he wanted her. One kiss, one meeting of lips, and he was hard and ready, even in a cramped carriage on his way to the bloody railway station.

He knew he should stop. Strike that—he knew he never should have begun—but he was helpless, a slave to his need for her. When she sucked on his tongue, he groaned, kissing her harder, deeper. They struggled over control. She kissed the way she did everything, with brazen vigor, and he could not get enough.

He tore his mouth from hers, hungry for more, for the taste of her skin, for the breathy sounds she made when she liked what he was doing to her. He dragged his mouth down her throat, kissing his way to the place where her neck and shoulder met. And there, he could not resist biting gently into her skin.

Lucien had never wanted another woman more than he wanted her.

"Hazel," he murmured, against the pounding of her pulse.

She could never again be Miss Montgomery to him now. Had he ever thought her an abomination? It seemed impossible.

"Arden." His name on her lips was a sigh, a prayer.

She must have removed his hat, because her fingers were tunneling through his hair, nails raking his scalp. He sucked harder, so hard, he was sure there would be a bruise on the tender, creamy flesh. Lucien could not resist skimming his hand over one of her lush thighs. He breathed into her skin, inhaling her scent, relishing her, this wild American spitfire, so submissive in his arms.

Up her inner thigh he traveled, and she parted her legs for him, granting him access. Higher still, to where her heat warmed the tips of his fingers. Higher, to the mound hidden from him by the billowing drapery of her trousers. He cupped her there, where he wanted to drive himself home.

She made the most erotic noise he had ever heard, half

growl and half mewl, as she arched into him. Pure, animal lust tore through him, sudden and fierce. Everything in him clamored to claim this woman. To make her his. But somewhere in the dim recesses of his mind, in the part of him that was a gentleman and the leader of the Special League, the part of him who still believed in honor above his own selfish wants, knew he could not possess her here. He could not tup her in his carriage as if she were not worthy of being worshiped.

For no other woman alive had been more made for worship than Hazel.

So instead, he took her mouth again. He kissed her lingeringly, making love to her lips the way he longed to do to her body. With great reluctance, he left the apex of her thighs and slid his hand higher, to the waistband of her trousers. Buttons, *thank Christ.*

He slid them from their moorings, one by one, as he buried his tongue in her mouth. The fabric gaped, and there remained only one layer now, between him and her warm sweet curves. Still kissing her, he found the slit in her drawers. Wet heat met his fingers as he parted her folds and found her pearl. She bucked against him when he circled the tender flesh with his forefinger, just the lightest of touches.

She moaned into his kiss, her tongue playing against his with greater urgency. Her hips rolled, silently begging him for more. And so he gave it to her, increasing his pressure, toying with the turgid bud. How desperately he longed to take her in his mouth. But that would have to wait. There was no time for leisurely lovemaking now.

But there was time for her to spend. And he was a greedy bastard when it came to Hazel. He wanted to make her come undone again. Wanted her husky cries of ecstasy, her head thrown back, her cunny thrusting against him. He wanted everything, and he wanted to be the man who gave it to her.

He wanted to be *her* man, even if it could only be for this fleeting moment, this carriage ride. This next ten minutes. This next breath, this next kiss. He would take it. He would take it all. He would take whatever he could.

"Hazel," he said against her lips, kissing her again, working her hungry flesh, before breaking away to gaze down at her. Her cheeks were flushed. Her eyes were glassy. Tendrils of her dark hair had come free from her loose coiffure. Her mouth was swollen from his kisses. But her eyes were closed.

"Hazel," he said again, stroking her harder, faster. "Open your eyes and look at me when you come."

Her eyes fluttered open, and a cry tore from her throat at the same moment her body convulsed against his hand. Wetness coated his fingers, and he could not resist delving deeper, circling her entrance, teasing them both. She was even wetter there, and the thought of plunging his cock into her tight passage was torment.

He wanted inside her so badly.

The carriage stopped.

So did Lucien. His sanity, or what remained of it, returned gradually. He withdrew from her, his fingers coated in her essence. Glistening in the light of day. God help him, but he had not bothered to draw the curtains over the windows, and anyone could have glimpsed what they were about.

She was still breathing heavily, flushed and gloriously disheveled, watching him with a curious expression he had never seen her wear before. Complete befuddlement, he expected, as if she were asking herself the same perplexing question he was posing to himself: *What the devil came over me?*

He could blame his lack of discretion and control upon lust, but he feared the way he reacted to Hazel Montgomery was caused by more than such a base urge. He respected her, admired her even, and he could not recall a time when he had ever appreciated another woman in the way he did her. His affairs had not been many, but when he had sought lovers in the past, it had always been based upon primal need, rather than anything else. He had never conversed for hours on end with his lovers. He could deny it all he liked, but Hazel was...different.

Which meant she was a risk.

He reached into his coat and extracted a handkerchief as his driver knocked discreetly upon the door. It was old habit, ordinarily unnecessary, but Lucien was grateful for Cobb's discretion today.

"A moment," he called, his voice hoarse and strained, even to his own ears. His erection was still raging, desperate for relief he could not indulge in; not now, and not ever.

Hazel's eyes had gone wide at the unexpected intrusion, and she instantly stiffened, her hands rushing to restore the buttons of her trousers to their proper places. He was about to wipe his hand clean, but it occurred to him, if this was to be the last time he ever touched her, he could not deny himself the forbidden knowledge of what she tasted like.

He raised his fingers to his lips and sucked them clean. She was earthy and musky, and squelching his groan of pure, libidinous enjoyment required all the effort he possessed. She looked back up at him as she smoothed her waistband into place and righted her bodice.

He ought to have been ashamed of himself. She was an unmarried woman. He was a gentleman. She was also his partner. But a rush of pleasure went down his spine and settled in his groin at the knowledge she was watching him savor the traces of her, which remained upon his skin.

"I should apologize once more," he told her, finally using

his handkerchief to wipe his hand. "But I cannot find a speck of contrition within me for what just occurred. Instead, I will promise you it will not happen again."

She stared at him, saying nothing, simply devouring him with her unnaturally pale gaze, until he wondered if he had robbed her of speech. Her lips, still dark and swollen from his kisses, parted at last.

"That is a pity, Arden," she said at last. "Because I can think of nothing I would like better."

With that parting volley fired, she rose from the bench and threw open the carriage door on her own, alighting without waiting for Cobb to offer her his aid. Lucien watched the tempting swell of her backside and her luscious legs as she descended, a grim sense of finality settling over him. Hazel Montgomery was more than a risk.

More lethal than dynamite. More tempting than the lure of the Sirens.

"Bloody fucking trousers," he muttered to himself, before he followed in her triumphant wake.

HAZEL STARED DOWN at the notes she had made in her journal the evening before, doing her utmost to remain impervious to the presence of the very large, very handsome, very proficient kisser seated behind the massive, elaborately detailed desk in his study. She was pacing the rug back and forth as she was wont to do when deep in the cobwebs of her own musings.

"There have been no sightings of Sean Flannery or Thomas Mulroney?" she called over her shoulder to Arden, progressing through the items on her list.

"Not one," he confirmed.

"Blast," she muttered to herself, continuing to pace to the opposite end of the cavernous chamber as she attended to the next item upon her list.

It had been several days since she and Arden had visited the damaged railways to examine the aftermath of the explosion. Broken glass had been everywhere. Carriages had been transformed into mangled wreckage, scattered like felled beasts in eerie silence. Pipes and telegraph wires inside the tunnels had been ruined by the blast, office windows shattered. Miraculously, no one had been killed, though many had suffered serious injuries. She still shuddered to think of the intensity of the damage left behind, to imagine how terrified the passengers must have been in the wake of the detonation, destruction all around them, everything plunged into darkness.

The Home Office's Chief Inspector of Explosives had determined the cause of the blasts, and it had not been a gas leak. Rather, Fenian bombs. London was a city clenched in the grip of terror. Police had been stationed on the railways to stave off further attacks, and the pressure to find and arrest those responsible for colluding to plan and carry out the bombings was tremendous.

"Has there been word from the agent I was working with in New York?" she asked next, irritated anew that Eli was not being permitted to send her telegrams directly. The Home Office regulated all messages containing sensitive information, which meant she had been forced to beg for information Eli passed on from either the Duke of Winchelsea or Arden himself.

Arden had taken note of her repeated requests to contact Eli, and she did not miss the manner in which his nostrils flared and his shoulders stiffened whenever she mentioned him. Eli Fairchild had been her partner in New York City for the last several months, and she was as concerned for his safety as she was eager for any new information he could offer her.

"Are you referring to Fairweather?" Arden asked from the opposite end of the room.

She spun about to face him and looked up from her notes, frowning. "Eli's surname is Fair*child*, as you well know."

"Hmm," was all he said, his attention riveted upon the documents he had laid out atop the surface of his desk.

His lack of concern for Eli's well-being nettled her as much as the manner in which he treated her as if she were another piece of furniture in his study did. "I wish to know whether or not he has been informed that Flannery and Mulroney recognized me. While I was in New York, Eli posed as my husband, and if word reached the Emerald Club that Eli's wife turned up in London under suspicious circumstances, he could well be in danger."

"Mr. Fairchild has been informed," was all Arden said, his tone cool.

"I would like to contact him myself directly," she said, though this was not the first time she had made such a request. Nor would it be the last if he denied her once more.

"Miss Montgomery, we have been over this matter already." He sighed, still looking down at the surface of his desk, shuffling through a sheaf of missives. "The Home Office will contact your fellow Pinkerton in New York. He has been made aware of everything that has occurred here in London. You may rest assured of that."

"Though you and Winchelsea have both denied my requests thus far, I have never been given a reason," she prodded, marching across the empty span of carpet between herself and his imposing desk. Even the chairs opposite it were rigid and unforgiving, and she could not help but to wonder if Arden had chosen them intentionally for just that reason.

He looked up at her at last, his face devoid of all expression. But his green eyes were cold, his jaw rigid. "Is he your lover?"

She stopped pacing, so stunned by his abrupt question, she could do nothing except stand there and gape at him, wondering if she had heard him correctly. "I beg your pardon?"

"Fairchild," he gritted. "Is he your lover?"

She almost blurted the truth, which was that Eli Fairchild was far more like a brother to her than a lover. But that would have been too easy. She did not like the manner in which Arden had so easily dismissed her after what had happened in his carriage on the way to Praed Street. Nor did she like his aloof mannerisms toward her, or the way he seemed to take every effort to avoid looking at her or speaking to her about anything aside from Special League matters.

"Would it matter to you if he was?" she asked, staring him down.

Let him be the first one to blink, the first to relent, she thought.

Only, this time, he did not. He inclined his head, stoic and regal as ever. "I asked you a question first, Miss Montgomery."

"An impertinent one," she countered smoothly. "My private life is none of your concern."

"It is my concern when I have enjoyed intimacies with you," he countered, rising from his chair at last.

She would wager it had eaten him alive to forego his gentlemanly training and remain seated while she paced. Indeed, she hoped it had. She was vexed with him. And frustrated. And fairly bursting with feelings and emotions she had not experienced in a very long time.

Hazel considered him solemnly. "Did you *enjoy* the intimacies you shared with me, Arden? I confess, I could not be certain."

"You know I did." He stalked toward her, his countenance darkening.

Damn him, he was handsome when he was angry. And when he was distracted. And tired. And happy. And even when he was solemn. Especially when he was in the midst of contemplating evidence, because he acquired the most endearing furrow between his brows. A furrow she longed to kiss.

Heaven help her. How could he not see he was all she thought about? How could he not know his hands and his mouth and every wickedness he could visit upon her were all she craved?

Already, he had banished her irritation, replacing it with a breathless anticipation. With a tightness in her belly, a quiver between her thighs where her body recalled how he had pleasured her in the carriage. How he had circled her entrance, the aching center where she hungered for him most, and yet he had not breached her.

"What if I say yes?" she dared to ask, testing him. "What if he is my lover?"

Never mind the notion of Eli in such a role was laughable. Arden did not know otherwise, and his response meant everything to her.

A muscle in Arden's jaw tensed. "Answer me, Hazel."

Ah, but she was too busy enjoying watching this strong, powerful, arrogant man squirm. He was an English aristocrat. She was an American orphan. He wore neckties and gold signet rings. She wore divided skirts and took on a role many considered a man's work. There could not exist two more disparate characters in all the civilized world.

He was near enough to touch, but she had been in closer

proximity to him on many occasions before. Somehow, the small distance heightened her awareness of him. Her nipples were painfully hard, and the ache in her core deepened. She wanted his touch there, stroking her as he had done before. More shocking, even, she wanted his mouth. His tongue. She had experienced some of the pleasures of the flesh with Adam, and she was not entirely innocent. Though she had fancied herself exempt from such weaknesses, the man before her had proven her wrong.

"Why does my answer matter so much to you?" she countered now, wondering if he would give her the truth she longed to hear.

"You know why," he said in that low, decadent baritone of his that never failed to send a trill of anticipation straight through her.

She hoped she knew why. But that did not mean she did not wish to hear it from his lips directly. The last few days had been a whirlwind of research, investigation, and recovery from her attack. He had resurrected the walls between them, and she burned to bring them down.

"Tell me," she whispered. She closed her journal with a snap.

"Because I want you for myself," he admitted, the concession sounding as if it had been torn from him. "I should not, but I do."

She met his gaze unflinchingly. She had lived her life without adherence to conventions. From the time she could first recall any memories, she had known she was different. She had not cared for dolls or dresses. She had longed for freedom and adventure. She had wanted to exceed the bounds she had been given as a female.

And so, she had.

Boundaries were meant to be defied. In this life, she was a

trespasser. She always had been and always would be. She had worked day and night, honing herself, educating herself, fighting for herself, to be the best Pinkerton she could be. She was an agent, a detective, a respected mind in her field despite every obstacle which had been placed in her path.

For all those reasons, she met the Duke of Arden's gaze without a hint of hesitation. "Then take me," she said.

Chapter Eleven

$\mathscr{I}$ T HAD BEEN a long time since Lucien had last had an
assignation with a woman, and he had never previously
had one in his own home. He was uncertain of the protocol.
In the wake of Hazel's bold invitation in his study, he had
been hit with the twin weights of duty and desire. He ought to
have turned her down, but from the moment the words had
left her lips, he had only been capable of forming one
response.

Come to me tonight.

A simple statement, a request of his own, and yet it had
changed everything. The tension between them, always
simmering beneath the surface of their every interaction, had
burst into an uncontrollable flame. Need had seized him, and
thank God she had taken mercy on him and excused herself
from the study, deciding to abandon their work early and
retire to her chamber.

Because from the moment she had offered herself to him,
the desire to possess her consumed him, along with an
absolute disregard for anything other than Hazel Montgomery
lying naked beneath him. Not even drawing life-giving breaths
seemed as necessary.

After she had gone, he had remained in place, standing
precisely where she had left him, staring at the closed door,
inhaling the lingering scent of her and willing his erection to

abate. He had known, of course, he could not run after Hazel, haul her into his arms, and carry her to his bedchamber like a pillaging Viking of old.

Instead, he had bided his time, walked calmly to his desk, and neatly stacked and arranged his correspondence, locking away sensitive documents as always. He paced, stopping to check his pocket watch every few minutes until finally a half hour had passed between Hazel's retreat and what would become his own.

And then, at last, he had ascended the stairs and found his way to his chamber, where he dismissed his valet and stripped to a dressing gown. He paced the confines of his chamber now, feeling a bit like a callow youth. Anticipation skittered through him, along with an endless barrage of questions.

What if Hazel changed her mind?

Why was he about to do something as foolish as bedding her?

What would it be like to have her beneath him, all feminine skin and smooth curves?

A subtle knock sounded. He wasted no time in hastening to the door and opening it. Hazel stood, wide-eyed and beautiful, on the threshold. She was still wearing her trousers and bodice, but her stockinged feet were without their customary black boots. He knew not if it was a sign she had indeed thought better of her rash decision in his study, but he wanted nothing more than to undress her himself. To peel those trousers down her legs. To undo the fastening on her drawers. To put his tongue on her.

Shaking himself from the licentious reverie, he stepped back, gesturing wordlessly for her to enter. Her gaze intent upon his, she moved swiftly forward, into his domain. He closed the door and turned to drink in the sight of her in his bedchamber. How oddly erotic it was to see her surrounded by his dark, masculine furniture. To see his bed in the background, just over her left shoulder, beckoning.

But he could not just pounce on her, and he knew it. Suddenly, everything he had ever learned about wooing a woman seemed to have disappeared from his mind. He forced his whirling thoughts to slow.

"Have you changed your mind, then?" he asked, his voice sounding rusty and unused.

She began plucking the pins from her hair.

His mouth went dry.

She did not stop until her hair had fallen around her shoulders and down her back in dark waves. She raised her fist, clenched around a handful of hairpins.

"Where would you have me put these, Arden?" she asked in her drawl.

The absurd thought that he wanted to keep them pricked the haze of lust clouding his mind. He extended his hand. "Here."

Her fingertips brushed his palm as she relinquished them. A frisson of desire skated down his spine. Her pupils were round, the fringe of her lashes thick and decadent framing the bright irises. He closed his hand on the hairpins, the metal already warmed from her skin.

Wordlessly, he walked past her, to a marble-topped chest of drawers. Instead of placing the pins on the surface, he slid them inside the first drawer and then turned back to her.

"I have not changed my mind," she told him. "Have you?"

He wasn't even certain he had a mind any longer. "No."

"One night," she said, startling him. "This can be nothing more."

Those were meant to be his words of caution to her. He ought to be relieved she had spoken them first. It was best if they knew where each other stood, after all. But somehow, the haste with which she limited their liaison nettled him.

"Have you done this before?" he asked, curious.

She raised a brow. "Would it matter if I have?"

He considered her question, allowing his gaze to trail over her form as he had not dared indulge before. "No," he said. "I merely wish to know how to proceed."

She smiled then, and it reached her eyes. He supposed he had passed her test.

"I am no delicate magnolia, Arden."

He stepped closer, needing to touch her. He traced the backs of his fingers over her cheek, absorbing the soft luxury of her skin, her warmth. "Lucien."

If they were to be lovers, even just for one night, he wanted to hear his name in her honeyed inflection. He wanted to hear her moan it when he brought her to her pinnacle. He wanted it on her lips when he buried his face between her legs.

Her smile deepened. "Very well. I am no delicate magnolia, *Lucien*. Do not treat me as if I am one of your sheltered debutantes. As you have said, I am not refined. I am afraid I am missing most of the graces a lady is ordinarily expected to possess."

He regretted the bitterness he had directed toward her on the first day he had met her. She had taken him by surprise, both with her appearance and her mannerisms, and he had been unpardonably rude.

"I am sorry I paid you an insult that day," he said, trailing his touch over her jaw. "I was angry at the prospect of being forced to accept a partner. Angry for the mistakes I made."

"Mistakes?" she asked.

He knew she was curious about The Incident. But now was not the time. Instead, he took her chin in his thumb and forefinger, tilting her head back. And then slowly, his gaze never leaving hers, he kissed her. Long and open-mouthed. He savored, ran his tongue against hers.

Here was the answer he would give her: desire. A leisurely introduction to what they would be doing all bloody night long. If he only had her once, he would make it count. Need blossomed inside him anew, and his prick was harder than it had ever been, his ballocks drawn tight, all while she was yet fully clothed except for the omission of her boots.

And even the reminder of her stockinged feet made him ache.

Her arms went around his neck, drawing him closer still. He stepped into her lush curves, every point of contact between them setting him on fire. Her generous breasts were crushed against his chest. Her belly touched his rigid shaft. With his free hand, he grasped the fullness of her hip, anchoring her to him.

He bit her lower lip, then soothed the nip with his tongue. *My God*, he wanted to consume her. One night could not be enough. He knew it instinctively, with this kiss. He knew it in his marrow. There was something elemental about the way he wanted her, something irrepressible about the magnitude of his need. And if her responsiveness to him every time he touched her was any indication, she felt it too.

They could fool themselves all they liked.

He kissed the corner of her mouth. "Sweet." He kissed her cheek. "So sweet." Then her ear, the dip behind it.

She sighed, and he absorbed the tremor that ran through her as he took a handful of her sweet-scented hair and held it back, revealing her throat. He kissed her there as well, dragged his mouth down, stopping when he reached the hollow where her pulse thudded.

The urge to see her wearing nothing but her trousers struck him. He raised his head, moving his hands to the line of buttons on the front of her smart bodice. The bodice was the color of cream today, its sole adornment the double line of shells and a tiny satin bow. Mindlessly, he worked the buttons free.

So many bloody buttons.

He lost patience and began to tear.

"Arden," she protested on a startled gasp.

He remained unrepentant as he looked down at his progress. The halves of her bodice hung open, revealing a modified chemise beneath. No corset. Her breasts were soft and round, the hard, pink peaks taunting shadows.

"Lucien," he reminded her, then found he could not tarry another moment.

He lowered his lips to her breast and sucked a hungry nipple into his mouth, ignoring the unwanted fabric barrier.

"Oh," was all she said, but her fingers were in his hair now, sifting.

He loved her hands on him. They made him feel as if she was as greedy for him as he was for her. Tenderly, he bit her nipple, and he was rewarded by her sharp inhalation, the score of her nails on his scalp. This was not going to be a tender bedding. It was going to be a wild and frantic fucking.

He released her nipple, and took her mouth again. He tore the rest of her bodice from her arms, sending it falling. He would buy her a dozen to replace it. He would buy her an entire *modiste* shop. *Damn it*, he would commission the finest dressmakers in London to make her a hundred more bodices, and twice as many trousers, as long as she would allow him to tear them all off her.

He forgot about his fantasy to see her in nothing more than the trousers, because her lips were clinging to his, and she was softening. Melting in his hands, losing all the starch and determination she carried about her like a shield. And she was touching him, her hands gliding over his dressing gown in caresses which were tentative at first, then grew bolder. His shoulders first, then his chest, and down his abdomen, until she glanced over his burgeoning cock.

He groaned into her mouth, resisting the instinct to mindlessly thrust against her. He wanted a far greater prize than her hand. And, more importantly, he wanted to last. He kissed her deeper as he found the fastening at the waistband of her trousers and opened it. The billowing fabric fell away. Her drawers came next.

She tugged at the knot on his belt, and he felt it loosening. Too soon. If he was naked, he would not be able to resist taking her to the bed and making her his. Rushing was not what he was after. Rather, a slow and thorough seduction was.

He tore his lips from hers, his breathing harsh, and stared down at her. Her cheeks were flushed, her mouth stung with his kisses, her lips parted. He had never seen a sight more glorious than Hazel half undone, clad in nothing but a short chemise, stockings, and garters, her hair a wild mass spilling down her back.

He reached for her hands, entwining their fingers. "Come." He tugged her to the sitting area by his fireplace, and she allowed it.

Her eyes held a new question as he stopped her before one of the damask-and-gilt chairs. "What are you doing, Lucien?"

Damnation, he liked the sound of her husky drawl saying his name. Anticipation pulsed through him. "Take off your chemise for me."

"Here?"

Of course she would question him, the stubborn woman. "Here," he confirmed. "Please."

He had never begged for anything in his life, but he would gladly do so, for the chance to watch Hazel strip away the last layer of fabric shielding her lithe body from him. Still watching him in that intense way she had, she gathered up fistfuls of the chemise and pulled it over her head.

"Christ," he rasped, his voice strangled.

A violent surge of want resounded through him. In her stockings and garters and nothing else, she was a vision. A dream. More beautiful than he had imagined, and he had imagined her many times. Many nights. But never this.

Pale and curved, hips lush, her breasts tipped with hard, pink nipples he already knew loved to be sucked. He had to touch. His hands were on her, stroking, worshiping, investigating. Her delicately curved shoulders, the protrusion of her clavicle, lower, over the fullness of her breasts, down her waist, cupping her bottom. She was all smooth heat and lush femininity.

He sank to his knees before her, his gaze locked upon hers, and kissed her knee through her silk stockings. He caressed her slim ankle, then grasped it firmly and urged her to lift her leg.

"Arden," she protested.

"Lucien," he reminded, intent upon his prize. Her mound was hidden by a dark, silky tuft of curls. He recalled how sweet she had tasted.

"Lucien," she said, breathless. "What are you doing?"

"Loving you." He guided her hands to his shoulders, then hooked a hand behind her knee when she continued to stand, unmoving. He rocked forward on his knees, blowing air lightly over her. "Trust me, Hazel."

With a jerky nod, she relented, allowing him to place her right foot upon the cushion of the chair at their side. She was open to him then, naked save for her garters and stockings, those willful blue eyes upon him, and he had the perfect view of her. Pink and pretty, glistening in the light of the gas lamps. Wet for him.

She saw the direction of his gaze and shielded herself with a hand. He caught her wrist in a gentle grip, brought it to his lips for a kiss. "Let me."

He drew her hand back to his shoulder, and he did not wait for her response this time. His head dipped. He kissed a path along her inner thigh, all the way to her sweetly spread cunny, then kissed her there too. Once, on her pearl. She stiffened, but made no move to push him away. He licked, just a flick of his tongue along the turgid bud, and she cried out, her fingers tensing on the muscles of his shoulders.

"Lucien," she said, half moan, half protest.

He suckled her, then licked again and traced her seam with his fingers. "Shall I stop, sweetheart?" he asked, blowing a stream of air onto her exposed flesh as he glanced up at her.

"No," she whispered.

He smiled, then buried his face between her legs once more.

THE DUKE OF Arden possessed a miraculous tongue. This was Hazel's sole, coherent thought as he devoured her with his mouth. Wicked and long and knowing, his tongue licked over the sensitive bundle of flesh at her center. Then he traced a path of decadence through her sex, lapping at her entrance.

Helpless. She was helpless to ask him to stop, to want him to stop. She *never* wanted him to stop. Her initial embarrassment at the depravity of her pose—foot upon a chair, her thighs parted to reveal the most intimate part of herself to his voracious gaze—fell away. What a beautiful sight, the high and mighty Arden, a man whose very dressing gown was of better quality than almost every garment she owned, on his knees before her.

He was, as he had said, loving her. Licking her, laving her, sucking, using his teeth to nip at her pearl until she moaned, grinding herself against him. More. She wanted more of everything he was doing to her. There was his tongue again, playing at her channel, subtle licks, circling, teasing. He wanted her as much as she wanted him inside her. That huge, hard maleness of him she had felt against her and beneath her hand would stretch and fill her there, and she wanted that too.

Wanted him.

He groaned. She felt the rumble against her eager flesh. A warm surge of wetness pooled between her thighs. She was slick, the sounds of him pleasuring her filling the silence of his massive bedchamber. Her foot slid on the damask of the chair, opening her to him more, and her hips instinctively thrust forward again and again.

He sucked her, then released her and drew back, his eyes darkened with pleasure, his lips red and glistening with the evidence of her desire. "Yes, Hazel. Show me what you want, what you like. Make me do your bidding. Tonight, I am your servant."

His words made a heaviness settle low in her belly, the tingling coil of desire tightening into a knot that drew tighter by the moment. She relished in this great and powerful man, urging her to use him for her pleasure. There was no time for thinking or hesitating. Her fingers found his hair—she loved his hair, so dark and luxurious, with a curl to it. She gripped handfuls and urged him back to her mound.

Humming his approval, he tongued her seam, licked over her channel, his tongue dipping inside her, then darting back out again in shallow thrusts that made her desperate for more. He buried his face deeper, his tongue traveling lower, sliding over another, equally forbidden part of her. She jolted at the unexpected contact as he lapped at her, varying long and slow licks with faster flutters.

"That is… You should not… Lucien…"

She could not seem to finish her thought. Some part of her knew she should protest, but what he was doing to her was transcendent. It was wicked. It was wonderful. It was…

Oh.

His fingers found her pearl, petting her in tantalizing strokes as he continued his shameless sensual torture. Everything within contracted. Sensations coursed through her. She was mindless, boneless, and breathless all at once. For the third time, Arden brought her to a shattering, beautiful release.

But this time was different. More intense. As she rode the first, blinding wave of pleasure, she screamed. She forgot about servants or Lady Beaufort overhearing her, forgot she was not meant to be in Arden's chamber, let alone naked and at the mercy of his skilled fingers and even more skilled tongue. She was wetter now than she had been before, and this too, he lapped up, moaning into her flesh, as if she were the most delicious feast laid before him.

As awareness and lucidity gradually returned in the wake of her release, she realized she was gripping fistfuls of his hair tightly, and she relaxed her fingers, exhaling slowly. Her heart pounded and the rest of her tingled everywhere. Even her scalp and the bottoms of her feet. *Dear God*, the way he had owned her body, wringing pleasure from her in places she had never dreamt could be pleasured in such wicked fashion…

He took his time, kissing her everywhere. Flicking his tongue back over her pearl until she jerked and shuddered, ready for more. And then he kissed her thigh, the prominence of her hip bone, the curve of her belly. He stood, his expression that of a drunken man, and it was heady, so heady, to realize *she* was the reason for that look. That he was drunk upon *her*.

"Hazel," he said, his gruff baritone making the already pulsing flesh between her thighs quiver anew. "Fuck, Hazel."

His curse did not startle her. Nor did it offend. She had heard coarser language in her years as a Pinkerton. She allowed her foot to slide back to the floor and looped her arms around his neck. He was taller than she was, but not so very tall she could not reach him. Not so tall she could not rise on her toes and kiss his mouth. His filthy, wonderful, beautiful mouth.

He tasted earthy. Musky. Of herself and something elemental. Lust. Intercourse. Man and woman, woman and man. He tasted like nothing she had ever tasted before and could not wait to taste again.

He caught her waist, lifting her feet from the floor, and she allowed it. And when he ordered her to wrap her legs around him, she did without hesitation. And when he carried her all the way to his bed, her core sliding over the silk of his dressing gown with every step, she could not stop kissing him. His lips, his face, his throat. *Ah*, his throat. So strong and vital. She dared to taste him, to run her tongue over the prominence of his Adam's apple.

He laid her on his bed as if she were as delicate as the magnolia flower she had assured him she was not. She was still wearing her stockings and garters, but she lay in the center of his bed and watched as he made short work of the knot on his belt she had been unable to free earlier. When he shrugged the robe to the floor, she could do nothing but admire him.

His shoulders were broad, his chest strong, delineated with muscles that bespoke a man who was active. Dark hair stippled his pectorals and arrowed lower into a mouthwatering trail that led over the hard plane of his stomach and straight to the prominence of his manhood.

She had known that part of him was large because of her previous encounters with him, but then, he had been clothed. Now, he was nude. And the full effect of the Duke of Arden naked and ready to join her in his bed was mouthwatering, astounding, and intimidating all at once. His cock was a thing of beauty, full and thick and long. Much larger than she had even supposed.

She stared at him for longer than was polite, she knew. If indeed it was polite at all to stare at one's bedmate's erection? She had no earthly idea. It was a concern that had not troubled her until this moment.

"Do you approve?" he asked, amusement lacing his perfectly clipped accent.

The accent that reminded her he was an aristocrat who belonged to a world she could not even comprehend while she was an orphan from the red dirt of Georgia, a woman who had made her way in a man's world, earning her own bread. He had been born to respect and luxury, groomed from birth and by the circumstance of it to be treated with the utmost respect. For a moment, the heat sliding through her cooled as she was reminded of all the reasons why this one night was all they could have.

Their lives were too disparate. One day, she would return to New York. He would remain here where he belonged, in a home with chamber pots that were fancier than all the crockery she had ever dined on prior to her arrival in London.

He seemed to sense the sudden reticence in her, because he joined her on the bed, stretching his long, lean body alongside her, and cupped her face. "We do not have to do this, Hazel. Not if you do not want it."

But he had misread her hesitation. She clasped his wrists, grateful for his tenderness, and lost herself in his eyes. "I want this. I want *you*."

"Thank Christ." On a growl, he buried his face in her neck, kissing her there, then opening his mouth and sucking.

It was as if he wanted to mark her. As if he wanted to brand every part of her body with his taste, his smell, his touch, his searing style of pleasure. And she wanted him everywhere.

She reached for him, pushing aside the doubts in her mind. They could be addressed later. Tonight was hers. Arden was hers. *Not Arden*, she reminded herself as she ran her hands over him, savoring the hot, sleek male flesh and the barely leashed strength lingering just beneath the surface.

Lucien.

She must have spoken his name aloud, for he ceased suckling her throat and raised his head. "What is it, sweetheart?"

Sweetheart. He had called her that before, when she had been injured, and earlier, when he had been pleasuring her with such depraved persistence. But something about the way he said it now, something about the deepness of his voice coupled with the intimacy of the moment—both of them naked, skin to skin in his bed—resonated with her. Broke something inside her.

But perhaps it was something that had been meant to be broken all along. Long ago, when she had been hopelessly in love with Adam only to lose him, she had sworn she would never again allow herself to feel anything for another man. She had always supposed a part of her had died along with him, never to be resurrected. Now, it seemed what had been inside her had been a monument to her grief, precious and precarious, fashioned of her own guilt, her own fears, and her everlasting sorrow.

The monument had lodged inside her, impenetrable and immovable, obstructing her ability to feel, until Arden had come along. Until he had dared her with his arrogant condescension to prove her worth. Until he had shown her he was just as vulnerable on the inside as she was. Until he had made her see she had not been honoring Adam's memory by closing herself off from the world.

She had only been protecting her heart.

"Hazel?" Lucien's brow furrowed, his gaze probing hers. "Tears?"

She blinked, realizing belatedly her cheeks were wet, her lashes spiked with drops. Leftover emotions she had never allowed herself to indulge in the wake of Adam's brutal killing swarmed her.

"We need not go any further," he said, kissing her cheek, the tip of her nose, her forehead.

His gentleness and concern pierced her armor. "It is not that," she reassured him, caressing him wherever she could—his back, his shoulders, his rigid jaw.

"What is it then?" He traced her cheekbone, then the whorl of her ear, with his forefinger.

It was as if every part of her was desirable to him, as if he needed to touch her everywhere. And she recognized the feeling, for she felt it too. It was the way she felt about him.

She took his hand in hers and turned her head to press a kiss to his palm. "It is me, realizing I can still feel after all this time."

"What happened to you, Hazel Montgomery?" he asked, brushing a tendril of hair from her face. "Will you tell me?"

But she was not ready to answer his question. Not now, not yet. Just as he had not been prepared to unburden himself to her.

"One day," she said, hoping she could keep her promise. "Not tonight. Tonight, I want you inside me."

"Jesus, Hazel." He kissed her slowly, lingeringly.

She had proven to herself that the part of her she had believed died alongside Adam had not. Lucien had helped her to resurrect it. First, with longing. And now, with something more. Caring and compassion. Tenderness.

Their kiss deepened. As one, they moved until Hazel was on her back and Lucien atop her, settled between her splayed thighs. His fingers dipped between them, working her to a new crescendo, before he withdrew.

He broke the kiss, his breathing harsh and ragged, his forehead pressed to hers. "Are you certain?"

She did not hesitate. "Certain."

His blunt tip met her slick and swollen flesh. He positioned himself at her entrance, poised to take her.

"How slow must I go, Hazel?" he asked.

She did not fully comprehend his question. "Only as slow as you wish," she answered, for it seemed the right thing to say.

No man had ever made love to her before. Not completely. There had been kissing, touching, teasing. There had been pleasure, to be sure. But there had never been another inside her. She had not wanted it after Adam. But she wanted it now, with Lucien. Only Lucien.

He moved. Thrust inside her, fast and hard. She had not been entirely prepared, and she stiffened beneath him, a burning pain tearing through her, momentarily supplanting the pleasure.

He stilled, his shaft buried deep inside her, her body stretched and aching all around him, and lifted his head. "You are a virgin?"

She was trapped in his glittering green gaze, and his face was strained, a reflection of the control he exerted to remain still within her. "I *was*."

"I thought—" He stopped whatever it was he had been

about to say and exhaled.

She knew what he meant. He had assumed she was an experienced woman, and he was not entirely wrong. She had done far more than was proper with Adam, but that had been years ago, and it had never been...*this*.

"It doesn't matter," she reassured him. Because it didn't. Not what he had believed her to be, not her past, not anyone or anything but the two of them.

But he was not appeased. He frowned down at her, looking torn. "Damn it, Hazel, did I hurt you?"

"No," she whispered, framing his handsome face in her hands. He was so beautiful in his concern for her, it almost made her heart ache to look at him. "You could never hurt me, Lucien."

But as she said those words, she knew they were not true. He *could* hurt her, but not physically, not intentionally. She had somehow, in spite of her resolve to keep what was happening between them relegated to the sexual rather than the emotional, allowed him to slip past her walls. He was inside her now in more than one way.

And now that her body had adjusted to the suddenness of his bold invasion, a new hunger pulsed inside her. She tested the instinct to move, moving her hips against his and bringing him deeper still. Pleasure and pain intertwined. She exhaled on a sigh.

"Do not move," Lucien warned.

He ought to have known by now she never took orders. She moved again, undulating her body beneath his. The friction made heat unfurl in her belly. The need had returned, taking control of her. She pumped her hips against him.

He groaned and dropped his forehead back to hers. "Hazel."

"Lucien." She kissed him. "I told you I am no magnolia blossom. I want you to make love to me."

At long last, he began a rhythm, withdrawing from her in long, slow strokes only to sink inside her once more. She could not be certain if it was her imagination, or if he had hardened even more. He was large, and each time he sank inside her channel, he filled her, the sensation exquisite almost to the point of pain.

They were kissing again, mouths fused, a messy, carnal kiss of tongues and teeth. Her body had never felt more alive. She was attuned to her every sense, ridiculously aware of all the places where they met, not just deep inside her, but elsewhere. Her breasts crushed into his chest, their stomachs melded, his lean strength against her softness, her inner thighs wrapped around him. He was so very masculine, dominating her, devouring her, pinning her to the bed, completing her.

There was no other way to describe his possession.

His questing fingers returned to her pearl, giving her just the right amount of pressure and stimulation. Her body had already broken open for him. He had introduced her to a raw, wicked pleasure, and she was still alive with it, tingling, ready to come again. Ready to give him anything.

To give him *everything*.

When he dragged his mouth to her ear, kissing her there, his breath hot and harsh and desperate, and he issued a command, this time, she could not help but to obey. "Spend for me."

And she did. Her inner muscles clenched on him, around him. The force of her climax took her by surprise. She cried out, slamming her hips into his, trying to drive him deeper inside her. So deep. Mewling sounds erupted from her throat. Sounds she did not even recognize as her own. A shudder rocked through her as he continued his pace, sliding in and out faster and faster, until suddenly he withdrew from her entirely.

Holding himself in his hand, he came with a roar of his

own, spurting all over her belly. His breathing was as ragged as hers, his eyes intent upon her. She could not look away. Licks of pleasure still rippled through her body.

"Are you...well?" he asked hoarsely.

"Yes." She watched him, trying not to ogle him and failing. She had never imagined a man could be beautiful. But the Duke of Arden was. There was not a hint of spare flesh on him. He was all lean muscle, angles and planes and sinews.

The way his eyes roamed over her made a new frisson steal through her.

"I like seeing you this way," he said. "Naked and flushed in my bed, my seed on your skin."

His admission was wicked and raw. She should be shocked.

"I like it too," she said, realizing she did.

Nothing could be the same now, and she knew that, too. But she kept that particular realization to herself as he left the bed and then returned moments later with a wet cloth he used to clean her despite her protestations she could tend to herself just as well. When she would have gone from his bed, he held her against him, his arms wrapping around her.

"Stay with me," he said into her ear, pressing a kiss to her neck.

How could she deny him? How could she not want to linger with this man?

"For a little while longer," she conceded, even though she knew it was foolish and futile. Even though she knew the longer she remained in his presence and in his bed, the more she would never want to leave.

But the dawn would come soon enough, and with it a return to responsibility. And for now, she had the steady, reassuring thump of Lucien's heart pressed against her back and the warmth of his mouth on her skin.

Chapter Twelve

*L*UCIEN WAITED FOR Hazel to join him in his study, doing his damnedest not to look at the small parcel sitting upon his desk, elegantly wrapped and tied with a sleek bow. He had risen in the midst of the night to find himself alone, nothing, other than the faint scent of Hazel and their lovemaking in his sheets, to remind him he had been inside her hours before. His cock had gone instantly rigid at the memories, and denied what he truly wanted, he had taken himself in hand.

By dawn, he had been awake again, trying to put a name upon the sensation of restlessness inside him. The urge to see her had been almost insurmountable, and he wanted nothing more than to let himself into her bedchamber and awaken her with his kisses. And later, with his tongue.

But he had agreed to one night, and she had left him in the darkness, which surely meant she intended to remain stern in her resolve. Instead, he had dressed himself, ringing for his valet, only for a shave. He had breakfasted alone, then had gone for a ride, attempting to clear his mind. His mind, however, would not be cleared of Hazel Montgomery. Nor could his body be freed from the need to have her, not just once, but again and again.

Instead of returning home following his ride, he found himself at a shop, which had just opened. He had not known precisely what he was searching for, until he had seen it, and he had brought it back home for her.

A gift.

She had been nowhere to be found upon his arrival, and he had attempted to busy himself with other matters, but the correspondence awaiting him did not interest him nearly as much as the prospect of watching Hazel open her gift did. Would she like it? Would she accept it? Had he been wrong to buy her something?

It did rather smack of a gesture one would make toward a mistress, and Hazel was most certainly not his mistress. She was...

Well, damn it, he did not know. There was not a word which could define her. The English language did not contain a means of conveying her spirit and her brash ways, the complex combination that made her who she was. Nor could it adequately describe what she was to him, the way she made him feel.

As no other woman before her ever had.

As he was beginning to suspect no woman after her ever would.

He rose, hands clasped behind his back, deciding he could no longer remain seated, staring at the bloody gift he had bought her. He rang for his butler, and almost instantly, Reynolds appeared, his face an expressionless mask.

"Has Miss Montgomery breakfasted yet?" he asked, attempting to allow only a note of cool disinterest to enter his voice.

Whatever happened between himself and Hazel, he would not have her the focus of belowstairs gossip. Her presence here at his home as an unmarried woman, even with Aunt Hortense as chaperone, was scandalous enough. He did not wish to add to the sordid mix.

"I believe she is breakfasting now, Your Grace," his butler

informed him.

It was nearly half past eleven, and Hazel ordinarily took her morning repast nearly as early as he did. He hoped she had been merely tired, and not feeling ill-used. She had repeatedly assured him he had not hurt her, but when he thought of how unprepared he had been for the barrier he had ruthlessly breached, he knew an arrow of shame.

"Very good, Reynolds," he forced himself to say, as if he could scarcely care what his guest was about. "When she is finished, would you tell her I require her presence in my study?"

"As Your Grace wishes." Reynolds bowed, then was gone.

Lucien distracted himself with more pacing. He straightened a picture on the wall. He gazed out the window. He picked up the parcel, imagined stuffing it somewhere, perhaps in one of the locked drawers on his desk. Hiding it, and never giving it to Hazel at all.

He worried it was too much, too soon, and too maudlin.

Far too sentimental.

Lucien did not believe in finer emotions between a man and a woman. He believed in physical needs being met. The gift in his hand seemed to suddenly be his albatross. It burned his hand, and he wondered why he had even bought it in the first place. What had he been thinking, buying Hazel Montgomery a gift, as if he were courting her?

He stalked back to his desk, the gift in hand, when a subtle knock sounded upon the door. He stopped, for he knew who it was. He recognized the sound from last night. He cleared his throat.

"Enter," he bid her.

The door opened, and she hesitated at the threshold. There was color in her cheeks, he noted, and she wore a gown instead of her trousers. Her dark hair was pulled into a

Grecian braid, coiled heavily, a few wisps framing her lovely face. The sight of her hit him like a fist to the gut.

"Good morning," she told him, in her sweet drawl.

"Good morning," he forced himself to say, as if she did not steal the very breath from his lungs.

She entered the study at last, the door closing at her back, but immediately stopped just inside and remained where she was, almost as if she feared the need to make a hasty escape. "Mr. Reynolds told me you were inquiring after me."

He did not bother to correct the manner in which she referred to his butler. There was no point. "Yes, I was. Are you... That is to say, how do you feel this morning?"

It occurred to him he was inquiring as to just how much of a brute he had been the night before. His ears went hot.

Her lush lips curved into a smile. "I am well, Lucien."

He was not yet returned to *Arden*, so there was that, at least. Except, he stared at her, and he knew not what he ought to say. He had been bold with her last night, because he had thought her experienced after the manner in which she had invited him to make love to her. And then, he had discovered, too late, she was not. He had taken her maidenhead, and this morning, he had bought her a bloody gift, as if any object he purchased with coin could compare to the priceless treasure she had given him.

He stood before her in the midst of his study after having summoned her, feeling a cad and a fool.

"Good," was all he managed. A single-word response. His grip on the gift tightened. He was sure his knuckles had gone white with the strain.

She swept toward him, and he noticed her hair was still slightly damp as she grew nearer. The scent of her soap hit him. Such a luxury he had been afforded yesterday, to touch her freely. To make her his.

His eyes could not stop roaming over every bit of her creamy skin. Her throat, so elegant. Her hands, the fine-boned fingers. Precious little was actually visible, in truth. Most of her was hidden from him today. He wondered if it had been intentional on her part. Her gown was a polonaise of deep burgundy. Ecru lace adorned the high neck and fell over her wrists. A tempting line of buttons ran down the front of her bodice.

Her lips parted, and for a heavy moment, she simply stared back at him, her head cocked as if she were studying him. "I think I must apologize for misleading you yesterday," she said at last.

He could have swallowed his tongue. "Misleading me how?" he queried with deceptive calm when he had regained his voice.

She swallowed, then fiddled with her hair for a moment, as if she were discomfited. "You were not expecting a virgin. I am not mistaken in that, am I?"

No, he had not been. He had bungled that matter very badly. It occurred to him now, quite belatedly and much to his everlasting disappointment in himself, that as a gentleman, he ought to offer for her. He had taken her innocence, without a thought for consequence. And this morning he had bought her a frivolity and summoned her to his study, as if she were a servant he could order about, instead of attending to his duty.

"I meant you no insult," he said, but it was no explanation, and neither was it an apology, and he knew it.

She smiled at him again, but this time, he was near enough to see the smile was on her lips, though not in her eyes. "You paid me none. I have lived a great deal in my twenty-eight years. I am by no means an innocent. And there was someone once, a man I loved, who I..." Her flush deepened.

"You need not explain," he interjected, not to spare her. To spare himself. Selfish reasons only. The thought of Hazel loving someone else made him want to smash his fist into the plaster of his study wall. It made him grind his teeth and clench his jaw, and clasp the symbol of his stupidity with such force, that had it been capable of breaking, it would have already snapped in two.

Fortunately for him, and the object in question both, it could not.

"It does not matter now," she agreed. "All I mean to say is, you need not feel a moment of guilt, Lucien. I am a woman with her own mind, and I knew what I wanted. My only regret is that I feel certain you would not have allowed yourself to indulge in what we shared had you known the truth. I suspect your sense of honor would not have allowed it."

She was right. Perhaps part of him had been eager to believe her experienced, for it made making love to her a feat infinitely more attainable. He had never dallied with innocents. His past lovers had all been skilled and seasoned.

"I have dishonored you," he found himself saying.

It was the truth, after all. The stupid gift in his hands could do nothing to expiate his sins. What manner of man defiled a woman he was meant to protect? Him, that was who. And for a man who had made so very many mistakes in his lifetime, this one somehow stung more than all the rest.

He had failed his mother.

He had attempted to do what was best for his sister, but had wound up driving her away from him instead.

He had accused another League member of treason, believing the lies of a man he had trusted with his life, a man who had deceived him with such treachery, it still left Lucien reeling to think of it, even though the perpetrator was dead.

"You have not dishonored me," Hazel said then, interrupting his turbulent musings.

He realized she had moved closer still. Close enough to touch. He wanted to kiss her. Wanted to haul her against him, bury his face in her neck. And yes, he wanted to raise her skirts and sink inside her once more, but bedding her was not the strongest need coursing through him. Simply touching her was.

Lucien recalled the gift clenched in his hands, and he offered it to her. "I saw this, and I wanted you to have it."

Her brow wrinkled in adorable befuddlement as she looked at the neatly wrapped, perfectly rectangular parcel. "I do not require gifts, Lucien."

"It is not…" He paused, struggling with his thoughts, a rarity for him. "I did not buy you a gift because of last night. I bought it for you because you make me happy, and I have not been happy in a very long time, and I wanted to return the favor, in a small way. A very small way, of course."

He stopped talking, lest he say anything more foolish than what he had already done. In truth, he did not recall a time in his life when he had ever been happy. But this, the rush going through him, the pulse of life beating inside him, the voracious, wild need he felt for her—it was different than anything he had known.

His childhood had been tumultuous and uncertain, his parents forever at each other's throats, his mother plagued by wildly vacillating moods until the day she had taken her own life. His youth had been spent attempting to shield his younger sister from the wrath of it all. And though he loved her and had strived to do his utmost to see Lettie settled and happy, he had driven her from him.

Hazel took the gift from him now, holding it in her small

hands. The hands that had caressed him last night. The hands that had raked his scalp and explored his back. The hands that had been all over his body. How strange it was to think he could not freely touch these hands by the grim morning light. Not unless she invited him to do so.

"You make me happy as well, Lucien," she said quietly, her head bowed over the gift he had given her. "It pleases me to know I make you happy, too. That is the best gift of all. I think you are a man who needs a reason to smile."

He had to swallow down a lump that had risen in his throat. "Open it, Hazel. Please."

Strange, how he had been tormented, part of him wanting to hide it away, part of him longing to give it to her, and now he could not wait until she tore open the wrapping and revealed it. He watched as she carefully untied the bow, sliding the ribbon away in a long, silky strand she kept clutched in one hand. With her other, she tore the paper open, revealing a journal.

Bound in the finest leather, it boasted mother of pearl and gold inlays on its cover and gilt on the edges of all its pages. The interior was lined and fashioned of fine, thick creamy sheaves of paper. Nothing but the best. It had cost him an exorbitant fee. But it had been worth it. *She* was worth it.

"Oh, Lucien," she crooned, lovingly stroking the cover. "It is beautiful."

She was beautiful.

And he was unaccountably nervous. He wanted, with a desperation as alarming as it was embarrassing, to meet with her approval. To please her. To be the reason she smiled.

"This journal is for you," he said needlessly, attempting to explain himself. "For your private thoughts. I have enjoyed reading your notes, which are not at all like notes, but rather stories in themselves. And I thought it would be lovely if you had something of your own, somewhere you could share your thoughts and have it be yours alone."

She was silent, staring down at the journal, sifting through its pages, running her fingers over the fine paper. And when she looked up, her eyes were glistening. A tear rolled down her cheek, then another, and another. She sniffed, then laughed, catching a fat droplet on the fleshy pad of her forefinger as she gazed at him.

"What are these tears?" he asked. "Have I made you sad?"

He would not forgive himself if he had. Making her sad had never been his intention, even if he could not be entirely certain what his intentions toward Hazel Montgomery were.

"Not sad," she said with another sniffle, before offering him that blinding smile of hers once again. "Honored. No one has ever given me a gift before, and this one is so unbearably lovely. I will treasure it always, Lucien. Thank you."

"You are most welcome, Hazel."

But he heard the words she left unspoken, and he knew she meant she would treasure the journal even after she had gone and they were no longer partners, no longer sharing the same roof and the same common goal. The time would inevitably come when they would part ways.

The knowledge left him cold.

The knowledge made him want to do everything in his power to change it.

But reality intruded, and he reminded himself they were here, sharing the same space, breathing the same air, for a reason. And it was decidedly not so he could woo her. Or lure her back to his bed for another night. Nor was it so he could ply her with gifts.

Neither of them could forget the lethal seriousness of the burdens upon their collective shoulders. But he also suspected neither of them would be capable of forgetting what had happened the night before. Regardless, he would do his utmost to pretend.

HAZEL SPENT THE remainder of the morning pretending the Duke of Arden's omnipresence at her side meant less than nothing to her. She pretended the gift he had given her had not made her weep. She pretended being in such proximity to him, without touching him intimately, did not affect her at all.

She pretended she did not want to kiss him.

That she did not remember the wicked wonders his tongue could work upon her flesh.

That she did not want to make love with him again.

After all, she was the one who had set the rules for their impromptu liaison, had she not? One night only. One night, and nothing more. One night, then back to focusing upon the incredibly difficult task of capturing the criminals responsible for the bombings on the railway.

She had thought it would be easy.

She had thought she could hunker over Arden's desk, examining a map of the railways, without wanting him to press himself against her from behind. She had thought, after she had gone to bed with him, she would no longer want him.

And she realized she had been wholly, thoroughly wrong.

As wrong as could be.

Her longing for him had only grown, compounded by his unexpected gift and equally unexpected admission that she made him happy. When had anyone ever said something more profound to her?

She could not recall, as she sat across from him in the dining room, where they were being served luncheon. Lady

Beaufort was feeling bilious today and suffering from an unfortunate attack of arthritis, which she blamed upon the cool, rainy weather, leaving Hazel and Lucien alone.

Like every dish set before her at Lark House, lunch was presented upon delicate china. Cold chicken and ham, curried eggs, and freshly baked bread, along with a jam tartlet and lemonade, which she was sure Arden had requested for her benefit. Her stomach growled in most unladylike fashion, and she surreptitiously pressed her palm over it, willing the most disagreeable and demanding part of her to quiet.

"That will be all, Reynolds, thank you," Arden said. "You may close the door behind you."

The butler and duo of footmen accompanying him bowed before taking their leave of the room. When the door was closed, she became acutely aware of the fact she was alone with Arden once more. Though they had just been closeted within his study all morning, there was a distinct difference between their earlier toiling on behalf of the League and now.

She vowed she would distract herself with food. She would not think of the kisses she had shared with him last night. She would not envision him without his clothes. Nor would she imagine his mouth and tongue, and the wicked pleasure of them both upon her most intimate and shocking places.

Her plate was laden. In grim silence, she stared, unseeing at it, and stabbed the first object within reach of her fork tines. Unceremoniously, she shoveled the sustenance into her mouth. Cold roast chicken, she realized, seasoned well. Her stomach rumbled again. Yes, it was far better to answer the hunger in her belly, rather than the other hunger.

That one was far more pronounced. And far more troubling.

"I was betrayed," Arden said suddenly into the silence.

Her gaze jolted to him at last. He was watching her with an indecipherable expression. She did not know what to say, and there was a lump of chicken in her mouth precluding her from speaking anyway. She swallowed, then took a sip of her lemonade. Then another, working out what she would say to him next.

A swallow, a breath. She attempted to regain her composure. If she had felt gauche before, she felt positively foolish now, reminded once more that, despite what had happened between them in the night, he was a duke, a blue-blooded aristocrat, and she was nothing but an orphan. She did not have his effortless manners. She was graceless and brusque, decidedly unfeminine, even when she wasn't garbed in her divided skirts, devoted to a vocation most of the civilized world considered solely male.

"Betrayed?" she repeated at last, after having swallowed two more bracing gulps of lemonade. His chef certainly knew how to perfect the drink. Not too sugary, not too tart. Just perfection on her tongue.

Much like Arden.

But that was a thought she needed to banish altogether.

"By a man I considered unimpeachable," he added. "He was my most trusted aid, in truth. He was gambling and suffering heavy debts. I had no knowledge of the difficulties in which he had found himself mired. Instead of coming to me and asking me for assistance, he turned to his cousin, a Fenian sympathizer."

She took another sip of her lemonade, fighting for the right words to say. "You are speaking of the reason for my presence here, are you not?" she dared to ask. "The reason why the Home Office suddenly required you to have a partner, yes?"

"Yes," he bit out, his eyes searching hers, his lips unsmiling. Firm, like his clenched jaw.

He looked every bit the forbidding aristocrat, the arrogant duke. He was beautiful, yet untouchable. Only, she had touched him last night. Had more than touched him. He had been inside her. She remembered his tongue, then she remembered she should never think of it again.

But such a decadent wickedness could never truly be forgotten, and she knew it.

"How did he betray you?" Her curiosity and her concern for him collided, overruling any hunger roiling through her belly.

"He planted evidence of Fenian collusion at the home of one of my agents. I mistakenly believed the agent was guilty, and brought him here to Lark House, keeping him under duress. He escaped and eloped with my sister, proving me wrong, but not before the bastard I trusted almost killed him, myself, and two other men I respect and admire. Not to mention my sister." He paused, his tone rueful, shaking his head. "Lettie saved us all that day, but the crux of it is, she would not have been capable of doing so, if not for the man I believed guilty of treason. He taught her how to shoot a pistol when I refused, you see."

Hazel absorbed everything Arden had just revealed. Part of her was shocked he had been duped, for he seemed so omnipotent. Part of her was shocked he was admitting to it, for he was exposing a weakness to her. But she was grateful, so grateful, he was entrusting himself to her. Here was his story, the information he had carefully guarded from her, laid out and open before the both of them, as plainly as the food gathered for their luncheon.

"The man you believed was guilty, his name has been cleared?"

"I saw to it," he said, his face devoid of expression.

She sensed how deeply what had happened affected him, however. He had revealed something else about himself she had not known until this very moment: he had a sister. "And your sister, she saved you all?"

Arden nodded. "She did."

Hazel could not contain her smile at the affirmation, for she could not deny she applauded the notion of a woman saving a group of men from imminent danger. "Your sister— Lettie, as you call her—she sounds like a lady I would admire and respect very much, Arden."

"Yes," he agreed, deadly serious now. "You would both admire each other, I suspect. I... I very much fear my actions have created a rift between us that cannot be mended."

"You have apologized, have you not?" she asked tentatively.

Arden did not seem the sort of man who would refuse to make amends for his sins, but he could also be arrogance personified, so she could not be entirely certain.

He grimaced. "Of course I bloody well apologized. I nearly had my brother-in-law sent to prison. As one can imagine, however, my relationship with the two of them remains strained. Lettie is headstrong and fiercely loyal, but she is also her own woman. It is a lesson I learned too late for it to do me any good, I fear."

"The evidence against him must have been compelling for you to be so convinced of his guilt," she ventured.

"It was, but I am afraid my actions, however well-intentioned, neither endeared me to the Home Office, nor to Lettie and her husband." His smile was self-deprecating. "All I wanted for my sister was her happiness, but in trying to secure that for her, I ended up pushing her away."

His revelations both hurt and warmed her heart. She was grateful he had trusted her enough to unburden himself, for she knew it was not easy for him to speak with such candor, particularly in regard to his own faults. And she also knew the time had come for her to share a painful part of her past as well.

"We all make mistakes, Arden," she said sadly. "At least the mistakes you made did not cost anyone his life."

She had not spoken of Adam, of what had happened, in many years. Her silence had not ameliorated her guilt or her sadness. Nor had it dimmed the profound sense of loss his death had caused.

Arden seemed to understand the seriousness of the truth she was about to convey. His jaw clenched. "You have already shared enough of yourself with me, Hazel. You need not feel obligated to share anything more. I told you about what happened with my sister and brother-in-law because you were right some time ago, when you told me you ought to know my weaknesses. It would seem I have far more of them than I had once supposed."

For a brief, heady moment, she wondered if he was implying she was one of his weaknesses, but then dismissed the thought as silly. She was old enough, and worldly enough, to understand what had happened between them last night had been an even exchange. They had sought pleasure and comfort in each other's arms. Nothing more, and neither would it be repeated.

But still, she could not deny the closeness she felt to him. Not just because of the intimacies they had shared, but because the Duke of Arden—*Lucien*—touched a part of her she had not known existed. She would never be the same Hazel Montgomery she had been before she had first clapped eyes on him, when he had been scowling and looking down his nose at her in his study, wondering where H.E. Montgomery was. A part of her would always be his.

And so, she was not telling him about the way she had failed Adam because she had made love with Arden. Rather, she was sharing it because she *needed* to. The time had come. She had held her tongue for far too many years. Telling someone felt right, but telling Lucien felt necessary.

"I want to tell you, Lucien," she reassured him, intentionally omitting her use of his title. "If you want to hear it, that is."

"I want to hear anything you wish to tell me," he told her, his expression and his tone both deadly serious.

She swallowed, daunted for a moment by his intensity. But then she forced herself to remember the enormity of the admission he had just shared with her. His secret had been closely guarded.

"I was on my seventh assignment as a Pinkerton," she began slowly. "A bank teller had been murdered, and one hundred thousand dollars had been stolen from the bank's vault. It was my first case involving a murder, and a brutal one at that. The teller had been beaten with a hammer. I was working the case with one other detective, my fiancé, Adam."

"Hazel," Lucien interrupted, his tone so tender, it made something inside her ache. "You needn't go on."

"I suspect you know already how this tale ends, do you not?" Though she tried to smile, she failed. Saying Adam's name aloud, even after all the time that had passed, pained her. She was no longer the girl he had once known and loved, but she would always miss him.

"I suspect I do," he acknowledged, looking grim, "but continue. Tell me, if it will lessen the weight you carry on your shoulders."

She could not be certain if it would, but all she knew was, she wanted to tell him. She continued. "The case seemed an obvious one. The bank teller often remained late to accommodate tradesmen who brought their deposits after their businesses had closed.

"One of the men who commonly arrived with evening deposits was the teller's good friend. Our investigation uncovered a great deal of debts that man had incurred. His motive was obvious. I was so certain of his guilt, I approached him with the evidence mounting against him, though my fiancé had warned me against doing something so foolish. But I…I had misread the suspect. When cornered, he did not confess his crimes. Instead, he attempted to shoot me. Adam stepped in front of me."

The violent discharge of that hated pistol would forever echo in her memory, as would the sight of Adam's body falling to the floor before her, the blood streaming from his mouth, the shocked look in his eyes, as he struggled for breath. A shuddering breath went through her now, as the same old fear gripped her, nearly a decade later. Adam's blood had been on her hands, warm and wet, such a sickening sensation.

"S-somehow, I was able to retrieve the pistol hidden in my reticule," she said haltingly. "I shot him before he could shoot me. I put my bullet in his head. B-but…it was too late for Adam. He died in my arms, and I have never forgiven myself for that day."

To her utter mortification, hot tears had begun to fall down her cheeks, sobs hitching her every breath. She had been so deeply dredged in the horror of the memories, which she had tamped down and repressed inside her for so long, she had not even been aware Lucien had risen from his seat opposite her.

Not until warm, strong hands hauled her to her feet and spun her about. She was confronted with a wall of broad, hard chest for a moment. And then, he swept her into his arms. He held her, his arms banded around her, his face buried in her hair, as he caressed a slow, soothing path up and down her spine.

"You were not to blame, Hazel," he said. "You were conducting your investigation, attempting to bring a man to justice. You had no way of knowing the bastard would attempt to kill you."

"It is my fault Adam was killed," she whispered, her ear pressed over the steady, reassuring thud of Lucien's heart. *Thump, thump.* A subtle, visceral reminder *he* was here. *He* was alive.

And so was she.

She could not undo the past. No matter how desperately she wished she could go back and make a different choice, time had already taken that ability from her. Adam was gone.

"It is not your fault, and you know it," Lucien countered, his arms tightening around her even more. "You were doing your duty, attempting to bring a murderer to justice. I know you, Hazel. I know you well enough to know you are one of the best agents I have ever been privileged to work alongside."

His words had a strange effect upon her, cutting through the grief and guilt, planting deep roots. How grateful she was, not just for his comfort, but for his belief in her. Sharing what had happened with him felt freeing. It felt right.

He felt right.

Her arms were wrapped around his lean waist, and she leaned into him, allowing herself to be vulnerable. Allowing herself to be consoled.

"Thank you," she whispered, meaning it to her marrow, and yet, incapable of saying more, for fear she may burst into sobs all over again.

His gentle touch continued to glide up and down her spine. "Thank *you*, Hazel. Thank you for telling me. I know what it cost you, how incredibly difficult it is to relive past horrors. I am honored you chose to share it with me."

For a long time, she said nothing, simply holding on to him, absorbing his heat and his strength. Breathing in the familiar, delicious scent of him. Listening to the sound of his heart pumping life through his veins.

Wondering how she could ever possibly limit herself to one night with this man, with this beautiful, complex, surprising, endearing man in her arms.

Wondering how she could ever possibly let go.

Chapter Thirteen

$\mathcal{L}$UCIEN COULD NOT sleep, which was not a new affliction. The reason for his insomnia, however, was.

He wanted Hazel.

Well, to be precise, wanting Hazel was not a new affliction either, because he had certainly desired her from the moment she had brazenly waltzed into his study and scathingly referred to him as *Mr.* Arden. But not being able to sleep because he knew she was beneath the same roof, and because he knew what she tasted like, what it felt like to sink deep inside her, because the sweet sounds of her release would forever haunt him to his dying day, that was all bloody well a new affliction.

Damn it.

One night, she had told him.

One night, he had agreed.

But one night could never be enough. He had known it last night, and he knew it better than ever as he tossed and turned, then lay on his back, staring at the plasterwork on the ceiling in the darkness of the night. Shadowy acanthus leaves mocked him, lit by the glow of the evening's unusually large moon.

Christ, he was not even certain that one lifetime could be enough. They had shared more than just their bodies. They had shared themselves, their weaknesses, their mistakes, their follies, their regrets. And he wanted her in a way that was different than mere base lust. He was old enough, experienced enough, to know the difference between a woman he wanted to fuck and a woman he wanted to fuck and hold when she cried, and kiss away her tears, and hold her hand, and protect her, and worship her as she deserved, and, and, and…

Emitting a low growl of frustration, he scrubbed a hand over his face and sat up in his bed. In his lonely bed, which still smelled faintly of Hazel and their lovemaking. He had taken himself in hand, but it had not been enough. Nothing but Hazel could be enough now.

He thought again of what she had shared with him over their luncheon. How personal her revelation had been. How unexpected. She seemed so controlled at all times, so unemotional and untouchable. But he thought he understood her better now. She was devoted to her work as an agent as a sort of penance, a means of making atonement for the lost life of her fiancé.

To his great shame, Lucien knew a spear of envy for her dead betrothed. The man who had thrown himself in front of her to spare her a bullet. Her feelings for the man had been apparent in the way she had spoken of him, in the reverence of her tone, the tears she had cried. For a brief, embarrassing moment as he had listened to her story and relived the awful trauma she had experienced along with her, Lucien had experienced a sudden stab of envy toward a dead man.

He recognized instantly how foolish his reaction was, how grounded in primitive instinct. After all, her betrothed had died, and Lucien had been the one to take her maidenhead instead of the martyr who had saved her life. He ought to feel guilty for that, but he could not summon up a speck of remorse. When it came to Hazel Montgomery, all he knew was that he wanted her, all for himself. He wanted to possess her, to consume her, to protect her, to make her his.

To hell with one night. He would begin with two. Two ought to satiate his relentless desire for her. Never mind his forbidding aunt was in residence and that it would not do to potentially cause a scandal that would embarrass her. If he was quiet and careful, if no one ever found out, what would be the harm?

He threw back the bedclothes and quickly donned a dressing gown in the semi-darkness. The household was asleep. Finding his way to her chamber undetected would be easy. Convincing Hazel to change her mind may not be, however. But never mind. He was prepared to persuade her. With his tongue, if necessary.

The last thought sent a bolt of lust straight through him.

He opened the door, strode over the threshold and into the hall, and promptly collided with someone. He instinctively reached for the person into whom he had crashed. His hands met with warm female flesh, undeniable beneath the barrier of a wrapper. She made a startled sound, her hands clutching at his shoulders for purchase, as the scent of her hit him. Soap and a hint of lavender.

"Hazel," he whispered, relief and gratitude washing over him as one. His grip on her tightened, but he could not help it. He was starving for her, and she had come to him. He could only hope her reason for flitting about in the darkness outside his chamber was the same reason he had been exiting his chamber.

"Lucien." Her buttery drawl was once more in evidence.

Just his name and nothing more, and yet his cock twitched with appreciation and remembrance. She had been so tight and hot around him, so wet, dragging him deep, milking him to release. He was a greedy bastard, and he wanted more.

"You were coming to me?" he asked, just so he could be certain.

"No, I was off in search of your kitchens," she said. "I have the strongest urge for a chocolate cake, and I thought to bake myself one."

He could not be certain if she was teasing him or if she was speaking truth. If any of his acquaintances were to wander to the kitchen to bake a cake in the midst of the night, it would be she.

"Truly?" Even if she did intend to do as she claimed, he would not allow her to flee him so easily. He drew her flush against his body, sucking in a breath when her bountiful breasts met his chest, and his hard cock connected with the sweetness of her curves.

"Not truly," she admitted. "I was looking for you."

"Thank Christ." He found her lips in the darkness, taking them in the kiss he had been longing to give her all damn day.

She opened on a sigh, her arms twining around his neck. *At last*, was all he could think as he moved them as one, back into the safe haven of his chamber. His mouth never left hers. Somehow, he managed to close the door before it occurred to him he did not know why she had been seeking him.

He ended the kiss and left her for a moment to turn on a lamp. Now that he had her where he wanted her, the darkness was not good enough. He had to see her in the light. And what a sight she was, with her lustrous hair unbound, her smart dressing gown belted at her waist, and bare feet and trim ankles peeking from beneath the hem.

He swallowed, moved by the sight of her. She was different here in the glow of the lone lamp, bereft of her armor. Even her demeanor seemed different. More tender. Adorably uncertain. He did not know which he wanted more—to kiss her or to embrace her.

"Why were you looking for me?" he asked, realizing he could not simply continue pawing at her, regardless of how inviolably strong the urge to carry her to his bed and go about the business of making love to her all night long was.

She closed the distance between them, her gaze never leaving his. "I…I did not want to be alone tonight."

The question his mind had been wrangling with—to kiss or to embrace—was decided. *Both.* He took her in his arms once more, drawing her close to him. Their bodies were flush, her curves melding to his sturdy frame. He dipped his head and brought his lips back to hers, kissing her thoroughly.

"Stay with me," he whispered against her lips. "Please."

She drew back, her bright eyes searching his. He did not know what answer she found there, if any. In truth, he had no answers for himself. He could not explain why or how he was so drawn to the woman in his arms. Lord knew he had never intended to be. Nor did he know what it meant, this all-encompassing need he had for her. All he knew was that it was there, a burning and aching thing.

"What happens between us, Lucien…" She halted, her words trailing off as she struggled to explain herself. "It can never be more than the physical, an exchange of pleasure. I do not allow myself to make the same mistakes twice."

He knew she was speaking of what had happened with her betrothed. It had marred her, scarred her forever. Death had a way of doing that to a person. He knew all too well. Scars were reminders that though the skin had healed over, a wound had once existed, and the body would never be the same. Death was no different.

Her eyes were solemn pools, laden with a sadness he wanted to chase. He ran the backs of his fingers over the curve of her cheek slowly, gently. He would not argue with her words, because the physical was all he dared seek from a woman. He did not believe in love, and he had no intention of ever marrying or siring children of his own. His mother had left him a legacy he would not pass on to the next generation.

"Whatever you want, Hazel, it is yours," he told her. "Take it. There need be no explanation."

She exhaled, then gave a jerky nod. "Thank you."

"Come to bed with me?" he asked, mesmerized by a tiny cleft in her chin, so small, it was scarcely visible to the eye.

He traced his thumb over it, wondering what other mysteries she hid. What facets he would learn. The prospect thrilled him. He had not taken her in the manner he would have had he known she was inexperienced. He had been too bold, then too abrupt. Tonight, he would make amends. He would learn every bit of her body, devote himself to what made her sigh, what made her moan, what made her lose control and spend.

"Yes," she said simply.

He kissed her again, long and slow, taking his time. He explored the velvety insides of her lips, sliding his tongue against hers. Her mouth was meant to be savored. He would not rush this, he promised himself. He would bide his time. Cherish every second. She was a rarity, and he appreciated her in a way he had never before been grateful for another woman. Her honesty, her vulnerability, juxtaposed with her undeniable intelligence, determination, and drive, undid him.

No other woman like her existed, and he was certain of it. Just as certain as he was that no other woman would ever compare to her in his arms. No other woman could ever match the incredible compliment of her capitulation, her hands upon him. Her mouth beneath his.

She was real, and she was true, and she was smart and fiery and fierce, and in this moment alone, she was *his*. All his. He intended to keep her that way for as long as possible.

Her tongue moved, slowly at first, then with greater intent. Their grapple for control had begun once more, and it was the sweetest aphrodisiac. He groaned as he slid one of his hands up her spine to just beneath the heavy, silken strands of her hair. Her nape was soft. He cupped the base of her skull and angled her head toward his as his fingers gently tightened on a handful of wavy tresses. Holding her still, he ravaged her mouth.

She made a sound, half-mewl, half-moan. Pure sensual frustration. Anticipation sent an arrow of heat to his groin. The knowledge she wanted him every bit as much as he wanted her was heady.

Hazel was not shy about her physical wants, needs, and desires, and he not only applauded her forthright nature…it made him so hard, he ached. She met him touch for touch, stroke for stroke, and kiss for kiss, thrust for thrust.

He could consume her as if she were the most decadent dessert ever laid before him. He wanted to bite her, to lick her, to fuck her, to kiss her, to own her. She overpowered his instinct, his sense of duty, his mind. He wanted her beneath him, atop him. He wanted her hair wrapped around his fist, her mouth on his cock. He wanted to spend his seed and watch as she swallowed it down.

But for now, he had to temper himself. To rein in his sweeping desires and intemperate longing. Control. He needed control. Coolness, calm. He could hold himself back. He could keep himself from blindly driving onward in full charge. They were not at battle, after all. They were lovers. She wanted nothing more than pleasure? He could give her that. *Hell*, it was all he could give her. They were two jaded hearts, finding mutual solace in each other.

He kissed his way down her throat. Smooth and taut, the cord of her neck a delicacy he nipped with his teeth before soothing with the blunt strokes of his tongue. Her pulse was fast. Beating like the wings of a butterfly. Delicate and intoxicating yet strong and sure, just as she was. He wanted more.

Proceeding slowly would be torture. His hands traveled over her body, shaping and molding her curves through the fabric of her dressing gown. After all they had shared today—the painful revelations of their pasts merging with the present—this intimacy seemed even more potent.

He took her hands in his then and led her. They moved as one to the bed, stopping just before it. For a beat, they stared at each other, neither one of them speaking. The first time had been wild and unexpected. They had clashed, exchanged words, and she had thrown out her challenge. *Then take me.* And he had accepted. The gauntlet had been tossed down. He had been helpless to resist.

This time was different. They were making a cognizant decision. A second night when there was to have only been one. A silent acknowledgment the passion burning between them could not be cooled after one delirious joining.

"You are certain?" he asked her, because the gentleman within him demanded it even though he already knew the answer.

"Certain," she said, fumbling to undo the knot on the belt at her waist.

He caught her fingers in his, moved them aside. "Let me."

His hands trembled, ridiculous though it was. He was a man of experience, and this was not the first time he was about to see Hazel nude. Anticipation swelled inside him, along with a rising tide of want. It did not matter that they had made love before. He desired her more now than ever. She was glorious, this eccentric American warrior goddess, bold and brash and unique, this Athena brought to life.

The knot came undone. He wasted no time in pushing the wrapper from her shoulders. Beneath it, she wore a nightdress of soft white cotton. It was plain, unadorned by either frill or lace, but it suited her, clinging to her curved hips and full breasts. Her nipples were already hard, prodding the fabric.

His mouth went dry. She was not even nude, and he was hard, his cock aching to be inside her. He cupped her breasts through the nightdress, his thumbs finding her nipples and grazing them in steady circles. Slowly, he reminded himself. He had been mad in his need for her before. He would woo her with gentle care, show her the tenderness he would have, had he realized she was far more inexperienced than he had supposed.

She sighed, and then her hands were on his own dressing gown, undoing the belt, sliding inside to caress a trail of fire over his chest. He was entirely nude beneath it, and he was thankful for that now, as her clever hands traced over him, taunting. Tantalizing.

He took her mouth again, kissing her, luxuriating in the sleek suppleness of her lips beneath his, in the way she surrendered, opening, her tongue seeking his. And then she surprised him by nipping his lower lip, as if she, too, was overrun by the desire to claim. To mindlessly consume.

Her palm slid down his abdomen, making his muscles tighten and his prick spring higher. He groaned into her mouth, deepening the kiss. Every vow he had made to take things slowly with her was banished by the onslaught of her desire. She kissed him back ferociously, her enthusiasm unbridled, and he was awash in need. Aching for her. When her fingers gripped him, his hips jerked.

Her clasp was tight and sure as she worked over him, pumping his shaft. *By God*, it was all he could do to keep from grinding himself against her, from spending in her hand and all over her simple nightdress.

"Minx," he muttered without heat.

He kissed down her throat, pinched her nipples lightly. A small row of buttons taunted him, keeping him from her bare skin. He could undo them, or he could tear, and with the violence of the need rising within him, spurred on by her hand stroking his cock, he gripped the modest neckline of her nightdress and tore it firmly in half. One line, straight down the center, until it hung from her in two pieces, and he was rewarded by a hint of pink-tipped breasts and the dark nest of curls shielding her sex from him.

"Arden," she protested, releasing his painfully erect shaft and glancing down at the tattered remnants of her nightdress in shock. "You have ruined it."

"Forgive me," he said, quite insincerely. In truth, he would do it all over again. "It was in the way of what I wanted."

That was the truth, undeniable, and he did not believe he had ever wanted anything or anyone more than he wanted Hazel Montgomery. His entire being pulsed with the desire to take her, to make her his. Slide home inside her welcoming, tight sheath. To lose himself in the depths of her wet cunny.

"It was a favorite of mine," she chided. "I have had it for five years now, and it has held up with remarkable aplomb. I do not believe I will find another to replace it."

"I will buy you a new nightdress." He kissed her neck as he drew the nightgown—or what remained of it—from her body. "A finer one."

He already owed her a bodice. He was making the destruction of her wardrobe a habit.

"No doubt you will," she said, sighing when he bit at the skin over her clavicle. Her hands flitted to his shoulders, not pushing him away but holding him in place. "But I will not accept your largesse, and that was badly done of... *Oh.*"

He had kissed his way to the tip of one breast, and now he dragged hard on her nipple, gratified by the way her words trailed off as she forgot her pique in favor of the pleasure he had to offer her. He lapped at the bud, playing his tongue lightly over it, then released it and blew a stream of hot air over the distended peak. She had the most beautiful breasts he had ever seen. Round and full, creamy and pink, more than enough to fill his hands, and they were so gloriously attuned to his touch.

He had a brief, wild fantasy of stuffing his cock between them, fucking her there. But that would wait for another day. He could not debauch her in one night. And neither was he sure it was his right to do so, even if there was something about her that drew out the primitive beast within. He wanted to claim her body as his own, to fill her and mark her and pleasure her in every way he could. He wanted her with a desperation he doubted could ever be satiated.

But for now, she was within reach. She was warm and sleek and curved and lush, a rare creature he had somehow ensnared for the moment. She was so completely unlike every other woman he had ever known. There was no artifice in her.

She had not led a life of pampering but one of toiling. Even her body was stronger than a female's ordinarily was, and he admired the muscles of her thighs, her buttocks as his hands swept over them anew, the taut sinews of her upper arms. No dainty, frail lady, Miss H.E. Montgomery. She was as graceless as a turnip, more beautiful than any woman he had ever met, and he reveled in her oddities and complexities, her blend of the masculine and the feminine, her uniqueness, so different, so refreshing.

Just, simply, *her.*

He released her nipple and laved the other one, listening for the hitch in her breath, for the mewls of pleasure he wrung from her throat. This woman was made for sin. Made for him. His fingers dipped into the inviting warmth blossoming between her thighs. He parted her folds to find her slick and hot and wet. So wet for him. The discovery made his ballocks tighten in anticipation.

Her hands were on him too, dragging the ends of his robe apart, pushing it down his arms. She glided her palms over his chest. Her nails rasped down his abdomen. She once more found his erect cock and squeezed.

Not hard, but with enough pressure to make him release her nipple and thrust his hips instinctively forward, seeking more of the oblivion she offered even when he was determined to do everything in his power to make the night last forever.

"Damn it, Hazel," he ground out.

He did not want to know how she knew how to pleasure a man so well. She had been a virgin, but he could not fathom she would know how to touch him with just the proper amount of pressure and tenderness, how to stroke him and bring him to the brink.

She did. God, how she did.

And he knew a fire of jealousy, lit deep within him, and envy toward the man who had earned her heart, the betrothed she had loved and lost, before ever marrying. Some part of him, the possessive beast who had fallen beneath her spell, envied that man, who had been the first to teach her passion. Envied that man, who had won her heart.

Christ. What was he thinking? The pleasure was making him mad. He did not believe in love. Or in the fickleness of hearts. He did not believe in anything other than pleasure. Bodies. Nature. His cock in Hazel's pussy. Yes, that was what he believed in. That was all he could afford to trust.

She stopped, either sensing the maelstrom within him, or uncertain of herself. "Is something wrong?"

"No," he bit out.

Yes, he thought. *Yes, by God there was.* Everything was wrong, because she was making him feel things. Things he had not felt in years. Things he had not believed himself capable of feeling any longer. She was…undoing him.

Slowly.

Surely.

Seducing him, transforming him, and he could not stop it, any more than he could stop the sun rising in the east. It was elemental, inevitable. Just as she was. Some mad part of him wondered if she had been destined for him, if their bodies were meant to be joined. And then, he told himself that was foolish. Nothing was meant to be.

She stopped stroking him, but did not ease her grip. "Should I not touch you?"

"Fuck." He muttered the epithet in a bitter tone, and he knew he ought not to say it before her, even if they were naked, and even if he was about to lose himself inside her body without the sanctity of marriage. "Always touch me, Hazel. Never stop."

"Are you certain?" Her tone was hesitant, a reminder that, regardless of whatever knowledge she had obtained from her betrothed, she was still very much an innocent. A fact he could personally attest to, since he had been the one to take her virginity.

"I have never been more certain of anything in my life," he gritted. "Stroke me. Do what you like with me. I am at your command."

As he said the words, a hot rush of excitement burned through him. It was what he wanted, he realized. What he longed for. He wanted Hazel to take control of him, to govern her own pleasure, and his. He wanted to be at her mercy, utterly and completely.

"At my command," she repeated slowly.

"I am yours," he said.

Her grip tightened on his cock. He nearly spent in her palm.

"Mine?" she asked, resuming her strokes. Up and down his shaft, her thumb finding the tip, rubbing over his sensitive head.

"Yours," he growled.

"What if I want you on your knees again?" she whispered, leaning into him, her mouth close enough to claim, her breath hot and sweet as it skimmed his lips.

"On my knees pleasuring you?" he asked, getting harder at the thought.

"Yes."

Suddenly, all his intentions fell away. Desire hit him like a locomotive, full in the chest, speeding down the tracks. There was no turning back.

"Tell me to do it," he told her. "Order me."

"Order you?" she asked, her tone suddenly hesitant.

"Yes."

Her response was instant. "Get on your knees."

"And then what?"

She flushed, her cheeks warming, and it spread, all the way to the tops of her breasts. "You know, Arden."

"Calling me Arden won't get you what you want, sweetheart." His hands were back upon her breasts now, teasing her hungry nipples.

"Lucien."

"Yes, love?" He rolled the stiff peaks between his thumbs and forefingers.

"Your tongue."

He kissed her, because he couldn't not. "Mmm?"

"I want it on me. I want you on your knees."

She was ordering him, just as he had asked, and he almost came, then and there. "Yes." He sank to his knees on the thick carpet.

Yes, echoed everything within him. Lust, desire, passion, need, whatever one wanted to call it, the crescendo rose, undeniable. His heart was pounding, his mouth was dry. The scent of her, musky, yet with a fragrant floral note, hit him.

On a groan, he caught her hips with his hands, urging her toward his bed. With his guidance, she settled her rump there, then he made a place for himself between her splayed thighs, all the better to worship her. But he took his time, savoring. He flattened his palms on the insides of her thighs, caressing her, feeling the subtle strength of her muscles, so delicately constrained, within her silken flesh.

She was revealed to him, pink and open, like a blossom. Wet and perfect. His. He kissed the inside of each thigh as his blood thundered through his veins. Slowly, he reminded himself. Slowly. He wanted to savor her. To draw out his seduction, until they were both desperate, consumed by lust so agonizing, it could only be answered in one way.

Her fingers sifted through his hair, smoothing over his scalp. The simple touch elicited a frisson down his spine. A warm rush of pleasure. And it was not just sexual in nature. Rather, it began somewhere deep within him and emanated outward. He liked the way she touched him, as if he were precious to her. Or necessary. As if she cared for him. No other lover had ever caressed him with such selfless tenderness.

He rewarded both of them by kissing higher, dragging his open mouth over her sensitive flesh, until he reached his prize. He parted her with his tongue, ran it reverently over flesh hot and moist with her dew. She tasted all the sweeter for her desire. He licked into her, sinking his tongue deep in an imitation of what he would do soon with his cock. She gasped and arched into him, thrusting herself against his face. Her fingers tightened on his hair, pulling slightly.

The almost painful pleasure heightened his hunger for her. He licked deeper, harder, using his forefinger to pet her engorged pearl. Beneath his other hand, he felt her body tensing, the firm muscles in her thighs going taut. She was close, already, to climaxing. And he wanted to give her that release, wanted her to spend on his tongue.

He was ravenous for her, determined to devote himself to nothing but her pleasure. Mindlessly, he licked up her slit, his mouth latching onto the bud of her sex as his fingers parted her folds. Gently, he used his teeth on her sensitive flesh, raking them over the distended nub. He sank a finger into her tight passage, groaning into her cunny when she gripped him with her inner muscles. Molten heat, slick, so good.

He fucked her as he sucked on her, adding a second finger when one did not seem like enough. And she came undone beautifully, climaxing on a gasp as she flooded his fingers. He played his tongue over her lightly as the torrent of her release wracked her. On a throaty moan, she shuddered until her body relaxed, the tension seeping from her.

He stood, transfixed by the sight of her, naked, legs spread, her lips parted, hair cascading down her back. Her breasts jutted outward like offerings, and the need roaring through him to pin her to the bed and take her could not be contained. Had he thought he could protract this? That he could seduce her slowly?

Not a chance. He was not sure which of them was the seducer and which the seduced. His body was clamoring for hers. His cock had to be inside her. Now. He settled himself between her legs, his cock against her cunny, and swept aside the dark curtain of her hair to press a kiss to her throat.

"Lucien," she said on a throaty sigh, tilting her head back.

He nibbled on the cord of her neck, bit lightly where her shoulder and her throat met. With one hand, he cupped a breast, toying with her nipple, squeezing until she moaned. He reached between them with the other, finding her slick and swollen flesh, teasing her bud again until her back bowed and she jerked toward him.

Tantalizing them both, he rolled his hips, running his thick length over her. He lifted his head to watch her. In her pleasured state, she was glorious, her skin flush, her eyes glazed. *By God*, he could lose himself inside her forever.

"Do you want me, Hazel?" he rasped.

"This way?" she asked, her eyes going wide. "Do we not need to recline?"

"This way," he confirmed, guiding his cock to the delicious warmth of her entrance. *Damnation*, she was dripping.

"Oh." She scooted her bottom forward, seeking more contact.

But he would not enter her until she said the words. "Tell me."

Her hands had found their way to his buttocks now, and with a sound of frustration, she gripped him and drew him closer. "I want you. Please, Lucien. I need you inside me."

She had not even finished her sentence, before he obeyed. Not hurried. Not deep, but deliberate, as if he could last all night. He was not a rutting beast, and he was mindful of the fact she was still a novice to lovemaking. His cock was large. He had no wish to hurt her. He withdrew almost entirely, then thrust deeper. Her sheath constricted around him, drawing him in. Her release had left her so wet, despite the tightness of her channel, he glided in and out of her with breathtaking ease.

Again and again, he plunged, then withdrew, each new stroke bringing him deeper, closer to losing himself completely. The effort to hold himself back made sweat pool on his brow and trickle down his back. Her fingers dug into his buttocks, her legs around his waist. Neither of them spoke, but their gazes were locked. Their breathing harsh. Their hearts, he imagined, pounded in unison.

No joining had ever been so personal, so intimate, so complete. He thrust deeper. Increased his pace in steady bursts, until finally, he was seated inside her all the way. She moved against him, a needy cry tearing from her parted lips. He forgot to be gentle when she clamped down on him hard, a ripple working through her and igniting a fire within him, which could be doused with nothing but release.

He withdrew, then surged inside her, again and again. Lucien reached between them, finding her pearl, pressing. Working it. He lowered his lips to her neck, sucking, licking, biting. Leaving his mark upon her as he took her body as his own. When she came again, it was almost violent in its strength. The spasms rocking her milked him, squeezed him.

He lost control.

With a hoarse cry, he pumped one last time and emptied his seed inside her. So deep inside her, there was no undoing it. No time for withdrawal. Pleasure licked down his spine, then rocketed through him like a fireworks display. He came so hard, his vision went dark around the edges, exploding with stars.

Bracing a hand on the bed, he collapsed against her, his face buried in the delectable crook of her neck. Awareness returned to him in stages. His heart raced. His breathing was as ragged as if he had been sprinting in circles around St. James's Square. Beneath his bare feet, the carpet was soft. The scent of Hazel and lovemaking was redolent in the air. He was still inside her.

He withdrew slowly, as inevitable regret hit him. He had been careless with Hazel, careless with her body, her future. He'd had no right to fill her with his seed. Shame seared him. What would he do if she became pregnant with his child? What would *she* do? He had never before lost his head so thoroughly with a lover that he had spent inside her. The world was filled with bastards and fatherless children enough, and he had no wish to add to their sad numbers. But what he had just done was undeniable.

There was only one way to answer for his sin. To atone.

"Hazel," he said hoarsely, knowing what he must do. "Will you marry me?"

Chapter Fourteen

$\mathscr{H}$AZEL WAS HAVING difficulty forming coherent thoughts. And not only that, but her heart was pounding louder than the hooves of a spooked herd of wild horses galloping across the planes. Surely the mindless bliss she had just experienced, coupled with her altered, pleasure-sated state, was the reason her ears deceived her into believing she had just heard Arden propose marriage to her.

No, surely she was mistaken. He could not have just asked her to marry him. Could he have?

He had withdrawn from her body, and she mourned the loss of his hardness inside her. Her flesh was throbbing deliciously. She felt so very thoroughly alive. More alive than she had ever felt before. She was still gasping for breath, aftershocks of euphoria ebbing through her, making her flesh tingle everywhere.

"Hazel?" he repeated her name, a frown furrowing his brow, his sensual lips compressed in a firm line.

His lips were glossy with the evidence of her desire for him, and just looking at them made a fire kindle to life inside her. For she could recall every delicious moment of those sinful lips upon her. Oh, what he had done to her. It was as if she had been slumbering for all the years since Adam's death, and now, for the first time, she had been awakened.

But she still could not speak. Words seemed beyond her.

She wanted only to feel. To bask in this luscious glow, the wickedness she had not known she possessed.

"Mmm?" she asked.

When he had withdrawn from her, she had been forced to relinquish her grip upon his bottom. She thought of how new the sensation had been, his firm rump, the muscles clenching as he pounded into her. She planted her palms on the surface of his bed now to keep her limp body from sprawling all over the fine coverlets. Strange to realize how visceral and carnal making love was. Shocking to think how much she had been missing, all these years of remaining chaste.

Why had she? She lived her life to suit herself. And was she certainly not a society debutante. She was a woman of liberty, who had fought hard to be regarded with respect in her avocation. Had it been the memory of Adam haunting her all these years, or had it been because no man, before the Duke of Arden, had ever interested her enough to take such a risk?

"Will you do me the honor of becoming my wife?" Arden asked stiffly now, breaking through her meandering contemplations with the same question she had convinced herself he had never spoken.

The words, and the tone of his voice, penetrated the fog of pleasure infecting her mind. She heard both quite clearly this time. There was no mistaking them. Nor was there any mistaking his lack of enthusiasm. He was not proposing to her in a fit of mad passion. No indeed, the question was one asked in obligation.

Which was just as well, because Hazel did not want to marry any man, and certainly not one as unsuitable as an English duke, for heaven's sake. There was nothing she could offer a man like him, aside from her mind and her body. She had no wish to simper and sit about pouring tea, or learning the proper forms of address. She did not know when to curtsy—often, it would seem—when to bow—never, it would seem—and when to offer her hand to shake—also, apparently, never.

Was he teasing her? Making a poor attempt at a joke? She searched his gaze, uncertain. He seemed sincere, but there was no telling. So much of the beautiful man before her remained an enigma.

"Don't be silly," she said at last, with a light trill of laughter meant to deflect his question and his intense regard both.

It was the wrong thing to say, and she recognized it too late, when he stiffened, his shoulders straightening, his lips tensing. "You laugh at me, madam?"

She could explain all the reasons she found levity in their current situation. For one thing, the Duke of Arden could be haughty, arrogant, and condescending even in the nude. For another, she could not stop admiring his body, her eyes slipping to the heaviness of his thick shaft, which, even spent, was large. Oddly lovely. She could not help but wonder how that part of him had possibly found a home within her.

But none of these sentiments bore repeating, not to the naked, peeved Duke of Arden, after he had just proposed marriage to her.

Instead, she scooted nearer to him, a foreign rush of tenderness bubbling up within her. She cupped his cheeks, feeling the decadent prickle of his whiskers against her palms. "I laugh at myself," she said, and this was true. "I am no duchess, Lucien, and you know it. You pay me an honor. A foolish honor, but an honor nonetheless. Thank you, but of course the answer is no. I cannot, nor do you wish for my answer to be yes."

"I pay you an honor too late." The set of his sensual mouth was grim. "Perhaps you are too much of an innocent to realize the consequences of what I have just done, but I am not. I will take responsibility for my actions."

"This is not the first time we have engaged in this folly," she reminded him. "I fail to see what makes this any different than the last."

"I spent inside you, Hazel," he ground out. One of his big hands splayed over her abdomen, warm and possessive. "You could become with child."

Ah. Understanding finally hit her. The hot spurt inside her had been his seed. She ought to have noticed he had not finished upon her body as he had the last time. But she had been too far gone, mindless in the pleasure he bestowed upon her, and she had failed to realize the difference.

A chill ran through her for a moment as she contemplated the changes to her life should she bear a child. But then she thought of how it would feel to hold a child in her belly, and in her arms, to gaze down upon an infant bearing Lucien's dark hair and strong nose, of how it would feel to keep a part of him with her forever, and she knew a strange pang of longing.

She suppressed that unwanted emotion, tamping it down inside her, for it would do her no good in this moment. And likely not in any that came after, either.

"It is doubtful there will be a child," she told him. "As of now, there is none. I thank you for the offer, but once again, I must gratefully decline."

"You must gratefully decline," he repeated, a new emotion edging his baritone.

Bitterness? Anger? Could it be he was offended by her refusal, even though he had not wished to make her the offer in the first place?

"Yes, I must." She leaned closer to him and pressed a firm, close-mouthed kiss to his lips. "Thank you for the honor you pay me. Some other woman, a fine lady, born and bred for the role, will make you a fine duchess one day. But that woman is not, and can never be, me."

"There will be no other woman." He shook his head slowly, his jaw as tense as the rest of him. "I will never marry nor have children if I can help it. I made the offer to you, because of my own lack of control. I will not allow you, or a child, to suffer because of me. I suffered enough at the hands of my own mother."

His admission he did not want to marry her was hardly a surprise, but even so, it should have stung. Instead, all she could feel was an ache in her heart for him. He was still hurting from what had happened, however many years ago. He had said he was a lad. She tried to imagine the Duke of Arden as a young man. Would he have been tall and forbidding even then, with a head full of dark, wavy locks? Or would he have been different, his heart unmarred by pain? Would he have been quicker to smile, to laugh, to love?

"I am sorry for the pain she caused you." As she spoke, she held his cheek in one hand and moved to stroke his hair with the other. She had noted how he seemed to like her to touch him there. Nothing carnal or sensual about it; the mere stroke of her hand over his head, a wordless way of showing him she cared.

"She was selfish and weak, and she left my sister and me behind, without thinking of the agony she would leave us in," he bit out. "Knowing she did not love us enough to live, that she chose to die. It is a pain I would not wish upon my mortal enemy. But she was also mad, Hazel. I have vowed I will never visit such suffering upon any progeny of my own." He stopped, sucking in a shuddering breath.

The hurt in his voice touched something deep inside her. She took him into her arms then, as naturally as if she had always done so. As naturally as if she would always have the right, even though she knew she would not. Her assignment here would end, and they would part. Perhaps even before then.

But for now…for now, she could hold this strong, handsome man in her arms. And she could comfort him. She ran her hands up and down the planes of his back, gliding over his well-muscled flesh, absorbing his heat. "I understand, Lucien. My mother abandoned me too, and I have spent many days railing against her. Other days, I feel sad. Still other days, I feel thankful. I feel that perhaps she gave me the best life she could have, that leaving me—whether right or wrong, for good or for ill—was, to her, the best decision she could make."

His arms banded around her then, crushing her into him. It was another rare show of vulnerability from a man she had come to believe was mostly impervious. His hot breath ruffled her hair, and his lips moved against her scalp as he spoke.

"I am sorry, Hazel," he choked out. "I have never lost myself and done something so bloody foolish. If I could take it back, I would. The best I can do is to offer you the protection of my name."

"It will be well, Lucien," she promised, because even if she could not be certain of the outcome, she knew she would make it right, however she must. She had been mostly alone in the world for all her life, and she had come to depend upon herself. She alone knew what she was capable of, and she alone had the power to accomplish it. "You need not worry on my account. I have been taking care of myself for a very long time."

"Promise me, if there should be issue from what happened between us tonight, you will tell me," he insisted, still holding her tight.

She wanted to say the words, to give him the promise and the benediction he required, yet, her lips would not move. If she became with child, she would not force him into marriage. And neither would she subject herself to a loveless union with a man who felt trapped. A man who had just confessed he never wished to wed or sire children of his own. She did not belong here in his glittering world. She belonged elsewhere, traveling, moving with the wind.

Perhaps not New York. Perhaps somewhere else. Paris beckoned, in fact, and she had never been to France. Wistfully, she imagined herself living there, only to wonder how she would earn her bread if she were to bear a child. She had saved funds, of course, and one of her reasons for taking on the position in the Special League had been the lucrative offer made to her by the Home Office. She had been able to take a leave from her position as a Pinkerton agent. She had always imagined she would return, take up where she had left off, but now, for the first time, the lure of something else called her.

"Hazel," he repeated, for he was not a fool, and he knew what her silence meant. "Promise me you will not leave if there is a child. Promise me you will marry me so the child can bear my name."

But she could not make such a promise. "Lucien, I cannot be a duchess. I do not belong here in your world."

"Hazel."

His voice was uncompromising. But she had not risen to the ranks of the most esteemed Pinkerton agents because she folded easily, like a gambler with a bad hand of cards. She was steely when she needed to be, which had been just about every day of her life thus far.

Still, she had no wish to argue with him. "Lucien, you cannot change the truth. I would make an abysmal duchess. I wear trousers, I am a Pinkerton agent, and I have no desire to be a debutante."

"That is just as well," he said, his body pressing more intimately against hers, so she felt the heavy thickness of his shaft rising against her. "Because I have never desired a debutante. But I do desire *you*."

Heaven help her, he wanted her again. The knowledge lit an answering fire of need within her. This was where she could meet him. The physical connection between them: they were electric together. It was uncontrollable, undeniable. And she could not resist even if she wanted.

Because she could not give him the promise he desired, she tipped her head back, her gaze meeting his. She could never become his wife, but neither could she deny herself the opportunity to know him. To run her hands over his body, to kiss him, to welcome him inside her. Joining with him fulfilled her in a way she had never previously imagined possible.

"Good," she said, running her nails over the blades of his shoulders, up his neck. "Because I desire you as well, and I fear we have already wasted too much time this evening in worrying over something that will never even come to pass."

"If it should—"

She pressed her mouth to his, ending their discussion in the best possible manner. She would never promise to become Arden's wife, because he did not want a wife, and she did not want a husband. No matter how much she wanted him, and no matter how deeply knowing Lucien had changed her, she could never marry him. She would not chain them both to a life of regrets.

To her relief, he kissed her back, forgetting—at least, for now—the promises he had demanded from her. They moved together to the center of his bed, mouths fused, bodies straining, ready for each other again. This time, when he entered her, they both sighed. It was not just a joining, but a homecoming. She clasped him to her, riding the waves of ecstasy as they pounded through her in time to his thrusts, and they reached their release simultaneously. He withdrew in enough time, spending himself all over her belly. She shook beneath him as the spasms of her own pleasure overtook her.

Afterward, he settled alongside her and drew the coverlets over them both, settling her back against his chest.

"I ought to return to my chamber," she protested sleepily. But her body was humming with sensation, and the muscled warmth of him at her back proved too tempting a lure.

"Hush," he commanded, his arm going over her waist, as if that was where it belonged. "Stay with me for a time."

She was tired, so tired her bones melted, her body sated in the most glorious fashion possible. And nothing could rival the feeling of Lucien's big body wrapped around hers, his heart beating against her shoulder.

"Only for a bit," she acquiesced, on a sigh of pure contentment.

"For as long as you like."

She felt his lips upon the crown of her head, a simple kiss that landed somewhere in the vicinity of her heart. She allowed the false joy to remain, even though she knew this was a fleeting happiness, that they came from opposite worlds, and all too soon, she would return to hers. Or to her next adventure. Whichever felt right. Whichever came first; the need for duty, or the need to wander. She had devoted herself to both in her life.

She would miss him, Hazel thought, when she left, and this realization, more than any other that evening, was a revelation. Hazel snuggled more firmly against him, taking what comfort she could get from him while it lasted.

LUCIEN AWOKE, BURNING with an absurd desire which refused to be ignored, along with an inevitable sense of realization. A realization something had changed inside him. Perhaps it had been gradually altering over the course of weeks. Perhaps it had been sudden, spurred by his weakness last night. He did not know.

It was a new sort of desire. Not one of the flesh. It nattered at him as he rose from bed. It battered down his defenses as he rang for his valet to help him prepare for the day. No matter how hard he tried, the desire would not dissipate. If anything, it gained strength and insistence, prodding at him, until he acknowledged it with a sigh as he tightened the belt of his dressing gown with an irritable yank.

He wanted to make Hazel happy.

There it was; that foreign, undeniable sensation, rising up within him. For the first time, he wanted more from a woman than the slaking of his bodily needs. He did not just want a bed partner. He wanted to make her feel protected and wanted and cherished.

He could do none of those things now as the sun rose over London. She was long gone, of course, having once more slipped from his arms and from his bed in the early hours of the morning, before the sun had risen. He had watched her in the moonlit shadows as she donned her robe and belted it firmly at the waist. Her pale curves were glorious, even in the darkness.

But it had not been her luscious feminine form which had stirred him the most. Rather, it had been the way she had quietly padded to his side of the bed and bent down to press a kiss to the top of his head. He had closed his eyes and feigned sleep for her approach, keeping his breathing even and rhythmic.

A simple gesture, a mimicry perhaps, of the kiss he had bestowed upon her before they had fallen asleep in each other's arms. But it had crept inside him, that kiss. She had lingered for a moment before leaving the chamber, and even then, not without kicking a chest of drawers and cursing beneath her breath, which was altogether Hazel, and somehow, also altogether endearing.

For a long time, he had lain awake after she had gone, staring blankly at the ceiling, her final, gentle kiss haunting him. She had kissed him as if he mattered to her. As if she cared. And it did not stop haunting him now, as his valet appeared and went through the motions of preparing him for the day. Fresh shirt, waistcoat, and neck cloth laid out, new trousers, and a shave.

Through his daily ritual, he ruminated in silence, wondering what this newfound desire to make Hazel happy meant. He had been accustomed to looking after himself and Violet. Was it the notion of potentially fathering a child, after all the efforts he had made to avoid doing so all these years, that had affected his wits? Or was it Hazel's unprecedented reaction to his proposal?

She had denied him. *Christ*, she had dared to laugh first. He ought to have been infuriated. Insulted. After all, they were as disparate as she suggested on the surface. She was an American; he was an Englishman. She had been raised in an orphanage, and he had been born the son of a duke. His wealth derived from the Dukes of Arden who preceded him. Hers was earned.

As she had pointed out, she was no debutante. She swore when she thought no one else could hear her. He had no doubt she could not play an instrument or sing, that she had never dabbled in watercolors or needlework, or any of the other feminine arts. Undoubtedly, she would not even know the proper manner in which one poured tea. She shook hands, she wore trousers, and she fell into her seat as if she were a sack of flour.

There was no reason why he ought to suddenly be seized by the urge to buy her flowers as if he were a suitor. Or to make her laugh. To make her smile. To watch her bright eyes light with inner joy.

And there was damn well no reason at all why he ought to feel disappointed she had turned him down. Why he ought to sit as his valet neatly shaved his jaw in swift, efficient strokes, and think about ways he could change her mind. He had vowed to never marry. The title could pass on to a distant cousin. The tainted bloodline would stop with him.

Yet, in the wake of his lapse of caution last night, the notion of siring a child had seemed real to him for the first time. Not just real, it had seemed *possible*. And as he had pressed his palm over the softness of Hazel's bare belly, envisioning it swelling with his child, he had been attacked by a vicious surge of longing, accompanying the familiar dread. The two opposing emotions had blended into a confused tangle he was still attempting to sort out by the light of day.

"Dobbins?" he said into the silence, as his valet finished the shave.

"Yes, Your Grace?"

"Why did you marry Mrs. Dobbins?" he asked.

Ordinarily, he preferred to keep to himself and did not attend to the matters of his domestics. He usually kept busy attempting to manage his investigations for the Home Office and the Special League. But his manservant was enough a part of his daily routine, and he knew Dobbins had gotten married in the last few years.

If his valet thought it strange Lucien had chosen to discuss his personal life with him, he did not allow it to show. His expression remained implacable as he restored the razor to its case. "I married her because I love her, Your Grace. I determined I wished to spend the rest of my life with her, to have children."

A normal response, Lucien supposed. Expected. In Lucien's world, most peers married to either preserve or restore fortunes and old familial dynasties. Ladies married to save their fathers and brothers the burden of supporting them. Romantic love was often an afterthought, if one even believed it existed. Which Lucien did not. He loved his sister and Aunt Hortense, but that was different.

"You believe in romantic love, Dobbins?" he queried next, striving to keep his voice even, perhaps a touch disinterested.

The servant looked surprised for an instant, before he schooled his expression. "Of course I do, Your Grace."

"Hmm," he said noncommittally, as he shrugged into his shirt. He was not certain how to answer a man who seemed to believe love was as real as the sky overhead. "What would you have done if Mrs. Dobbins had refused to wed you?"

Dobbins paused in the act of aiding him with his necktie. "I suppose I would have persisted, sir, until her answer was yes."

He mulled that over whilst he donned his waistcoat. Persistence in life was good. He and Dobbins could agree upon that score, at least. But persistence when one had already been dismissed was another matter entirely. It smacked of desperation, and he was not, nor had he ever been, a desperate man.

Did he want to marry Hazel? No, of course he did not. He did not want to marry anyone, ever. What the bloody hell was wrong with him? Where was all the maudlin sentimentalism heralding from? Why could he not shake this strange, incipient longing from his chest? Why was he now mired in this inexplicable notion that having Hazel in his bed every night, Hazel carrying his child, Hazel becoming his duchess, would please him in a way nothing and no one else could?

"How would you have persisted, Dobbins?" he asked at last, his curiosity driving at him with the force of a swinging cricket bat.

Dobbins was silent for a moment as he helped Lucien put on his coat.

"I would have courted her, Your Grace," he said at length, his tone thoughtful, as if to suggest he had simply won Mrs. Dobbins' hand outright, and it had required frightfully little effort on his part. *Lucky chap.* "I would have done everything in my power to make her smile and laugh."

Courting.

Lucien had never courted anyone. Had never even possessed the slightest desire to do so. Courting led to marriage, and marriage led to children, and children led to the possibility of him inflicting his mother's madness upon an innocent. And that, he could not do.

But there was that question again, that voice which would not be ignored inside him. Making him wonder what he would do if the outcome was already determined. What if Hazel were already carrying his babe? The die would have been cast, the decision made. If the choice was already out of his hands, what would he do?

He refused to examine it too closely just now.

Lucien smoothed a hand down each of his sleeves. "That is excellent advice, Dobbins. I thank you."

"Are you...are you wishing to court a lady, Your Grace?" Dobbins dared to ask, perhaps emboldened by the personal nature of their dialogue this morning, quite extraordinary.

And Lucien found he was not bothered by the query. Nor

was he bothered by his answer, though perhaps he ought to have been.

"I think I may be, Dobbins," he said, the admission filling him with a curious sense of rightness. "Perhaps."

ONLY ONE OTHER man had ever proposed marriage to Hazel, and Adam's request to make her his wife had occurred under decidedly different circumstances. He had been pleased to make the offer, for one thing. He had come calling to take her for a drive. She recalled the innocence of that long-ago moment quite fondly now, as she prepared herself to enter the dining room in Lark House.

The scent of breakfast wafted to her as she remembered how Adam's cheeks had been tinged with pink, how his hands had shaken upon the reins, and how he had seemed nervous. Smiling too much, talking too loudly. When he had given her his mother's ring, she had been moved to tears, an overwhelming sense of belonging blossoming inside her. The feeling that, at long last, after all her years without a home and a family, she would finally, *finally* have one of her own.

But that had not been meant to be, and the young woman she had been then would scarcely recognize the world-weary woman she had become. She still wore the ring upon her finger, but she had never been able to wear it as his wife. The ring and a *carte de visite* bearing his young, unsmiling countenance were all that remained, along with the love in her heart, which had never faded. But she had realized, somehow along the way, loving Adam did not mean she could not have room in her heart for others.

She hesitated outside the dining room, uncertain of how she should proceed after the duke within had proposed to marry her the night before. What if his aunt, the queenly Lady Beaufort, was present this morning? How would Hazel face her, without her face blushing crimson with guilt? What if Arden regretted his actions, his words? What if he wished he had never offered to marry her at all? Would it matter? Would she care?

There was such a contrast between the two proposals she had received, one from the heart and the other under duress. One receiving her instant *yes,* and the other her instant *no.*

And yet, she could not deny she was conflicted about not only Lucien's proposal, but her reaction to it. She had spent most of the night in his bed. She knew him in a way she had never known another man: his scent, the groan deep in his throat when he lost himself inside her, the taste of his lips, the weight of him, thick and heavy and firm in her hand, the taut sinews of his back, the silkiness of his hair. Some foolish part of her wished his proposal had been made in the same spirit as Adam's. Some part of her wished their worlds were not so disparate, that she could have said *yes.*

Silly, she knew. She was better on her own, just as she had always been. Life was simpler when she had no heart to worry after but hers. If she put herself in danger, she alone would pay the price. If she did not love Lucien, she would not have to lose him.

Realizing she could not continue tarrying at the threshold of the dining room, caught in the tangled web of her conflicting emotions and desires, she took a deep, steadying breath, and entered. She had taken care in her dress this morning, donning her divided skirt and bodice, instructing Bunton to confine her hair in a rather severe knot. She did not wish to look feminine. She wanted to remind Arden she was his partner, not his bedmate.

Last night could not be repeated, she admonished herself

sternly as she entered the room with its striped wallpaper and immense windows admitting the morning sun. At least Lady Beaufort was not in attendance, and there would be no glowers of disapproval this morning, though she did wonder if Lucien's aunt was avoiding her or if she was truly that ill. Hazel did not like to think of Lady Beaufort suffering. Perhaps she could check on Lucien's aunt later.

For now, she would forget the way her body reacted to Arden's. Pretend none of it had happened. It was only the animal within her, after all, a base need for pleasure. Pretending her thoughts were not so heavily burdened, she forced herself to smile at Reynolds, who was overseeing breakfast. He gave her an imperious look in return, his expression never wavering. The man seemed perpetually immovable.

Her gaze drifted inevitably to Lucien.

He had risen at her entrance, and offered her a courtly bow now, his emerald eyes burning into her. His formality rendered her immobile. She stopped halfway across the chamber, staring at him stupidly. Had he grown even more handsome overnight? With his jaw freshly shaven, his wavy, dark hair brushing the collar of his jacket, his charcoal waistcoat and perfectly tailored trousers, the crispness of his shirt and necktie, he was breathtaking.

He made her remember in vivid detail what had happened the night before. The way he had dropped to his knees, making love to her with his mouth. Between her thighs, she pulsed and ached at the memory.

She burned.

And yearned.

And hungered for more.

You cannot have more, she reminded herself sternly. It was impossible. Irresponsible. She had told him once that he made her want to break all her rules. But in truth, he made her wish she possessed no rules at all. How could she ever spend the next weeks, perhaps months, at his side without wanting to touch him? Without being tempted to kiss him or to offer her body to him once more? Without stealing to his bedchamber in the midst of the night?

Doing so seemed as likely as the Atlantic Ocean drying up in one day. So much intensity, such deep connection, could not be vanquished. But she had to protect herself. Too much more time in his arms, and she would lose her heart.

"Good morning, Miss Montgomery," he said in his impeccable aristocratic accent, one more reminder of why she could not run to him again this evening.

"Good morning, Your Grace," she returned with equal formality. She would have offered a curtsy, as she reckoned it was the proper response. But she was wearing her trousers, and dipping like a debutante seemed silly. So she bowed back at him.

His lips twitched. "That will be all, Reynolds," he announced to the butler without ever removing his gaze from Hazel.

The butler and pair of footmen assisting him disappeared with alarming haste, leaving Hazel alone with the man her body did not want to resist. She frowned at him for being so handsome, for using his tongue so well. For making her come undone so thoroughly, she had been nothing but a quivering, spent mass of woman in his bed. For showing her what she had been missing. For making her want something she could never have.

"You laughed at me," she accused, feeling in the mood to argue. Perhaps it would be a way to arm herself against him.

"You laughed at me as well, if you will recall," he countered, raising a brow. "Please, sit. We have a great deal to accomplish today, and I would like to get an early start so we have enough time to go on an excursion later. I know how grumbly Famished Hazel can be."

The lightness in his tone took her aback, for it was not at all what she had anticipated. Indeed, it was almost…intimate, for lack of a better word. Jarring, for certain.

"I laughed at the absurdity of your question," she reminded him, "not at you. For you know as well as I that it was a question you ought never to have asked me."

"Why not?" He skirted the table suddenly, moving past her in such proximity her swift inhalation encompassed his scent. He withdrew a chair and gestured toward her imperiously. "Have a seat, Hazel."

"I will sit when I wish to do so," she countered, for just because they had been lovers—past tense, she reminded herself, as it could not happen again—did not give him a right to order her about. She would breakfast when and as she pleased.

"You did not answer my question," he persisted.

"You know as well as I all the reasons why you ought never to have asked me to marry you. Everything about me is unconventional."

"That is one of the things I admire about you," he said seriously. "Sit."

"What are you doing?" she demanded.

This was not how they were meant to conduct their breakfast. They were meant to sit, attended by servants, so that nothing untoward could be said, and then focus upon their investigations, before returning to the site of the railway bombings and meeting with Winchelsea. Business. Impersonal. Formal. That was what she had wanted this morning.

How was she to contend with a Duke of Arden, who was looking upon her as if he wanted to consume *her* for breakfast, instead of the sausages and eggs?

"You would prefer I pretend not to admire you?" he asked innocently. "Strange indeed, Hazel, for I would think an independent woman such as yourself would demand her suitor admire her."

Suitor?

The word may as well have been a curse. Her heart thumped faster. Louder. Her palms began to sweat.

"You are not my suitor, Arden," she corrected coolly.

"What if I am?" he returned, his countenance deadly serious.

"You cannot be," she snapped, her tenuous grip on her own feelings making her irritable. "We have been over this tired discussion before. If there is something you need to know, I will tell you. If not, you need not worry about me. Very likely, I will be on my way soon enough anyway. We already know the identity of the dynamitards. Now it will be a matter of catching them, before they elude us."

"You see? Famished Hazel, baring her claws." He gestured toward the chair again. "Sit. Please."

Her stomach chose that second to deliver a loud, indignant, and wholly unladylike rumble. Bemused, she pressed a clammy hand over her belly, wishing for once she had worn a corset, for perhaps the infernal contraption would have staved off the sound.

Her cheeks went hot. Arden said nothing, merely regarded her calmly. Knowingly.

Well, she was hungry. There was no denying it. And he seemed content to continue their impasse, he at the chair, she standing in the midst of the dining room like a fool. So she did the only thing she could think of doing. She strode to his vacated chair and seated herself with as much elegance as she could muster. She was aware she possessed precious little grace, but she could force herself to conform when the situation required it.

She laid Arden's napkin neatly in her lap and regarded him from the opposite side of the table. "I am quite famished, Mr. Arden. Thank you."

She took care to drawl the words, lifting his untouched coffee to him in a mock toast, before she took a sip. The decadent, dark liquid rolled over her tongue, bitter and rich and delicious. She had to admit, he had excellent taste in coffee. Even if he was an overbearing, arrogant duke.

He inclined his head and lowered himself into the seat he had been offering her. "Touché, my dear. I only hope you like kippers."

She glanced down at his laden plate with dismay, discovering a grouping of the revolting, smoked herrings the English so favored upon the fine china. "I adore them," she lied with a brilliant smile.

"Excellent." There was a smile in his voice, but she refused, on principle, to look back at him.

Her stomach growled again. Grimly, she snatched up a fork. She had been hasty in her decision to steal his place at the table, that much was plain. But by no means would she retreat now. At least, there was also a poached egg and some sausage. She would simply consume the disagreeable creatures first, while breathing through her mouth, then drown them with delicious coffee, before ending the meal in epicurean delights.

She stabbed at the thing, then cut off a bite-size portion and stuffed it into her mouth, chewing hastily. Hazel swallowed before washing it down with coffee.

"Excellent indeed," she gasped, for her gulp of coffee was hot, and the flavor of smoked fish remained redolent on her palate, much to her chagrin.

"Hazel."

She glanced up at him at last, her eyes watering from the combination of the dreadful kippers and the hot coffee. "Yes?"

"You do not have to eat the damned kippers to prove a point." He looked as wry as he sounded.

"I enjoy them." She speared another bite, lifted it to her lips. Even the texture of the thing was enough to make her want to gag. Truly, how could he eat this wretched fare? She would sooner eat the bark of a magnolia tree.

"Hazel."

She swallowed more coffee to mask the untenable flavor in her mouth, just a sip this time. "Arden?"

"Lucien," he corrected gently. The smile he gave her was disconcertingly tender. "I do believe we are beyond formality at this point, are we not? And please, for the love of all that is holy, cease eating the kippers, lest you vomit all over the breakfast table."

Yes, they were well beyond formality.

Yes, the kippers were horrible.

She sighed. "What do you want from me, Lucien?"

His sensual mouth hiked into a deeper smile. "Many things. But to begin, I would like the honor of your company this evening."

"This evening?"

This time, he grinned at her with such ruthlessness, twin divots appeared in his cheeks. Heavens, the Duke of Arden had *dimples*. And they were a revelation. As was the man himself.

"Yes, that is what I said just now, I do believe, my dear," he said calmly. "I would like you to accompany me this evening."

Was this his strange way of attempting to get her to reconsider his proposal, because of his own guilt? If so, he was destined for disappointment.

"I will not go to one of your balls or society functions, Arden," she warned. "It is out of the question. I have no notion of your fancy rules and fancy ways, nor do I have any wish to. I am as you see me, unapologetically."

"No ball," he said smoothly, reaching for a plate of Bayonne ham and liberating a slice for his new plate. "Just an excursion."

"What manner of excursion?" she demanded, eyes narrowing as she studied his calm façade.

He looked almost princely as he glanced in her direction. Certainly too handsome and too blue-blooded for her. "Agree to join me, and you shall see."

She clenched her jaw. Oh, the rotten man. He knew her well enough, far better than she sometimes expected. And he knew she would not be able to withstand the mystery of where he planned to take her. If she refused him, the question would persist, taunting her, making her wonder. If she agreed, she would know.

And she wanted to agree. Of course she did. The Duke of Arden could offer to escort her to the gates of hell, and she would gladly accept.

"Perhaps," she allowed.

"There is no 'perhaps,' sweetheart," he countered. "There is only 'yes' or 'no.' Which shall it be?"

"My pride demands that it is 'no,'" she said. "But my pride also demands that I eat these revolting things you call kippers. I do not think I can stomach the latter, so my pride may well have to go to the devil."

Indeed, she rather feared it had already gone there.

"One word, Hazel. Say it."

She sighed. He would give her no quarter, as always. And she would expect nothing less. "Yes," she grumbled. "Very well. I will accompany you on this excursion, whatever it may be. But only if I do not have to eat this nonsense."

He grinned. "No one ever said you had to eat the kippers, my dear. Perhaps you ought to stop heeding your pride."

She was sure her pride was the only thing she ought to listen to. But for now, there only was one voice her heart wanted to hear, and it belonged to the Duke of Arden.

Chapter Fifteen

*H*AZEL KNOCKED ON Lady Beaufort's chamber door half a dozen times before she finally received an answer. She and Lucien had returned from a full afternoon of investigations and interrogations—questioning the staff of the hotel, the railway workers, and other bystanders and witnesses. Lucien's aunt had been once more absent from dinner, and this time, Hazel had been too concerned to avoid seeking the older woman out to make certain she was well.

"I told you, Greaves, I am not hungry," came the unmistakable voice of Lucien's aunt at last.

"It is not Greaves, my lady," Hazel ventured, bracing herself for the stinging censure Lady Beaufort would once more hurl her way. "It is Hazel."

"Miss Montgomery?" Lady Beaufort's voice was hesitant, edged with a note of disbelief.

Hazel suppressed a smile. Of course Lady Beaufort would refuse to refer to her with her given name. Formality was her mantle of protection. "Yes, my lady. It is Miss Montgomery. May I enter?"

"No."

Well, she supposed she ought not to have expected any different. Still, she was nothing, if not determined.

"Please, my lady?" she tried, lacing her voice with sweetness. Even the English were susceptible to a drawl, she found.

There was silence on the other side of the door.

"I am mightily stubborn, Lady Beaufort," she warned without heat. "And my constitution is hearty. I can stand here, asking for you to let me in, for the next few hours at least. Why, on one of my cases, I pretended to be an invalid and stayed at the home of a suspected murderer for an entire week, spreading droplets of false blood all over his hallway floors, until he finally confessed to his crime, believing he was being haunted for his sins."

It was a true story, and one she was not necessarily proud of, for she preferred not to resort to trickery to wrangle her quarry. But as it turned out, it was just the bait she needed to dangle before Lady Beaufort.

The door opened.

Lady Beaufort faced her, pale and drawn. Her eyes were swollen, bloodshot, and even her hair was bereft of its usual severe—if outmoded—style of two loops worn over her ears. She was not even dressed in her typical mourning, but wrapped up in a plain gray robe, a simple cap on her head.

And she had been crying.

The realization took Hazel aback.

"Come inside, if you must," Lady Beaufort announced coolly. "I cannot bear the notion of the domestics hearing you carry on about such vulgar nonsense."

There was the Lady Beaufort Hazel knew. She flashed a smile, ignoring the insult as she entered Lucien's aunt's chamber. She noted at once the small nuances which told her this chamber must have belonged to Lady Beaufort for a long time.

The wallpaper was gray damask, but the walls were hung with a vast array of elaborate needlework framed in gilt housing, and portraits of a gentleman she could only imagine must be Lord Beaufort. From the coverlets to the smell of the room to the very carpet, every inch of the handsomely appointed chamber bespoke it was Lady Beaufort's domain.

Lucien had clearly been taking care of his widowed aunt for years, and the knowledge settled in Hazel's heart. It was plain to see he was a good man. But she had not sought out his aunt so she could fall deeper beneath the Duke of Arden's spell.

Rather, she had come here to ascertain for herself the state of Lady Beaufort's well-being. She spun about to face her ladyship, who was walking, as usual, with the aid of her handsomely decorated cane. But aside from her halting gait, there appeared no heightening of her illness.

"Why are you hiding in your chamber, my lady?" she asked.

Lady Beaufort's chin snapped up. "I do not hide. I am ill. Can you not see?"

"I can see you have been weeping," Hazel said. "Why?"

"Curse you," Lady Beaufort spat with great feeling, her eyes—the same green, Hazel noted, as Lucien's—brimming with hellfire. "How dare you speak to me with such impudence, you vulgar American vagabond?"

Hazel suppressed a wince. "Even vulgar American vagabonds can feel concern for someone who is suffering, my lady," she persisted. "What is the cause of your grief? Is it me?"

"You possess an awfully high opinion of yourself to imagine I would concern myself over you, Miss Montgomery," Lady Beaufort said. "Of course, I worry about Arden's reputation, but he can weather any scandal you decide to cast in his direction. No, these tears are purely selfish. They are for me alone."

Hazel had not been expecting such brutal honesty, but she could respect it. "The tears are for you?"

Lady Beaufort sniffled. "To be precise, they are for my beloved Beaufort. Today marks the day of my Arnold's death."

It was as she had suspected then. Hazel's heart gave a pang. "I am sorry, my lady. I know how difficult the death of the one you love can be."

"How can you know, Miss Montgomery?" Lady Beaufort demanded. "I daresay you never knew love in your life, else you would have been married already at your advanced age."

The advanced age comment did smart, but she supposed it was not altogether incorrect. Hazel was twenty-eight years of age or thereabouts. She would never know for certain.

"I would know, because I loved and lost the man I was going to marry," she said, though her voice trembled a bit under the force of remembrance. "He was shot in front of me, and he breathed his last breath on this earth as he lay dying in my arms. *That* is how I know, my lady."

Lucien's always dignified aunt appeared to crumple before her. "I am sorry, Miss Montgomery. I ought not to have said something so horrid."

"I understand the bitterness grief brings." She paused, offering Lady Beaufort a gently reassuring smile. "Do you care for company?"

Lucien's aunt was quiet for so long, Hazel braced herself for a rejection and a request for her to leave. Instead, Lady Beaufort sighed and gestured to a sitting area near the hearth. "We may as well sit, Miss Montgomery."

Her grudging invitation made Hazel's smile deepen. Here, at last, was evidence Lady Beaufort did not loathe her entirely. "Thank you, my lady."

They settled into the overstuffed chairs by the cheerful little fire crackling in the grate. The autumn day was cold and wet, and the warmth of the fire felt good to Hazel after a day spent in and out of the carriage and traipsing about in the railways. She recalled Lady Beaufort's absence at dinner, and her assertion she was not hungry, when she had assumed Hazel had been her lady's maid.

"Have you eaten, my lady?" she asked, as she arranged her divided skirts in a concession for Lady Beaufort's sensibilities. "May I ring for some tea?"

Lucien's aunt was staring pointedly at Hazel's trousers, but to her credit, she made no comment on them. "No, thank you, Miss Montgomery. I have already taken my tea for the day, and I have no desire to eat. This day has been a dark one for years. I allow myself a few days of sorrow, and then I go on."

Hazel rather suspected Lady Beaufort had not, in fact, gone on. Her perpetual mourning attire, the brooch she wore pinned to her bodice each day, even the style of her hair and dress, outdated by decades, suggested a part of her remained trapped in a happier past. That part of her had never moved on from losing her husband. And Hazel saw a great deal of herself in the older woman, if she were brutally honest. The love she had lost had made her close her heart. She had devoted all her time and energy to being a Pinkerton agent.

"Sometimes," she said tentatively, "talking about what happened can help to ease the pain. Would you like to tell me?"

She knew she was prodding, that there was a chance Lucien's aunt would recoil and demand she leave at once. Still, she hoped the opposite would be true.

After another lengthy silence, punctuated by nothing more than the crackling fire and the rain pattering on the windows, Lady Beaufort took a deep, shuddering breath. "It was a carriage accident. And he suffered. I know he did. They did not find him for hours, and even then, he was still alive.

When they brought him back to me, I was convinced he would live. I just knew it in my heart."

Hazel said nothing, understanding there was more to the story, and that she needed to allow Lady Beaufort to tell it at her own pace. That she needed to unburden herself.

"He fought. For an entire night, he fought." Lady Beaufort's voice broke. "But he could not survive the injuries."

Her heart ached on the older woman's behalf.

"I am so sorry, my lady," Hazel said.

"As am I, Miss Montgomery," Lucien's aunt said, sounding weary. Almost defeated.

"Call me Hazel, if you please," she urged.

Lady Beaufort extracted a handkerchief from a pocket in her robe and dabbed at her eyes. Even that motion was elegant and refined. "I prefer Miss Montgomery."

Hazel almost smiled. It was a relief to have proof Lucien's aunt was still her redoubtable self, even in her grief. "As you wish, Lady Beaufort."

"You will not tell Arden about this undignified display, madam," Lucien's aunt warned her next. "He has suffered enough sadness in his lifetime."

"You refer to Arden's mother," Hazel guessed.

Lady Beaufort's brows rose. "He has spoken of the duchess with you?"

"Some," she admitted. "I can see it pains him."

"As well it ought," Lady Beaufort said sharply. "When I think of what that woman did to those poor children, leaving them as she did... And poor Arden, the manner in which he searched for her. He had no rest until he found his mother's body washed ashore. He carried her back to Albemarle himself."

Her heart ached anew at the thought of what Lucien had suffered. At the knowledge he had set out to find his mother, and had not stopped, until he carried her home himself.

"You have my promise I will not carry tales," she forced herself to say past the lump in her throat. "The last thing I would wish is to cause upset for either you or Arden, my lady. While I may be incapable of meeting your standards of comportment, I hope you will at least believe I hold your family in the highest of esteem."

Her ladyship treated her to a long, searching glance, before she finally gave a sniff—though whether of approval or disapproval, Hazel could not say. "Perhaps you might ring for a tray of tea for me after all, Miss Montgomery."

This time, Hazel did smile. "Of course, my lady."

Time did not dull the pain of a loss, but sometimes, the caring of others could replace the cold with a flood of life-affirming warmth. It was yet another lesson Hazel had learned since her arrival in England, and it was a good one, she decided, as she rose and headed for the bell pull. It was a lesson she would carry with her in her heart, even when Lark House, Lady Beaufort, and Lucien were nothing but memories.

LATER THAT EVENING, Lucien and Hazel arrived at their Portman Square destination, the carriage stopping on Baker Street.

"Will you tell me where you are taking me now?" Hazel asked.

Her lilting drawl made heat slide through him. He rather suspected she could recite poetry in Latin and still make his prick go hard, with nothing more than the rasp of her voice and the sweet trill of her accent.

"You will find out soon enough," he told her, hoping she

would like her surprise.

He had never before had an interest in playing the tourist in London, but for Hazel, he was willing to make an exception to his rule. It was a disturbing pattern he had come to recognize. How one woman could suddenly have so much power over him, was a vexing question he would interrogate later. For now, all he wanted to do was please her and make the smile return to her lips.

And kiss her.

And lift her skirts.

And sink home inside her.

But all of those, like the matter of her supremacy over him, would be examined another time. She had been adamant in her refusal of his proposal. She had been fiery at breakfast, prickly through their day of navigating the bombing scene, and then their meeting in Scotland Yard with Winchelsea and others. This evening, she was a different, softer side of Hazel. She had finally relented, at least as much as Hazel Montgomery ever deigned to relent.

He descended from the carriage and offered her his hand, which she promptly ignored, being Hazel. If his driver was laughing at him, Cobb certainly gave no indication. Just as well. Lucien would hate to have to sack the fellow, for then they would be obliged to obtain Hazel's favorite mode of London transportation, the hired hack.

He had put a great deal of effort into conjuring up the ideal manner in which a gentleman would court an unconventional woman such as Miss H.E. Montgomery. The Waxworks were gauche, it was true. Common also. A haven, no doubt, for garish spectators to spend their hard-earned shillings on a quick distraction. He had it on good authority that the optimal time to attend was under the cover of darkness, when the gas lamps were lit. Perhaps it added to the realism of the whole affair. Perhaps it was merely an ambience.

Either way, he was here. He had brought Hazel here. And he hoped like Hades it wasn't a misstep on his part. He wanted her to enjoy herself tonight. He offered her his arm to escort her into the building, and thankfully, she at least accepted that much from him. Her head tipped back to observe the structure they were about to enter.

"Madame Tussaud's Waxwork Exhibition," she read aloud. "How did you know I have been longing to visit?"

"A guess." He smiled back at her enthusiasm. "You are pleased?"

In truth, Hazel-when-happy was as easy to read as Hazel-when-hungry.

"I am very pleased, Lucien," she told him warmly.

Christ help him. He was lost for this woman.

He cleared his throat, attempting to gather his composure. "Good. Shall we be on our way?"

"Oh yes!" She clapped her hands together, much like a child who had been given a gift.

Her excitement was infectious, and he found himself grinning like a fool as he paid a shilling for each of them to enter. Hazel argued she wished to pay her own fee. He ignored her. She muttered "*damned arrogant lout*" beneath her breath. He ignored that as well, as they stepped through a turnstile and approached an attendant, who collected their outerwear and offered them a ticket in return. Another attendant, watching the procession of visitors with a stony glare, turned out to be a wax figure himself, though credibly lifelike in appearance.

"Oh! I thought he was real," Hazel murmured to him.

She was brimming with happiness, and he reveled in it. Basked in the glow of her as they made their way through the exhibit, wandering past the royal family, where fellow visitors had gathered to coo over the lifelike qualities of the wax assemblage. He had to admit the Duke of Connaught was represented especially well.

"Here," Hazel said then, *sotto voce*. "Look at your world."

"I am not a member of the royal family," he countered firmly, steering her away from the exhibit.

Devil take it, he had brought her here so she would enjoy herself. So she would focus less upon the disparities between them, and more upon the similitude. He guided them into the Hall of Kings, where most of the wax exhibits looked to be from centuries long gone.

"You are nobility," she countered at his side, when they stopped before a new exhibit. "Even your chamber pots are fancy."

Her observation wrung a startled bark of laughter from him.

"I do not think I have ever taken note of the chamber pots," he noted, reflecting on what she had said. "After adding the bathrooms and renovating, one hardly needs to even use them."

"Not unless one has been encouraged to consume an unthinkable quantity of port by the Duke of Arden," she said archly. "And one cannot make it to the bathroom in sufficient time to retch."

Guilt skewered him anew at his behavior. He had been an arse, and he knew it. "I deeply regret the manner in which I treated you upon your arrival, Hazel," he told her, his tone grave, for he meant every word of his apology. "I was wrong, and I am sorry."

"I do believe it had Athena depicted on the outside, and it was rimmed with gold."

It was not what he had expected her to say, and he turned to her askance. "I beg your pardon?"

"The commode," she elaborated. "It is white porcelain, rimmed with gold, and bears Athena on the outside. Who would bother with such extravagance for an item that is tucked beneath a bed, mostly gathering dust?"

She sounded bewildered, and he wanted to kiss her, but he did not, for they were in public, and there was a startlingly lifelike effigy of William of Normandy staring at them through his highness's rather lifelike glass eyes.

"I suppose it is old by now. Perhaps even a familial relic," he teased. "But entirely appropriate, if the goddess depicted on it is indeed Athena."

She frowned at him. "Appropriate how?"

"You are rather like a warrior goddess yourself," he admitted, before he could think better of the words.

A charming flush crept into her cheeks, but she smiled shyly and looked away, eyeing poor, stoic William. "Hardly a goddess, though I will admit the warrior has been apt, at times."

Her shyness charmed him. The more time he spent in her presence, the more he fell beneath her spell. He did not think he could ever find a more intriguing woman. It was not just her beauty and liveliness that drew him to her, it was…everything. Every part of her, each facet, all the nuances. All the wit and wonder, bravery and determination, the intelligence and wiliness, the brashness and the vigor, that comprised Hazel Elizabeth Montgomery.

"A warrior goddess," he repeated. "You must take me at my word."

"Must I?" She turned back to him, her brow raised, and the smile on her full, inviting lips would have been coquettish on any other woman. On Hazel, it was natural and artless. Breathtaking.

He was staring at her, mooning over her like a lovesick

puppy, and he did not give a good goddamn. There was no one about who knew him, and neither his fellow visitors milling about the wax exhibition nor the eerily still figures themselves held him in thrall. Only she did.

"You must," he said. "On account of all the instances in which you have astounded me, you must defer to my superior knowledge of the matter."

Her smile turned wry. "Astounded you, or confounded you?"

"Astounded me." His voice was gentle. Admiring. Just as he intended it to be. With his eyes, he told her what he did not dare say aloud with so many people about to overhear.

Her expression turned serious, her eyes darkening to a blue so deep, it was almost violet. Or perhaps it was a trick of the gas lamps. He could not be certain. Whatever the effect, he found himself lost in the still pools of those vibrant depths.

"Lucien," she murmured, half protest, half plea.

"I admire you greatly, Hazel," he told her unapologetically. "Surely you can see that by now. Surely I have made my esteem known. If I have not, I am a greater lout than I had supposed."

Her lips twitched. "You *can* be a lout at times."

Her observation smarted, even if it was true. *Because* it was true. But he would not shy away from it. Rather, he would face and acknowledge it, head on. He owed her so many apologies, he realized, he little knew where to begin. "I am sorry for the way we began. I was an utter ass, and I know it. You are incredibly talented, intelligent, and capable, and it has been my honor to work alongside you."

"Thank you." She bestowed one of her rare, truly blinding smiles upon him then, as if he had pleased her immeasurably. "It has been my honor to work alongside you as well."

They were silent for a beat, simply staring at each other,

an unspoken agreement passing between them. Gradually, awareness of their surroundings returned to Lucien as he felt the uncompromising stare of William of Normandy upon him. Not far from his side, the equally lifelike wax figure of William II stood, also gazing.

Perhaps in disapproval? How strange to think that a life could be remembered so many centuries after a death, so many vicissitudes of fortune later. What a uniquely human trait that was, the collection of thousands of years of memories. *History.* At once, a blessing and a curse.

"Have you seen enough of the Hall of Kings?" he asked her.

"I would dearly like to see The Chamber of Horrors," she said. "After all, you paid an extra six pence for the privilege, did you not?"

He was surprised, she had noticed, but he ought not to have been. Hazel was an observer. She studied the world and people around her, constantly absorbing and learning. What she saw, she used to her advantage, whether in private, or in the midst of an investigation.

"I did," he acknowledged. "Though I was not certain you would wish to enter a chamber bearing such a grim designation."

"That is the *only* reason I wish to enter." She paused, appearing to think better of her response, before continuing, "Well, that and the prospect of seeing Napoleon's traveling carriage. Of course, there is also the guillotine. Is it true that it is an actual, working guillotine, used during the French revolution?"

Yes, he decided, he had certainly made the right decision in bringing Hazel here. She was not the sort of woman who could be contained in a drawing room, or content to dance the quadrille. She was the sort of woman who thrilled at the prospect of walking into a chamber hung in black, notorious for its macabre collection.

"There is only one way to truly tell," he said. "After you, Miss Montgomery."

WEARY AFTER A day of investigations, followed by their impromptu trip to Madame Tussaud's, Hazel crossed the threshold of her guest chamber at Lark House on a contented yawn. Her evening with Lucien had been surprising. His desire to please her with the visit even more so.

His words returned to her now, making her smile anew. *I admire you greatly, Hazel.*

She knew the feeling all too well. Because not only did she admire Lucien, but she was beginning to fear she was losing her heart to him. It had happened gradually at first, spurred by his nearness, his kisses and caresses. But this evening, there had been something indefinable in the air. A current of knowledge that what was between them had changed.

Still, she was not prepared for that change. It frightened her, for she knew, regardless of how she felt for him, there could never be a permanent place in his life for someone like her. He had not broached the topic of his proposal again, and she was grateful for it. But he had certainly played the role of suitor well, charming her, making her laugh, escorting her about as if she were a queen on his arm.

She would remember this night and cherish it forever. She would—

Someone had been inside her chamber.

The realization interrupted the wayward bent of her musings. She knew it to her marrow. Years as a seasoned Pinkerton had taught her to have a heightened cognizance of her surroundings. But it was not just the instincts honed as an agent. Her mind liked order. She preferred organization. A clear scheme at all times.

Her writing surface, for instance. Wherever she was, regardless of the case she was investigating, she kept her journal on the left side of her desk, the ink at the right. Newspapers and other resources were stacked tidily at the top, leaving her writing space open and clean.

The disorganization on the writing desk in her guest chamber stood out first. She strode toward it, the hackles on her neck rising. To an impartial observer, nothing would appear out of order on the immaculately polished surface of the burled walnut desk. But her journal—the gift from Lucien with the handsome, creamy pages upon which she had yet to write a single word—was in the center of her desk. The newspapers depicting descriptions of the railway explosions were on the left. Her pen and ink were two inches out of place.

Someone had been shuffling through her personal effects.

The detective in her spun with questions. All the earlier merriment of the evening fled her. Icy fingers of dread gripped her gut. Who? Why? How?

And, most importantly, what else had that someone been doing?

Carefully, Hazel began a search of the chamber. Her garments were still hung with neat precision in the massive wardrobe. A peek into the adjoining bathroom revealed nothing untoward. Her soaps were laid out, a stack of clean towels awaiting her use.

Whoever had been within her chamber, their purpose had been clear. None of her personal items—not her sparse jewelry collection, not her brush and hairpins, not her stockings and shoes—had been moved or touched. The travel-battered carpetbag she had been carrying with her for years rose to her mind then. Although she had given the bulk of her notes to Lucien, there remained some important information contained within it still. Journals, notes on Emerald Club members, snippets of conversations she had overheard, newspaper clippings, a handful of telegrams she had managed to pilfer, amongst other pertinent documents.

She always kept the satchel beneath her bed, wherever she traveled. Out of the way, not immediately visible to others. Safe. Dread swirling in her gut, she dropped to her knees. In the low light of the gas lamp, she could not readily see through the murk beneath the bed hangings. Blindly, she groped, reaching forward, until her hand connected with an object.

But it was decidedly not the object she had been seeking. Nor was it an object that felt familiar. Her fingertips struck something hard. Wooden, she thought, and not finely fashioned either. Not polished, but rough. A box.

No, she realized as she slid the item from beneath her bed in dawning horror. *Good, sweet Lord in heaven.* Not a box at all. Her carpetbag had been stolen, and in its place, someone had left a bomb. She had to warn the household. Had to get to Lucien.

Heart pounding, she raced from her chamber and ran down the hall to find him.

Chapter Sixteen

"*I* T IS FORTUNATE indeed, Miss Montgomery, that you discovered the device when you did," announced Colonel Olden, the Home Office Chief Inspector of Explosives. "You had but an hour to spare before detonation."

An hour.

Fucking hell.

A flurry of Scotland Yard investigators and Special League agents had combed Lark House in search of the villain responsible for the device Hazel had found beneath her bed, and for the possible existence of additional bombs. Their exhaustive explorations had turned up nothing, and no one.

Which meant the bastards responsible were still out there, somewhere. Still capable of attempting to hurt Hazel again.

A chill settled over Lucien. Though he stood in the familiar confines of his study along with Hazel, Colonel Olden, and Winchelsea, the four walls seemed suddenly foreign. Someone had trespassed upon his home. Someone had infiltrated his staff, breached his defenses, and roamed the halls of Lark House in his absence, with the intent of murder and destruction.

There was no truer way to bring home the grim reality of the war they were waging against their faceless foes than this. The battle had been waged beneath his roof. But this battle was personal, because it had been an attack, not just upon him, but upon Hazel. Someone had hidden a bomb beneath her damned bed.

Someone had meant to kill her. The thought of Hazel sleeping peacefully in her bed when the device beneath it exploded sucked the air from his lungs. He felt as if a vise was squeezing his chest. A great roaring sound rushed in his ears, and for a moment, his vision darkened.

"Arden?" prompted Winchelsea.

He cleared his throat, realizing belatedly he was staring at Hazel, consumed by old fears and ghosts that were mingling with new. She was pale, all the joy from their earlier romp at Madame Tussaud's vanquished by the horror of having discovered the bomb beneath her bed. Thank God she was as skilled an agent as she was, and she had taken note of the subtle indications someone had intruded in her chamber. Lesser detectives than she may never have noticed.

But three pairs of eyes were upon him now, awaiting his reply, and he could not afford to continue to wallow in the unexpected feelings assaulting him. He cleared his throat. "I beg your pardon, Winchelsea. What was the question?"

"The timing of the invasion of your home," Winchelsea elaborated, looking as grim as Lucien felt. "What would you aim it to be? You mentioned that both yourself and Miss Montgomery had been away on an outing this evening. Do you believe it occurred then?"

"Unquestionably." He nodded, resisting the urge to pace the length of his study. Or worse, to take up some helpless object and send it hurtling through the mullioned windows overlooking the street.

"I do not believe you mentioned the nature of your excursion," the duke said.

Blast.

"Miss Montgomery and I had concluded our investigative

toiling for the day, and we aimed to seek some distraction by paying a visit to Madame Tussaud's Waxwork Exhibition," he explained, careful to keep his tone and expression neutral. The last complication he needed was to cause issues for Hazel by allowing the Home Office to discover they had been intimate.

"Waxworks?" Winchelsea's brows lifted simultaneously.

"At my request, Winchelsea," Hazel chimed in, lying, presumably to protect him. She worked her lips into a thin attempt at a smile. "Arden was kind enough to indulge me in my childish fancy to explore London as a tourist for a few hours."

"Ah," Winchelsea said, his expression guarded, his gaze quizzical as it met Lucien's. "How *good* of Arden."

Devil take it. Winchelsea was not a stupid man.

"Arden is very kind," Hazel said, her accent more pronounced with her heightened emotions. "I am thoroughly sorry I am the cause of such danger being brought to Lark House. If those men had not recognized me at the hotel, this never would have happened."

"You cannot blame yourself for your attack," Lucien countered. "Your courage and intuition in attempting to find the suspects has given us the best information we have thus far in finding the men responsible for the railway bombings. You suffered enough as a result of that mishap."

Though the wound on her head was nicely healed, the reminder of her suffering filled him with a surge of impotent rage. Coupled with the fury resonating within him—the daring of these bastards, infiltrating his home with the intent to do Hazel harm—he was left feeling as if he needed to smash something. Or someone.

"Miss Montgomery, we are grateful for your presence," Winchelsea assured her, smiling smoothly in Hazel's direction. "Your service has been invaluable. Our goals moving forward are twofold: to find the criminals responsible for these outrages, and to keep you safe. It is apparent Lark House will not be suitable any longer."

"I must agree," Colonel Olden said. "The devices are getting more complex, and the danger is real. The bomb discovered here this evening is the first I have seen of its kind, with a mechanical means of enabling delayed detonation. An alarm clock was rigged to a pistol inside the box. The likelihood of severe damage is undeniable. If they are capable of breaching the defenses here at Lark House and planting bombs such as this, I shudder to think what else they are capable of."

So did Lucien. An even greater fear was blooming inside him, the fear the men who had recognized Hazel and attacked her in the hotel would not give up until they got what they wanted. And that appeared to be her eternal silence, since they had failed previously.

"I propose you stay at my townhome," Winchelsea told Hazel, "as an honored guest. We will keep your whereabouts a secret, and no one will be the wiser as to where you have gone."

"No," Lucien found himself saying quickly. Far too quickly.

But the thought of Hazel sharing a roof with Winchelsea? The possessive beast inside him roared in denial. He would not allow it. She was his responsibility. After all, she was his partner, was she not? She was his to keep safe.

He ignored the part of him, deep inside, the primitive beast, that said she was *his*. That she was his, full stop.

He had no right to lay any claim upon her. And neither did she wish him to. She had been clear in her rules. He was clear in his. Except somehow, along the way, his rules had become rather murky. Somehow, the incessant need to have her, to touch her, to kiss her, to be inside her, had driven his blasted rules into the muck.

He ought to allow Winchelsea to harbor her at his town-home. It would be the sensible thing to do. Rational. Reasonable. Best for the both of them, quite likely. He could turn his full attention back to the gravity of the menace facing them, and the real possibility the men responsible for the railway bombings were still in their midst.

To hell with that.

Sensible, rational, and reasonable could sod off. He wanted Hazel at his side. Not just in his bed, but…he had rather grown accustomed to sharing his days with her. He looked forward to seeing her each morning, to dining with her, to sharing part of himself. More than just the physical. They had a deeper joining. And it ought to alarm him, but damn it, he could not deny the way he felt.

"I will see to Miss Montgomery's safety," he added hastily, lest Winchelsea add further logic to bolster his position.

"I can see to my own safety," Hazel interjected, scowling at him, as of course she would.

Yes, he and Winchelsea were fighting over her as if she were a prized painting which needed preservation and an armed guard to stave off thieves, rather than a woman with a reputation a mile long as one of the best damned agents in America.

"Of course you can, Miss Montgomery," he reassured her apologetically. The apology was for the delivery, though not the sentiment. He still intended to look after her, whether she liked it or not. And whether she needed it or not.

"Perhaps I will stay at a hotel," she said, frowning and crossing her arms over her middle in a protective gesture.

The bomb hidden beneath her bed had affected her. He could not blame her, for it had done the same to him. The notion one of the villains who had bombed the railway and brutalized Hazel had infiltrated his home with the intent to murder her was enough to make him want to tear the plaster from the framework of his study with his bare hands, until no trappings of civility remained. Nothing but sticks of wooden framework.

"You will do nothing of the sort," he snapped at her. "I forbid it."

Her eyes flashed, heralding the return of the fiery woman he had come to know and admire. "You *forbid* me, Arden?"

"Yes," he bit out. "You will not be safe on your own."

"You do not have the right to forbid me to do anything, Your Grace," she told him with the icy aplomb of a queen.

He would be damned if he was going to allow her to put herself in danger to assuage her pride. "I beg to differ," he told her, forgetting they had an audience for a moment. He settled for conveying the rest of what he had been about to say with his gaze.

Her chin went up. "You may beg to differ all you like, Arden. I alone am responsible for myself."

Her tone remained cool. Her independence was important to her. But her safety was equally important to him. He would make certain no one could get near enough to her to cause her harm again.

"We did not bring you to England to aid in our investigations so that you would become the target of attacks yourself, Miss Montgomery," Winchelsea interjected then, eyes traveling between Lucien and Hazel in a manner which suggested he suspected there was something simmering beneath the surface of their dispute. "I must insist you defer to reason. The Home Office is responsible for your well-being, and I hold the duty in the highest regard."

"I would argue the Special League is responsible for Miss

Montgomery's safety," he said to Winchelsea.

This, here, was where he drew the line. He would not reveal the nature of his relationship with Hazel. But neither would he allow the duke to sweep her away. She had nearly been killed on his watch, and he would stop at nothing to protect her. Winchelsea was a statesman. Lucien was a warrior. The difference was distinct.

"And again, I would argue that I am responsible for myself," Hazel interrupted. "The two of you can speak about me as if I am not present in the room all you like; it will not change the way I feel on the matter."

The colonel, who had stood silent for the bulk of the discourse, chose that moment to intervene. "Wherever you choose to go, Miss Montgomery, you must be vigilant. The nature of the device hidden in your chamber leaves no question that someone wants you dead."

But Hazel did not shrink from a challenge. She was no wilting flower beneath the heat of a summer sun. She was more like a rattlesnake, prone to striking when riled. Her shoulders were stiff, color blazing on her cheekbones, and she was ready to fight. Lucien was grateful the shock of the discovery of the device beneath her bed had dimmed, and she had returned to herself, but he was not going to allow her obstinacy to determine the outcome of this argument.

"A word alone with Miss Montgomery," he said suddenly, "Winchelsea and Colonel Olden, if you please."

Olden inclined his head. "I must see to the testing of the explosives in the device. The sooner we are apprised of the quality and type, the better for our investigations. I suspect it is American in origin, but time will tell."

Winchelsea's lips compressed into a fine line as he cast Lucien a disapproving glare. "I do not see the necessity, Arden."

"I do," he returned smoothly. "A moment, if you please. That is all I require—the opportunity to speak with my partner alone. You will grant me that, will you not, Winchelsea?"

Winchelsea's jaw clenched. He certainly looked as if he wanted to argue, but in the end, he did not. Lucien watched with satisfaction as the other two men left his study. He waited until the door was firmly closed at their backs to descend upon Hazel.

He reached her in three strides. And though he had intended to be gentle and coaxing, to persuade her with logic and reason, now she was within his reach at last, he could not keep himself from touching her. His hands were on her waist, hauling her against him, and then, he was embracing her.

Burying his face in her dark, sweet-scented hair. Holding her to him as if he feared she would be wrenched away at any moment. Perhaps that was part of the emotion squeezing his chest. Perhaps it was the reason for his shaking hands stroking over her back, up her spine.

That old fear, the one that had nearly swallowed him whole when he had been a young lad, searching for his mother's lifeless body on the shores.

"Lucien," she said on a sigh, but her arms tightened around him too, and for a beat, they simply held each other.

"Hazel." He kissed the crown of her head, unable to help himself. If something had happened to her tonight… "I want to look after you. Will you not allow it?"

"I look after myself, Lucien," she said. "You know that. Nor can I thank you for the manner in which you and Winchelsea were all but growling at each other over me, as if you were dogs in competition for a bone."

"Come now, sweetheart." He continued stroking her, as much to console her, as himself. "You do not resemble a bone

264

in the slightest."

He was not certain where this newfound capacity for levity originated. But he wanted to hear her laugh. Wanted to bring her a moment of lightness in the midst of such darkness. And he succeeded at that, his reward the hitch of her breath and a reluctant chuckle, before she squelched the sound.

"You know what I meant to say," she returned without heat. She showed no indication of pushing him away. Indeed, her arms had tightened.

He held her now as he should have earlier. But her discovery of the device beneath her bed had led to a frantic race to notify Scotland Yard and Winchelsea. Thank Christ the colonel lived nearby. If he had not been present to disable the infernal death machine...

Concern for someone beyond the circle of his small family—essentially his sister Violet and their Great Aunt Hortense—was foreign for him. He did not like it. Vulnerability had not been a mantle he had worn in years.

"I know what you meant to say," he answered her at last, his voice thickened by worry and guilt. "But please understand me, Hazel, the thought of you being injured or killed on my watch is enough to make me want to retch. Already, you were attacked by these bastards, and now they have trespassed in my home with the intent to murder you. Let me make this right."

"We must make it right together," she said, a stinging note of censure in her voice. "We are equals, Lucien. Partners, if you will recall."

"We are partners, yes, but that does not mean I do not want to see you safe," he returned, his words muffled by the top of her head.

He inhaled her scent, holding it in his lungs. She was special to him. More than just his partner. More than a fellow agent he respected and admired. He did not merely care for her. She had somehow come to mean so much more to him. She had smashed through his protective turrets with her cannon balls, and he was not certain he wanted to rebuild them.

"I do not need anyone else, Lucien."

But though she protested, she was still clinging to him, as he was to her, as if they were adrift together in the sea, and releasing each other would be the end of them. She was stubborn…and strong, so strong.

Stronger than he was, he began to suspect.

"Hazel," he said, pulling back so he could look down into her face and meet her gaze. He cupped her cheek in one hand, unable to resist tracing the high arch of her cheekbone with his thumb. "I have never met another woman more capable of taking care of herself. Nor have I known another as fiercely determined. I admire you, I respect you, and in the time since you first walked through the door of this very room, you have astounded me. But you cannot truly believe I will simply allow you to leave me now, after all that has happened between us."

"I gave you my body, Lucien, not sovereignty over me," she countered in return. "You cannot *allow* me to do anything."

"You are correct." *Devil take it*, he was making a hash of this. When had he ever blundered so much? "You entrusted yourself to me, did you not?"

Her striking eyes burned into his. "Yes."

"Then trust me now, Hazel." He would not plead, would not beg. But neither could he let this go. Let her go. He wasn't ready, and he could not shake the feeling, if she either set out on her own or stayed with Winchelsea, she would be forever lost to him. "Trust me, please."

"Why do you care so much?" she asked, searching his gaze, as if she would find the answer there.

He did not think she would, when he little knew the answer himself. In lieu of a response, he pressed a reverent kiss to the cool smoothness of her forehead. "Please," he repeated.

She sighed, then nodded resolutely. "I trust you, Lucien."

Relief and gratitude flowed through him. He would have kissed her lips, but for the presence of Winchelsea on the other side of the door. Instead, he settled for a chaste kiss on her cheek. Just one.

"Thank you," he said, and he had never meant two words more.

Chapter Seventeen

$\mathcal{T}$HE HOUR WAS late by the time Lucien escorted Hazel and Lady Beaufort to the townhouse of the Duke of Strathmore. His august aunt was fidgeting with the ribbons of her black bonnet, clearly in high dudgeon after the unprecedented events of the evening. Hazel could not blame her, for she felt shaken herself.

Beyond shaken, if she were honest.

"How are we to ever believe we are safe again, Arden?" Lady Beaufort demanded of Lucien, who sat opposite them, grim and silent in the low lamp of the carriage light. "Now they are hiding dynamite in your very home. When will it end?"

"Strathmore will make certain you are safe. I dare not entrust the welfare of you and Miss Montgomery to another," Lucien said, though the admission sounded grudging, as if torn from him. "You cannot remain at Lark House until I can determine precisely how the blackguards were able to enter undetected and plant a bomb in Miss Montgomery's chamber. As for when this will end, I very much fear none of it will until those responsible are commended to prison where they belong."

The reminder of the reason for their impromptu flight sent a chill through Hazel. She did not believe in fear—a woman in her profession could not afford to dwell on it—but she did know something of shock. She felt it now, making her mouth dry, making her hands tremble. Making her go cold and numb. She had felt this extreme possession only once previously, when Adam had been murdered before her, and she had held his lifeless body in her arms.

"I still cannot approve of the manner in which Strathmore stole your sister from us, hauling her out of Lark House with a blade fashioned from a dinner plate held to her throat. The finest china, and that miscreant turned it into a weapon. Thank heavens the servants did not spread tales. Only imagine how the gossips would sink their talons into such a monstrosity," Lady Beaufort grumbled.

"We do not speak of it now," Lucien said tightly. "I was in err for persecuting Strathmore unjustly. The mistake was mine, and I am thankful Lettie and Strathmore were able to prove me wrong."

Lady Beaufort fixed Hazel with a threatening stare. "You will not repeat a word of what I just said beyond this carriage, Miss Montgomery."

"I trust Miss Montgomery implicitly, my lady," Lucien defended Hazel before she could say a word, his voice sharp.

"Yes, and did you not also trust Mr. Swift?" Lady Beaufort demanded, a harsh note of censure in her voice, which was no doubt the product of her fear.

"How do you dare, madam?" Lucien went pale, his jaw going rigid, and Hazel was left to surmise Mr. Swift was the man who had betrayed his trust. "You will not place Miss Montgomery and that treasonous scoundrel in the same thought again, my lady."

"Enough," Hazel bit out. "I will not be spoken of as if I am not present in this carriage. Lady Beaufort, as I assured you earlier today, I hold your family in highest esteem. I would never dream of besmirching their name or carrying unbecoming tales about them. Furthermore, it is most ungenerous of you to fling Arden's past mistakes at him, when he has already paid for them mightily. And Lucien, cease growling at your aunt. I can fend for myself well enough."

Silence descended upon the carriage, and she became aware of two pairs of eyes staring at her in shock. Belatedly, she realized she had referred to Lucien by his Christian name, rather than his title.

"Oh, hell," she muttered to herself, before she could hold her tongue.

"I beg your pardon, Miss Montgomery!" said Lady Beaufort, her tone scandalized.

Hazel was not certain which of her gaffes had just offended Lucien's aunt the most: chastising her for holding Lucien's past errors in judgment against him, referring to him as Lucien, or saying an epithet and being overheard. Ordinarily, she cursed aloud solely when she was certain she was alone. She could only blame her lack of caution upon the events of the evening.

After all, it was not every day she discovered a bomb hidden beneath her bed.

"Forgive me," she said at last, rather lamely. "I meant no insult."

"There is no insult," Lucien assured her. "Tonight has been deeply troubling for all of us."

"One does not refer to a duke by his given name, Miss Montgomery," Lady Beaufort rebuked. "And neither does a lady issue oaths."

"Nor," Hazel could not help but add dryly, "does a lady have a box of dynamite laid beneath her bed, I would wager."

Lucien mumbled something beneath his breath which sounded rather like an epithet himself. But the carriage had gone mercifully still.

"We have reached our destination," he announced. "I sent word ahead to Strathmore and Lettie. They are expecting us, despite the lateness of the hour."

At long last, Hazel was going to meet Lucien's sister and brother-in-law. Curiosity mingled with nervousness. She had already proven herself hopelessly inept at wrangling English manners and customs. To make matters worse, she was arriving at their home, an unwanted guest, after being chased by a bomb from her previous lodgings.

Lucien leapt down from the carriage first and was now offering gentle assistance to his aunt, who clearly experienced some degree of difficulty maneuvering the carriage step as she alighted. He offered her his hand next, and she took it, grateful for the warmth of him burning through the layers of their gloves. For a whimsical moment, she wished she could throw herself into his arms and embrace him, but she recognized the foolishness of such a gesture.

His green gaze searched hers. "You are well?" he asked.

"Yes," she said, careful to keep her voice low. "Lady Beaufort is another matter, however. This has upset her, quite understandably, and you must be patient with her."

"The arthritis has affected my joints, not my ears, you insolent girl," the lady in question snapped from just ahead of them on the promenade.

Hazel and Lucien exchanged another look, before he rushed to offer his aunt his arm. Hazel followed in their wake, deciding Lady Beaufort's quip was a good sign her spirit was returning, dispelling the fear. Hazel took in the impressive exterior of the townhome as they approached—which was in a neighborhood that looked similar to Lucien's home, and was every bit as equally formidable. An implacable butler greeted them at the door, as though late-night visits in the wake of Fenian bombs was a common occurrence.

They were escorted into a sumptuous entry hall, then into a salon, where a handsome dark-haired man and an equally lovely raven-tressed woman awaited. The butler announced them, standing upon ceremony, despite the alarming circumstances surrounding their arrival.

Hazel noted the resemblance between the Duchess of Strathmore and Lucien. She also saw instantly the love burning brightly between the duke and duchess. It was there in the protective manner in which he stood at her side, the loving glance he exchanged with her, before turning his stare to settle upon Lucien. The tense set of his expression and the rigidity of his jaw suggested he had not yet forgotten Lucien's mistaken pursuit of him.

The duchess rushed forward, even before full introductions were made, and embraced Lady Beaufort and Lucien, then stopped in front of Hazel. Feeling foolish, Hazel's cheeks went hot, for reasons she could not define. She dipped into a curtsy, grateful she had chosen to wear a gown for her excursion to Madame Tussaud's, a gay frivolity, which seemed as if it had happened a lifetime ago by this wretched hour of the evening.

It was not as if Lucien's sister could look upon her and know she had been intimate with Lucien, but somehow, Hazel felt as if her vivid green gaze, so like her brother's, saw far more than Hazel wanted it to.

"You must be Miss Montgomery," the duchess said with a welcoming smile. "I am so pleased to finally make your acquaintance, though I must admit, I do wish it was under far more cheerful circumstances. Both Arden and Aunt Hortense have sent notes to me hailing your many virtues."

The color on Hazel's cheeks deepened. This was news to her. Indeed, she was certain Lady Beaufort would be more inclined to bemoan her deplorable American manners, her scandalous penchant for wearing divided skirts, and working alongside men. As for Lucien? Initially, his notes would have been much the same, she had no doubt. But now, she could not be so certain. Either way, she did not dare risk a glance at Lucien or Lady Beaufort, for fear her ears would turn red as well.

"It is a pleasure to meet you, Your Grace," she told the duchess. "I cannot think of any virtues they may have extolled concerning me, but I thank you for saying so, just the same."

"Nonsense! Arden in particular has written a veritable novel's worth." The Duchess of Strathmore sent a pointed look in Lucien's direction.

Hazel was fascinated to discover he too was flushing. But he hastily clasped his hands behind his back in a forbidding stance, and forced his countenance into one of severity. "You need not tell all my secrets, Lettie," he cautioned his sister quietly.

But there was such tenderness, such love in his voice, that it was unmistakable. So too the manner in which the duchess smiled at Lucien. Brother and sister loved each other very much. Hazel recalled his sadness when he had spoken of their rift, of hoping their differences could be mended.

The duchess hummed noncommittally and turned her attention toward her handsome husband. "May I present my husband, the Duke of Strathmore?"

The duke bowed formally, but when he rose, he was grinning. Hazel did not know what she had expected, but it had not been precisely this rakish, dashing duke with a teasing air. After all, had Lady Beaufort not mentioned something about him turning the family porcelain into a dagger?

"Formerly known as the Duke of Duplicity, according to Lady Beaufort," he added with an affable air, having the daring to wink at the lady in question. "Or may I call you

Aunt Hortense too, now that we are family?"

"No." Lady Beaufort sniffed. "You may not."

"Some things never change." Strathmore pinned Lucien with an arch look. "Speaking of which, forgive me for reveling in the day the mighty Duke of Arden has sought me out for assistance. I regret that it involves dynamite, and I am heartily relieved the bomb was discovered in time and no one was injured, but I must admit to a certain satisfaction in the irony."

A muscle twitched in Lucien's jaw. "I still do not like you, Strathmore. The only reason I sought you out was for the sake of Miss Montgomery and Aunt Hortense."

"I am aware." Strathmore grinned. "It is a pleasure to watch you squirm."

"My love." The duchess shot her husband a quelling look. "Now is not the time for gloating."

"Forgive me, Vi," Strathmore said instantly, his tone penitential.

Odder still to see how much the duke was in his duchess's thrall, Hazel thought. But she was beginning to gain a clearer idea of the family dynamics at play. She knew why Lucien and Strathmore would mix as well as tea and tar. Lucien was controlled and rigid, while Strathmore was brazen and irreverent.

"Whilst this dialogue is most engrossing," Lady Beaufort interrupted acidly, "I am old, and I am tired. These ancient bones have been roused from sleep and paraded about half of London. Where might I find my chamber, Violet darling?"

"I will see you and Miss Montgomery settled," the duchess said instantly. "Do forgive me, Aunt Hortense. Come, you must be weary."

Only Lady Beaufort could insult her hostess, then be instantly shepherded to her bed for the evening, with sympathy no less, Hazel thought wryly. She had developed a keen sense of respect and admiration for Lucien's aunt, however. They had a great deal more in common than Hazel would have supposed, and she knew the tenderness which lay just beneath her wizened, reserved façade. Beneath the older woman's cool hauteur, beat a broken heart.

Hazel glanced to Lucien, wondering when the two of them would reconnoiter.

"You need your rest," he told her. "Go."

"But we need to dig into the investigation," she protested, partly because for so much of her life, her work had been her life's blood, and partly because she needed to bring the men responsible for the railway bombings and the bomb beneath her bed to justice.

He came to her, not daring to touch her before mixed company, but the emotion in his eyes felt like a caress. "Miss Montgomery," he said, his formality feeling so unutterably wrong, "please. Go with my sister. I will make certain the perimeter of this house is safe. We have guards stationed, and we took great care to make certain no one followed us here. You have suffered a shock, and after everything you have endured, what you need most is to sleep. The investigation will wait for tomorrow and the sunrise."

"Are you going to rest as well?" she countered. While she was grateful he cared enough to want to see to her well-being and safety, she could not shake the feeling he was treating her now as if she were a defenseless woman. As if he were her protector.

She had not been defenseless from the moment she had first learned to shoot a pistol, and she had no intention of becoming defenseless now. Nor would she simply trail in Lady Beaufort's wake like a lost puppy who had been ordered to her bed.

Lucien sighed, then compressed his lips, staring at her. "I need to speak with Strathmore. Alone. And then I too will seek my rest for the evening, back at Lark House, after I finish questioning my staff. We will be sharper, our investigation far more clear-headed, if we attempt to get some sleep. If we wear ourselves ragged, those villains will outsmart us, and we cannot afford to allow that to happen."

She studied his handsome face, wondering when it had become so beloved, and decided he was right. Though she wanted to protest his returning to Lark House after what had occurred, she had no claim upon him, and she knew it.

Likely, he wished to address what had happened with Strathmore and lay it to rest once and for all. And she knew better than anyone, conducting an investigation on little sleep was a poor plan indeed. The night before Adam's murder, she and Adam had stayed up until dawn analyzing evidence. They had separated for no more than four hours of sleep each, and she had always known that lack of proper rest had left her weary and under-prepared for the depth of evil she would face later that day.

If she had been prepared, Adam may still be alive.

But if Adam were still alive, she would be his wife, and she very much doubted the Duke of Arden would be looking down at her now, with such intense concentration, as if she were the focus of his entire world. Nor would she want him to.

The knowledge was bittersweet, because she was beginning to realize what she had found with Lucien—however fleeting—was every bit as valid and necessary as what had happened so long ago between herself and Adam.

Because she loved Lucien too. It was a different love than the one she had possessed for Adam. She was older now, changed. Wiser. Harder. But as she stood in the gilt-bedecked salon of the Duke of Strathmore, she knew it without a doubt.

She had lost her heart to the man standing before her.

For the first time in as long as she could remember, she was going to do what a man had asked her to do, and it was because she respected him enough to do it. Not because she was deferring to him.

She nodded. "You are right, Arden. Every investigation is best served by acuity. I will bid you good evening."

He inclined his head, then offered her a slight, gentlemanly bow, as if they were strangers. "Please rest knowing you are safe here, Miss Montgomery."

She would have to accept Lucien's decision and trust his judgment.

"I bid you good evening as well, Your Grace." She turned to the Duchess of Strathmore with a smile. "Thank you so much for your hospitality this evening. Please do not allow my poor American manners to hold us here any longer. Lady Beaufort is in need of her chamber, and I find I am quite weary as well."

"Of course, Miss Montgomery," said the duchess, her eyes traveling from Lucien to Hazel, then back again. "Follow me, if you please."

There had been a question in Lucien's sister's eyes, but Hazel had no intention of answering it. Blindly, she swept away from Lucien, and followed his sister and aunt.

HE HAD BUNGLED matters with Hazel, and he knew it. But as Lucien watched the women retreat from the salon, leaving him alone with Strathmore, he did not see any other way he could have proceeded. Hazel was not the sort of lady who appreciated being dismissed or lumped together with her fellow sex. He knew better than anyone she prided herself upon being a man's equal, upon performing a job most considered wholly in the male sphere.

She had fought hard for the reputation she had earned. She was an incomparable. And she was an excellent investigator, as capable as any man, and then some. He knew leaving had been difficult for her, but he hoped she could see the impending interview had everything to do with the situation between himself and Lettie's husband, and nothing to do with Hazel herself.

"I never thought I would see the day the great Duke of Arden was brought to his knees."

Strathmore's voice, part-victorious, part-amused, interrupted his tumultuous thoughts. He faced his brother-in-law as a prize fighter would, chest to chest, the stance of a man about to go to battle. Though he had no intention of sparring this evening, Lucien had no notion of what to expect from the duke.

"Laugh about it as you will, Strathmore," he quipped grimly, "but there is precious little levity in a bomb being laid beneath an innocent woman's bed. Miss Montgomery was the victim of a potentially deadly attack, and I will thank you to show some concern."

"On that, we are in accord, Arden," Strathmore acknowledged grimly. "I do not find bombs, dynamite, or murderous intentions humorous in the slightest. What I do find entertaining, however, is you requiring my aid."

Lucien gritted his teeth. He had wronged his brother-in-law badly, and he knew it. But that did not make swallowing his pride any more palatable. It went down as easily as a mouth full of wriggling worms would. He had apologized profusely in the aftermath of The Incident, but he knew as well as anyone, apologies could not ameliorate some wounds.

Words could oft be inadequate.

"Undoubtedly," he allowed, "and I do not blame you for holding me in contempt. But I did not drag two ladies here in the midst of the night so that you could laugh at me, however tempting the prospect may be to you."

"I have forgiven you for what happened," his brother-in-law said then, his tone easy. An absolution. There was no bitterness, no anger.

"You have?" he asked, startled by Strathmore's calm acceptance.

After all, his suspicions and his merciless determination had nearly landed Strathmore in prison. He could have been hanged, *by God*. And all because Lucien had been blinded to the maneuverings and manipulations of his most trusted man. A man who had turned out to be an insidious devil.

"Of course I have," Strathmore said. "You are my wife's brother, and I love my wife more than I love my next breath. She tells me you are not altogether horrible, and I believe her. She tells me you have good intentions, and I believe that too. I know you love her, and that you did your utmost to see her well-settled and happy, even if you are an overbearing arse."

He bristled at being called an *arse*. "Careful, Strathmore. I may be at your mercy now, but I will not be insulted by you."

Strathmore remained unapologetic. "I speak only the truth. But fortunately for Vi and myself, she has a mind and heart of her own, and she followed both straight to me."

Vi.

Lucien had always called Violet "Lettie." But of course, Strathmore had decided upon a nickname of his own. The diminutive was yet another reminder his sister had flown from the nest and had begun a life of her own. Her happiness pleased him, of course, but he felt a keen stab of envy for the joy she had discovered in her marriage.

"I am glad Lettie has found happiness," he forced himself to say, his voice sounding rusty. "I would not have it any other way."

"It is my duty to make her happy for the rest of our lives," Strathmore replied, his tone growing serious.

"Your damned right it is," Lucien growled.

He had been protecting Violet since she had been a girl, and it still nettled he had been so summarily replaced, even if he had always known the supplanting would be inevitable.

"Tell me what happened this evening," Strathmore said, effectively changing the subject.

Though Strathmore remained a member of the League, he had been on unofficial leave in the wake of The Incident and his marriage to Lettie.

Lucien sighed. "The abridged version of it is that the railway dynamitards are after Miss Montgomery. She was recognized here in London, and somehow, the bastards infiltrated Lark House and planted a bomb beneath her bed, while she and I were away this evening."

Strathmore cursed. "Thank God she was not hurt, or worse."

Ice returned to his veins at the thought of harm befalling Hazel. But he would not allow that fear to consume him now, for what he needed to do most was focus upon apprehending the men responsible, before they made yet another attempt upon her life.

"It is a credit to her impeccable instincts and experience as a Pinkerton agent that she was not," he said, his throat going thick. "She noticed someone had been in her chamber and was instantly suspicious enough to perform a thorough search of her room. That is when she discovered the bomb."

"You admire her."

Strathmore's assertion startled him. Not because it was

untrue, but because he had not thought himself so damned transparent when it came to his feelings for Hazel.

He met his brother-in-law's gaze, unflinching. "Yes."

Strathmore's eyes narrowed, his stare turning speculative. "You more than admire her, in fact."

He ground his molars. "What does it signify? Miss Montgomery is my partner. If I do not have faith in her abilities as an agent, I am putting myself at unnecessary risk. Of course I admire her intelligence and her daring. She has uncovered more about the Fenians since her arrival here in London than I have in months. Her instinct is impeccable. We are fortunate indeed to be able to avail ourselves of her expertise."

"You speak with the vigor of a lover, rather than that of a peer," Strathmore assessed.

Correctly, damn it all.

"Do not make me blacken your eye in your own home, Strathmore," he growled. "How dare you suggest I have acted as less than a gentleman in regard to Miss Montgomery?"

"I suggested no such thing, but your guilt is betraying you." Amusement laced Strathmore's tone now.

Sodding hell.

He had walked rather neatly into Strathmore's trap. "If you say one word to besmirch her honor, I will do far worse than blacken your eye."

"Come now." Strathmore made a clucking sound. "Why would I wish to besmirch the honor of my future sister-in-law?"

The notion of marrying Hazel returned once more. He waited for the inevitable, accompanying sense of dread, but it failed to arrive. In its place, all he felt was the searing warmth of contentment. The slow, steady rush of peace. The fledgling hope that perhaps all was not lost for him. That perhaps he could find happiness with Hazel, if he but dared.

"I am not marrying Miss Montgomery," he sputtered at last.

Only because she had refused his suit. But Strathmore need not know that.

"Pity. You ought to," the duke said, his expression grave.

He was not joking or making light of Lucien this time. His brother-in-law appeared utterly serious. "I have no wish to marry.

Still, even to his own ears, and most importantly to his own heart, the denial rang false.

"Why?" Strathmore asked. "Because of your mother? You need not look surprised. Vi has told me all about her madness and how her loss affected you both. But you must know that the unhappiness of your parents need not be visited upon you. Marriage does not have to be a hell, and neither does your life. Do you truly want to spend the rest of your days alone, when the woman you love is within your reach?"

"Love is a fiction," he spat, because it was what he had believed for so long.

His mother had claimed to love him, and she had left. His father had claimed to love his mother, and yet he had confined her to a life of misery at Albemarle, until she had killed herself. There, in the scars of his past, lay irrefutable, incontrovertible proof that love was nothing more than a chimera, invented by the weakhearted, and clung to by the masses.

Did it not?

Why then, did it feel as if Hazel had reached inside him, filling a void he had not known was empty? Why did the thought of his life without her in it paralyze him with dread and fear?

"Tell yourself that, if you must," Strathmore said. "But you have only to look at the world around you to see that love is, indeed, real. Do not blot out the sun to spite yourself. Let it burn brightly. Take the chance that it will burn. Allow yourself, for once, to ease your grip upon the reins of the past, and if you dare, let them go."

Damnation.

Not long ago, he had been determined to see the Duke of Strathmore thrown into Newgate prison for crimes he had wrongly believed he had committed. And now, here he stood, waxing poetic about love and life. Worse for Lucien's already battered pride, Strathmore was not wrong in a single, bloody word he had spoken.

Hazel was the sun. She was the source of the warmth in his life, everything he needed to sustain himself.

Nevertheless, he could not afford to wallow in these new-found realizations. The hour was late, but he could not rest until he learned how those bastards had gained entrance to Lark House with the intention of harming Hazel.

He cleared his throat. "I have no wish to argue the vagaries of human emotion at this time of the night, Strathmore. I need to return to Lark House and continue overseeing the inquisition of my staff. I trust you will keep the ladies safe until my return?"

Strathmore inclined his head. "I will protect them with my life."

"Let us hope it does not come to that," he said grimly, another chill seeping into the very marrow of his bones.

He would fight these villains and bring them to ground, or he would die trying. Either way, he would do everything in his power to see they could never again harm Hazel, or anyone else.

"HOW LONG HAVE you been in love with my brother?"

The Duchess of Strathmore's question gave Hazel such a shock, she almost tripped on the sumptuous carpet of the guest chamber she had been given. After escorting Lady Beaufort to her chamber first, the duchess had accompanied Hazel. Fortunately, she had waited until they were ensconced in the room, away from the vigilant ears of Lady Beaufort, to pose the query.

Hand flying to her heart, Hazel spun to face Lucien's elegant sister, who watched her with a knowing air. "I am not in love with Arden," she denied, though part of her knew it was futile.

Still, how strange it was to think someone whose acquaintance she had just made that evening, a woman whose company she had been in for less than a half hour's time, could see the truth so plainly, when it had taken Hazel herself weeks to discover it.

"You are," the duchess countered. "I could see it in the way you looked at him. But you need not fret, because he is in love with you as well."

This assertion shocked her even more than the first.

But what left her most stunned was the sudden, almost painful rush of longing the duchess's words brought to life within her. She *wanted* Lucien to love her. But that was foolish yearnings, the product of her reckless heart. She ought to be wise enough to know such an impossibility could never come to fruition.

"It does not matter," she told the duchess, careful to keep the sadness from her expression and her voice both. "Arden and I are two very different people, from two vastly different places."

"What has any of that to do with love?" demanded the duchess.

Lucien's sister possessed the heart of a true romantic. She also had the lack of caution of a person who had been given everything she wished her whole life. As the daughter of a duke, she had undoubtedly been coddled and spoiled. What must life be like for a woman who could be anything she wished to be, who was assured of her role in society, her place in life, who had never had to struggle or fight? Hazel would never know, because she had been destined from birth to have to claw her way through the world. She had been born to be nothing, but she had made herself into something.

"Love is an impractical emotion for a woman like me," she explained. "And I am a woman who does not dare be impractical. I hold your brother in the highest regard, Your Grace, but I am no fool. I do not belong here in your gilded world. I am but a fleeting visitor, though it is a visit I will never forget."

Indeed, she would cherish the memory of the arrogant duke who had stolen her heart for the rest of her days. He had awakened her from sleep. He had shown her passion with his touch. He had worshiped her with his body. And she would always love him. Always.

"Forgive me," the Duchess of Strathmore said, moving toward her in a silken swish of amethyst skirts. "I must argue with your fatalism. I know you must be weary after your travails this evening, and the hour is late, but do you think we might sit for a moment?"

"Your Grace," she protested, "I am already imposing upon you enough by my presence here in the middle of the night. I would not dream of importuning you further."

"Nonsense," said the duchess with a friendly smile. "And you must call me Violet. I insist. *Your Grace* and *Duchess* are far too formal for us, for I think we shall be fast friends, you and I. Do you not agree?"

Her air was easy and light, and she possessed none of the starch and sternness that were the hallmarks of her formidable aunt. She made Hazel forget the disparity in their social classes.

"As you wish, Violet." Hazel smiled back at her, and relented, allowing herself to be led to the chamber's seating area. "And you must call me Hazel."

What would it be like to belong to Lucien's family? To have this brilliant, lovely woman as her sister? To have Lucien as her husband?

She banished the questions, for they were a moot point.

"This is far better." Violet settled her skirts into place and sent another tentative smile in Hazel's direction. "I find myself becoming tired so easily in my delicate condition." She laid a hand over her belly.

Comprehension dawned on Hazel. Lucien's sister was going to have a babe. "Good heavens, I had no idea! You ought to be in your bed, getting rest. Not here with me."

"Nonsense." Violet waved a dismissive hand. "I am perfectly well, but do keep it a secret for now, if you please. I have yet to tell Arden, and I want to surprise him with the news he is to be an uncle."

"I will not breathe a word," she promised.

An odd thought wound its way into her mind then. She could have a babe of her own, even now. This thought, like the questions and longing rising in her heart, she quashed.

"Thank you." Violet's smile faded. "I want Lucien to find the same happiness I have, Hazel. For so many years, he has closed himself off to anything other than duty. First me, then the Home Office. He has carried so much weight upon his shoulders. He deserves love. He deserves a life and family of his own."

"I hardly think seeing us together, for but a few minutes

this evening, could suggest either Arden or myself is desirous of a future together," she said stiffly.

"He wrote to me of you, as I said," Violet said. "We have not been as close as we once were since I married Strathmore, and it has grieved me mightily, but I still know him well. His admiration for you is undeniable. I have never known him to be so in awe of any woman, and it gives me hope he can find contentment at last."

She wanted to look away, but could not seem to wrest her gaze from Violet's uncompromising green stare, so like her brother's. "Your Grace—*Violet*, your brother is an honorable man, and I enjoy working alongside him, but I cannot be the woman to give him the life and family he deserves. I am an American orphan, who has spent her life working in a profession most of the world believes is more suited to a man than a woman. I know nothing of your customs or manners, and as your aunt would be quick to tell you, my comportment is abominable."

"When our mother drowned herself, Lucien swam into the sea after her. He swam until servants went after him, dragging him, fighting all the way back to shore, before he collapsed from exhaustion himself. And even then, he walked the shores until he discovered her, wet and pale and lifeless, still wearing her finest morning dress. He carried her home that way." Violet's voice trembled by the time she finished the harrowing recollection. "That is the sort of young man he was, the sort of man he is. He will do anything for the ones he loves. Give him a chance, Hazel, please. That is all I ask."

Hazel did not know she was crying, until she felt the wetness of tears trailing down her cheeks. It was the same story Lady Beaufort had told her, but this time in greater, more haunting detail. Her heart broke all over again for the frightened young man he had been, and for the man he had become.

"I have already given him a chance," she told Violet. "I let him into my heart."

The trouble was, she very much suspected he was destined to break it.

Chapter Eighteen

$\mathscr{H}$AZEL JOLTED AWAKE at dawn, startled to find herself in unfamiliar surroundings once more, until she recalled where she was and why. She had slept fitfully in her new and temporary bed at the Duke of Strathmore's townhome. Indeed, she would be surprised if she had even managed two consecutive hours of slumber. Sleeping without the comforting heat of Lucien's big body already felt foreign.

She yawned and scrubbed a hand over her face as her wits returned. Long after her conversation with Lucien's sister had ended, Hazel had paced the room, unable to sleep. The events of the evening had weighed upon her. So much had occurred, almost a lifetime's worth in the course of hours. She had realized she had fallen in love with Lucien. And she had discovered inarguable proof that someone—or to be more apt, the Emerald Club—wanted her dead.

Most frustrating of all was her inability to act upon any of her newfound knowledge. There was nothing she could do with her love for Lucien except hold it inside her, just as there was nothing she could do to defend herself from an unseen foe.

She sighed, for though she was bone-weary, she knew there would be no more sleeping for her this morning. Even with the little slumber she had managed to nab, her restless mind was spinning. First and foremost, she was a Pinkerton, and she had not forgotten the duties which came with such a distinction.

Hazel rose from bed, performed her morning ablutions, and hastily dressed herself, for though Bunton would surely arrive if she rang for her, Hazel was accustomed to doing for herself. And she needed the reminder the charmed existence in which she found herself—bombs and murderous Fenians out for her blood notwithstanding—would eventually come to an end. She would once more return to her modest life of rented rooms the size of the guest bedchambers in which she stayed, of no servants to cater to her whims, and of breakfasts she prepared by her own hand.

Pacing the floor some more, she set her mind to unraveling the mystery of Sean Flannery and Thomas Mulroney, and any of their unknown confederates. Because most of her journals had been inside her carpetbag when it was stolen, she was bereft of her lists and copious notes. She had not realized how very much she had relied upon them, until they were gone.

On another perambulation of the chamber, she noted the small writing desk set up near a window, with a sheaf of papers and pen and ink upon its glossy surface. She would just have to make her lists again, she decided, storming to the desk with purpose and settling down to begin.

Known Fenians

Thomas Mulroney

Sean Flannery

Drummond McKenna

The Nightingale

Her pen paused after the last, something about the code name used for the Fenian connection in England bothering her.

"The Nightingale," she repeated aloud.

As code names went, it was damned odd. Nightingales were small and uninspiring in appearance. Dull and drab, with portly bellies and a sweet call they trilled cheerfully in the spring and summer months. Was The Nightingale unassuming? Commonplace?

Hmm, that did not seem right.

Perhaps, she reasoned, tilting her head as she contemplated, The Nightingale was female, and that was the reasoning behind the code name. Or The Nightingale was a man who was short in stature. Or maybe The Nightingale had brown hair. Or he was exceedingly garrulous.

"Hell," she muttered to herself.

She could not help but to feel now, as she had all along, that uncovering the identity of The Nightingale would unlock the mysteries of the case. If she could find out who The Nightingale was, she would be able to determine the whereabouts of Mulroney and Flannery, and any of their cohorts, she was certain.

Unless…

No. It could not be. Surely that would be too easy. Too simple.

But still, the thought would not leave her, prodding her with the persistence of a swarm of angry bees. She rose from her chair and went to the hastily packed valise which had accompanied her the previous night during her flight from Lark House. Opening it, she discovered the map of London she had been utilizing in her research, one of the few documents in her possession which had not been thieved by the villains who had attempted to kill her.

She hastened back to the writing desk, map in hand, and unfolded it, spreading it out atop her list. Her forefinger traveled over the portion of map devoted to the London docks. She traveled over dozens of streets and lanes. Saint George, Pennington, High, Wapping, Cable and Betts, Princes Square, and so many more, until finally her finger connected with precisely what she had been seeking.

"Nightingale Lane," she said aloud, as she took up the pen once more and drew a circle around the street upon the map.

If she was right, The Nightingale was not a person at all. Rather, it was a place. A street, to be specific, which meant it was the source for Fenian funding and dynamite. And if her instincts did not fail her, she had no doubt the conspirators would be found somewhere on Nightingale Lane, near the docks.

There was no time to waste.

Calmly, she located her pistol and tucked it inside a reticule, along with enough coin to see her about the city. Hired hacks would do, and she would worry about Lucien's disapproval later.

He wanted to protect her, she knew, but she did not need his protection. If anything, she wanted to protect *him*. He had already suffered enough in his life. He had a sister who loved him, and a niece or nephew who would love him as well all too soon. She was no one, just as she had always been, with no family of her own. No place she belonged.

Yes, she decided with a bittersweet smile. If either of them was to invite danger into their lives and put themselves at risk, it would be her. But with a little luck and some clever sleuthing, she would not need to worry about danger at all.

At least, that was what she hoped.

LUCIEN ARRIVED AT Strathmore's townhome later than he

had intended. He had spent the bulk of the evening conferring with Scotland Yard and sitting in upon interrogations of his staff. At dawn, one of his youngest footmen had finally broken and confessed he had enabled entrance to a man with an American accent, who had claimed he was a family member of Miss Montgomery's and that he wished to surprise her with a gift.

Conal, the lad in question, was vehemently apologetic. Not that it mattered one whit. He had allowed a stranger— and not just any stranger, but a Fenian madman who intended to harm Hazel—into Lark House. Lucien had been obliged to sack him, for in this climate of danger, he could not allow a domestic susceptible to outside interference to remain upon his staff. Conal had been a diligent worker by all accounts, so Lucien had cut him free with six months' worth of wages and letters of reference.

Exhausted, he had fallen into his bed upon a pillow which still smelled faintly of Hazel. But he had been alone and miserable without her, and with the heavy weight of dread sitting upon his chest, he had tossed and turned, unable to obtain the rest his body required. When he had finally fallen asleep, it had been mid-morning, the sun streaming through a gap in the window dressings.

Upon waking, he had rung for his valet, only to discover an urgent summons had come for him from Strathmore. Fear and rage had locked his heart in a fervent, unrelenting grip for the entirety of his punishing ride to Strathmore's address. He did not even bother to knock. Instead, he strode through the front door, much like a lion stalking its prey.

He had not far to roam, for Strathmore appeared instantly, his expression pinched with worry. Lucien's gut clenched. "Where is she?" he demanded, not bothering to elaborate.

Strathmore knew. "Miss Montgomery is…missing, I am

afraid."

"Missing," he repeated, his mouth going dry.

One word, his greatest fear. Hazel. Gone.

He could not speak.

Perhaps it was the lack of sleep. Perhaps it was the intensity of his feelings for her. But all of a sudden, he went dizzy, as if he had suffered a powerful blow to the head. He was not even certain he could stand on his bloody feet. He staggered under the weight of it. Nearly stumbled and fell.

Strathmore was there to catch him with a steadying hand. "Good God, man, are you ill?"

"Tell me," he gritted, "how it is possible that she is *missing*. Did someone take her? Did she leave of her own free will? Was there a struggle? Did your domestics or any of the guards witness anything? Jesus Christ, man, I know you loathe me for what I put you through, but have mercy. I need answers. I need to know more."

The world was still spinning. He focused on Strathmore with great care.

Strathmore had not looked this grim when he had been facing the prospect of prison and the hangman's noose himself. "If I had answers, I would offer them. All I know is that she was already gone when her lady's maid went to attend her this morning. Nothing is out of place, and there is no hint she left in any way other than of her own free will. No one saw her departure, I am afraid, but her chamber is immaculate, nothing but a map and a list on the writing desk."

The notion of the Duke of Strathmore in Hazel's chamber rankled, but he could not dwell upon it now. "Take me to her chamber," he said hoarsely.

He ought to have known better than to leave her here while he remained at Lark House. He ought to have damn well never strayed from her side. Self-recriminations flooded him as he followed in Strathmore's wake, striding through the entry hall and up the elegant, twisting staircase.

"Lettie and Aunt Hortense," he asked of Strathmore as they walked down the upstairs hall, "they are well?"

"Perfectly." Strathmore slanted a glance in his direction. "I know you do not wish to hear this, Arden, but all signs point to the lady leaving of her own volition. I have no desire to be the one to point out you are an arrogant, overbearing arsehole, but—"

"You have already done so on more than one occasion," he interrupted Strathmore coldly. He had done his penance for wronging his brother-in-law, and if there was ever a day when he could not withstand Strathmore's mockery, this, *by God*, was that bloody fucking day. "She would not leave me."

He said the last with more conviction than he felt. In truth, Hazel Elizabeth Montgomery was a law unto her own. No one could tame her. Nor should any man dare. Least of all, Lucien himself.

"Leave *you?*" Strathmore asked pointedly, as they reached a door and he opened it.

Lucien stormed past him, ignoring the raised brow and the question both. He hadn't time for games. He was single-minded now. He needed to find Hazel. Immediately.

The chamber was, as Strathmore had described, immaculate. No sign of disturbance. No overturned furniture, nothing out of place, nothing broken. Her valise lay at the foot of the bed, and the chamber still smelled faintly of her scent. He stalked to the writing desk situated by a window and found a map opened over its polished surface.

London was laid out in tidy streets and squares, the River Thames curving through it. She had drawn a circle around a street, he noted. Nightingale Lane. He lifted the map and discovered a paper beneath it bearing a list, written in her tidy scrawl.

Known Fenians
Thomas Mulroney
Sean Flannery
Drummond McKenna
The Nightingale

"Of course!" he said aloud, realization dawning on him. "The Nightingale."

The code name for the English Fenian, who had been supporting the Emerald Club with funds and shipments of dynamite. It all made sense. They had all been convinced The Nightingale was a person. But, if what he suspected Hazel had surmised was correct, The Nightingale was not a person at all.

Rather, The Nightingale was a place.

More specifically, a street.

And on that street, he would find Fenians. And on that street, he would find Hazel. Supposing he wasn't too late. The thought made his blood run cold as ice and his gut clench. He let the list drift from his fingers, allowing it to flutter back to the desk.

He glanced up at Strathmore. "She's gone to Nightingale Lane. I need to get there to find her. Now."

But his brother-in-law blocked his path. "Stop, Arden. Miss Montgomery has been gone for hours, perhaps since first light. If she has not returned in all this time, the indication is strong that she has met with trouble. And if she has met with trouble, we will require all the reinforcements we can get. We need to summon Scotland Yard and all the League agents available to us."

"Fuck you," he growled, pushing at Strathmore's chest. Nothing would stand in his way. He needed to protect his woman, damn it. He needed to be certain she was safe. To see her, touch her, hold her, kiss her, *marry her.*

Yes, damn it all, he would marry the woman. Just as soon as he upbraided her for doing something as foolish as attempting to take on a band of dynamite-loving criminals on her own.

But Strathmore had brute strength and gripped Lucien's shoulders, fighting him for power. "Damn it, arsehole, listen to me for the first time in your life. If we want to give Miss Montgomery the best chance to escape these bastards' clutches unscathed, we have to bring a bloody army and go to war. Do you understand me?"

The violent bloodlust coursing through his veins subsided enough for his brother-in-law's words to penetrate Lucien's mind. And damn it all, he had to admit Strathmore was not wrong in this. Rampaging into a den of Fenian vipers would likely only get both himself and Hazel killed.

If she hadn't already been murdered by them.

Lucien refused to contemplate it.

He clenched his jaw so hard, his bloody ears popped. "I understand you perfectly, Strathmore. Let us assemble the damned army."

"THIS CAN BE easy and as painless as possible, Miss Montgomery, or this can be painful and difficult. The choice is yours."

Hazel gazed down the barrel of the pistol Sean Flannery held trained upon her head, before meeting the cold, flat eyes of Thomas Mulroney. "Painless and easy for whom, Mr. Mulroney?" she dared to ask defiantly.

Defiance was an easy choice, when one was faced with the potential knowledge of one's impending death. She had nothing left to lose. The implacable man before her was going to attempt to dredge all the information he could from her, before he lodged a bullet in her brain.

"Arrogance does you no credit, Mrs. Mulligan," Flannery snapped. "Or should I call you H.E. Montgomery?"

They knew who she was. But Hazel was not surprised. Of course they did after their run-in at the hotel and then thieving her carpetbag and her notes. She knew who they were also, and having faced death on many occasions before, she had the advantage of facing Mulroney and Flannery without shock or fear.

She tipped back her head, the only part of her body she could move, aside from her fingers and toes. "You may call me whatever you wish to call me, Mr. Flannery, just as long as you stop pointing that pistol at my head. Until then, you can go to hell."

The bitter sting of failure hit her. She had taken a hired hack to the area and directed her driver to leave her, before she entered Nightingale Lane. Although she had made her way painstakingly through the maze of massive warehouses lining the docks, she had been overtaken from behind by Mulroney.

One moment, she had been navigating a warehouse, and the next, the barrel of a weapon had been jammed in her back, and Flannery had appeared before her, pistol at the ready. She had been out-manned, outgunned, and essentially, helpless. Her training told her that her best chance was to prolong her interaction with the two men. Fighting back would likely result in her being wounded, or worse.

And truly, there had been no opportunity to defend her-self. The two men had forced her deep into the interior of the warehouse, to a small store room which appeared to serve as an office. They had confiscated her reticule, discovering her pistol with ease. Her hands had been bound, and her limbs had been lashed to an uncomfortable chair. The warehouse was cold and smelled of tobacco, sea brine, and mildew. It was not the place she wanted to meet her end, but then, her life had never been one of choices, so perhaps it would be fitting.

"Brave and foolish to the last, Miss Montgomery," Flannery said, his tone snide. "Both will prove to be your downfall."

Mulroney approached her, grabbed a handful of her hair, and pulled with such force, tears stung her eyes. The cold barrel of his pistol jammed into her temple. "Where is the great H.E. Montgomery's bravery now?"

"You can both still go to hell," she bit out, refusing to give in or show her fear.

Mulroney slapped her. The pain was sudden, ferocious. "I warned you," he growled. "This can be painful, or painless. It can be even more painful if you force our hands. The choice is yours."

"You can start by telling us about the Special League," Flannery demanded. "Beginning with Arden. What does he know?"

"He knows nothing," she lied flatly. Her cheek stung. Already, she could feel her flesh swelling.

The pistol barrel dug into her temple harder, and Mulroney pulled on her hair a second time. "Try again."

She decided to go on the offensive. "He knows you are both responsible for planting bombs on the railway. He has your names, and he has agents in New York investigating the Emerald Club as we speak. Indeed, I would be surprised if arrests had not already been made. When was the last time you had word from McKenna?"

"Just yesterday." Mulroney slapped her again. "And that is how I know you are lying, Miss Montgomery. I will give you another opportunity to tell us the truth, and if you do not oblige me, I will start breaking those pretty fingers of yours, one by one."

She would have to tide them over. Pacify them with information, even if it was wrong, and pray Lucien would somehow come looking for her. Pray he would find her. But as the thought hit her, she knew it was futile. Even if Lucien discovered her missing, he would have no way of knowing where she had gone.

If only she had left him a note. Or waited for him. If only she had never left the Duke of Strathmore's townhome on her own that morning. If only she had not followed her instincts.

Her instincts, ever infallible, had not betrayed her. No, rather, her own pride had. And now she had no choice but to continue to distract the two men.

"What do you want to know?" she asked them, trying her best to pretend pain wasn't blossoming from her cheek where she had been hit.

"Wise choice. I would hate for the Duke of Arden to find your dead body covered in hideous bruises." Mulroney stroked her cheek, almost tenderly. His expression, however, was harsh. Murderous.

She struggled not to flinch away from his sickening touch, even as her stomach lurched at the thought of Lucien discovering her body much as he had his mother's. He had already carried one lifeless woman. And because she had been too hasty and clumsy in her investigations, it was entirely possible he would now have to relive that horrible day from his past all over again.

This time, with her.

Instinctively, she fought against the ropes on her ankles and wrists, but they were tight. They held firm. She had no hope of escape, other than using her wits, and they were failing her fast.

"The Duke of Arden will not give a damn how my dead

body looks," she evaded.

"Lying again." Mulroney gave her hair a violent jerk. "Do you truly believe we haven't been watching Lark House and following you and your lover about town? How naïve you are. You have shown us your hand repeatedly."

Though she had done her best to be vigilant at all times, she had never noted anyone trailing them. Fear, true and real, caught her heart in a cruel, icy grip. What if they intended to harm Lucien next?

"We had heard, of course," Flannery added, "that a Pinkerton had been sent to London. But we never would have known H.E. Montgomery and Mrs. Mulligan were the same, until that day in the hotel. And then to discover you are the Duke of Arden's whore! Why, imagine our surprise."

"I am assisting Arden in investigations," she allowed coldly. "That is all."

"There is more between you than that." Mulroney's smile was feral. "You ought to realize by now, that lying to us will only hurt you."

He delivered another brutal slap to her face, but this time, her skin was already numb from swelling and previous pain. She was prepared for the blow.

"Tell me the names of his New York City agents."

"I do not know," she said honestly. And even if she did have that information, she would never betray a fellow agent and deliver them to certain death, even if it meant avoiding her own.

Before Mulroney could inflict further torture upon her, an explosion rocked the warehouse, jarring the walls and ceiling of the room they inhabited. Dirt rained from overhead, and the building itself gave a loud groan, almost as if it were a giant creature that had just been wounded.

"Damn it," Mulroney cursed. "We have to go, Sean."

"What will we do with her?" Flannery asked, jutting his chin in Hazel's direction.

Mulroney's lip curled as he cast a hateful eye over her. "Leave her to burn."

With that ominous statement, Mulroney released his grip on her hair and withdrew his pistol from her temple. He lowered his face to hers. "I could have put a bullet in your head so you wouldn't suffer, but I'm not going to."

She had never felt the force of such anger, and it left her hollow, even in this grim moment, as the certain realization she was about to die hit her. She would not beg for mercy, because she recognized all too well he possessed none. Instead, she held her head high and maintained her silence. Creaks and groans sounded around them, and the building shuddered as the undeniable scent of burning wood reached her nose.

Mulroney turned to Flannery. "We have to go before the roof collapses."

Flannery nodded, his light-blue eyes trailing over Hazel, almost apologetically, before both men turned and fled from the room, leaving her to die by flame.

Chapter Nineteen

*H*E HAD TO find Hazel.

It was the only thought in Lucien's mind as he fought his way through the smoldering inferno of the warehouse on Nightingale Lane with Strathmore at his side. They had indeed gathered an army, but he had discovered an army couldn't hold a bloody candle to dynamite. Scotland Yard and Special League were in full force, dozens of men having been called into action to apprehend the villains responsible for the railway bombings.

But when they had descended upon the road in the docks Hazel had circled on her map, they had been met with an explosion. One of the large warehouses shook, flame bursting through the roof, windows raining glass on the street. He could still feel the concussion of the blast in his chest, as he threw a hand over his face and worked his way through fallen rafters and the oppressive heat of the flames.

Around them, the building groaned, a full collapse imminent.

He turned to Strathmore, yelling over the din. "Go back! It isn't safe, and if anything happens to you, Lettie will never forgive me."

But Strathmore shook his head. "If anything happens to *you*, Vi will never forgive me."

Stubborn bastard, but Lucien was damned grateful for

him. His heart was pounding, his body pouring in sweat. Christ, if he lost Hazel—

No. He refused to think of anything other than locating Hazel, of the hope she was yet alive. She had to be somewhere in this damned warehouse. He felt certain of it, and he would not rest until he found her.

Through the smoke and the shipping crates before them, two figures came into sight ahead, moving with haste. In the haze and lack of lamplight, Lucien had just enough time to distinguish the glint of pistols before the building gave a shudder, and the floor overhead gave way, falling down on the men and burying them in burning rubble.

He and Strathmore rushed forward, but the men who had been felled by the wreckage, whoever they were, showed no signs of life. That was when he heard a shrill scream he recognized.

"Hazel," he called out, shielding his face with his arm as he moved blindly toward the source of her cry.

The terror in her voice had been undeniable, and it matched the terror clawing at him from within. The flames grew higher with each labored breath he took. The possibility he would not locate her in time, or that they would all perish in the rampaging fire was strong. The building gave another groan.

"Move!" Strathmore shouted, pushing him out of the path of a falling, burning floor joist.

It fell harmlessly between them, leaving a hole in the rafters overhead and a perfect view to the escalating fire raging through the level above them. If Strathmore had not acted when he had, shoving him before the joist had hit him, he could have been knocked unconscious and succumbed to the flames and smoke.

"Thank you!" he yelled, then turned his head back toward

the direction of Hazel's scream. "Hazel!"

"Lucien!"

Her frantic response reached him over the crackling fire. Either he was delusional, or she was still alive. Either way, he moved toward the sound of her voice. He was an automaton, going toward her come hell, Fenians, dynamite, or a burning warehouse. She was his, damn it, and he loved her. He could deny it no longer. He *needed* her. She was the woman he would not fail. *Could* not fail.

This was her life, but it was also his and Strathmore's.

His brother-in-law, bless the fearless bastard, followed him through the rapidly rising flame. Through the smoke, he found her at last, bound to a chair which had been upended and lay on its side. She was attempting to use a piece of splintered wood that had rained from overhead to cut through her knots. It was so damn like her, this endless determination and her boundless courage, he almost cried in relief.

But the groaning shell of the warehouse reminded him they had not reached safety yet. He dropped to his knees at her side.

"My God, Hazel." He extracted a knife and began sawing away at her binding. Strathmore was not far behind him, and he too withdrew a blade and started work upon the ropes capturing her legs.

"Lucien?" she gasped, coughing.

Her face was streaked with soot, tracked with tears, but she was alive, *thank God*, and she had never been more beautiful. He freed her wrists and arms.

"I am here, my love," he soothed. "Strathmore and I will take you to safety."

"Done," Strathmore announced. "Let's get the hell out of here before the roof falls on our bloody heads."

"Can you walk?" he asked Hazel.

She scrambled to her feet. "Yes."

"I will go first," Strathmore hollered over the tumult. "Arden, put her between us. We need to stay together, stay calm, and move toward the door as quickly and efficiently as possible. Ready?"

Strathmore had endured the hells of torture and imprisonment. Of course he would be cool and calm in the midst of a deadly blaze. Once more, Lucien was grateful for his brother-in-law, a man he was quickly coming to admire.

"Lead the way, Strathmore," he hollered, planting his hands on Hazel's waist. "Here we go, darling," he said into her ear. "Hold on to Strathmore, and I will hold on to you."

There was no time for her to respond, for Strathmore had already begun moving. Time was against them, so too the flames and the thickening of the deadly smoke. His lungs burned, and the three of them were gasping for air. The heat was intense as they meandered slowly through the path they had just taken, avoiding fallen floors and beams, working their way around a fresh blaze.

Finally, at long last, they reached the doorway. The cold, crisp air of late autumn was a welcome burst on his face and in his lungs. Strathmore guided them into the street, and the three of them collapsed as one, gasping for breath, shuddering coughs wracking them all.

But alive.

Mercifully, blessedly, *alive*. Lucien looked toward his brother-in-law, nodded his thanks, then gathered Hazel in his arms. He buried his face in her hair, not giving a damn who saw his unseemly display of emotion. Not giving a damn about the tears streaking down his cheeks.

All he cared about in that moment was the woman in his arms. Words failed him, so he didn't say a bloody thing. He simply held her close, relishing the pounding of her heart against his chest, the way she clutched him back. Now that he had her where she belonged, he had no intention of ever letting her go again.

"TILT YOUR HEAD back, sweetheart."

Hazel obeyed Lucien's command, tipping her chin toward the ceiling. She offered no protest at his term of endearment, just as she had not offered any protest when he had held her in his arms for the carriage ride back to Strathmore's townhouse. Just as she had not protested when Lucien had announced to his worried sister upon their arrival that he would attend Hazel in her bath.

Brother and sister had indulged in a private exchange just out of earshot. Presumably, Violet had argued against the scandalous notion of Lucien assisting an unmarried female whilst she was nude, submerged in a tub. Also presumably, Lucien had run roughshod over his sister's protests. In the end, Lucien had escorted Hazel upstairs, drawing the bathwater for her and undressing her himself, before joining her in the tub.

His every touch had been reverent but practical. He had stripped her dress, chemise, stockings, and drawers away and plucked what remained of the pins binding her hair. He had scrubbed her skin free of the soot and smoke, though she felt certain the awful, putrid scent of it would never leave her. After the shock and tumult of the day, the presence of his powerful body at her back, surrounding her in the warm, lavender-scented water, was precisely what she needed.

Gently, he worked a lather into her hair now, his long fingers kneading her scalp.

"Is your cheek paining you?" he asked, his tone grim.

She had not seen herself in a mirror, but the pain in her cheek and jaw was enough to tell her she suffered bruising from Mulroney's slaps. "It is well enough," she said, closing her eyes as he continued his massage.

His hands upon her, after all the hell she had endured, felt like pure heaven.

"I would kill them again if I could, for what they have done to you." His voice was a low growl now, and she did not doubt he meant what he said.

It was the first acknowledgment she had received that Mulroney and Flannery had perished in the fire. "Are you certain?"

"Certain that I would tear them apart with my bare hands?" he asked. "Christ yes. I will hurt any man who hurts you. It kills me that I was not able to protect you as I should have."

"Certain they are dead?" she elaborated. "That the two of them died in the fire?"

Lucien cleared his throat, continuing his tender ministrations. "Yes. When the Fire Brigade doused the flames, two dead were discovered in the rubble. Two men meeting the descriptions of Flannery and Mulroney were found side by side, buried beneath fallen debris. The man acting as lookout, and who also caused the blast when he saw the arrival of Scotland Yard, was captured as well before he could escape. He is the same man I chased at the hotel that day when Mulroney and Flannery attacked you. You are finally safe now, thank God."

Hours had passed in the wake of her rescue from the burning warehouse. As the Fire Brigade had arrived in their steam fire engines, she, Lucien, and Strathmore had been swept to the periphery of the scene. A physician called for by Winchelsea had attended all of them there in the street. They had answered the questions of Scotland Yard. And then at long last, they had returned, all three of them, to Strathmore's home.

Lark House still required additional safety measures in an abundance of caution, Lucien had explained, in the wake of the incursion and planting of the bomb in her chamber. And that was how she had managed to find herself ensconced in a hot, restoring bath, the Duke of Arden waiting upon her as if he were her personal servant.

"I am not glad they are dead," she said at last, a tremor in her voice she wished she could have suppressed, "though I am grateful they cannot harm anyone else. But I would not wish such a demise as what they suffered upon my greatest enemy."

"They left you tied to that chair, knowing you would perish in the flames, those craven bastards," he reminded her. "It is only fitting they received the end they would have forced upon you."

Lucien was right. Mulroney and Flannery had consigned her to die in the fire. And if the fire hadn't begun when it had, they would have killed her themselves in another fashion. But she had no wish to dwell upon that now. The evils of others would be answered for, and she had faith in that, if not human nature.

She was a Pinkerton agent, after all.

But she had much to be thankful for, because she had failed herself today, and unquestionably, she would have died in the fire as Mulroney and Flannery had intended, had it not been for the selfless intervention of Lucien and the Duke of Strathmore. Though she had thanked them both profusely in the street, gratitude rose within her again now, and she could not contain it.

"Rinse," he said then, and she felt the lukewarm caress of water bathing her head, washing the suds free. Once, twice, thrice. He sifted the heavy strands of her hair, cleansing any lingering traces of the trauma she had faced earlier that day.

"Thank you for finding me," she told Lucien. "And for saving me."

"We all need saving sometimes," he said.

Sweetly floral notes filled the air, warring with the scent of smoke she realized must still be emanating from their discarded garments. It seemed a miracle they had escaped the burning, badly damaged warehouse together. A miracle they were both relatively unscathed. A miracle for the protective strength of his body all around her, his worshipful touch and tenderness soothing away the horrors of the day.

"Who saved you?" she dared to asked, eyes still firmly closed.

"You," he said simply.

No one had ever said something so deeply moving to her, so personal, and she knew what such an admission must cost Lucien. She sat up in the bath and turned in his arms. Everything inside her came loose. The fear, the terror, the pain, the hope, the joy…all spiraled into one, effervescent sensation. Gently, she cupped his beloved face, stubbled in whiskers, committing it to memory. Their gazes locked and held.

"I love you, Lucien," she told him, because she could not keep the words to herself any longer.

They were bigger than she was, huge and demanding, needing to be spoken.

His mouth was upon hers in the next breath, moving tentatively at first, then with greater hunger. The kiss turned carnal—lips and tongue and teeth and desperation. She sucked the fullness of his lower lip. Hours ago, she had faced the looming prospect of her own death, and now, she felt so very alive, with the mouth of the man she loved on hers. With his big, powerful body surrounding her, with their breaths mingling, their tongues moving languidly together.

Later, she would worry about consequences. Tomorrow, she would remember all the reasons why they could not be together. She would worry about the disparity between their social stations. Today, she did not want to fear. Today, she only wanted to be the woman who loved Lucien West, Duke of Arden.

Their kiss deepened, and she was ravenous for him. Perhaps it was the shock and the trauma she had endured. Perhaps it was simply the freedom of admitting her love to Lucien. Hazel could not be sure. The reason did not matter. Only the want did.

Her hand glided through the silken water, and she found him, thick and erect. His deep groan echoed in the tiled expanse of the bathroom. She gripped him, pumping his shaft. The tenderness inside her splintered, mingling with savagery. With the need to claim and be claimed. Deep inside, she hungered to be filled.

Hazel broke the kiss, losing herself in his verdant gaze. She was breathless, and his mouth was puffy from the ardency of their kisses. His dark wavy hair was wet, just beginning to dry. He had never been more gorgeous.

"I want you," she told him, not bothering to mince words. "Now."

He clenched his jaw. "I promised my sister I would not defile you in her house, damn it."

She was determined, her hand stroking him with greater intent beneath the water. He grew firmer. His cock was a thing of beauty, and she wanted it inside her. *Just one more time*, whispered her heart. What could be the harm?

"Your sister never has to know," she said.

"Bloody hell." He took her wrist in a gentle grip and

moved her hand away, before standing suddenly. "I am attempting to be honorable, Hazel. You have suffered so much today, and I will not be a rutting beast."

Hazel looked up the impressive expanse of his body, taking in every sinew, every muscle. Water rolled down his broad chest and flat abdomen, down his thick thighs, dripped from the end of his rigid length. Entranced, she rose to her knees.

"I see no beast here," she told him, and then she took him in her hand again.

She wanted to taste him. To pleasure him as he had done for her. If she never had another chance after today, she would not squander this one. Tentatively, she touched her tongue to the tip of him.

His quick inhalation sliced through the stillness of the air from above. "Hazel."

She ignored the warning in his tone. Tilting her head back so her gaze locked with his, she took him into her mouth. She hummed her approval deep in her throat. An answering ache pulsed to life between her thighs.

"Fuck," he ground out.

The leashed desire in his proper baritone spurred her on. She took him deeper, wanting more of him. His fingers were in her hair, cradling her skull. His hips moved, and he thrust into her mouth. Allowing her instinct to guide her, she ran her lips down his length, swirled her tongue over the tip of him until he moaned, then took him in her mouth again. He surged into the back of her throat. She withdrew, catching her breath, and flicked her tongue over him once more.

"No more." He caught her arms, pulled her until she stood before him, dripping and naked as he was. "You are enough to tempt a saint."

But there was no censure in his gaze. Tenderly, he helped

her from the tub, then stepped out himself, before toweling the both of them dry. When he had finished, he kissed her long and hard, then took her hand in his.

Wordlessly, he guided her into the guest chamber. Hands linked, they made their way across the plush carpet and fell onto the bed together. She kissed him as he rose over her, settling himself between her spread thighs. His fingers dipped into her folds, parting her, petting the bud of sensitive flesh, and sending wild sparks of desire shooting through her.

Her nails dug into his shoulders. Her hips were moving restlessly, and this time, she did not want patience. She did not want prolonged, tender lovemaking. All she wanted was Lucien, deep inside her.

He slid a finger into her channel, testing her readiness. She bowed from the bed. It was as if every sensation within her had been heightened. Making love with him had always been a revelation, but this was a celebration. It was life and love.

"Please," she whispered against his lips, "I need you."

And he gave in, removing his finger, guiding himself to her entrance. She was impatient beneath him. She kissed down his throat, gently bit into the strong cords of his neck, over his Adam's apple.

He held still for a moment, gazing down at her with an expression so affectionate, she could do nothing but frame his face in her hands. "I love you," she told him again.

It was all the spur he required. Lucien thrust inside her, deep and hard and fast. She was filled, stretched. Completed in a way only he could complete her.

"You are mine," he told her, withdrawing, then slipping inside once more.

"Yes. I am yours." She pulled him to her for another kiss, telling him with her lips what she could not bear to say aloud.

That she would be forever his. And how she wished he too could be hers. But they were not meant for forever, and she knew it.

They moved as one, their joining wild, almost furious. When he stroked her pearl, she fell apart, seizing on him as a violent wave of pure bliss broke over her. Her climax thundered through her like a summer storm, and she fell headlong into the velvety abyss as he thrust home inside her one last time. He tensed beneath her questing fingertips, his body stiffening, as he reached his pinnacle as well. The hot rush of his seed filled her, and she clutched him to her, sated and spent, their hearts pounding in tandem.

Chapter Twenty

"*H*AVE YOU ASKED her yet?"

Lucien heaved a sigh and glared at the interloper who had dared to disturb him as he pored over documents in Strathmore's study. The early light glowed, making his sister look particularly radiant this morning, even if she was interrupting him and poking her nose into his affairs, where it decidedly did not belong.

"Good morning, Lettie," he greeted wryly. "I did not realize, when your husband offered me the temporary use of his study that it would mean you would trespass whenever you wished."

Violet smiled at him, imperturbable as ever. Her disposition had always been sunny, and her happiness only heightened it now. It was good, he thought, to see her well-settled with Strathmore.

"You did not answer my question," his sister pointed out tartly, settling in to one of the chairs arranged before Strathmore's desk, quite uninvited.

"Have I asked who?" he asked, feigning ignorance. "And what shall I ask her?"

In truth, he knew precisely what Lettie's query was about. In the aftermath of the warehouse explosion and fire the previous day at the docks, Lucien had returned to Strathmore's townhome and had promptly spent the rest of the day tending to the woman who loved him.

Yes, Hazel loved him.

And he loved her, but he had found the words strangely difficult to say in return.

Because they terrified him. He had spent his life believing romantic love was nothing but a fiction which led to everlasting misery.

"Miss Montgomery of course," Lettie said. "After the scandal you created yesterday, you must marry her."

She was referring to his insistence he accompany Hazel to her chamber and tend to her himself. He did not regret his actions, though he acknowledged the rashness of them. He inclined his head. "I have every intention of marrying her. I already asked her previously, in fact."

Lettie's brows rose. "And what did she say?"

"She declined." He frowned then, recalling her response.

What if she denied him again? He wanted Hazel, and yet, she was forever determined to see the differences between them.

"Did you tell her you love her?" Violet asked gently, ever perceptive.

"No," he admitted.

"What are you waiting for?" his sister demanded. "You could have lost her yesterday. Do not lose her to your pride."

Lettie was right, of course. But damn it if the notion of his little sister giving him counsel did not rankle. "Thank you for your unsolicited advice, sister dearest. I will take it into consideration. For the moment, I have work to do."

He gestured to the papers he had been poring over. Some of the documents in the possession of the Fenians had remained intact, kept inside a strongbox. Winchelsea had tasked him with reviewing them for any information which would be of use to future investigations.

"Always the League," Violet said then. "Always duty. For once, Lucien, put yourself and your heart first. You deserve to be happy, and so does Miss Montgomery."

Did he?

He sighed again. "How can you know I will make her happy?"

His sister smiled. "Because I can see the way she looks at you, and the way you look at her. Stop lingering here with these dratted papers! Go find her, and ask her to be your wife. My babe will be fortunate indeed to have a brave auntie like Hazel."

The last of his sister's words hit him then. "Your babe? Are you...? Lettie! Why did you not say so before? This is wonderful news."

Her smile deepened. "Yes, it is." She rose from her chair abruptly in a swish of lavender-colored skirts. "Now, I must get back to my crocheting. I'm trying my hand at a blanket for the babe. Do cease being a stubborn arse and go secure yourself a wife."

Bemused by the prospect of Lettie becoming someone's mother, he watched her go, before turning to the documents he had extracted from the strongbox. Hastily, he began to restore them to the box, knowing they could wait, that he had a far more important task at hand.

He was just about to return a small leather-bound journal to the strongbox when he opened it instead, for the journal looked familiar. He was startled to find his name written prominently within, penned in Hazel's tidy script. Clearly, the journal belonged to her and had been thieved from her chamber at Lark House.

He knew he had no business reading her private musings, but part of him reasoned he could not avoid reading it, for it was a part of his duty. The journal had become integral to the investigation, and it must be examined. Moreover, it appeared to be written in the form of a list. His eyes scanned the lines.

> *Lucien West, Duke of Arden.*
> *Arrogant.*
> *Forbidding.*
> *Suffering from an abundance of self-confidence.*
> *Strongly objects to being referred to as "Mr. Arden."*
> *Easily manipulated.*
> *Pompous.*
> *~~Strong.~~*
> *Dark hair.*
> *~~Emerald eyes.~~*
> *~~Possessed of an authoritative manner.~~*
> *Exceedingly rude.*
> *Arrogant.*

She had listed "arrogant" twice, and he could not help but to grin when he noted it. That was his Hazel, the woman who had stormed his battlements and overtaken him completely. He could not deny he owned each fault she had written. He could see from the manner in which she had crossed out some of the lines she had been conflicted about him at the time she had constructed the list.

It was, he supposed, an oddly prescient representation of the way he had felt for her as well. Initially, he had been vexed. He had been determined to make her cry off from being his partner in the League. From the beginning, he had been attracted to her, for she was not merely a beautiful woman, she was also capable, fierce, intelligent, bold, and daring.

She was Hazel, uniquely wonderful. Utterly intoxicating.

And he had been smitten. But his feelings for her had changed. Oh, how they had altered. As he worked at her side and watched the fascinating firing of her mind, he had been in awe. From the moment his lips had first touched hers, she had owned his heart.

Lucien had just been too damned stupid, prideful, and stubborn to see it.

He eyed the list and thought, forgetting the investigation, as Lettie had urged him. Forgetting everything but Hazel and the way he felt for her. The list was missing a few key points, he realized. Here, at last, was the answer he had been seeking.

He retrieved a pen from Strathmore's desk, dipping it in ink to add one more item to her list.

The man who wants to marry you.

He eyed the list, then realized, much to his dismay, he had neglected to include the most important item of all, the one which must not be forgotten.

The man who loves you.

There. That would do.
That would do quite splendidly.

HAZEL LOOKED DOWN at the gold band she had been wearing upon her hand since Adam's death. She stood by the window in her guest chamber at Strathmore's townhome, the morning sunshine kissing her face. Earlier, with the aid of Bunton, she had dressed and her hair was styled artfully. Her reflection in the looking glass had revealed a woman with a bruised cheek, but a determined air.

The time had come to move on, in more ways than one.

With a deep breath, she tugged at the ring, twisting it from her finger. She raised the thin metal—warmed from her skin—to her lips for a kiss, then tucked it inside the small pouch where she kept all her jewelry.

"I will never forget you," she whispered, putting the jewelry inside the valise where she had already seen the rest of her meager possessions packed.

In a few minutes, she would emerge from the chamber and face the rest of what she must do. Goodbyes were never easy, and this one would be the most difficult of all. She did not think her heart would ever recover. But she also knew it had to be done.

She had fallen asleep last night in Lucien's arms, only to wake at dawn to find herself alone. She'd had ample time to lie in bed and contemplate her life and what she wanted from it. She loved Lucien enough to let him go. With Flannery and Mulroney dead, and their cohort arrested, her work in London was finished.

She had not stopped the bombings from occurring. Nor had she brought the perpetrators to justice. But she had found, all the same, a sense of peace. A realization as well, that perhaps the time had come for her to cease being a Pinkerton agent and living an unsettled life of danger.

Losing her heart to Lucien had led to an unexpected discovery: she did not want to spend the rest of her life alone. She wanted a husband. Children. She wanted the deep, abiding contentment she had seen in the Duchess of Strathmore's eyes.

And she was going to return to America to find it, if she could.

A knock sounded at the chamber door. She knew without having to ask who it was.

"Enter," she called to Lucien.

The door clicked open, and he crossed the threshold as if he belonged there, shutting the door at his back. She wondered for a moment what Lady Beaufort and the Duchess of Strathmore would say at his trespass in broad daylight, without the excuse of their near-deaths yesterday to bolster his actions. And then she told herself it mattered not, for she was leaving this gilded world she little understood far behind.

But how difficult it would be to leave.

Nigh impossible, she thought, as she watched him stride toward her in his confident way. He was dressed informally, wearing only shirtsleeves, waistcoat, and trousers in stark contrast to his immaculately groomed dark hair. He had shaved, she noted. Her heart gave a pang.

"Good morning," he greeted tenderly.

"Good morning," she forced herself to return, as if she was not breaking inside.

"I believe I found something of yours."

Belatedly, she noticed he carried a small journal in his hands that she recognized as her own. "My journal! But where did you find it? It was in my satchel that was stolen from Lark House."

Naturally, Flannery and Mulroney had not stolen the handsome journal Lucien had gifted her, for its pages had been blank. She reminded herself now that she needed to return to Lark House for the remainder of her belongings. She was keeping the journal, for it would be the only piece of Lucien she could carry with her.

"I found it in a strongbox liberated from the rubble of the warehouse," he told her, offering the small leather-bound volume to her. "You may wish to have a second look at the list you made inside, however. I fear you were missing a few important things."

Her cheeks went hot as she recalled the first list she had made within it.

"Oh, hell," she grumbled, before she could stop her wayward tongue.

"I propose heaven, rather than hell," he said with an enigmatic smile. "Take a look for yourself."

Perplexed, she flipped it open to the first page. There was her infernal list, just as she had originally drafted it. However, there was a difference. Her small, precise scrawl had been joined by a slanting, masculine script. She read the last two lines of the list.

The man who wants to marry you.
The man who loves you.

She stared at the page, unseeing, as an intense burst of emotion hit her. Her gaze lifted to his, and he was still smiling, so fully, his rarefied dimples made a heart-melting appearance.

She struggled to string together words against a rush of hope so strong, it nearly toppled her over. "You love me?"

He nodded. "I love you, Hazel. When I thought I was going to lose you yesterday, I realized no pain or grief I had ever suffered in the past could be as strong as what I would feel if you were gone from my life forever. I cannot bear to lose you, and I cannot live my life without you in it, by my side, as my wife. Will you do me the incredible honor of marrying me?"

The journal fell from her trembling hands to the floor, but she paid it no heed. All she could see was the man before her becoming blurry and indistinct through the tears clouding her vision.

"Oh, Lucien," she said on a choked half-sob of love and

regret. "I cannot marry you, and you know it. I would embarrass you horribly."

His arms came around her then, firm and strong and reassuring. He pressed her head to his chest, just above the beautiful thudding of his heart. "You will only embarrass me if you refuse my suit a second time, my love."

Her arms were around his lean waist, and she breathed in his scent, musk and citrus, beloved. How would she ever let him go?

"You are not thinking clearly," she told him.

"On the contrary," his voice rumbled beneath her ear. "I have never been so clear-headed."

"I wear trousers," she reminded him.

"I love those trousers," he countered. "Your limbs and your rump look deliciously fetching in them."

"I have no notion of your societal rules and customs."

He kissed the crown of her head. "I consider that part of your charm."

"I cuss."

"So do I." There was a smile in his voice.

"I am an orphan who has spent her entire life roaming, with no true home of her own," she tried.

"And I am the man who wants to be your home at last." His voice was solemn.

Something inside her shifted. Gave way.

"You cannot mean that," she said, too afraid to hope. Terrified of the love she felt for him. Of the possibility she could actually have this man as her own. That she could be his wife.

"I have never meant anything more. Look at me, Hazel."

She tipped back her head, meeting his gaze. "Lucien."

He kissed her. Slowly. Sweetly. Nothing more than a gentle feathering of his lips over hers. "I love you. I admire you. I respect you. And I need you by my side. Stay with me, Hazel. Be the duchess of my heart."

Nothing else mattered when she was in his arms. Her fears, her doubts, all fell away. Because she loved him, and he loved her, and this time, he had asked her to marry him with his whole heart. He had braved his own fears to ask for her hand.

And there was only one answer she could give him.

"Yes," she said, smiling through her tears.

Epilogue

*L*UCIEN WATCHED HIS wife as she spun about in the entry hall of the building he had brought her to view that afternoon. She was not wearing her trousers today, for her burgeoning belly had rendered them too uncomfortable by her standards. She had bemoaned the retiring of them, and so had he, but she assured him she would wear trousers for him once more after the babe was born. With or without her divided skirts, she was so lovely, she made him ache.

He still could scarcely fathom she was his. That she loved him. That their child grew within her womb. He allowed himself a moment of simply savoring the sight of her, before recalling the reason for their visit.

"What do you think of it?" he asked. "Will it suffice?"

"The building appears to be sound," she said, "but I confess I do not understand your sudden interest in purchasing edifices."

Smiling, he moved toward her, drawn to her warmth. "You told me you wished to begin a school for lady detectives, did you not?"

Though she had continued to act as his partner in the League, the discovery she was with child had necessitated a change of occupation for her. He had not forced the matter; Hazel had made the decision herself, but he was grateful for it. He had no wish to spend his days worrying over the safety of his wife and his unborn babe.

But in the absence of her work as an agent, she had struggled to find her new purpose, until she had finally settled upon the notion of opening a school for young ladies interested in becoming detectives, just as she had. In typical Hazel fashion, she had already thrown herself into the task of locating lady detectives who could offer training to her students. As with anything she set her mind to accomplish, Lucien had no doubt Hazel's lady detective school would not just succeed, but thrive.

Her eyes widened. "Oh, Lucien! You cannot mean to tell me you purchased this building as a home for my school."

"The transaction is not complete," he allowed, taking her into his arms and devouring her upturned face with his gaze. "Naturally, I would never dream of making a decision so important without your approval. That is why we are here. I have had my man looking for some time now, for something I thought would be suitable—a large enough building capable of being outfitted to your requirements, a neighborhood in which I need not fear my wife traipsing about in trousers…"

"You love my trousers," she protested. "You have told me so yourself on many occasions."

"I love peeling you out of them," he corrected, his hand drifted lovingly over her belly, cradling the life growing within. "Here is the evidence."

"Wicked man," she said, without heat.

"I do not recall hearing you complain." He dropped a kiss on her lips, groaning when she deepened it, her tongue slipping inside his mouth.

She pulled away then, smiling up at him. "Why would I complain, when I have a life so wonderful, I could never have even dreamt it?"

"Even though you married a man with fancy commodes?"

he could not help but tease, affecting her honeyed drawl.

Hazel laughed. "Of course, and even though I swear a mockingbird could imitate my accent better than you can."

He kissed the bridge of her nose, right over the smattering of freckles he found endlessly bewitching. "I shall have to try harder, darling. Fortunately for me, I have the rest of our lives to perfect it. But tell me what you think of this building for your Lady's Detective School. I can bear the suspense no longer."

"How I love you." She cupped his cheek. "I think it is utterly perfect. Thank you for supporting me in this endeavor. I do realize it is not precisely the thing a proper duchess does, and Lady Beaufort is rather horrified by the notion."

"Aunt Hortense is horrified by everything and everyone," he countered easily. His aunt had taken Hazel under her wing and had done an excellent job of teaching Hazel the vagaries of London manners. "You know that I am only happy when you are happy, Hazel. I will never seek to cage you."

He was blessed with strong women in his life, who had taught him a woman's independence was to be reveled in, even if much of the civilized world would still seek to repress her. Hazel, with her wings spread, was a glorious sight indeed.

And her legs, for that matter, but that errant thought was decidedly unwanted, for the spear of desire it sent to his groin.

His intrepid wife was somehow instantly aware of his discomfort. She palmed him through his trousers. "There is another way you might make me happy, Lucien."

He was rigid. Ready.

"Here?" he asked, his voice hoarse.

The Duchess of Arden was a wanton. And he loved it. He loved *her*. Lucien cast a glance about their surroundings. They were alone in the building, and there was an accommodating old chaise lounge in a salon to his left which had been left behind by the previous occupants. He could position her before it, lift her skirts, take her from behind…

"Here," she echoed, and then his brash American duchess tugged his head back down to hers for another searing kiss.

THE END.

Dear Reader,

Thank you for reading *Shameless Duke*! I hope you enjoyed this fourth book in the League of Dukes series and that you loved Hazel and Lucien's story as much I loved writing it. I'm not supposed to have favorites as an author, but I will admit these two characters touched my heart in an extra special way. After so much struggle in their pasts, they found their home, their hearts, and their happily ever after in each other.

One historical note: while the bombings on the Praed Street (now known as Paddington) and the Charing Cross stations depicted in this book are firmly based in fact, they occurred in October of 1883 rather than in autumn of 1882. Aside from tweaking the date to fit my fictional timeline, however, I relied on eyewitness accounts to describe the aftermath of the bombings with strict attention to historical detail. I'm also much indebted to nineteenth century travel guides for all the minutiae concerning the London railway and Madame Tussaud's. (Sadly, Napoleon's traveling carriage was destroyed in a fire in the early twentieth century!) And, in case you were wondering, yes, there truly were lady Pinkerton agents, the most famous of whom, Kate Warne, served as inspiration for Hazel.

As always, please consider leaving an honest review of *Shameless Duke*. Reviews are greatly appreciated! If you'd like to keep up to date with my latest releases and series news, sign up for my newsletter here or follow me on Amazon or BookBub. Join my reader's group on Facebook for bonus content, early excerpts, giveaways, and more.

If you'd like a preview of my upcoming standalone *Scan-*

dalous Duke, Book Five in the League of Dukes, in which the Duke of Winchelsea meets his match in a scandalous American actress with dangerous secrets, do read on.

Until next time,

Scarlett

Scandalous Duke
League of Dukes Book Five

By
Scarlett Scott

Felix Markham, Duke of Winchelsea, has devoted his life to being the perfect statesman and raising his daughter after his beloved wife's death. But when devastating bombings on the railway leave London in an uproar, he is determined to bring the mastermind of the attacks to justice. He will lure the fox from his den by any means.

In her youth, Johanna McKenna donned a French accent and stage name to escape the clutches of her violent father and became the darling of the New York City stage as Rose Beaumont. Her past comes calling when her brother's reappearance in her life leads her into a dangerous web of deceit. She finds herself hopelessly trapped until she receives an offer she cannot refuse from London's most famous theater.

Felix's plan is clear: bring the famed Rose of New York to London, secure her as his mistress, and drive his quarry to English shores. But the more time he spends in Johanna's company, the more he realizes nothing is as it seems, least of all the woman who feels as if she were made to be in his arms. When he finally learns the truth, it may be too late to save both his city and the enigmatic lady who has stolen his heart.

Chapter One

1883

ROM THE MOMENT he first saw Rose Beaumont grace the stage that evening, Felix had known why she was the most celebrated actress in New York City. He also knew why Drummond McKenna, the Fenian mastermind behind the explosions on the London railway, would want her in his bed. And he knew he was going to do his damnedest to use the beauty to lure McKenna to the justice awaiting him.

But for now, he would settle for champagne.

He took a sip, watching his quarry from across Theo Saville's sumptuous ballroom where the company of *The Tempest* and the city's most elite patrons of the arts had gathered to fête the famed Rose of New York. Trust Theo to throw a party lavish enough for an emperor. The servants were aplenty, the food was French, the champagne likely cost a small fortune, and the company was elegantly dissolute.

As a duke from a line that descended practically to the days of William the Conqueror, wealth and ostentation did not impress Felix. As a man who had lost the only woman he had ever loved, women did not ordinarily impress him either.

Rose Beaumont, however, did.

In the light of the gas lamps, she was a sight to behold. Dressed in an evening gown of rich claret, her golden hair worked into an elaborate Grecian braid, there was no doubt she commanded the eye of every gentleman in the chamber. Rubies and gold glinted from her creamy throat, her lush bosom and cinched waist on full display.

And though he observed her to hone his strategy, he could not deny he was as helplessly in awe of her as the rest of the sorry chaps gaping at her famed loveliness. He had watched her perform, so mesmerized by her portrayal of Miranda, he had forgotten he was attending the theater to further his goal. For a brief beat, he forgot it anew as she tilted her head toward Theo and laughed at something droll he had no doubt said.

Theo looked pleased, and well he should, for though he had brought Rose Beaumont to his stage as a favor to Felix, there had been so much fanfare surrounding the arrival of the famed Rose of New York, that his already much-lauded theater was enjoying an unprecedented amount of attention. But he was also favoring Miss Beaumont with his rascal's grin, the one Felix had seen lead many a woman straight to his bed.

Felix had not painstakingly crafted his plan just so Theo could ruin it with his insatiable desire to get beneath a lady's skirts. No, indeed. Felix finished his champagne, deposited his empty glass upon a servant's tray, and then closed the distance between himself and his prey.

As he reached them, he realized, much to his irritation, that Rose Beaumont was even lovelier than she had been from afar. Her eyes were a startling shade of blue, so cool, they verged on gray. Her lips were a full, pink pout. Her nose was charmingly retroussé. Hers was an ideal beauty, juxtaposed with the lush potency of a female who knew her power over the opposite sex.

Their gazes clashed, and he felt something deep inside him, an answering awareness he had not expected, like a jolt of sheer electricity to his senses. There was something visceral and potent in that exchange of glances. A current blazed down his spine, and his cock twitched to life.

She smelled of rose petals. Rose had been the scent Hattie favored. The realization and recognition made an unwanted stirring of memory wash over him. He banished the remembrance, for he could not bear to think of Hattie when he stood opposite a woman who had shared the bed of a monster like Drummond McKenna.

"Winchelsea," Theo greeted him warmly. "May I present to you Miss Rose Beaumont, lately of New York, the newest and loveliest addition to the Crown and the Thorn?"

Her stare was still upon him. He looked at her and tried to feel revolted. But the disgust he had summoned for her when she had been nothing more than a name on paper refused to return. Her beauty was blinding, and he told himself that was the reason for his sudden, unaccountable vulnerability. That and the scent of her. Not just rose, he discovered, but an undercurrent of citrus. Distinctly different from Hattie's scent after all.

He offered a courtly bow. Though he no longer chased women, he recalled all too well how to woo, and he reminded himself now that this was a duty. One in a line of many he had spent in all his years as a devoted servant of Her Majesty.

"Miss Beaumont," he said when he straightened to his full height. "My most sincere compliments on your performance tonight. You were brilliant."

"Thank you," she said, her gray gaze inscrutable as it flitted over his face. "You are too kind."

Her husky voice reached inside him, formed a knot of desire he did not want to feel. Why did she have to be so damn beautiful? He cast a meaningful glance toward Theo, who had been his friend for many years. And who knew what was required of him in this instance.

"If you will excuse me," Theo said smoothly, "I must

check in with my chef. The fellow is French and quite temperamental. Miss Beaumont, Winchelsea."

Theo departed with the sleek grace of a panther, leaving Felix alone with Miss Beaumont. His friend's defection occurred so abruptly, Felix found himself unprepared.

"That was badly done of him," Miss Beaumont said in the same voice that had brought the audience to their knees earlier that evening. It bore the trace of a French accent, one which had been notably absent from her earlier performance.

"I beg your pardon, Miss Beaumont?" he asked, perhaps in a sharper tone than he had intended.

He was out of his depths, and he knew it. He had procured mistresses before. He had been a statesman for all his life. He had been involved in complex investigations, harrowing danger, the aftermath of brutal violence. He had witnessed, firsthand, the wreckage of the rail carriages in the wake of the bombs, which had exploded several months before.

But he had never attempted to make a Fenian's mistress *his* mistress.

"Mr. Saville," Miss Beaumont elaborated. "He was giving you the opportunity to speak with me, was he not?"

"I cannot say I am capable of speaking for Mr. Saville's motivations," he evaded.

The statement was a blatant prevarication, for Felix did know precisely what spurred his friend in every occasion: money and cunny with a love of the arts thrown in for good measure.

"Forgive me, but I have already forgotten your name," she said. "Was it Wintersby?"

"Winchelsea," he gritted, though she did not fool him.

He had seen the light of feminine interest in her gaze. She felt the attraction between them—base animal lust though it may be—as surely as he did. Some time may have passed since he had last engaged in the dance of procuring himself a bed partner, but it had not been that long, by God.

"Of course." She smiled, but it did not reach her eyes. "Winchelsea. I am not a naïve young girl. I know what you want."

His heart beat faster, and a chill trilled down his spine. She could not know who he was or what his true intentions were. Surely not. "Oh? I pray you enlighten me, Miss Beaumont. What is it I want?"

She stepped closer to him, her red silk swaying against his trousers. "You want me."

She did not elaborate. Nor did she need to.

Her proclamation was the immediate source of both relief and anticipation. Here was a game he could play. He lowered his head toward hers, not near enough to kiss but near enough to tempt himself to close the distance and seal their mouths. Her lips were so full. Her eyes so wide. He did not think the luminous sheen in them could be feigned, though her fluency as an actress was undeniable. How shameful that such a creature should belong to a soulless villain.

"And if I do want you, Miss Beaumont?" he dared to ask, allowing his gaze to devour her face. Part of his task would be easy. His desire for her was inexplicable, yet real. "What would you say?"

Those inviting lips curved higher. Her smile revealed two dimples. "I would say though you flatter me, you cannot have me."

Damnation.

He ought to have known getting the Rose of New York to fall into his arms would not be an easy feat.

Want more? Get *Scandalous Duke*!

Don't miss Scarlett's other romances!

(Listed by Series)

Complete Book List
scarlettscottauthor.com/books

HISTORICAL ROMANCE

Heart's Temptation
A Mad Passion (Book One)
Rebel Love (Book Two)
Reckless Need (Book Three)
Sweet Scandal (Book Four)
Restless Rake (Book Five)
Darling Duke (Book Six)
The Night Before Scandal (Book Seven)

Wicked Husbands
Her Errant Earl (Book One)
Her Lovestruck Lord (Book Two)
Her Reformed Rake (Book Three)
Her Deceptive Duke (Book Four)

League of Dukes
Nobody's Duke (Book One)
Heartless Duke (Book Two)
Dangerous Duke (Book Three)
Shameless Duke (Book Four)
Scandalous Duke (Book Five)

Sins and Scoundrels
Duke of Depravity (Book One)
Prince of Persuasion (Book Two)
Marquess of Mayhem (Book Three)

The Wicked Winters
Wicked in Winter (Book One)

Stand-alone Novella
Lord of Pirates

CONTEMPORARY ROMANCE

Love's Second Chance
Reprieve (Book One)
Perfect Persuasion (Book Two)
Win My Love (Book Three)

Coastal Heat
Loved Up (Book One)

About the Author

Amazon bestselling author Scarlett Scott writes steamy Victorian and Regency romance with strong, intelligent heroines and sexy alpha heroes. She lives in Pennsylvania with her Canadian husband, adorable identical twins, and one TV-loving dog.

A self-professed literary junkie and nerd, she loves reading anything, but especially romance novels, poetry, and Middle English verse. Catch up with her on her website www.scarlettscottauthor.com. Hearing from readers never fails to make her day.

Scarlett's complete book list and information about up-coming releases can be found at www.scarlettscottauthor.com.

Connect with Scarlett! You can find her here:
Join Scarlett Scott's reader's group on Facebook for early excerpts, giveaways, and a whole lot of fun!
Sign up for her newsletter here.
scarlettscottauthor.com/contact
Follow Scarlett on Amazon
Follow Scarlett on BookBub
www.instagram.com/scarlettscottauthor
www.twitter.com/scarscoromance
www.pinterest.com/scarlettscott
www.facebook.com/AuthorScarlettScott
Join the Historical Harlots on Facebook